The WEST FAÇADE

LAUREN C. JOHNSON

sfwp.com

Library of Congress Cataloging-in-Publication Data

Names: Johnson, Lauren C, 1985- author
Title: The west façade / Lauren C Johnson.
Description: Santa Fe, NM : Santa Fe Writers Project, 2026. | Summary:
    "It's 1348, and the enchanted statue of Sainte Geneviève longs to be
    more than just an object on the Notre-Dame Cathedral. She wants to
    explore Paris, to understand her human makers, to love, and to live
    for herself. But when she gets what she wants, she is faced with an
    impossible choice: Remain mortal or return to her original form and
    live for eternity"— Provided by publisher.
Identifiers: LCCN 2025026357 (print) | LCCN 2025026358 (ebook) |
    ISBN 9781951631550 trade paperback | ISBN 9781951631567 ebook
Subjects: LCSH: Gargoyles—Fiction | Identity (Philosophical
    concept)—Fiction | Paris (France)—History—To 1515—Fiction |
    LCGFT: Fantasy fiction | Novels
Classification: LCC PS3610.O3626 W47 2026 (print) |
    LCC PS3610.O3626 (ebook) | DDC 813/.6—dc23/eng/20250721
LC record available at https://lccn.loc.gov/2025026357
LC ebook record available at https://lccn.loc.gov/2025026358

Published by SFWP
369 Montezuma Ave. #350
Santa Fe, NM 87501
www.sfwp.com

Praise for *The West Façade*

"Imaginative and immersive, *The West Façade* is a sensuous fairy tale all about the delights and horrors of the human body. I will never look at statues the same way again."

—Rita Chang-Eppig, author of *Deep as the Sky, Red as the Sea*

"Luscious and strange, *The West Façade* captivates with statues and gargoyles struggling to "resist gross, fleshy impulses." And thankfully failing. Lauren C. Johnson crafts a visceral, detailed novel about being alive."

—Tomas Moniz, author of *All Friends Are Necessary*

"Lauren C. Johnson's debut novel, *The West Façade*, steeps readers in a historical fantasy world that's subtly resonant for our current times. The medieval city of Paris comes alive, "filled with a manic energy that makes people want to sing and eat and buy things." Johnson's literally and symbolically rich, beautiful writing takes us on a journey for knowledge and purpose with the protagonist Geneviève, as her self-awareness deepens. The story is so well wrought and such a delight to read that the themes of feminism, the environment, pandemic, class and social hierarchies, antisemitism, and domestic abuse come through softly. Though Geneviève is a statue, she illuminates central questions of humanity's vulnerability and mortality. Johnson writes a rawness of the body that matches the historical time, but also accepts indelicate things, showing how people exist in cycles of life, death, and creation. In this book you'll learn what it sounds like to hear a gargoyle laugh, and you'll never look at statues the same way again."

—Heidi Kasa, Author of *Split*, *The Beginners*, and *The Bullet Takes Forever*

"*The West Façade* draws us into Paris at the onset of the Black Plague, if through the eyes of Sainte Geneviève, a statue with an insatiable appetite for life. A saint who transgresses and a character who yearns, Geneviève pierces her enchantment and sets out to find out what it means to be alive in this lush, sexy dream of a book for fans of *Piranesi*, *Fingersmith*, *Circe*, and the *ACOTAR* series."

—Yohanca Delgado, O. Henry Prize Winner, co-author with Janelle Monáe: The Memory Librarian

"*The West Façade* is a soaring novel that will take you from the spire of Notre-Dame down to the streets of Paris during the Plague and through the labyrinths of the human (and non-human) hearts. It is both an exhilarating adventure and a profound meditation on community, hope, and the kind of love that makes you brave enough to risk everything. Filled with delight, wonder, and so much yearning, this book reawakened me to the joy and preciousness of being alive. Un Enchantement!"

—Syr Hayati Beker, author of *What A Fish Looks Like*

"Lauren C. Johnson's *The West Façade* is an insightful meditation on what it means to be alive. The characters—both those made of limestone and those made of flesh—long for experience and friendship and community and love. Johnson shows us humans and statues at their best and at their worst, set against the tumultuous backdrop of plague-ridden Paris. A beautiful novel."

—Cari Luna, author of *The Revolution of Every Day*

To Matt Scott Carney, my partner and greatest champion

To Becky Durham, one of the first who encouraged me to write

To my parents, Sarah and Stuart Johnson, for everything

Prologue

Are you drawn to ugly things? I watch you walk the cathedral grounds, despite the rain, and stop to look at my teeth and eyes. Water spills from my mouth, and you tilt your chin towards me as if you'd like a drink. Your lips nearly part.

I see that I have your attention now.

I am Strix. I'm named for the birds that nested along the rooftop of the Cathédrale Notre-Dame de Paris when nights were still completely dark. I've clung to this wall for over six hundred years and believed in humanity and its revolutions. I've loved the things people have made; I've loved the way you harnessed energy and light. Your phosphorescent disco lights—I've loved those, too. The way you learned to fly and breach the black expanse beyond the atmosphere. I heard about that golden record you flung into the stars. You call it the Voyager message and it tells your story. You are committed to telling your story.

But now, your kind has changed the seasons.

I don't impress like the other gargoyles: the ones reclining from the balcony above the West Façade, elegant wings folded, showing their mouths to Paris. They are beloved because they are beautiful and new. They have been here for only two hundred years. As for me, I am just a long, slender face. I am all teeth. An old girl receding into the wall, c'est vrai. But don't pity me; I speak with pride. I've been here for a very long time, after all.

And you? You interest me. You're a tourist, aren't you? I can always tell. I've watched you come back to the cathedral day after day. You came to Paris seeking beauty and awe, and yet, here you are circling a gargoyle. Most visitors look at me with flat, dull eyes or gawk and regard me as trash from the Dark Ages. But you don't.

Ha, the Dark Ages. Of course, I remember the stink of the tanneries and the slaughterhouses. The plague's miseries, the stench of human illness, and how disassociation becomes the only way to look at so many funerary pyres.

But people are just as chaotic as they ever were, and I don't need to tell you how polluted your air has become. Now, long days of sun dry and crack me. Then, when the rains finally come, they bring more dissolution. I watch myself crumble, falling to the ground in pieces.

So now, before I lose another tooth, I speak. Écoutez-moi.

Notre-Dame has always been beloved, though most people prefer the limestone statues on the West Façade. There, the saints have kind faces, and the demons charm with twisted smiles. Hundreds of angels watch you from the arches. You're a little bit afraid of them, aren't you? Maybe there's pleasure in that fear.

But did you know why the West Façade is famous for its ornate beauty? Because the people who built this cathedral feared the Last Judgement. Back then, they believed the horsemen would come from the west, because that is where the sky swallows the life-giving sun at the end of each day. And so, the masons created a fortress of statues to protect the cathedral's western face.

The West Façade looks so alive, but now it is silent. Placid smiles and still lips. Cold hands and talons reaching out for you as if they'd like to draw you near. Long ago, they could. Long ago, on the night of the new moon, the buttresses, portals, and spires would murmur when the stars were the only source of light. They would wake. On these special nights, *The Wakenings*, the statues could turn their heads and speak.

Each month, they received one night of life, from dusk to sunrise, for protecting the cathedral. For letting the people believe their outstretched hands could break fevers, could fill ships with silk, could end drought and war.

They were stories carved into stone; with their posed bodies, they taught the people who couldn't read the written word.

For this great labor, the guardians received a gift. And for most of these statues, one night of life each month was enough.

This is where my story begins, because my story is bound to my maker's, a woman called Geneviève Donnadieu. Unlike the men credited for building this cathedral, her name is not immortal, so I trust you to remember it.

Geneviève was a statue who crossed the threshold into the mortal world. Each day she walked, she confronted her own death because that is what mortals do. Don't you want to know why she did it? Wouldn't you choose immortality if you could?

While you are here, I will repeat her story exactly as she told it to me, for she gave it to me to protect. It is my hope that you are worthy of her story, too. You, who loves gargoyles and seeks beauty and light amongst macabre things. Maybe I can give you a piece of awe after all.

No, this is not a love letter to the cathedral. This is a love letter to you—your kind. Despite everything, I know what you are capable of building.

Look now. It's raining again! My fragile body will not withstand this weather much longer. I speak with urgency before my mouth erodes.

PART I

CHAPTER I

Feast Day of Sainte Geneviève, January 1348

The girl came to me at Vespers, drunk, with a mouth full of grief. Her breath warmed my cheek as she squeezed next to me in my door jamb. I was so accustomed to the cold that her body heat startled me. She smelled like the almond cakes the bakers liked to sell in the parvis and beneath that, her stale breath. Her lips brushed my ear, and she dropped a gift into my outstretched hands; it rolled along the edges of my fingertips, warm and sticky, before it settled against my palms.

"Sainte Geneviève, I need help," she said through chattering teeth.

Snow flurries rose around her head and caught the waning light. She gripped my shoulders. From this height, she could not touch the ground with her boots, but if she fell, she would not break bones. Reaching my niche would have been a troublesome climb, but certainly not impossible for someone limber, like this young woman. Though I could easily see and hear anyone who approached the cathedral, I stood too high up for most to touch without a step ladder.

The girl had a round face, round eyes, and a woman's voice. Still adolescent: eighteen years at most. Her body shook, and her voice was a pressured whisper—a flurry of prayers. Her tears dampened my face and rolled towards the corners of my mouth.

"My parents are missing. Let them be alive!" She bit her lip so hard, I thought she would bleed.

She spat words about a merchant ship that had landed in a port called Messina, steered entirely by dead sailors. The ship carried illness in its cargo, and now people were dying throughout the south. She had family in Messina, and she'd heard the illness had claimed both parents and her eldest sister.

"Sainte Geneviève, I ask you to intercede! Protect my family. Let them live! But if you can't, if it's too late, at least let me speak to the dead." She squeezed the soft thing she'd placed in my hands. "Oh, Geneviève. I know it's wrong. I know I should never ask for such things."

I couldn't reassure her. I was not really Sainte Geneviève. I wasn't a saint at all. I was just a statue. A statue that stood outside the entrance to the Notre-Dame de Paris.

I tried to listen, but I got lost in the sensation of her touch and hot breath on my face. So rare was it to feel warm arms embrace me. I wanted to taste her tears so badly. If only one would fall between my parted lips!

I had always loved the feeling of being touched and tended to. Once or twice a year, artisans from the masons' guilds repainted the cathedral's West Façade, where I stood. Though no one had ever held a mirror to me, I knew how I looked. I could see the colors on the artisan's brushes, and Bathsheba, my favorite companion, told me herself, as if she were my mirror. I was given orange hair that curled around my face, brown eyes, and pink lips. I had round cheeks and round eyes. Every statue had childlike eyes and an expressive mouth. These exaggerated features helped the people see our faces in the architecture.

The masons painted my arms, hands, and face beige. My chemise, cote, and mantle were humble gray. I hated gray, so dull and solemn, but I had long learned to accept it. Some artisans had a gentle, steady hand and some were hurried and careless. I could tell a lot about a person from their touch.

And beneath that paint, I was limestone, porous enough to absorb light, heat, scent, and sound. I was all seams of bone-colored rock. I was soft-bodied, chalky, and old. Older than the hunched men playing tric-trac in the parvis. Older than the Avignon papacy. Older than Paris. Older than the Île de la Cité.

I could not remember my natal quarry or the faces of the men who had cut and hauled me into the sunlight. But in my body, I felt echoes of my separation from the earth.

"Find a way to let them speak with me," the girl begged. "Send a bird, a bird to fly between the worlds."

The doors swung open, releasing the flood of high, sweet voices singing within the cathedral into the crepuscular air. A monk poked out his ancient face.

"God's blood," the girl cursed, squeezing my neck.

"Get down from there, demoiselle!" The monk demanded. "You're disgracing the cathedral! During Vespers prayer, no less!"

Inside, the choir sang that wise men and fools, the rich and the poor, would all perish.

The girl smeared her tears with the back of her hand. "Forgive me," she muttered.

The monk withdrew into the cathedral and the girl whimpered.

"The devil may hear me, but I don't care, Sainte Geneviève. Please help me speak with my family. I need to believe I can speak to them. Send the bird!"

She gripped my hands and sleeves for support, yet I heard her leather boots rasp against the masonry when she slipped and tumbled, cursing all the way down.

The monk burst through the doors again.

"Miserable girl, what is the matter with you?" He eyed the girl's mantle lined with budge fur. "You look like a young woman who would know better. What is your name? I will tell your father you will not come inside to pray."

The girl stood, and I could see her well. Her brows were dark and straight, and her black hair hung past her shoulders. I knew her face, didn't I? This was the same girl who had placed candles beneath my alcove on Noël. On la Toussaint, she'd stared at me with lips moving silently in prayer. I'd seen her before that, too; on the Feast of Saint Michel, she looked up at me and smiled. Now, here she was again, with blood droplets beading her hands like gems. And as she sucked her palms, I felt that old longing: what did blood taste like? What did it feel like to bleed?

The girl suddenly sprinted across the parvis while the monk shouted after her. She elbowed her way through crowds milling around the hot wine and sweets stalls, bumping into a fashionable woman with a horned silk headpiece. The woman stumbled and cursed the girl, who barely glanced backwards to apologize. I would have laughed if I could. I kept my curious gaze on the demoiselle's back until she slipped into an alley beyond Rue Neuve Notre-Dame. Then I remembered the soft thing the girl had placed in my hands.

The gift was a citrus: a bitter cooking fruit. I absorbed its smell through porous stone, and I felt its weight settle in my palms. A delicacy as precious as a pouch of spice from across the sea. The girl hadn't gone inside to pray. She hadn't left candles at any of the altars, nor had she sung with the congregation. Instead, she had reached for the patron saint of Paris—what she *believed* was Sainte Geneviève—and she had meant for me, and me alone, to hold her offering.

I didn't know how to help her speak with the dead. I didn't know how to summon the bird she asked for. I only knew I wanted to press my fingertips into the fruit's skin and mark its flesh. I wanted to press it against my nose and mouth and inhale its acrid scent. This was an organic thing. A thing that could be eaten.

Evening deepened into night, and the bells rang for Compline prayer. Candlelight winked within windows of the tall, narrow houses that faced the parvis. Occasionally, a figure stood silhouetted in one of those dim openings. I longed to see beneath the steep, pointed roofs, and I strained to see inside the windows. But I could only hear the inhabitants. The clatter of pots, jars, and knives. Shutters squeaking on metal hinges. Laughter. Stray notes from a lute. Children fighting for possession of a tin knight. A feminine sneeze from one of those high-up windows.

Eventually, the parvis emptied, and I inhaled as a mortal would. It always felt so good to breathe. To welcome cold air between my teeth and let it fill my body. Old flecks of paint peeled from the corners of my mouth, and I could move my hands and feet once again. Folds of the sculpted mantle draped across my shoulders softened, and I sighed as I turned my head.

Smoky charred wood smells drifted from the houses and mingled with the scent of carthorses and manure. A breeze blew across the Seine, stinking of the tanneries—the unmistakable cow urine and quicklime. But I loved it all; this was Paris. Fecund. Alive.

I rolled my eyes upwards to note the position of the stars above Notre-Dame. Altair, the eagle's eye, winked from the sky's dome. Hours remained before daybreak. The watchman's footfalls echoed in the alleys. A torch-bearer's light bounced beyond the houses lining Rue de Oubloures, and slivers of light from prayer candles slipped beneath the cathedral's bolted doors, along with myrrh resin incense, an afterglow from the feast-day services at Vespers and Compline. But otherwise, darkness sheltered us.

In the door jamb that faced me, the angels Uriel and Gabriel stretched their gold-painted wings and caught starlight on their flight feathers. Saint Denis drew his tight-lipped, severed head close to his body and crossed himself as he always did when he began to breathe. In the centerpiece between the two wooden doors, pretty-faced Lilith, all red lips and cheeks, coiled around the Tree of Knowledge with a rattle of her scales. Bathsheba stirred beside me. We shifted our weight and looked at one another. The new moon had finally arrived and with it, all the gifts of our enchantment.

"Pleasant wakening," I said.

Bathsheba's pink lips cracked into a smile, and I could see her pointy little teeth. The green veneer on her eyes had peeled, revealing gray stone, but they were still kind. A year ago, her crown had been yellow, and her hair the color of a raven, but the spiteful sun and weather had faded both. Brown lines of paint creased around her mouth like aged skin. Still, if she were mortal and not stone, she would have been very beautiful. I thought she was, at least.

"Geneviève, what is that?" Bathsheba breathed. "Did that girl give you an offering? Give it here, let me see it!"

I reached out, ready to show Bathsheba the citrus.

Bathsheba and I stood next to each other in the door jamb facing the Portal of the Virgin. Saints Jean and Sylvestre stood on either side of us, and the four of us knew all there was to know about each other. But Bathsheba was my favorite. We told ourselves stories about how our bodies had come from the same quarry—that we had been cut from the same stone, split at our seams and planes. We called ourselves sister stone. Notre-Dame was a pillar for Parisians, and Bathsheba was a pillar for me.

I shared everything with Bathsheba. Of course, I would share this offering.

But just as I began to open my fingers, I changed my mind and darted my hands back into my mantle, concealing the fruit inside my newly softened clothes: a loose chemise worn beneath a loose, modest cote with a long skirt. The girl could have lit a candle or opened her alms purse inside the cathedral. Instead, she brought the statue of Sainte Geneviève an offering on her feast day. She asked Sainte Geneviève for help.

This gift was special. This offering was just for me. I didn't want to share it.

"It dropped from my hands. I didn't get the chance to look."

"What? You dropped it? An offering? Offerings are *rare*—only Michel and Marie ever receive them. How could you have dropped it?"

"I don't know," I said, my voice thin. "It must have fallen when the girl climbed down the façade."

"I didn't see anything fall!"

I looked away from Bathsheba and shifted my feet, creating as much space as I could between us. This was the first time I had ever lied. Yet, this was the first time something had belonged to me.

"No one has ever left me a gift," she said, her longing plain. She tilted her head to search the ground with her eyes, and I felt guilty. Bathsheba believed me. The desperate, grieving young woman believed in me too. She believed I could send her flocks of spirit birds and keep her family safe. She believed I really was Sainte Geneviève. I shifted awkwardly and felt the peel of the fruit split against my fingers. I tucked the citrus deep into my chemise, hoping no one would smell its fragrant flesh.

"Did you hear what the girl said?" I asked Bathsheba. "It was the strangest story."

Bathsheba shrugged. "She was crying and sniffling so much, I could barely understand her."

Jean leaned in, and Bathsheba flinched when the carved curls of his yellow beard grated against her shoulder. "I heard her. She said her father was on a trading ship that sank."

"That ship didn't sink," Sylvestre said, shaking his head until his pope's hat nearly slid off. "She said everyone on that ship died before it reached the port. It carried illness in its cargo."

"That's not what I heard," Jean said, now leaning over both Bathsheba and me.

"You must have misheard again. You're always mishearing people!"

"How could I have misheard? I was right here."

Sylvestre folded his arms over his white and gold fanon. Oh, how I envied Sylvestre's golden paint! "Jean, you are growing more and more unpleasant to stand beside with each year, and it's been a century!"

"Well, Geneviève, what did you hear?" Bathsheba asked. "After all, you're the one she prayed to."

I didn't want to talk anymore. I wanted to play with the citrus. "She heard the ship's crew was dead when it landed in the port and now death is spreading throughout the southern lands. She talked about Messina—that's where her parents and sister were."

"Merchants," Bathsheba said. "That offering must have been very rare and expensive indeed. Let me help you find it!" She looked like she wanted to climb from the façade and search the snowdrifts for the phantom fruit. She knelt on her pedestal, catlike, stone fingers gripping the door jamb ledge. Her kneecaps slid beneath sculpted fabric.

The Wakening gave us the flexibility of any living being. Porous, chalky stone softened. We could climb from our pedestals if we dared, but fear kept us in our proper places in the architecture. We all knew it was easy to break the enchantment. We all knew what had happened to the statues of L'Ecclésia and Saint Etienne. I grabbed Bathsheba's arm and tugged her upright. I hated how I'd lied to her. Already, she felt further away from me.

Sylvestre leaned in close and lowered his voice. "Where's Messina?"

"I don't know," I admitted. "I've never heard of it."

"Well, how are we sure it's a real place? She might have made it up," said Jean.

If there was something I had learned from standing still and watching humanity for over one hundred years, it was that people lied. For infinite reasons, people lied. Self-protection, convenience, or to impress one another. But I didn't know why someone would deceive a statue. The girl believed her story. I felt fear in her shaking hands. I absorbed the smell of fear in the sweat that had beaded on her forehead. But what was the original truth and how many people had embellished it before it reached her ears, then mine? She wasn't lying but, for her sake, I hoped it was a rumor.

And if it wasn't?

No one had ever come to me like this for help before, and I didn't know how to give her the thing she'd asked for. But I wanted to.

From high above in the architecture, within the pair of towers so great they cast shadows in darkness, the bells rang twelve times. We statues fell silent. This was Matins. Monks and nuns rose from their cloister beds, interrupting their sleep, to pray at the cathedral. We would wait until their hour-long vigil had ended and the clergy returned to their dormitories before we spoke and moved again.

Rows of Benedictine and Cluniac monks walked through the parvis towards the cathedral. Their heavy black tunics swept the ground and blended with the darkness, and their black hoods concealed their faces. Snow flurries swirled overhead, and a fine mist shrouded the monks along with the shadows and nighttime. I could only distinguish individuals when they stood one by one before the Portal of the Virgin and chanted, "Oh Lord, open my lips."

I recognized the moon-pale teenager who always kissed his book of devotionals. I recognized the aging, puffy faced one who always wore a massive gold cross inlaid with red and blue stones. I even saw the ancient one who'd scolded the girl who gave me the offering. Everyone washed their hands in a basin outside the double doors before stepping into Notre-Dame.

Next came the nuns, dressed in black habits nearly identical to their brother monks. Some wore leather belts cinched at their waists and plain wooden rosaries. I could tell which ones were novices by the white veils they wore beneath their hoods.

In a way, this procession mirrored the statues on the West Façade. Monks, nuns, and statues—we all served Notre-Dame. With their voices, the clergy brought the cathedral to life. The clergy made the cathedral sing. Meanwhile, we statues brought the cathedral to life through everything we represented.

And these monks and nuns were mysterious to me—unknowable in their dark clothing. Who were they beneath their habits? What did they desire in the privacy of their hearts? Perhaps I was just as mysterious to them as they were to me. Did they ever look up at the West Façade and wonder if we statues possessed our own hidden worlds?

Or not. Perhaps honoring the passing day with prayer hours was enough for them. Maybe the simplicity of their days freed them from the striving I'd witnessed among people.

After the last nun entered the cathedral, I turned my eyes to look up at the trumeau. Marie and The Child stood here between the double doors on a pedestal encircled by Adam, Eve, Lilith, and the Tree of Knowledge. Marie's blue robes—her coveted blue robes!—yellow crown, and light brown face were cracked from neglect. We all needed new paint, even The Child in her arms: the round-faced sculpture of a boy with one or two years at most, cherubic and smiling. His rosebud cheeks and lips, black eyes, and brown hair that curled around delicate ears had all begun to crack and fade from the weight of sun, snow, heat, and cold.

Above this Marie rose a triangular gable populated with earnest faces representing Heavenly Jerusalem and the Ark of the Covenant. Here, three layers of statues were carved into the wall. The first row depicted three prophets and three Old Testament kings. The next row housed an aged Marie, prone on her death bed, surrounded by the Twelve Apostles and two nameless angels preparing to carry her to the Sky. A third Marie graced the top layer, seated next to her son—youthful, resplendent, restored—on their thrones. Hundreds of curious cherubim watched down from the high, pointed arch, all vibrantly painted.

There were two more entrances that led into the cathedral from the West Façade: the Portal of the Last Judgment in the center and the Portal of Sainte-Anne on the right. Each was populated with hundreds of guardian statues I had never seen with my own eyes. Each statue— including me—had been created to relate Biblical stories to the people who couldn't read or write, which was most. We told stories with our posed bodies, smiling faces, and the objects we held. Parents would point to the façade and tell small children, "C'est la Vierge Marie."

Most days and nights, we were Sainte Geneviève or Bathsheba or Angel Gabriel, but on the new moon, we were ourselves. Our voices fell in place with the watchmen's footsteps, laughter from the Rive Gauche and the boats crossing the Seine, the dogs, goats, and sheep; a soft sound, like water running over rocks, like the lapping of the Seine against the shore, like the bells, like the dawn chorus of the birds. Just another cathedral sound, same as all the other sounds of Paris at this hour.

Sometimes, I would ask Bathsheba, "Don't you wish you could remember who made you? Don't you ever wonder if you're anything like your sculptor, your *maker*?"

Since the first wakening, I had always wondered who made me. If my traits matched theirs, like my bright hair and round cheeks. The things that always caught my eye in the parvis, like the woman who bartered with the beef seller, gesturing with broad hands as a child clung to the chaffed nipple. Or the falconer on horseback with her straight back and stern peregrines.

Bathsheba would say, "Oh, Geneviève, how many times have I told you it's best not to worry about the makers. We can't remember them, and we'll never know who they were, so let's forget about that."

"Then what about the quarry where we came from?" I'd ask. "Don't you want to know where it is?"

"What good will that do us?"

"Aren't you curious?"

"No! Everything I see in front of me is good enough. I'm happy enough to be alive one night each month. So should you. Don't you think it's painful to ask questions that can't be answered? Can't we just accept the gifts we have? Think of all we get to witness. We watch, and watch, and watch, and never die!"

I loved Bathsheba for appreciating our gifts. The present moment was good enough for Bathsheba, and I thought she was wise. But I saw the masons haul their carts to the cathedral, repairing fallen wall and façade, and I wondered whether any of these people had made me. I wanted to understand who I was.

Now this girl had picked me and given me an offering. In her grief, she asked me for something as tender as protection for her family. She asked me to speak to her dead. She had visited me three times before this night. Who was Sainte Geneviève to her?

Matins prayer ended, the clergy exited the cathedral, as silently and orderly as they had entered. When we had the night to ourselves again, I decided to address Marie.

Marie and I rarely spoke. Marie was important and intimidating, not just because of the figure she represented, but because she had a way of holding herself. She stood tall between the double doors, proud as the falconers, certain of her purpose on the cathedral. And her memory! She could recall the faces and names that belonged to each person who passed through the parvis. Which maker had gifted her with this grand ability?

"Did you see the demoiselle who climbed into my niche?" I called. "Do you know her name?"

I had to speak with more force than I normally did for Marie to hear me. Laughter floating up from alley taverns masked my voice.

Marie graced me with a smile and called back to me. "Yes, I saw her, and I've seen her before. Her name is Isabelle de Grantrue. She's the youngest child in a rich merchant family. You should pay more attention to the people."

"I was right," Bathsheba said, clearly proud of herself. "I wonder if she lives in a big house on the Pont au Change."

It was hard to pay attention to names and faces when the parvis was filled with so many curious things to watch and think about. But I wouldn't forget Isabelle's name.

Isabelle. Isabelle de Grantrue.

I reached into my clothes and squeezed the fruit with my fingers. I tried to feel the soft parts beneath the skin. There were bumps and ridges to run across my fingertips. A spot at the top where all the skin seemed to gather in the center like a nipple. I fought an urge to dig my fingernail there and break it open.

I would fight this urge to peel the fruit apart.

In the opposite door jamb, Constantin looked up and cleared his throat. "I overheard someone else pray about that ship!"

Beside him, Uriel nodded and lifted his slender hands. "I heard the same story, but the boat landed in Genoa, not Messina."

"Where's Genoa?" Sylvestre whispered.

I shook my head. I didn't know.

"North." Jean put his hands on his hips, smirking.

"Not true," said Gabriel, flicking his wings. "Genoa is in the south. But more to the point, I've heard these stories, too."

"It might have been Lucifer," Denis said gravely. He pulled his detached head even closer to his body.

Denis was always the one to remind us of the boundaries of the enchantment. Never wander far from our pedestals, never explore the edges of the cathedral. Remember that we were made to protect mortals, but we were not mortals ourselves. Do not let the people hear us, do not let the people see us move. Do not eat, do not drink, do not laugh so wildly. Most importantly, resist feeling and expressing emotions. Joy. Fear. Sorrow. Wonder. Grief. These were sensations for mortals, not the dignified cathedral guardians.

Remember the horrible thing that happened to L'Ecclésia and Etienne. How they gave into pleasure, all those wakenings ago, and now stood lifeless in the architecture. Two stone corpses. Ordinary, sun-crumbling statues.

Resist gross, fleshy impulses.

The moment Denis began this fretting, Gabriel and Uriel would use his severed head as a plaything, as if it were a simple ball in a game of la Soule.

Uriel sighed. "Oh, Denis. You and your Lucifer. You always think it's Lucifer!"

"It's probably a big story," Constantin snorted. "You know how people exaggerate. The merchants are the worst of them."

"Even if there is some truth to it, Genoa must be very far away," Jean said, waving a calcareous hand. "We don't have to worry about places like that. What happens there has nothing to do with us."

"Besides, illness comes for Paris every year and takes many people," said Uriel.

"Yes, but this sounds different," Denis said.

"Well, we can't get sick," said Constantin. "It doesn't matter to us."

"Oh yes, it does," Denis protested. "If too many people get sick and die, who will take care of us? Who will believe in us? Who will give us our purpose?"

Everyone began to murmur. Snorts and cackles from high up in the archivolts fanned over the double doors. I wanted them all to shut up and leave me to touch the citrus in peace.

Marie cut the noise with a gesture of her arms. "We will pray for Isabelle de Grantrue and her family."

This was what I'd wanted. Isabelle had asked for divine intervention from Sainte Geneviève, and though I wasn't Sainte Geneviève, this was the only way I could help her. Yet, I fumbled the citrus inside my mantle. I smelled it, fragrant and tart. I wanted to put it in my mouth.

No, Geneviève, don't eat it. We're not meant to eat. Remember L'Ecclésia and Etienne; remember the rules! Don't break the enchantment!

"Geneviève!" Bathsheba hissed, nudging me. I realized both she and Sylvestre were reaching for my hands. I muttered apologies and hid the fruit behind my back, pressed against the wall.

"Protect Isabelle de Grantrue's family from illness," we chorused.

The Child crawled from Marie's arms up into the archivolts. The cherub faces helped him, lifting his arms and legs as he ascended. He was our grimpeur, our climber. One of the only guardians who wasn't afraid to climb the architecture and move about freely, for the fact that he was such a little statue. He was swift and nimble as the gargoyles that clung to the cathedral walls, and the gargoyles that flew high above the cathedral to warn us of dawn before the first prayer bells.

The Child climbed past the archivolts and the Kings of Judah who stood in the upper balcony of the West Façade, high above the doorways. Then he joined the Archangel Michel before the great Rose Window and repeated those prayers to the constellations and the Sky. We believed that was how human prayers were heard.

The bells rang again—six times to herald Lauds and the sun's slow return, though the sky would remain dark for nearly two more hours. We released each other's hands and went still as the monks and nuns filed back into the cathedral, heads bowed as they chanted, "Oh God, come to my assistance." For the people, Lauds was a celebration: it represented a return to life after the long night, and the psalms and hymns were all about resurrection. But I hated Lauds because it meant The Wakening was ending for another month. And Good Sky, I hated how their prayers interrupted what little time we had left of The Wakenings.

Eventually, the clergy retreated, as they always did.

Denis' head made a spitting noise.

"Pray all you want, but trouble approaches," he insisted, lifting his head and swiveling it all around, trying to lock eyes with each of us. "This is about more than just the girl. If there truly is an illness spreading throughout the south, I hate to imagine what will happen when it reaches Paris—"

Poor Denis. Gabriel snatched Denis' head before he could breathe another word. "Nonsense," he said, holding the head up out of reach. "People are always getting ill. This moment will pass."

"You are all too somber," Uriel laughed, catching the head. "It is The Wakening. Those gooey, runny-eyed monks are all gone now! Be alive!"

Denis' body reached for his head, pushing blindly at the wings of the two angels. "Please," his head pleaded. "Do not break me!"

Uriel passed Denis to a cherub in the wall behind him, and the cherub threw him to one of the many imps perched above the doorway.

We reserved our game of Denis Soule for that rare silence between Lauds and Prime, when even the most devout monks were asleep in their chambers, resting for the day ahead, and the parvis was empty. Certainly, thieves were awake at this hour, but they either stuck to the taverns on the Rive Gauche or the brothels nestled in various alleyways beyond the Place de Gréve, on the Rive Droite. Certainly, lovers met for trysts on the banks of the Seine, but the cathedral and its population of statues was the farthest thing from their minds. We had this dark, ecstatic hour to ourselves. I savored it.

We had all played Denis Soule so much, that the paint had nearly peeled off his head completely. Between The Wakenings, Denis was a calcareous body clothed in red and violet painted robes and beige hands holding a poor bare-faced stone head.

Oh, I knew the game was cruel, but still I played along. We only had one night of life each month. And it was fun. I liked the feeling of hands reaching and grabbing. The way our stone made rustling sounds, feeling nearly short of breath. The way we almost forgot we were made of stone altogether.

I didn't want to play now, though. I wanted to roll the citrus in my hands. It should have been enough just to hold and protect it, as Isabelle intended. I shouldn't have dug my fingers into it. Why was I so determined to destroy it?

"That's enough!" Marie bellowed. "Leave Denis be."

Everyone sighed, a sound like a zephyr winding through the cathedral's cavernous halls. Bathsheba gave Denis to Sylvestre, who passed him along to the adjacent statues, and eventually his head was returned to his outstretched hands, ending the fun.

"I am grateful I can provide you with a distraction," Denis said, bearing chipped teeth. "We should enjoy our nights of play while they last."

"Sometimes, I think you wish for misfortune," Uriel murmured.

"I only wish you would listen to me," sighed Denis.

All too soon, we heard the familiar sound of wings strike the air. It was the somber gargoyle, flying from the East to West Façades to warn every companion guardian of dawn. The gargoyle never descended and never spoke to us. Gargoyles were solitary guardians; it was said that they spoke only to each other when they spoke at all.

From my position in the door jamb, I could only see shadows cut the sky and the slightest suggestion of wings. If I didn't know better, I would have thought I'd only seen a raven or a crow. But I did know better. Soon, we would hear bells and music swell within the cathedral for Prime and spill into the streets beyond the parvis.

No one watched me. I couldn't resist any longer. I turned over the fruit and peeled back its flesh. My fingers pushed open Isabelle's offering and pulled soft insides apart. What if I was more to Isabelle than just another object on the cathedral wall? What if she could see beneath the paint and the figure I represented, down to my seams? I felt sorry for destroying her offering.

But not sorry enough.

I closed my eyes and brought the fruit to my lips, concealed behind my hands. The tartness stung, and I delighted in my teeth and tongue as the sky turned pale. Juice filled my mouth and dripped down my chin. I bit and I chewed, and I bit, and I swallowed, and I chewed, and I bit, and I ate, and I felt delirious.

Bells rang from every side of Paris, from the church of Saint-Séverin on the Rive Gauche, to the church of Saint-Gervis on the Rive Droite. A booming, joyful response echoed here on the Île de la Cité—

or, simply, the City, as the people called it and as us guardians called it, too—from the bell towers of Notre-Dame and Saint-Chappelle. As the sky turned pink, my limbs stiffened, and my body returned to the form I was carved into. I was Sainte Geneviève again: a statue whose placid gaze promised peace and prosperity. Rigid and limestone with generous upturned hands. My palms forced open, and my fingers released the torn remains.

I did not know if I had broken the enchantment or if I would wake with the next new moon. I did not know if I had doomed Isabelle. My mouth twisted into its carved smile as the peel fell.

CHAPTER II

My lady keeps a viper in her heart
Which plugs her ear with its tail
So that she does not hear my sad complaint:
For this, no more, it always watches and listens.
And in her mouth lies unsleeping
The scorpion which stings my heart to death

From "Une vipere en cuer ma dame meint" by Guillaume de Machau
(c. 1300–1377)

I began to stink, not like scraps of old meat broiled in the sun, more like the cabbage heads abandoned from pushcarts and market stalls after feast days. Icy air tempered the worst of it, but I could smell sour rot on myself, and a sickly floral stench seeped through my smiling lips.

I knew Bathsheba, Jean, and Sylvestre absorbed the smell. How could they not, the way we stood pressed together? Surely, the imps carved into the wall behind me smelled it, too. I knew they liked stink, like good imps, because they always told me so. But did they know it was me this time? Had anyone seen me give in and eat the citrus moments before dawn?

I had eaten with both hands and pushing my teeth into something soft and earth-made felt so good. Filled my curious mouth. Ran my tongue across stringy, chewy veins. The satisfaction was far more delicious than the fruit, which was rather tart and acrid.

I wondered what my companions thought about the stench while they stood silently in harsh daylight. I wouldn't know until the next wakening.

If I was to have another wakening.

I still didn't know if I had broken the enchantment. Aside from the rotting thing inside me, I felt the same as I always did. I absorbed sights, smells, sounds, and the chill of winter air through porous skin. My thoughts and memories still belonged to me. But I didn't know if I would breathe and speak again with the next new moon. So, I could only watch people move through the parvis and wait out the days while the chewed-up thing lodged inside some hollow of my body decayed or was absorbed by limestone.

I looked for Isabelle de Grantrue in the throngs but never saw her. I worried for her and for her family in Messina; I felt protective of the young woman who had singled me out among all the stone saints to give an offering. I spent hours hoping those dark rumors weren't true and that Isabelle had been reunited with her parents, wherever they were. But I mainly passed the time inside my memories.

I remembered the first wakening. As the people said, it was in the Year of Our Lord 1220, and the masons had just completed the Portal of the Virgin. I turned to Bathsheba and ran my fingertips over her brow, eyes, nose, and mouth to understand what she was—to understand what I was. I awoke knowing my name—Sainte Geneviève—and nothing more. But as months passed, I began to understand words. Soon, on The Wakenings, my companions and I could speak in mortal language.

We learned that we were stories carved into stone but didn't know why we came to life each new moon. No one remembered the names of the people who had cut our bodies from raw limestone. We had soft, slippery memories of the natal quarries, but we couldn't place the hands that had hoisted us onto the cathedral wall. We didn't know if the neighboring Cathedral Sainte-Chapelle and Église Saint-Séverin were also watched by rows of living statues or if we were all alone.

We were all amused by the cheery, obscene songs written by troubadours and poets. I liked how the troubadours always attracted merry gatherings in the parvis, and the good singers could make the people go purple with laughter.

One song was particularly popular: *L'Evesque Qui Benei Le Con,* a loud, rude song about a priest.

Dist li prestres: <<Je n'en doubt rein.
Vous foutés, car je le voi bein!>>

Bathsheba and I loved these giggly, irreverent songs because they helped us understand the people, our makers. Every person who crossed my line of sight was fascinating to watch and hear and smell, but I found some particularly alluring. I had it in me to want to bite mouths or kiss necks or pull stockings towards ankles. Slip my hands beneath a working man's tunic or undo the metal belt that secured a lady's cote. I could do none of these things—sometimes, my longing drove me mad. Sometimes, I thought I would salivate. I even longed for Uriel a little bit, for just a handful of weeks, until I realized he didn't seem to notice me—not in a way I wanted—and the feeling passed.

Then, one wakening, Bathsheba leaned close to me and asked, "Do you think we look human beneath these long, loose gowns?"

The people were mostly suggestions hidden beneath linen, wool, and silk, but I could imagine what bodies looked like. I saw plenty of women breastfeeding babies. I saw swollen nipples every day. Some breasts were long and stretched, others short. Some pointed straight out, while others went east and west.

Sometimes, I saw ass cheeks when the men pissed behind market stalls. Some rounded with muscle, others flattened with age. Covered with red splotches from the pressure of sitting in one place too long or marked with acne scars.

Had the person who sculpted me given me more than what I could see? On The Wakenings, my garments softened just enough for me to shift in my niche. Was there more sculpture, more body, beneath? Did I have sloping breasts and stretch marks on my belly, too? Bathsheba's question made me curious, a little afraid, and very self-aware.

"I don't know. How long have you been thinking about this?" I asked Bathsheba.

"All month," she sighed.

"Should we look underneath our chemises?"

Across the portal, none of my other companions appeared interested in their bodies. They all happily accepted that they represented saints, angels, and divine beings.

Bathsheba lowered her eyes.

"Let's wait until the next wakening," she said.

"Why?"

"Because we don't know what we'll find," she said. "What if we don't want to know the truth? Maybe some things are meant to be mysteries."

Months passed and we never grew courageous enough to look beneath our clothing. As the masons completed the cathedral towers and East Façade, we learned much more about human bodies. Bodies made of skin were fragile. Sometimes, bodies made of skin fell from scaffolding and broke open on the rough earth. Sometimes bodies got crushed beneath falling masonry.

It was better to be made of stone.

Still, I grew fascinated with the mortal world. I learned how to distinguish the heady scent of bread from butchered meat. I could smell blood. And beer and wine.

I learned that women bled each month—a cycle tied to the dance between life and death.

People had preferences for different kinds of food, and I began to understand why. Through porous stone, I absorbed the smells of turmeric, saffron, and even salt, and tried to imagine the routes these goods had traveled to reach Paris. I stood in my alcove with a curious mouth.

I learned that people could love one another.

Hate and fear each other, too.

Then, on the Feast of Fools, ecstatic men and women stripped off mantles, cotes, tunics, stockings, and linen underpants and ran howling through the streets—balls, bellies, and breasts bouncing merrily—until the night guards caught and fined them.

I learned how the people were supposed to love this cathedral. They were supposed to love something called faith. A great kingdom of the Sky. The people had built the cathedral for their god and made the statues for their god. But we preferred the sky. Sky above and the earth from which we'd been pried, those were our deities—if we were to have deities at all.

And what about loving a tongue hanging from a pretty mouth? A kiss? I loved the skin-bodies, how everyone looked so different from each other.

I thought everyone was so beautiful.

And I wondered what it would feel like to climb down the wall. What would it feel like to live among the people I watched over?

One year later, in the Year of Our Lord 1221, or was it 1222 or 1223?—sometimes, my recollection of a particular year and date failed me—The Wakening fell on the Chandeleur. Crowds gathered in the parvis and converged into a raucous procession towards the cathedral. On the Chandeleur, it didn't matter which families people belonged to; Bishop Guillaume de Seignelay would bless anyone's candle for protection against famine and illness in the coming year, though both felt like distant, faraway threats. Problems for other cities to worry over, not Paris with its paved streets, ever-growing wall, flourishing guilds, and university. Paris' wealth would last forever and ever, as would the cathedral and its statues.

People squeezed against the West Façade all day, jamming their bodies into any place they could to watch the musicians in the parvis. I caught snatches of conversation in French and Latin—languages I understood—and languages I had learned to recognize, from months of watching and listening to parades of merchants and dignitaries visit the City, as Ethiopian, Coptic, Castilian, Greek, Tuscan, and German. The nervous energy made it easy to imagine what getting drunk on ale and hot wines would feel like. Frenetic laughter swirled with smells of lavender and sweat-drenched clothes. The flash of pale buttocks here and there as men adjusted their leggings to piss against a wall or tree.

The people were so alive. How bewildering to know they would one day die. All of them. And yet, I would not.

Goliards played the pipe, tabor, and five-stringed rebec, making people laugh with bawdy, silly songs about priests with lovers. For hours, we heard *Le Preste et Le Leu*, *Le Preste et Alison*, *Le Prestre Crucefié*, and *Le Prestre Qui Ot Mere Magré Sein*, followed by *Le Prestre Qui Abevete*, each song rowdier and obscener than the last. There were so many songs about priests, I could hardly tell when one ended and the next began.

I once overheard Bishop de Seignelay complain about these songs, but he knew there was very little he could do to stop people from writing and singing what they wanted. The Church had tried to forbid these songs before, and that seemed to make the people want to sing them more.

I studied Uriel, Gabriel, and Denis in the opposite niche. Freshly painted blue, green, and ebony eyes and gold-trimmed robes. Their colorful paint made me seethe with envy. Why did they get to have all the fun while I was stuck with boring gray? Uriel shifted as if he fought a temptation to stretch his wings. I twitched impatiently, too. I wanted to touch the people streaming in and out of the cathedral doors as they passed beneath me. No one noticed; no one heard the rolling crack of stone come to life. Or perhaps, if anyone did, they laughed and whispered under their breath that flickering candlelight could make any statue look like the living.

I wondered if the little imps carved into the wall behind me wanted to blow out all those lit candles—I certainly did—just to see what would happen. I wanted to touch ermine-trimmed points on the noble ladies' hats. My fingers twitched and craved the feel of silk. I fought to keep myself from pulling out a young girl's ribbon.

It was the crowd. The smell of alcohol and songs that sounded more violent as the hours passed. Mostly, this great gathering was orderly, yet there was a wildness running through the throng. Anything could break the tension, turning people animal.

The constellations Cepheus and Cassiopeia danced, spinning around each other in the sky. Then, finally, the bells rang for Compline, and the people grew weary. The night guards took up their torches and patrolled the alleys, but some people remained until Lauds had ended. When the parvis fell quiet, only two hours remained of The Wakening.

The cathedral walls shuddered abruptly, and Bathsheba and I lifted our heads. I gripped the walls to steady my balance. Denis crossed himself.

The cathedral was shaking! Not something inside the cathedral but within its structure. Not the sound of a falling pillar or crumbling piece of the edifice—nothing that simple. The walls were moving as if they, too, could wake and breathe. Bathsheba, Sylvestre, Jean, and I held each other's hands.

I looked across the parvis and saw them. The allegory, L'Ecclésia, and the monk, Saint Etienne. Both statues had climbed down the façade.

"Join us!" they said. "Let's enjoy the gifts of The Wakening. Let's take what the people left behind."

I knew L'Ecclésia and Saint Etienne stood separately in the porticos between the portal entrances. But I had never seen them before that night. They were tremendous—twice as tall as me. L'Ecclésia was a vibrantly painted woman with a plump, feminine body and Saint Etienne was an obedient-faced monk with a respectable tonsure, bald except for the thin circle of hair crowning his head.

They moved through the detritus as if they were people and fussed over bouquets of crumpled violets and picked over food scraps from the empty market stalls. Half-chewed beufz pasties, bowls of bog beans, and sugared flans. The statues' thighs pushed against their painted skirts, moving like muscle and fabric with The Wakening's touch. Their laughter ripped through the parvis.

Even they were adorned with colorful paint!

My chest tightened. I wanted to climb down and join them, but I was afraid—afraid of breaking the enchantment. Why weren't they?

Why couldn't *I* be like them?

Bathsheba grabbed my hand and pointed towards Saint Etienne, now a silhouette ambling towards the shuttered shops on Rue Neuve.

"Someone's going to see them," she breathed. "It's nearly dawn."

The gargoyle circled the cathedral, and the chanting monks approached from the East Façade for Prime.

"He's not going to return," I said, with obvious admiration and jealously.

"What's he going to do out there?" Denis asked though he knew just as well as I did. Etienne did not intend to return. Instead, he would cross the threshold between the cathedral grounds and City.

I wanted to climb down the façade and see beyond the parvis. I longed to drink the wine spilling from toppled cups. I wanted to join Etienne but couldn't follow him; I couldn't bring myself to leave my safe niche.

Just before Etienne disappeared beyond the row of houses along the parvis, he turned around and looked at the cathedral. Meanwhile,

L'Ecclésia returned to the façade, morning's first light on her back. I thought of the old stories I sometimes heard poets and troubadours tell in the parvis—the ones the Church tried and tried to forbid but couldn't because they were too ancient and too beloved. Pagan stories about goddesses of bounty, Juno and Ceres. A pomegranate-mouthed goddess called Perséphone. L'Ecclésia looked even more like a fertility goddess when she lifted her cup to drink, and I admired the carved outline of her buttocks beneath her robes. Before she climbed back into her portico, I saw the smile on her face. Not the simple smile her maker had given her but a genuine, mortal smile. Paint creased around her eyes as if it was skin.

Saint Etienne returned to the cathedral on the back of a cart the following evening. He was just as powerless in daylight as the rest of us, silent and still. The masons lowered Etienne back into his portico and wondered over the thief that had left him lying sideways before the Hôtel-Dieu, in Rue du Sablon.

For the next three weeks, the watch took special care to patrol the parvis. But no other statues were stolen, and the vigilance wore off. By the next wakening, we spoke freely without concern that the people would hear us.

Saint Etienne and L'Ecclésia would not wake. The rest of us moved, breathed, and spoke, but the portico statues had become lifeless and ordinary. They had broken the enchantment; they hadn't returned to their proper places in the architecture before dawn.

That night, Archangel Michel addressed the entire West Façade from the Portal of the Last Judgement. Here is how I imagined he did it: He turned to the statues that stood to his right in the Tympanum, figures I'd heard had been carved with crowns and pale, draping garbs, their hands clasped in prayer and their faces tilted skyward. These statues represented The Pure.

Michel asked The Pure to repeat his message to the statues in the lower lintel below, men and women pushing through their tomb lids for resurrection. Then, The Resurrected spoke to the faces of ancient kings and church doctors in the arches. The Foolish Virgins swinging empty oil lamps from the cathedral wall whispered Michel's words to The Apostles in the door jambs.

The Apostles turned to the imps and cherubs and whispered Michel's message until his words reached the Portal of the Virgin. It was an urgent message passed between guardian statues, but to the ordinary ear, our voices sounded like the language of crows.

The West Façade burst into riots of questions.

Could the portico statues ever wake?

Could they still see and hear us?

Had their minds gone silent too?

Were they dead?

Could *we* die?

"We must all atone!" Michel said through the lips of other statues. "We are in sacred agreement with the Divine to protect the cathedral. Now two fewer guardians will be left to protect Notre-Dame on Judgement Day. We must atone for this great loss."

"How do you know?" Marie responded. "How do you know it is our role to protect the cathedral?"

Sylvestre clutched his pope's crown and leaned over the divide that separated the Portal of the Virgin from the Portal of the Last Judgement. He repeated Marie's question to the imps and cherubs carved into the wall there, and those statues relayed the message to The Apostles. The Apostles passed Marie's message on until it reached Michel.

Michel responded through the layers of statues.

"I am the Archangel Michel. I am your Alpha and Omega."

Bathsheba looked at me with big round eyes. Marie pursed her lips together. Before we could ask another question, Michel told us we must choose a grimpeur, a climber from each of the three portals to carry prayers to the Sky. He told us we must pray to the Sky to bring our companions back to life.

"But how?" we asked. "How will we climb? How far shall we climb?"

"The three guardians will climb the façade until they reach the Virgin's Balcony. There, they will pray for L'Ecclésia and Saint Etienne. They will pray to restore the enchantment. The grimpeurs will return to their proper positions in the architecture before dawn. They will trust that the cathedral will support their climb because statues and façade are one."

"I will be grimpeur," said The Child. "I'm small and nimble; no one will notice my climb."

"Nonsense," Marie scoffed. "Michel's idea is foolish. You can't climb; if you fall, you'll shatter into a thousand pieces."

"You will not tell me what to do," said The Child. "You are not the Holy Mother. You are not my mother; you are just a statue."

"I ought to drop you," said Marie. "You know this Michel isn't the true Archangel Michel. He is not 'the alpha and omega.' He claims to know why we waken and the true nature of our role on the façade, but he's just as much in the dark as we are. Michel is a statue, just like me and you."

The Child opened his mouth and bit the crook of Marie's arm, breaking a tooth with a snap.

"Oh!" he cried.

Denis gasped.

"Serves you right," Marie spat. "Fool."

Bathsheba and I looked at each of them with our round, surprised eyes. The violence was so unexpected. Then, despite ourselves, we began to snicker, hiding our mouths behind our hands.

"Well, personally, I find it a relief that one of us has figured out why we waken each month," Jean said. "Of course, we're here to protect the cathedral! That's the only logical answer!"

The statues that made up Heavenly Jerusalem and the Ark of the Covenant nodded their agreement and mouthed affirmative sounds.

And so, Michel convinced us to elect grimpeurs.

Years passed, and the grimpeurs climbed. Marie worried over The Child but released him with less reluctance each wakening. Soon, she stood with her back and shoulders straight.

When the gargoyle passed over, warning us of Prime, The Child returned to Marie, and the pair whispered about everything he'd seen and heard above the Portal of the Virgin. I often heard them cackle with laughter.

The sleeping statues never woke. Eventually, we accepted they were ruined, and it was their fault. They should have been able to control their desires—resist feeling anything like desire, just like the rest of us. We didn't talk about climbing down the wall and leaving the cathedral grounds again. We were satisfied in our niches, though I observed that the most satisfied among us were the ones who had the best view of the parvis, those statues in the trumeau above the double doors: Heavenly Jerusalem, the Ark of the Covenant, Three Prophets, Aged Marie, The Son, and Twelve Apostles. Meanwhile, between The Wakenings, Bathsheba, Jean, Sylvestre, and I could only stare at the houses on Rue Char-Rori. I tried not to feel resentful of that fact.

And whenever I hungered for one of those pretty-faced people in the parvis, I swallowed down my longing and told myself it wasn't real. I was a guardian statue, after all, incapable of desire.

Bathsheba developed a beautiful singing voice and could remember most of the poets' and troubadours' songs. But she stopped wondering if her maker had sung beautifully too. She stopped wondering if Uriel and Gabriel's makers had been as roguish as the two angels and whether a smelly, impish man had carved the little imps in the wall behind me. She stopped wondering what our bodies looked like beneath our clothes.

But Bathsheba did notice how moss blanketed our arms between paintings, soft and hoary, and she noticed how spiders adorned us with their lacey webs. She pointed out families of sparrows that built their nests in the archivolts; she didn't even mind their droppings. I hadn't noticed the beauty in this growth, and I was grateful to Bathsheba for showing me.

One night, I told Bathsheba I wished I could see the other side of the cathedral.

"Why would you ever want to leave the West Façade? It's the best place there is. It is the most beautiful place in the world."

"How do you know?" I asked.

"Look at everything in front of us, Geneviève. We are so lucky to be what we are. We have infinite time to learn all the songs and all the languages. I wouldn't trade my perfect body for a body that decayed."

I nodded and convinced myself Bathsheba was right. I would never see beyond the parvis, but I would live forever. All the other statues believed that was good enough. For a long time, I convinced myself it was, too.

CHAPTER III

Approximately the Chandeleur, February 1348

The spice merchant, Monsieur de Berry, held court in the parvis again. When he was in Paris, he moved between the markets at the Halles, Place de Gréve, and the Porte-de-Paris. But he always returned to the parvis, where the clientele loved him best; everyone left mass with tongues burning for sweets.

Monsieur de Berry was a rather plain-looking man with fair skin, prone to sunburn. His face was always chapped. His hair was wheat-colored, and his features were thin and unremarkable. But he overcompensated for his appearance with fine clothes: red wool tunics and ermine-lined mantles. When he wasn't in the markets, his associates said he could be found in any number of taverns and brothels in the Rive Gauche.

Today, he had arrived from Venice bearing crates of Mecca ginger, cinnamon, lump sugar, cloves mixed with grains of paradise, candied orange peels, lemons, and red anise. People crowded his booth, eyes bloated with adoration, eager for stories from abroad.

I heard him go on about the cursed ship that had washed up in Messina. It was all anyone could talk about. When the ship arrived in the port, most of the crew was dead, but a handful of sailors had managed to steer home. Unfortunately, those survivors fell ill in a matter of days too. A week later, a second ship filled with dead sailors landed further north in Genoa. Monsieur de Berry spewed big stories when drunk, but I knew this was true.

"Fais moi confiance, you do not want this illness," he said. "I've seen it with my own eyes. It's a curse. The eggs of demons grow beneath your armpits—and crotch. The spots grow and grow and grow and turn black and pop into stinking, oozing sores. Imagine, if Lucifer had a goshawk. No, a serpent! A serpent that could hatch eggs beneath your skin. That's what this looks and smells like."

The audience coughed uneasy laughs. I looked for Isabelle de Grantrue in the throng but didn't see her. I hadn't seen her since the Feast Day of Sainte Geneviève, and I was worried.

Monsieur de Berry's teeth poked through his smile, reminding me of foxes and hunters. I knew he savored the attention. Sometimes, when I watched him, I wanted to snatch the eel pasties from his clean hands. The Church preached humility and modesty, but here was the spice merchant, proud and unashamed of his humanity.

Because he was a man. And not just any old man trudging along behind a pushcart or sheering wool, but a relatively wealthy man. I couldn't help but notice how the Church and society were willing to look the other way a lot more for men like the spice merchant than poorer men, much less any woman.

Meanwhile, it seemed that women, no matter how wealthy—no, especially the wealthy!—faced scrutiny from the Church and social circle gossips. The people believed women were naturally wanton and prone to corrupt men, just like Eve from the stories. Eve was weak-willed. Why else would she take a gift from a nasty serpent? Only when women devoted themselves completely to their families and the Church could they transcend their nature.

So, it seemed that women learned to fear their own humanity. Meanwhile, this spice merchant could say and do whatever he wanted without a second thought. I wondered what that kind of freedom felt like. I envied him. I wondered how many mortal women envied him, too.

"Oh, you are wicked," the lamprey monger laughed. "What a wicked tale."

"But it's the truth!" said Monsieur de Berry.

When the din softened, the baker, Monsieur Bondavid, spoke. "But have you heard any news about the flagellants?"

"God's bones, no," the spice merchant reached for his hip flask. "The flagellants went away ages ago. That's one thing we don't have to worry about."

The baker shrugged. "Well, I heard they're on the move again, coming on foot from the Kingdom of Hungary."

"What do you know about the Kingdom of Hungary?" asked the merchant. "I've heard many rumors on the trade routes, but I haven't heard a breath about those idiot fanatics."

The spice merchant yawned, displaying the inside of his damp, cavernous mouth and thick tongue. He didn't even bother to cover his mouth behind his hand.

My abdomen clenched with pain.

Twice, I had seen the flagellants' cheerless progression down Rue Char-Rori and through the parvis. Great mobs of men striking their own bodies with many-tailed ropes and spiked clubs. They said they'd been born to suffer, just like their savior who'd died for them. Split open tender skin, split open like butcher's work, like parted lips, like blossomed flowers, like the citrus I'd squeezed apart.

I'd seen them taunt people who wouldn't join them. I'd seen them pull an unwilling man into a circle and split his tunic. If they were so willing to destroy flesh, what else would they abuse in their passion? The cathedral walls? A beloved statue?

I kept looking for Isabelle from the cathedral wall, but she did not return.

I grew more and more anxious as Compline approached. Soon, I would know the repercussions of eating the citrus. Soon, I'd see if I'd ever waken again. No matter what happened, I sensed that this night, this wakening above all wakenings, would mark the moment when my existence changed irrevocably. I couldn't imagine what would happen next, but I feared change.

The night sky bathed the City in darkness, and I inhaled with a loud and greedy gasp.

"Geneviève?" Bathsheba asked.

"Pleasant wakening!" I cried, ready to throw my arms around Bathsheba and kiss her on both cheeks.

Pain suddenly burned through my body. Sour juice shot up my throat and filled my mouth. Stringy and tender. Pressure bearing on my chest, forcing my lips apart. I cupped my hands to my mouth and fought the lump in my throat. A mass pushed against my tongue. One cough and out came the remains of the rotting citrus fruit, splattering to the ground.

Bathsheba shrieked. "What was that?"

"I think it was bird shit," I whispered, my throat slick.

"That was no bird," Bathsheba hissed.

I curled my lips. "Yes, it was."

Bathsheba faced me with her eyes wide and owlish. "Did it land on you? You're shaking!"

"I'm fine."

And it was true, I did feel better. My body didn't ache anymore. In fact, I felt elated. I hadn't broken the enchantment.

She nudged Jean and Sylvestre. "Didn't you see that?"

But our companions were not paying any attention to us. I followed their pointed fingers to the ground between the double doors. A youth gazed up into the Portal of the Virgin with wet green eyes. He clutched a lit candle that illuminated his blue mantle, covered in countless golden stars.

I realized he wasn't a youth at all but another statue. A painted limestone angel holding scales in one hand and the candle in his other.

His eyes weren't flesh; someone had recently painted them green. His hands and face were silver instead of beige or brown paint. I knew him at once. He was Archangel Michel.

I had heard the others describe Archangel Michel many times before. Michel with eyes painted of emerald. Michel cut from lovely porous stone, malleable and oursin-bone bodied. Calcareous. Michel was the Portal of the Last Judgement's grimpeur, and The Child often talked him up with great respect. I remembered the night he spoke to all the statues, passing his messages ear-to-ear, lip-to-lip. Ever since, I'd imagined that Michel was tremendous, like L'Ecclésia and Saint Etienne. But I hadn't imagined he would be so delicate and lithe.

Bathsheba inhaled sharply. So did I. With his gold and silver paint glimmering behind candlelight, Michel looked like he had swallowed an ember. He radiated power, despite his diminutive figure. He was a masterpiece. He was the most beautiful statue I had ever seen.

"Pleasant wakening, children of the Portal of the Virgin," Michel said, bowing deeply.

Awestruck, we all bowed in response. No one had touched feet to ground since the two portico statues.

A woman and her companion swept past the cathedral, too close for my liking. "The cathedral always looks so pretty around the Chandeleur," she said. "Look how the statues hold candles!"

The pair chattered and walked on without noticing Michel. I knew they were much too involved in their conversation to be observant, but if they did see Michel, they would tell themselves later that their eyes had been playing tricks on them. That was how most people were.

"I come to you with a grave message," Michel said. "Things are so serious, I must see and speak with you myself."

Bathsheba squeezed my hand, rotten pulp now forgotten. "I can't believe he climbed down the wall," she whispered. "How bold!"

"A deadly illness is spreading from the south. It infests the human body and causes the skin to rot and break open. The people call it the

Great Death, and it's coming for the papacy in Avignon and then Paris. It is evil. Not only does it threaten the people, but it also threatens the cathedral. It threatens all life. I heard it from the lips of Bishop Foulques de Chanac. We are in terrible danger.

"That is why I've left my niche tonight to talk to you," Michel continued. "I've never seen your faces and you've never seen mine, but this is urgent. I believe we must do something. The Wakening is a gift. Let's use it to do something good."

Everyone spoke at once.

"We've heard the people talk about the illness too," Uriel said. "It begins with the common sweats then eggs grow beneath the skin."

"And they break open and smell fetid," Gabriel said.

"The tongue turns black and dries up in the mouth," Uriel said.

"And tears turn to blood," Gabriel continued.

"Balls burst open!" cried Uriel.

"So do cunts!" shouted Lilith. "And don't forget about assholes. Aren't you glad you don't have an asshole?"

Michel's upper lip twitched into a sneer, and he wrinkled his nose, silver paint bunching into the center of his face.

"Enough!" said Marie.

Gabriel and Uriel laughed behind their fingers.

"Do you believe we guardian statues can catch it?" Constantin asked.

"I don't know," Michel said. "But does that matter? Think about the people. They must be horrified. Can you imagine waking up and every day another neighbor is dead? Can you imagine losing your entire family? How could you stand to rise in the morning?"

The walls and arches became a jumble of jutting faces crying, "We must do something! We must stop this illness!"

"Yes, we must do something," Michel said. "We should choose more grimpeurs. Each portal should have two. Then surely, we can help the people's prayers reach the Sky."

"Two more grimpeurs? Someone will see us," Marie said.

Michel nodded thoughtfully before he replied.

"I understand your fear, Marie. But I'm standing here before you, holding a lit candle I snatched from an altar outside the entrance, and the people haven't noticed me."

"We don't know much about this illness; we haven't seen it for ourselves," Marie said. "I think we're doing all we can do right now. Climbing is dangerous for stone beings. The Child makes a sacrifice each wakening when he climbs. I don't think we should send a second grimpeur to the Sky."

"Furthermore, the people find us comforting to look at," she continued. "The ones who cannot read written words—mind you, that's most of them. They look to us to learn their lessons. We are stories carved into stone. Isn't that enough?"

Michel must have felt my gaze sweep the soft arch of his neck. He looked up and our eyes met just before I turned my head.

The bells rang for Matins, and we fell silent. That familiar rhythm of cloister doors swinging on hinges, heavy footsteps, and the hum of chanting voices filled the parvis. I held my breath, certain at least one keen-eyed monk would see Michel. How could they not? He stood out of place beside the double doors in the Portal of the Virgin.

Lithe, silver-faced Michel, clutching a lit candle and staring at the monks as if to dare them, paint glistening.

No one said a word.

Not one person noticed the bold little statue of the Archangel Michel. The monks prayed inside the cathedral, and when they finished one hour later, they treaded past Michel.

How did he do that?

"You see, the people don't pay us any mind at all. We're safe to climb," said Michel triumphantly.

"No," Marie replied. "Climbing is dangerous, and we don't know if it will do any good. No, I won't send another grimpeur from my portal. Not until we know more about this Great Death."

Michel pressed his lips together and closed his eyes as if searching inside himself.

"I think you should reconsider," he said.

Heavenly Jerusalem and Ark of the Covenant began to protest. "Listen to Michel! Listen to the archangel!"

"Look what he can do!" shouted Sylvestre.

"He has strange powers over the people," Jean said, fussing with the sleeves of his pale blue robes.

"He does not!" Marie said. "We already know the people do not seem to see us when we stand still. Michel was the only one either daring or foolish enough to test the limits of the enchantment in another portal."

"The Portal of Sainte-Anne has chosen a second grimpeur," Michel insisted. "You must too. What do you think will happen to the cathedral if there's no one left to take care of us? Do you think these walls will remain standing without human care? Who will paint your pretty, blue mantle?"

Marie shook her head no and dismissed him. "Thank you for visiting the Portal of the Virgin," she said.

With one short breath, Michel extinguished his Chandeleur candle and dropped it. He pressed his hands together and bowed a final time.

"We must be good, companions. Especially you, Marie, for all that you represent," Michel said, pointing a finger at her. "No jealous thoughts or jealous deeds. The people depend on us to represent their saints. We must embody purity of heart and mind and body. I know we can. I do believe in us."

When he walked towards the Portal of the Last Judgement, the cherubim cried for him to come back.

"She sent him away!" Sylvestre hissed. "Why did Marie send him away?"

"Marie is too solid; I've said it a thousand times. No porosity." Jean said.

Michel was a wonder to me. He had climbed down the wall and touched the ground with his feet. His feet! The grimpeurs climbed, but they never parted from the cathedral walls.

Michel wasn't afraid to part from the cathedral wall. He wasn't scared to leave the Portal of the Last Judgement. Where did he find this courage? This courage missing from the rest of us?

The monks returned for Lauds, and we slipped into silence again. I thought only of Michel. I was awestruck. When the prayer hour ended, Bathsheba touched my shoulder and nudged me to face her.

"What do you think of Michel?" I asked. "He's fascinating. Why did Marie dismiss him?"

"Tell me the truth," Bathsheba whispered, ignoring me. "What came out of your mouth?"

"Nothing came out of my mouth."

"But I saw it!"

"No, no, it was nothing." Hot with shame. "It was a bird. You imagined it."

"I'm scared you have the illness," she said through gritted teeth.

"Oh, Bathsheba. I promise you I do not have the illness. That's not possible."

"How do we know?"

"Because we've never been ill before."

Bathsheba lowered her eyes.

"You've never lied to me before," she said, slowly as if to consider each word. "I know you wouldn't lie to me now."

I ignored her sideways glance and wrapped her in a hug. Stone against stone did not grate. Instead, the ridges and divots in our bodies fit together as if two halves were whole again.

"I admit, I'm worried," she said. "We have witnessed so much since the first wakening, but something feels different now." She turned her chin towards the stars, fixing her gaze on Cepheus and Cassiopeia. "Doesn't it feel like everything is about to change?"

"Yes," I sighed. "It does."

It was true. I hadn't broken the enchantment, but I felt unsettled.

"Do you think everything will be okay?" I asked.

"Yes," Bathsheba said. "Because it has to be."

Spring

Paris filled with a manic energy that made people want to sing and eat and buy things. The young baker and her brothers sold all their almond biscuits each morning before Terce. Soon, the saltwater fish seller ran out of Marne carps, sole, and salmon. The butcher sold all his ox cheeks.

People talked about the illness, but it was all parvis gossip.

Did you hear that Master Jehan died on Tuesday? Such a shame.

He was very kind, but I suppose he was an old man.

Monsieur du Bois needs a new horse steward now, but he can't find a good replacement. Do you know anyone? Someone who's not planning to leave the city?

Mon dieu, Esther. Everyone I know talks about leaving these days. But perhaps that's not a bad thing. Perhaps it will bring down the price of bread and make it easier to buy a market stall in the Halles.

Ah—there's one I'm eyeing, too.

So, it went. Illness was a problem for other cities to worry over, not Paris with its wealth and walls. Illness in other cities didn't make the cinnamon soups and red sugar pastries any less sweet. Worse things had happened in Paris and the people always survived.

A song became popular that spring: *Dit des quatre oiseaux*. It told the story of a falconer who raised four sparrowhawks and released them as soon as they were old enough to breed. His preferred bird returned to him. The melody spread from the Rive Gauche to the Marais, and soon the students were picking up drums and singing in the streets. I knew it had something to do with love given freely, but the metaphor was lost on me. What was love given freely? Was it the sculptor's hand freeing my face from rock seams?

The song made me think of Isabelle, too. *Send a bird to fly between the worlds.* Was this what she meant? A bird that knew how to come home?

"I hate it," Bathsheba said, though she had learned most of the words and sang as beautifully as any of the cathedral's choral singers. "It's too simple. I like the one Marie de France wrote about the wolf."

Quite a few men become garwolves,
And set up housekeeping in the woods.

"I know that one," I said, remembering. "About the woman who loved a knight until he confessed the moon turned him wolf each month. Then she left him for another lover. Why do you like that poem so much? Is it because the man is enchanted, like us? Bound to the moon in a similar cycle?"

"No," Bathsheba said. "I like that there are no heroes in Marie's poems. Everyone is somewhat selfish and there are a lot of liars, but that's a more honest way to write about the people. All these men and their simple, stupid poems about women they don't even know. Marie de France was far more intelligent—she was the greatest poet of the past two hundred years."

"I love the things you notice, Bathsheba," I said. "I'm so grateful to stand next to you."

I remembered how a pair of finches once built a nest in the crook of Bathsheba's arm. For days, they flitted back and forth between the façade and parvis, gathering bits of straw, string, the feathers of other birds, twigs, and clumps of horsehair. Though the birds delighted her, Bathsheba knew she'd have to stand still until the nestlings fledged. She could not enjoy The Wakening while the birds were in the nest. I thought that wasn't fair, so I decided to stand still as well. For as long as the birds were there, I wouldn't even breathe.

But I couldn't help it. I couldn't resist The Wakening and the air and rain on my tongue. I inhaled, accidentally elbowing Bathsheba, nearly spilling the nest, eggs and all. I gasped, afraid the adults would fly away and abandon their nest, and Bathsheba would scold me. Neither happened. Bathsheba simply smiled and gave her head the slightest, most imperceptible shake.

When the birds eventually left, weeks later, Bathsheba and I found ourselves covered in shit. We laughed until it became a happy memory.

What did it mean to lie to my closest friend on the Portal of the Virgin? Someone who had stood next to me for over one hundred years. Did it mean she couldn't trust me? That we weren't truly sister stone?

I was supposed to be better than all of this, wasn't I? I was the likeness of Sainte Geneviève. Saints didn't lie.

But sometimes in the lengthening days between The Wakenings, my mind and tongue remembered how it felt to eat. My throat wanted *more*. Another citrus. A cup of wine. And my mind often wandered to Archangel Michel. How, for just one moment, our eyes had met.

CHAPTER IV

"Anyone who has received from God the gift of knowledge and true eloquence has a duty not to remain silent: rather should one be happy to reveal such talents."

From The Lais of Marie de France, Prologue (c. 1155–1170)

May 1348

Vespers was a peculiar time of day. Clouds bloated with rain and turned the dusk sky gray and hazy. These days marbled the awkward in-between before summer's full-throated heat. Likewise, Vespers marked threshold hour, that liminal space between daylight and The Wakening.

A sunbeam struggled but finally broke through the gray overhead. For one peaceful moment, I forgot I was a cathedral guardian. Like any other living being, I became a simple thing soaking in the heat. Some mortals would have exchanged places with me, trading warm beds, lovers, and even children for eternity on the most cherished cathedral.

I absorbed the most delicious scent drifting through the parvis. *Delicious* because I didn't have a better word to describe the sensation. Cloves and iris petals and some other spice I couldn't name. Fragrant but not as heady as incense in the swinging chain censers. I heard the slap of footsteps on the earth as the scent drifted closer. Some kind of perfume?

Yes. Spice, fruit, and petals, and beneath that, the unmistakable odor of human skin, milky and pleasant. The person who wore the most delicious-smelling fragrance approached, and I was surprised to see that he was a scholar in long Benedictine robes. His scent betrayed his robe's simplicity.

He didn't bother to cover his head, and I saw that he was young. I took him for twenty and five years, maybe less. He'd tied a linen smelling-cloth over his face to protect himself from the evil vapors people now feared, but it slipped, and I saw full pink lips that sat on mostly-straight teeth, delicate nostrils, and dark hair curled over his ears. So much hair despite his tonsure. Soft, rosy cheeks. An attractive man, beautiful even.

He looked familiar though there were so many scholars, so many Benedictines in particular, I could never recall them all or learn their names. He stood beside the Portal of the Virgin as if he were waiting for someone, and I could see that his tonsure was a shaven patch no bigger than a coin. The most minimal tonsure allowed.

I was surprised to see him here. The Great Death had taken Lyon and would reach Paris by summer. Bishop de Chanac had decreed city-wide curfews and urged people to pray within their homes. The wealthiest were fleeing to countryside villas and chateaus.

Queues of people desperate to leave Paris blocked the roads to the city gates and the parvis had never felt so empty. All that remained were the dogs and rodents sniffing the once-bustling market stalls and a few bold sellers who defied orders and rolled through Paris selling mutton, eel pies, and carp—things that were expensive and perishable.

I had also heard rumors that some of Paris' lords blamed the illness on the leprosy hospitals. Now they demanded that the Church quit funding these refuges. Everything about Paris felt eerie and lonely now, and the nights were unsafe.

I worried about the scholar standing by himself, his eyebrows furrowed with anxiety, hands fidgeting, rubbing each fingernail with ferocious determination. He tried the doors, but the cathedral was locked. So, who was he waiting for? A hidden lover? Why else would he wear such a sweet fragrance? He was a scholar, after all, and everyone knew how students struggled to keep their vows.

He raised his hand and cried out to a man hurrying past the storefronts on Rue Char-Rori. The man, another Benedictine, stopped and returned an enthusiastic wave.

"What are you doing out here, Celestine?" The man was breathless. "Why aren't you at prayer? What about tomorrow? Have you finished packing?"

He was also young, perhaps younger than his friend, with a broad, open face and sturdy shoulders. His hood had fallen, and I could see he took the tonsure more seriously than Celestine, but he still had more than enough reddish hair to look boyish. And with his hooded blue eyes, he looked roguish, too—like the most tempting kind of trouble.

"I'm waiting on my sister," Celestine said. "She asked to meet me here before I return to Jumiéges tomorrow. You?"

"I wanted to buy another tablet and a copy of *Le Tretiz,* but everything is sold out." The man shrugged with exasperation. "No one can get into Paris to sell anything, and everyone here is trying to leave."

Celestine grunted. "I'm sure there will be tablets and more books than you could ever hope to read at Jumiéges."

"Let's hope. Kind of an inconvenient place to meet your sister, no?"

"She's gone to live with her fiancé's family in the Marais," Celestine said. "You know the guards won't let anyone who doesn't live in the neighborhood pass through."

The other Benedictine offered a grim, tight-lipped smile and put a hand on Celestine's shoulder. "I'm sorry about your family."

"Ce sont des choses qui arrient," Celestine huffed and brought his hands to his face, pulling down his eyelids. "I just hate to leave her behind in Paris, Louis. I know she's not alone. Well, I know she's with her new family now, but I think they're so foolish for staying."

"It's only natural to worry about your sister," Louis said.

"My only living sister," Celestine said sharply. "And I'm going to convince her to leave Paris. She and her fiancé should just go—even if his parents refuse to listen to reason. They can stay with Nicholas' family in the countryside."

"Yes, why won't they do that?" asked Louis.

"Bof. They don't want to burden him with more mouths to feed."

Louis crossed his arms and wore the embarrassed look of someone who knew he had nothing appropriate to say.

"Besides, the fiancé's family believes the illness is only coming for the Jews and the nonbelievers. The idiocy! They know it took our parents!" Celestine balled up his right fist, and for a moment, I thought he would hit Louis. Instead, he struck his left palm so hard, the sound echoed. "God's blood," he cursed.

"We must trust in God," Louis chided.

"You know, to be honest, I'd rather pull out my own tooth than return to that stinking abbey," Celestine said, shaking his index finger.

"It is so damn cold there," Louis sighed. "And boring. I'll certainly miss Paris but at least we'll be safe at Jumiéges."

"Maybe I can find a reason to stay behind—to watch over Isabelle," said Celestine.

Louis' mouth dropped open. "No!"

The cathedral bells pealed and the parvis swelled with their familiar, comforting sound. There were thousands of Isabelles. Surely this person was not the same Isabelle who had given me the offering?

I recalled everything I'd learned about the de Grantrue family. I knew they were wealthy. Wealthy enough to afford the dowry the University of Paris demanded for someone like Celestine.

Celestine crossed and uncrossed his arms then waved his hand dismissively. "Ignore me, I'm thinking out loud."

"Convince Isabelle to go to Nicholas. Don't stay behind—you do not want to be here when the Great Death arrives."

"What if she refuses? How can I leave her?"

"Remember your commitment to the monastery. To the university. To God. I know it's tempting to stay, but you cannot. You could lose your position and everything you've worked for."

Celestine rolled his eyes.

"Celestine, you are going to become a canon! This is what your father and mother wanted from you. This is your duty as their son. And you need something to look forward to and work towards. God will take care of your sister."

"Coureuse de remparts," Celestine cursed under his breath.

Louis wagged his finger. "I'll pretend I didn't hear that."

Celestine threw up his hands. "She's an hour late!"

"And you already checked for her inside?"

"Of course I have, Louis."

"Well then, would you like me to wait with you?" Louis' voice had grown thin, as if he suddenly decided he would rather do anything else. Celestine looked weary, as if he couldn't decide whether he wanted the company.

"Go on. I will see you tomorrow morning at Saint-Séverin."

"Promise? Promise me you won't do anything foolish or let Isabelle convince you to stay? If you decide to stay now, it will be hard to leave the city later. Bandits are on the roads, and you look like prey."

"I know, I know. I promise I'll meet you tomorrow, Louis."

They agreed on their plans for departing Paris in the morning and exchanged farewells. Louis turned to the Pont Neuf, and though I could no longer see him, I imagined him casting uneasy backward glances every few steps.

Celestine paced the parvis for another hour. I watched him peek into the book seller's shops on Rue Char-Rori before he returned to the cathedral. Finally, Celestine tried the doors and stepped inside. Moments later, he emerged alone, releasing musky altar incense through the swinging doors. I watched him collect a fistful of stones from the ground, stray sandstone and sediment.

I grew anxious, too. Anxious for Celestine to stop pacing and anxious to see whether this Isabelle was the same who had given me the citrus.

Come, Isabelle. Show yourself!

Celestine fidgeted the stones in his shaking hands and gazed into the architecture as if suddenly aware of the pantheon of statues.

As if he knew we watched him.

He seemed to look at me—me in particular—and for a moment, I was certain he saw me for what I was, that he saw beneath my painted face, this mask of paint, this painted skull. He narrowed his eyes, and I was sure he saw me down to my stratifications, the seams and slips of porous stone, oursin bone-made stone.

And he saw himself through my eyes: a man with dark, delicate beauty and an amorous intensity behind his gaze. Someone desirable and forever out of my reach.

The moment passed. But I knew. I knew he was Isabelle's brother. My Isabelle.

Not just because he resembled her, though he did. He shared her dark eyes, dark curls, and straight dark brow. Not just because I knew Sainte Geneviève was special to her, so it made sense that she would give instructions to meet her here.

It was his smell. The smokey, floral cologne. Something a noble— or perhaps, a merchant's son—would own. And beneath that, the smell of skin and shared ancestry. Shared bone. I could feel Isabelle with me in the door jamb again.

Celestine curled back his lips to show all his teeth, like the feral dogs that roamed the parvis. He unfurled his hands and pitched the rocks he'd collected.

"Fuck you!"

The stones tumbled towards the double doors, some the size of pebbles, others crown jewels, spraying the Trumeau, Marie and The Child, Heavenly Jerusalem, and the Ark of the Covenant. I felt the impact and saw stray sediment and flecks of paint fly from the wall.

"Why did you have to take both parents and a sister in the same month! Foutre dieu, fuck you!"

Celestine bent down to gather more rocks and hurled them at the façade again and again as sweat beaded his forehead. A piece of stone struck my cheek and bounced off my face.

"I hate you!" Celestine hissed. "I hate you! I hate you!"

If I could, I would have reached for Bathsheba's hand for fortification. As one stone, we would be more difficult to destroy. Where had all these rocks and fragments come from? Were they old scraps from the mason's worktables? I felt angry that standing and smiling was the only thing I could do.

"I've been cursed! Someone's put a curse on me, and you didn't protect me! I hate you!"

Celestine lobbed another rock at the Portal of the Virgin. When I heard the crack, I knew he'd landed a significant hit.

"Chiabrena," Celestine said, spittle stringing from his lips, chest heaving.

His back disappeared into the alley that led to the Pont au Change and the Marais. I suspected Celestine thought he could bribe the watch to let him into his sister's neighborhood; that's what I would have done if I were him. A dangerous gamble, especially for a scholar. Bribing the wrong guard could cost him his robes and position within the university.

So could throwing rocks at the cathedral, but he had obviously reached the point of indifference.

In this city, who hadn't?

If Celestine reached the Marais and found that Isabelle had died? Well. He could return to the cathedral and deface its statues. How safe and smug we felt in our tidy niches, watching illness, famine, war, or whatever else haunted Paris while we believed we were safe.

We were bound together—creations with the people who made us. If the people wanted to destroy us, disfigure us, we couldn't stop them.

Over and over, I heard Michel's voice: *The people depend on us to represent their saints. We must embody purity of heart and mind and body.*

I remembered the sweetly vile pulpy mound trapped between my sculpted teeth. A gobby mound that had once been a beautiful offering. While I ate, I had felt more alive than ever, but at what price?

Was it possible—

Did I curse this family when I ate Isabelle's offering?

Why hadn't I been able to look at the offering with loving eyes? Why hadn't I been able to hold the offering in gracious hands and extend goodwill to this family, like a *perfect saint*? I did not know how to protect a family or send a bird between the worlds, but I knew it was wrong to eat. The real Sainte Geneviève would have resisted.

A choir of voices flooded my mind. *That girl prayed for her family, and you selfishly ate her prayer. Shouldn't you know by now what the saints mean to the people? Do you still think you're worthy of the name Sainte Geneviève?*

After Compline, The Child held out his hands so we could see how they were broken from fingertip to palm. His little red mouth, once plump, was now smashed in. Celestine's throw had also taken Marie's left eye.

"There will be no more prayers or grimpeurs. The Child cannot climb," she said, cupping her shattered eye. "Pray silently from your niches if you want to pray for these ungrateful people. As for me, I will not."

Confusion blossomed into protest.

"But you don't mean that," Denis said.

"I certainly do."

Denis continued. "Well, The Child has been climbing for nearly as long as we've stood on these walls. Perhaps it's time to elect new grimpeurs. Perhaps The Child should share the great honor and responsibility."

"No," Marie said, balling her free hand into a fist. "Climbing and praying to the Sky didn't bring back L'Ecclésia or Saint Etienne. A small enough thing. The Sky certainly isn't going to stave off the Great Death. I think we're doing enough for the people by standing right here in these walls."

"But what about Michel?" asked the little Eve figure. She craned her neck to look up from beneath Marie's pedestal. "Michel said we need two grimpeurs. Now we can't even have one?" Her fig leaf slid against her hips as she spoke. I often wondered if she and Adam felt chill in the winter, carved as they were.

"Michel was right, we need more grimpeurs," Denis said.

"No one is agile enough to climb," Marie protested. "If you fall, you will shatter into oblivion."

Denis gripped his severed head so tightly, his fingernails scraped off flecks of paint. "You talk as if we're simple ornaments," he said. "We are *not* ordinary statues! I agree with Michel: we must find a better way to use our gifts."

Jean piped up. "We shouldn't disobey Michel."

"Disobey?" Marie scoffed. "We're not disobeying anyone. Michel governs the Portal of the Last Judgement. *I* make decisions for the Portal of the Virgin."

Jean leaned close to Bathsheba, Sylvestre, and me. "I know what this is all about," he said, poking us with his stiff yellow beard. "She doesn't want anyone else to climb besides The Child. They think they're superior to the rest of us. Such odious little figurines."

Sylvestre placed his hands on his hips and asked, "What do you even know of figurines?"

Marie pivoted to fix her one good eye on Jean.

"Do you know how solid and heavy The Child is? I want him to climb, because I get tired of holding him. When The Wakening arrives, I can rest my arms. You don't understand the relief. Now, I suppose I'm trapped holding him forever."

"Is that really true?" Denis asked. "Your makers carved your arms around The Child. You should love holding him. All mothers love holding their children."

Marie laughed until her shoulders shook.

"I'm no mother, and he is no child," she said. "And if you're so certain we need a grimpeur, I elect you. But only that very wise head of yours."

"My head can't climb!"

"Of course it can!" the cherubim sang from the archivolts.

"Well, we should choose someone," Uriel said.

"How about you?" offered Gabriel.

Bathsheba began to snicker behind her hands. "This is absurd," she whispered. "Listen to us all, a bunch of stone bodies arguing over climbing the cathedral wall. The people really have no idea, do they?"

"If we don't elect another grimpeur, Michel is going to be so displeased," said Denis.

"Let him be displeased," Marie said.

"But this is how we've been doing things for nearly one hundred years, this is how it's always been," Denis said. "If we can't carry prayers to the Sky, what do we even have to offer?"

"We must choose a grimpeur," intoned Heavenly Jerusalem.

"We must choose two grimpeurs," intoned Ark of the Covenant.

"I said no!" Marie stamped her platform, shaking Adam, Eve, and Lilith. "It's too dangerous. Not one of you can climb like The Child could."

The Holy Men in the canopy leaned over their fresco and cupped their hands over Marie's mouth. "Quiet!" they hissed. "The people will hear you."

With one swift motion, Marie turned, reached up behind her and struck a bearded prophet's jaw.

"Sad clay pot," she said.

Bathsheba doubled over with laughter. "I'm telling you," she whispered to me, "it's like we're watching a mystery play! You would think we were human."

The Child suddenly slipped from Marie's arms, and she cried out. The Child couldn't scream for his mouth was smashed shut. He turned flips through the air, plump arms reaching, wrinkled feet kicking the void. With a horrific cracking sound, Marie bent at the waist and grabbed The Child by the neck, pulling him to safety and his rightful place on her hip.

We all had nothing else to say for a long time after that.

Matins and Lauds came and went. I noticed fewer monks and nuns present than usual and wondered how many had fled to places like Jumiéges and how many had caught the illness. Every face I could see looked so solemn—more solemn than usual. Some gazed up at the West Façade with a hollowed, burned-out look in their eyes and recited verses from the Seven Penitential Psalms. *Miser factus sum et curvatus sum usque ad finem tota die contristatus ingrediebar.* I noticed that some clergy covered their mouths and noses with strips of clothes.

The night passed, and I shifted my feet, letting my toes hang over the alcove. I wondered what would happen if I stepped out into empty air. Would the façade reach out to catch me? Or would it let me fall?

I lifted my curious foot from the alcove's lip and let it hang in the empty space before me. What if I didn't have to be Sainte Geneviève anymore? What if I could let this all go? I didn't have to represent a saint. I didn't have to be an effigy. I could let myself fall, break apart, return to ground. Wasn't I just a pinched-up piece of ground after all? Pinched-up ground shaped into the form of a woman. I could become something else.

The idea beckoned. It felt like freedom. A release from the weight of watching so many people from the architecture. I wouldn't have to smile as if I had all the answers to the world's troubles. Freed from citrus fruit shame.

Freed from this ache to *eat*.

But I thought of Isabelle de Grantrue. I didn't know if she was still alive, but if she was, I imagined how hopeless she would feel when she learned that the statue she had prayed to—her Geneviève—had been destroyed. No. She needed me and that gave me purpose. I ate her prayer, so now I was bound to her. I did not know how to send a bird, but I had something else to offer.

I finally spoke.

"I can carry the prayers to the Sky," I said.

Bathsheba turned her head and sputtered. "Have you lost all your good sense?"

Again, with force. "I will carry the prayers."

I liked the way my voice sounded. I liked the taste of air on my tongue, how my tongue cut the air and pulled all the attention towards me. The cherubim wedged into the highest points of the arches tilted their faces in my direction. The Child arched his eyebrows. I knew I babbled absurdities. Of course, little nimble statues like The Child and Archangel Michel could climb all the way up the façade.

But me? I was one of the larger, heavier statues that stood in a door jamb. And yet, I would climb. I would carry Isabelle's prayer to the Sky myself. I would undo the curse I'd placed on her family when I'd eaten her offering. This was how I'd intercede on her behalf.

The Child turned his cracked face towards me. What was that expression in his narrowed eyes? Doubt and contempt? Or envy?

"If you fall, you know you can never be replaced," said Marie. "And if you let the sunlight strike you before you return to your niche you will become an ordinary statue for all of time."

"I know."

"Don't be stupid!" Bathsheba hissed.

I took her hands in mine. Her fingers were slender, and my hands engulfed them.

Jean and Sylvestre fidgeted and shifted their feet. They both cleared their throats, released shallow breaths, and made contemplative sounds.

"What is it?" I asked. "Spit it already."

"The people might notice you climbing the façade."

"You've never climbed before. What makes you think you can?"

"How will you know you're climbing correctly?"

"Are you trying to draw attention to yourself?"

"Why do you want to be special?"

Bathsheba held my gaze. "Why do you want to do this?" she asked. Her furrowed brow softened.

Marie raised her hands and finished the conversation.

"You wanted a grimpeur, well now you have one," she said. "Geneviève will become our portal's next grimpeuse. She represents the Patron Saint of Paris. She will be very good, and she will not fall, because we will not let her."

"But what if the people see her climb?" asked Lilith. "She is so much bigger than The Child."

"She'll climb during the dark, quiet hours, between Matins and Lauds."

"You're hiding something," Bathsheba said, shaking her head. "You've never had much to say about prayers or the Sky before." She lowered her voice. "In fact, I always thought you didn't really care about all of that."

I exhaled. I wanted to tell Bathsheba the truth, but I couldn't force the words from my mouth. I bit my lower lip instead, harder than I'd intended, and the scrape of stone against stone made me wince.

"I believe Michel," I replied. "I believe there's more we can do with our gift of The Wakening. I think we barely understand the limits of the enchantment. Michel knows something we don't, and I want to learn from him."

Marie eyed me. "I've watched you during The Wakenings," she said. "I know you have a wandering mind, Geneviève. You will need to overcome your unfocused disposition. A grimpeur must remember every single prayer. A grimpeur must trust the cathedral; you must trust our oneness with this structure."

I closed my eyes and nodded. Then I felt the full force of the commitment I'd made. I craned my neck and stared at the façade's flat surface; it expanded upwards, nearly without end, finally terminating in those long, expansive bell towers. From the top, I could touch the very sky itself. Bathsheba and Marie were right, climbing this wall would be dangerous—and foolish.

How could I have offered up myself so recklessly?

CHAPTER V

Feast Day of Saints Peter and Paul, June 1348

Bathsheba and Sylvestre pressed their hands against my back so I wouldn't fall. I turned on my pedestal with one cautious foot behind the other, and my toes made rough scraping sounds, stone against stone. I feared I stood on the edge of a great mistake, but it was too late to change my mind.

At least the streets and alleyways beyond the parvis looked empty. One less thing to worry over. The night guards enforced a curfew for days to keep people inside and safe from the Great Death. But as grotesque stories of illness spread through Paris, it seemed that even the guards were afraid to keep watch. Not one torchbearer wandered the streets. So now my companions and I had the night entirely to ourselves.

I reached up. My fingers grasped the triangular gable that protruded from the wall, and I evaluated the full length of the façade. I felt very foolish; I was so big and clumsy. I looked back and caught Marie's eye. Was that a smirk?

"Geneviève, you don't have to do this," Bathsheba said. "Forget the illness and stay in the door jamb with us. We're stronger as one stone."

Bathsheba should be the grimpeuse, I thought bitterly. She was a much better statue than me. She was more patient. Better at listening to the people. I didn't know if Bathsheba was better at representing a *saint*, but I didn't particularly care. Wasn't being a good statue the same thing as being a good saint?

What would Michel think? Wouldn't he be disappointed in the new grimpeuse who gave up before she even tried to climb? What about Isabelle de Grantrue?

One of the patriarchs carved into the archivolt reached over the gable and grabbed my hands. Bathsheba and Sylvestre took hold of my legs and pushed me upward. Jean crossed his arms over his chest, muttering his displeasure. I no longer stood on my pedestal. The limestone bricks made room for me, and the wall seemed to come to life.

Uriel and Gabriel cheered, breaking the tense silence that had fallen over the Portal of the Virgin, and clapping spread from the door jamb niches to the highest points in the archivolts. It was the secretive applause of statues, no louder than the sound of doves or ravens in flight, but everyone from the Portals of the Last Judgement to Sainte-Anne understood: there was a new grimpeuse. Thrill and wonder overwhelmed me; I had seen The Child climb many times, but I'd never imagined the cathedral would move for me.

I reached the Tympanum and gripped more helping hands. I was in awe of the way the façade created space, as if I had always stood there, carved between the Ark of the Covenant and Heavenly Jerusalem.

"You shouldn't do this, Geneviève," said one of the prophets.

"You might fall," said one of the others.

I looked down at my empty niche. Bathsheba, Sylvestre, and Jean huddled close as if I'd never stood there at all.

"Be careful!" Denis cried.

"She might slip after all," Uriel said. "Now that would be something. I wonder what she would look like if she broke open."

"Hush," Marie said. "She will be just fine."

Bathsheba squeezed her eyes shut, as if she couldn't bear to watch.

The prophets spoke at once. "Turn back, Geneviève. You were not made to climb."

"I'm climbing now."

"Why do you trust yourself?" the prophet asked. "How can you?"

Why *did* I trust myself? I stood still in the Tympanum, my concentration broken. I didn't have much reason to trust myself. I'd never climbed.

I couldn't even be trusted to hold an offering.

Or tell Bathsheba the truth.

The prophet narrowed his eyes. Had he seen me eat the citrus?

But I had to trust myself. I was the only one willing to climb, and this was my opportunity to help Isabelle. I was obligated to her now.

"I represent the patron saint of Paris," I told the prophet. "If The Child can climb, so can I."

I stepped on the prophet's knees and enjoyed the crunch of my body weight, sediment crushing sediment. Then, I pulled myself into the next level of the Tympanum. Another Marie reclined on a slender bed, stone angels at her head and feet.

I had tried my best to ignore Heavenly Jerusalem, the Ark of the Covenant, Constantin, and worst of all, Bathsheba's scared face, but their doubts filled my mind, and they were much louder than the names of all the people and prayers I had forced myself to remember since May. My feet suddenly felt clumsy. I closed my eyes and searched my memories for all the prayers I'd heard.

Fewer people came to Notre-Dame now, but I still caught snatches of conversation in the parvis. The Great Death stood outside the walls of Paris, in Roissey and Gonesse. Thousands of people had perished at the Abbey of Saint-Denis, and it was only a matter of time before the illness crossed the city gates. Parents were scraping together family money to send their children to monasteries in the countryside, into safety, while they stayed behind in Paris and lit candles.

The people were scared and angry, and they wanted someone to blame. More than once, I heard the ghosts of old rumors resurface that people with leprosy were poisoning the fountains, wells, and wheat stores. Many years ago, the lords and royal officials of Anjou and Touraine claimed that leprosy shelters had launched a coordinated campaign throughout France to murder healthy Christians or turn them into lepers. According to the chroniclers, lepers dumped concoctions of human blood, urine, and snake venom into communal food and water sources in the deepest hours of the night. These lords even persuaded King Philip V to arrest and execute hundreds of people. Most of the violence happened outside of Paris, but some victims were sent to Paris and hung on gibbets at Place de Grève.

And it was going to happen again. What cruel, idiotic rumors. I could see the truth so easily from the cathedral wall. Those lords were resentful of the leprosy shelters for all the donations they had accumulated. *Why should ill beggars have so much?* they wondered. *Why should they live in fine, expensive shelters as if they were lords? We are the only lords.*

How had The Child remembered so many prayers, especially the ones that sounded the same? I tried to listen and hold onto everything I could, but straining after every conversation had grown tiresome. And yet, The Child had never once complained. Marie said The Child was solid, but perhaps he was far more porous than me. How else was it possible to hold so many voices in one's mind? How could I retrieve this knowledge from him now that he could not speak?

The reclining Marie poked a sharp finger into my back, startling me. "Grimpeuse, you have to climb," she said. Her voice was hoarse and scratchy—the voice of an old woman. A comically old woman. The imitation of an old woman. The reclining Marie played a part, she had taught herself to speak this way.

I wondered what her real voice sounded like.

Then I felt a rush of hands and teeth, taking my arms, biting into my robes as if they were wool, pulling me up, supporting me, eager to help. I didn't think about Heavenly Jerusalem and the Ark of the Covenant again.

Once I had passed the archivolts, climbing began to feel pleasurable. In the twist of my hips, in deciding where to place my hands and feet to gain purchase on the wall. And my connection to the wall! Marie was right: the entire cathedral was part of the enchantment, not just the statues. The wall responded to my touch; the limestone extended just enough to offer steps and ledges. Feeling very free and very bold, I looked back over my shoulder to glimpse the dark Seine hidden beneath the bridges and rooftops crowding the riverbank. I had heard so many stories about the river, had even heard the sound it made when it met the shoreline, but it was another thing to see it. It was overwhelming in its enormity, wide and writhing, every bit alive as me.

I felt alive. I was made of living things that once breathed and then died and turned into something else altogether—me, a statue on a loved cathedral. I was the next life. Calcaire. When I looked at the Seine—just visible enough for me to admire it—I knew this all was true. I could stay here all night and think about my existence. The wonder of it all. The Child must have felt this way, too. Perhaps that was the real reason he wanted to climb for all these many years.

My hands struck the smooth bottom of the balcony, and I was alarmed to find I had nowhere to put my fingers. A stone head with a painted yellow crown peered down from the wall, eyeing me without affection.

"Who approaches the Gallery of the Kings?"

"Sainte Geneviève. Grimpeuse from the Portal of the Virgin."

Silence. Then an incredulous, "Grimpeuse?"

"Yes, The Child has been damaged," I said through clenched lips. My hands felt weak. The enchantment was strong, that was true, but so was the earth's pull, and I couldn't stay suspended much longer. When I kicked the wall to secure my footing, debris crunched against my feet and tumbled below.

"Help me, and I will tell you everything," I said.

The figure retreated into the balcony. I heard his whispers as he consulted with his companions. I rested my forehead against the wall, breathing its cool, damp scent, and tried to draw strength from the stones. "I am cathedral. Cathedral will not let me fall," I repeated, my own prayer for reassurance.

Prayer to the chalky mucky limestone beds that I had never seen with these carved eyes, yet I knew existed. Prayer to the living things that had died and became mineral, reborn in the likeness of the patron saint of Paris. A prayer to myself.

The king reached down and offered his hand, and I took his arms gladly.

"Pleasant wakening," I said.

"I am Asa, third king of Judah," he said, narrowing his skeptical eyes. "What happened to The Child?"

"Someone threw stones at the façade and broke his hands and mouth."

"And now, you're the grimpeuse," said a second king. He folded his arms over his stone chest and leaned close to Asa, whispering something I couldn't discern. I thought I heard Marie's name. Asa responded with the slightest of gestures, a nearly imperceptible shake of the head.

"I am the representation of Sainte Geneviève, the patron saint of Paris," I said, with as much force as I could summon. "You must let me climb."

"We know who you are," said Asa.

Though my body was tired, I felt alive with my own strength. I almost wanted them to challenge me the same way everyone else had.

"And you are?" I asked the one beside Asa.

"Jehoshaphat, my lady."

My lady? I was a statue. I was the representation of a saint. I was porous and lovely, a figure cut from living stone to be admired and respected. I had thoughts and feelings; I was enchanted. People put offerings in my hands. I was calcaire. I was many things, but I wasn't a lady.

I nearly laughed.

"Ignore Jehoshaphat," Asa said, rolling his eyes. "He takes the poets and musicians and Marie de France seriously. I tell him sentiment is for mortals, not the cathedral's guardians."

Jehoshaphat shrugged. "I'm happy you're not afraid to climb," he said. "We need to keep sending prayers to the Sky."

"Especially now that people want to damage the cathedral," said Asa.

"Has Michel already reached your balcony tonight?" I asked.

"Yes," answered Jehoshaphat.

"Well, where is he?" I asked, hearing the edge in my voice.

"Michel has climbed beyond this point, and he's on his way to the Virgin's Balcony. That's where he goes each wakening."

"Thank you," I said. "Then, that is where I'll go, too. I appreciate your help. Pleasant wakening, guardians."

I reached up, ready to continue my climb, but Asa grabbed my hood.

"Not yet," he said. "Since you are here, please enjoy the view from our humble balcony."

"I insist," Jehoshaphat added with a nod.

"I would like that, but I need to find Michel. I need to speak with him, and I have many prayers to give the Sky before dawn."

"Dawn?" Jehoshaphat scoffed. "There's plenty of time before dawn! We haven't even heard the bells ring for Lauds!"

"Now look," Asa said, taking my arm in one hand and gesturing with the other towards the dark tangle of rooftops that stretched beyond the parvis. "That spire you see straight ahead belongs to Sainte-Chapelle, a sad and skinny little chapel. Far inferior to our Notre-Dame."

"It only took a handful of years to build that foolish church," Asa sighed, shaking his hands. "Can you imagine? It took centuries to complete Notre-Dame!"

"Look to the right of that steeple—" Jehoshaphat began.

"That sad, doleful excuse for a steeple!" Asa interrupted.

"Indeed, pathetic," Jehoshaphat continued. "But look, to the right, do you see those towers with roofs that look like ladies' funny pointed hats, the ones that were in fashion forty or fifty years ago?" Jehoshaphat continued. "That's the Palais de la Cité and the Palais de Justice."

I nodded as they prattled on, speaking at once, speaking over each other about the kings that had inhabited those buildings, military decisions that had been made over the past hundreds of years, the dignitaries who had visited from places like Egypt and Andalusia, emeralds, a crown made of thorns, a tiny locket with a splinter from a cross tucked inside, raw silk from Constantinople, and so on, and so on, and so on. I tried my best to remember these names and places, but as I looked down at the parvis—from this tremendous height—my mind traveled across the bridges that connected the Îl de la Cité to the rest of Paris.

I could hardly believe I could see it all with my own eyes. All this time, I could only see what lay just beyond my niche in the Portal of the Virgin. Now, I gazed at places I had only heard about on the people's lips.

To my great amazement, the City was surrounded by the Seine's waters on all its sides. I knew we were on an island; I had heard the word *island* before, but now I saw—truly *saw*—what that word meant.

I couldn't wait to tell Bathsheba. I knew she would appreciate this view. I wished she was here with me to absorb it.

When my mind returned to the conversation, Asa and Jehoshaphat were carrying on about Les Halles, a labyrinthine market on the Rive Droite, and the barrels filled with eels sold there.

"What do you suppose an eel's face looks like?" Jehoshaphat asked with a small smile. "I would imagine like a fish's, but I realize, I've never seen a fish. I've only seen the way their scales catch the sunlight far, far below this wall."

Asa snorted.

"I would imagine an eel's face would look a bit like your maker's."

"I imagine an eel's face would look a bit like your maker's cunt."

Good Sky, I thought. *They're going to steal all my time.*

"How do you know the names of all these places?" I interrupted. "Can you hear the people this far up from the ground? How do you know that place is called Les Halles?" I gestured towards the long buildings that housed the market shops. "I can hear the people talking from my niche, but sometimes it's hard even for me."

"Ah, The Child should have told you," Jehoshaphat said. His voice softened and he lowered his eyes.

"Told me what?"

"As the grimpeur, The Child not only shared prayers with the Sky, but he visited the Gallery of the Kings and told us everything the people talked and cared about," said Jehoshaphat.

"He talked about all of you statues, too," Asa said.

"Oh, he was a phenomenal gossip," Jehoshaphat said.

"He spent most of The Wakening here in our balcony. Sometimes, we talked so much, he never gave the prayers to the Sky at all."

My mouth fell open. So that was the reason The Child never complained about remembering every single prayer! That was the reason The Child always looked so content and why he and Marie exchanged their furtive whispers! Surely, the kings were lying.

Or were they?

No wonder Marie had resisted the idea of a second grimpeur. A second grimpeur would have held The Child accountable to delivering the prayers, depriving Marie of her gossip partner!

Asa and Jehoshaphat erupted into wild laughter and didn't stop until I could hear bits of stone and dried paint rattle in their throats.

"And we expect you to do the same, Geneviève," Asa said.

"But I have to speak with Michel!" I brought my fingertips to my forehead, overwhelmed and worried. God's bones, they meant to keep me here all wakening.

"Tell us more about The Child. What exactly happened to him?"

I exhaled and hastily explained how the scholar Celestine had thrown stones at the cathedral.

"That reminds me of Jacques de Molay," said Jehoshaphat, crossing his arms over his chest and straightening his back.

It took me a breath to place that name to the story. Then I remembered. Oh no. Not this again. I cupped my face and shook my head. I had to escape this conversation, or I would be here all wakening.

De Molay was a Templar, and if there was something I had grown tired of hearing about, it was the Templars. They were a military order that had been disbanded for over thirty years. As for Jacques de Molay, he had been brave and powerful and beloved until the day he wasn't. Prince Philip had accused him of heresy, which de Molay admitted to beneath inquisitors' hands. What exactly constituted heresy? I wasn't sure. I only knew that heresy was the word on every person's lips in those days.

Eventually, de Molay put on a good enough show to be set free, only to be arrested again when he publicly declared his admissions had been lies. King Philip and Pope Clement had him burned alive on the Île de la Cité by Pont Saint Michel.

Though I couldn't see the execution from my niche in the Portal of the Virgin, I could watch people expand in the parvis, the chaotic swell as they pushed each other to watch the funerary pyre. I absorbed their curiosity, their fear, and their ecstasy. I learned something about humankind that day; I learned that they could thrill in mercilessness. That they could take absolute delight in watching someone burn. De Molay's execution was the biggest party of the Year of Our Lord 1314.

Coincidently, King Philip IV and Pope Clement died within a year of the execution. Rumors spread throughout Paris that de Molay had cursed the kingdom and papacy. It was true, that year had been painful, and the people needed an explanation. But I knew Jacques de Molay was an ordinary man, and, in my eyes, the Templars were among the most typical. Common in their ambition to rise in power and travel the land. Many thought they were doing good by protecting the roads and the pilgrims; many were in it for money. The Templars were as mortal and human as humans could be—there was nothing particularly mystifying about them. It bored me to talk or think about them excessively.

"How?" Asa said, sounding every bit as surprised as me. "How does this remind you of Jacques de Molay?"

"Because he was destroyed, just like The Child."

"Indeed, The Child can't climb, but he hasn't been destroyed," I said. "Why are we still talking about the Templars? That was many years ago."

"It doesn't take much for people to turn," Jehoshaphat said without answering me. "Not even statues are safe."

Asa crossed his arms and fixed his eyes on the dark horizon.

"What if the illness is a curse?" he asked, his voice slow and contemplative. "What if Jacques de Molay cursed Paris with the illness?"

The word *curse* made me stand up straighter.

"You idiot, that illness started in Messina," Jehoshaphat scoffed, "de Molay didn't curse the southern cities."

The thought crossed my mind that maybe it was too late, and that Michel may have already climbed to the Balcony of the Virgin, repeated his prayers to the Sky, and descended to the Portal of the Last Judgment.

"Please tell me the best way to climb to the Balcony of the Virgin."

"Why do you need to climb up there? The Child never climbed further than this," Asa said.

"I need to speak with Michel."

"About what? Anything you want to tell him, you can tell us."

"No. I need to climb to the highest point I can reach. I want the Sky to hear me."

"Leave the prayers with us. We'll take care of them. We're kings, after all," said Jehoshaphat, shaking a thick finger in my face.

"This balcony is not high enough," I said.

"What do you mean it's not good enough?" cried Asa. "This is the Gallery of the Kings!"

"I never said it wasn't good enough," I sighed.

"The Child rarely climbed any further."

"But Michel does!"

"You are not Michel," said Asa.

"No, I'm not. But I am Geneviève."

What gave them the right to stop me? I wanted to ask them, do you know you're not really kings?

I held my tongue.

"I am following Marie's orders. She told me I must go to the Rose Window. She has a message for Michel."

It was a lie, and I hoped I wouldn't get caught. The kings exchanged tight-faced looks that made me want to hold my breath. But before they could respond, another voice called my name. A warm, beckoning voice. I looked up and saw Michel reaching for me over the railing of the upper balcony. Starlight crowned his elegant silver face, golden hair, and golden wings. All wide eyes and plump cheeks and a broad smile.

He was horrifying in his perfection.

He looked like everything the people wanted him to be. Gentle and deadly; serious and kind. Innocence embodied in a living sculpture.

I reached up until our hands met.

CHAPTER VI

The Northern Crown at zenith above the West Façade

At Michel's insistence, the stubborn kings offered their hands and shoulders for me to climb. Michel gripped my waist as I pulled myself over the railing and onto the Balcony of the Virgin. My knees met the flooring with a loud crack. Michel kneeled beside me and coaxed me to look.

"I can't." I covered my kneecaps with both hands and squeezed my eyes shut.

"Now, Geneviève, you speak just like a mortal child who's stubbed their toe playing games in the parvis. You must look; you are the grimpeuse."

His breath warmed my face, floral and smelling faintly of the frankincense burned at mass time. How strange. Neither Bathsheba nor Sylvestre nor Jean smelled of incense, and I suspected I didn't either, only of damp stone and moss. Perhaps Michel, carved in the likeness of an archangel, was the only one pure enough to smell of cathedral prayers. I wondered if I still smelled like citrus rot and felt even more self-conscious.

I shook my head no.

"I promise it's not as bad as you think it is. As a climber, you must expect these injuries. You cannot expect your body to remain perfect.

We age, too, along with the cathedral. Especially when we move."

He looked boyish sitting on his hands and knees, all wide, earnest eyes and silver face catching the moonlight. "Geneviève, this was what you wanted. You wanted to become grimpeuse. Now, you must get up."

I wasn't supposed to feel fear. I wasn't supposed to indulge in this kind of emotion. I was a guardian statue. If I broke, I would have to accept that fact; I would have to accept that I couldn't climb down.

"I cannot look."

"Then I will look for you," Michel said.

Sweet-smelling smoke tendrilled from his mouth.

"Oh!" I said. "How did you do that?"

He lifted his tongue, revealing a coal of lit incense. "Don't tell anyone," he said, smiling. "I found it on the cathedral steps and took it for myself."

He gently took my hands in his and uncovered my legs. The tops of my hands felt so warm and alive in his cool palms that I forgot about the break for one moment. Michel smiled.

"Oh, this is nothing, Geneviève," he said, touching the hem of my garment. "You simply scratched your cote—a blemish, nothing more. It only needs new paint. You'll see."

Michel was right. I saw a superficial scratch in the gray paint itself when I looked down. I lowered my eyes and pursed my lips, embarrassed. "Thank you," I said.

"Now what did Marie want to tell me?" Michel asked. The bite in his voice was subtle, but I didn't miss it.

"Marie didn't really have a message for you," I admitted with a sigh. "I only said that to convince the kings to let me finish climbing."

"That was smart thinking," Michel said, releasing my hands. I smiled, feeling warmed from his praise. "Those old sacks of clay talk far too much. Let's give your prayers to the Sky."

Upright, Michel stood as tall as my hips. But he pulled himself onto the balcony railing with surprising strength so that we could meet each other's eyes. Though the wind beat the air with force, Michel looked comfortable seated on the ledge. Birdlike, I thought, taking in the particularities of his delicate face, his short, pointed nose, and the domes of his almond-shaped eyes. The way he let his wings hang open against his back. I wondered, yet again, in whose likeness he had been carved?

He caught me watching him, and I turned my head to stare at the gables of distant rooftops. I clutched the guardrail, suddenly dizzy. I had never imagined I would see Paris. And I hadn't quite imagined I would get what I wanted: to stand beside Archangel Michel. He sat so close to me, our arms nearly touched.

"Do you remember all the prayers?" He had such a forgiving voice. An understanding voice. He might understand why a guardian statue would eat a citrus if he was willing to steal smoke. I imagined telling him, imagined the relief I'd feel at last when I shared this shame with someone else.

But not yet. I had to give the Sky every prayer I'd heard last month. I tried to focus on the prayers. Not Michel's grand, sculpted wings nor how he bit his round lower lip with pearl-like teeth.

Focus on the prayers.

Focus on the people.

Remember Isabelle and her brother, Celestine.

Why was Michel so beautiful?

I opened my mouth and let go of prayers from people without work, people without anyone to sell their bread, fish, and butchered meat. Prayed that Les Halles would flood again with fruit and cattle, vegetable sellers, fishmongers, shoemakers, and so many people. People with family members who had died or were taking their last breath, people whose bodies were betraying them every moment of every day. Disaffected students who couldn't finish their studies and people parting from their families, seeking safety outside the city walls. I tried to remember them all, but so many sounded the same.

I thought of the citrus. The citrus had tasted so bitter, but I tried to make my voice as sweet and honeyed as the cathedral choirs. I wanted to give Isabelle's eaten prayer to the Sky, but I didn't think my voice sounded good enough.

"Protect Isabelle de Grantrue and her brother Celestine. Though the illness has already taken her parents and siblings, please send a bird that can fly between the worlds and allow her to speak with them."

When I opened my eyes, Michel was staring at me, but I couldn't read his face. What did he make of me? What did he make of Isabelle's strange, heretical prayer?

And how could I do this with him watching me so intently?

"I have a prayer of my own," Michel said. "I want to pray for the beguines who care for the ill at the Hôtel-Dieu." He turned to me. "Oh, you don't know about the beguines, do you?"

I was relieved that Michel didn't ask me about the bird and seemed satisfied enough with my performance to direct his thoughts elsewhere. I shook my head no. Though I had heard stories about the beguines— average women who chose to live like nuns, devoting their lives to charity, I didn't know much about them. And because I couldn't see the Hôtel-Dieu from my niche, I knew little about their service.

"They're the ones who do the most difficult work," Michel explained. "They wash the bedding of the ill. They shave the faces. They cut the toenails."

Before I could answer, he took my arm and pulled me closer. "That is the Hôtel-Dieu," he said, pointing towards the structure on the riverbank, imposing with its high, gable rooftops and walls that stretched on and on—beyond even that little bridge joining the City with the Rive Gauche. "Can you imagine how many ill and dying people crowd those walls? It must be hundreds."

It was almost too much to give names to the island, bridge, and land on either side of the river. It was almost too much to see the scope of the island with my own eyes, to know the city was so much bigger than I had imagined. But it was too much to think about that dark, sprawling building that housed the ill. I couldn't imagine its corridors. Not yet at least. It was too much to simply gaze upon its rooftops.

The bells rang three times for Lauds, and I leaned over the balcony railing to watch the monks gather in the parvis. I counted only twenty hooded figures approaching the cathedral from the cloisters on Rue Char-Rori. They looked so diminutive from this height, just shadows holding candles through the gloom. I wondered how I looked to them. If they were to look up, would they perceive me peering down?

"Oh no, I've stayed here far too long!" I cried suddenly. "The Child always came back before Lauds and Marie told me to do the same. I should have just repeated those prayers and climbed down!"

"Forget what The Child used to do; you're the climber now, so you should do what you think is right," Michel said. "I always stay until the gargoyle flies over. You're welcome to join me."

"Should we be still and quiet?" I whispered.

Michel tilted his face towards the sky and closed his eyes. And then he opened his mouth as if to answer, but no—he sang. He sang! A low, melancholy voice that climbed towards the cathedral's towers.

I watched the arch of his throat and the ecstatic flutter of his eyes. The longer he sang, the more powerful his voice grew. I was afraid the monks would hear him, but I was so taken with his song I didn't ask him to stop. I couldn't wait to tell Bathsheba; she would appreciate this talent! Her voice was full and clear, that was true. But Michel's voice was smoother, and he reached notes she could not. I wished she was also on the balcony so she could hear his song.

I couldn't quit looking at the particularities of Michel's face. The arch of his lips over his wide teeth. I wanted to reach for him and hold my hands over his wings, daring to graze the long flight feathers, those intricate, flightless, beautiful wings.

His song was so painful that I wanted to touch his elegant hands with their square fingernail beds. I wanted to embrace him. It was a perfect prayer. An ideal offering to the Sky. I had simply repeated Isabelle's prayer—now, I wondered if I should have composed a song. Perhaps Bathsheba could help me prepare one for the next Wakening.

"No mortal can hear us from the Virgin's Balcony," he said, finally turning to me and opening his eyes. "And that was prayer for the beguines. I have more respect for the beguines than any of those people do. The ill need to be cared for, and the beguines are not afraid of them. They are far braver and more noble than these fleeing priests."

Listening to Michel made me wish I had paid more attention to the beguines. I wanted to say something that sounded equally compassionate.

This was the moment to tell him about the citrus. But what if the truth angered him?

"Our city is beautiful, isn't it?" he said. "I could never weary of this view. Not even after one hundred years."

"You're not carrying your scales!" I said, suddenly noticing. "Where did you leave them?"

Michel always carried heavy scales with tiny statues of the good and the damned. Peculiar and hopeful little faces.

"I let Lucifer hold my scales when I climb," he said. "Lucifer is good. I trust him. And the scales are cumbersome. To be truthful, holding them hurts." He rolled his shoulders back. "It is unfortunate how we can feel pain, even if we don't want to. Perhaps that's the price all living things must pay."

"What about the burning coal?" I asked. "Doesn't that hurt your tongue and mouth?"

He laughed and spat cold ashes.

"Yes, but it never stays lit for long."

Michel felt pain! A statue as otherworldly and powerful as Michel could know pain. I felt such a tenderness for him, I wanted to place my hands beneath his sculpted shoulder blades to soothe him.

"But surely the people notice the statue of Lucifer holding the Archangel Michel's scales of judgment?"

"You should know by now that their minds are too full to pay close attention to these things," Michel replied. "Lucifer can hold my scales. We're the same cathedral; what is Lucifer is me."

He shifted his weight towards me, and for a moment, we met each other's eyes.

"It is such a relief to tell someone how much it burdens me to hold those scales all the time," he said.

"I understand. Marie also says it's a burden to hold The Child all the time. It hurts her, too."

Silver paint creased between his eyebrows. "But Marie should love to hold The Child. He is part of her."

"Your scales are part of you, too," I said.

"It's different." His face held a look of confusion.

"Yes," I said, though I wasn't sure how. I hesitated a moment before speaking. "I have a confession of my own," I said. But my voice was too soft. As I began to speak, Michel interrupted me.

"Well, did you enjoy the climb itself?" he asked. "I love when it is my turn to be grimpeur. I love the way my body twists and moves. The agility in my body and the limits of my body. I like to figure out where to put my feet. Of course, I believe in the work of a grimpeur, but I enjoy the climb itself."

I felt my face brighten.

"I felt it, too," I replied. "The joy of climbing and forgetting all that has been troubling me."

"For so long, I have been the only grimpeur who lingers long past Lauds and dares the dawn," he said. "Except for you. Perhaps, you will dare the dawn, too, and keep me company."

Many moments passed before either one of us said anything

more. I felt my breathing quicken. *This was it*, I thought. This was my moment to tell Michel about the citrus.

"What do you think of Marie?" he asked, breaking my thoughts.

"Marie?"

I wasn't sure how to answer. Marie had allowed me to be grimpeuse, sure enough. But didn't part of me suspect she wanted to see me fail? I remembered her crushed-in, blinking eye on her otherwise haughty face, and the thought almost made me snicker. Sometimes I resented Marie, but I didn't want these thoughts to reach her ears. I didn't know how she might punish me.

"Whatever you have to say is completely safe with me. I won't tell anyone," Michel said, an easy smile on his lips.

His wings extended just enough to barely brush my back.

I felt a stab of worry, but Michel seemed to trust me.

"Marie's been angry lately," I said, unsure how to respond.

"It must be strange to see her so vulnerable. And The Child can't climb. You must be scared," Michel said.

"Well, we're guardian statues. We're not supposed to be afraid."

"We're not supposed to feel fear, I've said so myself. Yet, between the two of us, I know we feel these things all the same." Michel's voice was deliquescent. "In fact, I'm scared all the time. That's why I spend my wakenings near the Sky."

When I wasn't sure what else to say, Michel continued, "Marie doesn't respect me."

"She laughed at me," I said. "And I don't think she wanted me to climb."

I *was* angry at her, though at first, I didn't know where these feelings came from. But talking to Michel made me realize how much I was trying to embody the spirit of the Sainte Geneviève. Perfect, selfless, and controlled. Someone who would never steal an offering for herself.

"And the kings told me something very curious," I added. "They said The Child spent most of The Wakenings in their balcony gossiping!

And sometimes he never even gave the Sky his prayers at all!"

Michel rolled his luminous green eyes, and the stone made grinding sounds against sculpted sockets.

"He has become so lazy over the years," Michel said. "I'm happy you've replaced him."

He looked at me and pursed his lips, as if he had something else important to say. Then, he touched my upper arm, sending a pleasant chill through my body. I didn't want him to ever move his hand.

"I don't know what I'm doing either, you know. I am Archangel Michel, and there is so much weight on me to have answers and always be good and do what's right. I am trying to do the best I can."

"I feel the same way," I said.

I could trust Michel with my secret; he had trusted me with his.

But before I could say another word, I heard wings strike the air. Michel and I looked up, high beyond the double bell towers, and saw the gargoyle's shape. The Wakening was over.

"We must descend," Michel said. "Do you know how to climb down?"

I shook my head, peering over the edge. It was such a far way down.

"It's very much like climbing up, but the descent is easier. The stones extend to become a stairwell. Put one foot before the other, and you do not need to use your hands at all. Once you reach your niche, the other guardians will help you."

Then Michel balled his hands up into tight fists. "I cannot believe it," he said, his lips forming a straight line.

"Cannot believe what?"

"Marie didn't tell you how to climb and left you to figure it out on your own." He shook his head in disgust.

My mouth dropped open. "Maybe she didn't know?"

"You must be careful, Geneviève," Michel said. His hand slid from my arm, and his perfect smile appeared. "You know, your company is much more agreeable than The Child's. Will I see you again next wakening?"

I smiled back, forgetting about the citrus, feeling free, feeling alive. "Yes."

CHAPTER VII

"'Lady,' he said, 'where are you? Come forward and speak to us. With bird-
lime I have trapped the nightingale which has kept you awake so much.
Now you can sleep in peace, for it will never awaken you again.'"

From The Lais of Marie de France, Laüstic (c. 1155–1170)

Summer 1348

The clergy flocked to countryside monasteries or sequestered themselves in their dormitories and private apartments. Rumors spread that
Pope Clement feared the Death King so much he enclosed himself in
his papal chambers with France's finest doctors and a ring of tall-burn-
ing hearth fires. And our brave king, Philip le Fortuné? He was so
obsessed with the war with England, he kept taxing his subjects, illness
be damned. Then, he set sights on acquiring territories near the Medi-
terranean. It was almost as if he believed the illness would disappear if
he refused to acknowledge it.

The people wanted to know, where were all the God-fearing leaders?
Who could be called on to give last rites? Even Bishop Foulques de
Chanac had shied away from his congregation.

The body collectors, however, were plentiful. For anyone brave—
and opportunistic—there were pretty coins to earn pushing carts
through Paris' streets to gather the day's corpses, and there was no
shortage of this work. Hardly an hour passed when I didn't hear those
ominous wagon wheels grind against the cobble-paved Rue Neuve.

Or smell them. Once-familiar aromas like turmeric and fennel, violets and lilies, warm bread and roasted meat, hot wine, and mead decayed into the peculiar, sweet stench of putrid fruit, bile, and shit. The wind carried the stink of the carts and the funerary pits near the city walls.

I was well-acquainted with the stench of rot, a days-old carcass hanging from a careless butcher's stall, the sharp, acidic smell of the tanneries crossing the Seine. I had witnessed executions and knew the smell of the dead, but none of this compared to the stench the illness brought to Paris. Like sewage, but strangely perfumed. A great decaying flower in a rotting garden. A heady smell. How could I describe it? It was more than carrion beneath the midday sun and the eye-watering ammonia in animal waste. More than the menstrual blood I would never experience myself, though it was certainly that, too.

I couldn't bring myself to look into those carts. Even when they rolled past my eyes, I tried to keep my gaze on the living body collector. Like everyone else who was lucky enough to walk and breathe, the collectors had taken to covering their noses and mouths with strips of cloth to protect themselves from evil vapors; I overheard the living say that stench came from l'enfer, and anyone who inhaled it would get sick, too.

That's what made the body collectors so interesting: they could get sick, yet they all took this work. The married couples doing what they could to replace wages once earned selling bread or sheep; the young peasants who came into the city to make their fortune at a time when everyone with means had left. If they survived, they would buy property in Paris. Their children would live far better lives than they had.

Sometimes the body collectors were accompanied by children. Little boys and girls skipped ahead of their parents' carts, kicking and rolling wooden balls or playing with tin figurines. But the eldest children in the family always helped to lift and sort the bodies.

Sometimes, I overheard strands of laughter from the carts before realizing the collectors were joking with each other, referring to the disfigured bodies as "mon mari" or "une grand beauté." When I first heard them, I thought their jokes were foolish. Foolish to call a corpse ugly when it was so easy to land on the cart. But I knew people wanted to laugh when life was most horrific.

As weeks passed, I grew grateful for the sound of laughter, anything to remind me of a time when Paris was healthy. And indeed, cart pushers and body collectors fell ill, too. Then, they were readily replaced with more healthy and hungry people who wanted to work.

Sometimes I couldn't help it: I'd glimpse the limp, ashen arm of the newly dead. I'd see blackened, dried blood caked from the tremendous sore beneath an armpit, and I'd recoil as the smell and taste of rotten citrus fruit returned to me. Worst of all, I often recognized the people in those carts—faces I was once so used to seeing in the parvis. The mason who lived with his two little boys in a shabby hut on Rue Char-Rori. The girl who sold almond cakes. The old monk who scolded Isabelle.

What kind of cathedral guardian was I to look away? As Michel said, I was made to watch over everyone, the living and dead. But I had no loving gaze to spare those carts, even though I knew my body was safe from rot.

And then I wondered if climbing the cathedral wall really helped anyone.

But when I saw Michel, he smiled, and his face went soft and gentle. He looked at me like I had given him the greatest delight he had ever known. I saw warmth on his lips, lovely despite the chipped pink paint.

As the Feast of Sainte Anne approached, I met Michel's companion grimpeur, a blue imp with horns. There were two grimpeurs from the Portal of Sainte-Anne: Joaquim and Sainte Anne herself. They stood as tall as Michel, with their arms and faces painted golden and robes brilliant shades of green and gold.

After Matins, when Serpens was still coiled at the top of the sky, the five of us stood together in the Virgin's Balcony and repeated prayers, all of which sounded the same. Joaquim, Anne, and Michel's companion grimpeur never lingered on the balcony, and I exhaled after they left, relieved to be alone with Michel before the Rose Window. I watched him bite and twist his lower lip when I told him things Marie had said.

"Marie is wrong," said Michel. "We must keep bringing our prayers to the Sky."

He told me to remember the beguines, those women who had taken up drab, nunnish habits in the name of charity, service, modesty, and, most important of all, chastity. Michel knew the Sky heard his prayers because the beguines remained at the Hôtel-Dieu, finding beds, warm broth, and water for everyone. The clergy may have abandoned their flocks, but the beguines were there for Paris.

And hadn't I heard Pope Clement finally condemned all who blamed the Jews for the illness? He had condemned them all, saying they had been "seduced by that liar, the Devil."

"We must trust the Sky," Michel said. "We must trust that if we keep talking to the Sky, we can do good."

Sometimes we heard the strands of a faraway melody drifting across the Seine from some distant tavern, and Michel would sway beside me. He didn't touch me, and I never touched him. And I would want—Good Sky, I would *want*—to place my hands on his wings.

"All will be well, Geneviève. There is still so much life left in the world!"

Sometimes, he looked at me and said, "You have such long fingers. Your maker created you with the most beautiful hands."

Every time I began to tell him about the citrus, the quiet gargoyle cast shadows between the towers, warning of the first light. I felt relieved and disappointed as I descended.

By August, the graveyards began to overflow, and Paris stank with pyre smoke. The burial fires burned near the city walls, and though I couldn't see them from my niche, the smell clung to me. Every day, ash floated through the air, catching sunlight like dust motes, and landed on my fingertips, collecting in my upturned hands, the very hands Michel called *beautiful*. With their heat and low, constant roar, the fires seemed to burn with their own life force.

I spent more daylight hours thinking about Michel than the people. Part of me didn't want the illness to end—no, not the illness, but The Wakenings I spent in the Virgin's Balcony. I wanted this time with Michel to go on forever.

On the feast day of Saint Barthélemy, at the end of August, a strange star hung low on the horizon. After dusk first settled, I hardly paid it any mind for it flickered discreetly, as an ordinary star would. But as midnight approached, it grew bright and burned red. I stood beside Michel, as he sat perched on the balcony railing as always, and together we watched it traverse the sky.

"What do you think it is?" Michel asked. I'd never heard him sound so uncertain. "An omen?"

Was it simply a star that came loose from the heavens? We had seen falling stars before. Common as doves and larks. But now, after seeing everything the Great Death could do, I didn't know. If guardian statues could come to life, and a citrus could be a prayer, maybe a dancing star could be a warning from the Sky.

"Maybe it's not enough," Michel said, stone eyelashes long against his downcast gaze. "Is it not enough to climb to the cathedral to pray to the Sky? Wakening after wakening, nothing brings an end to the illness. Why is the Sky so indifferent? What does the Sky want from us?"

Michel cupped his face in his hands.

"If only I could fly myself," he said. "If only I could take prayers to the Sky. Why can't I fly like the gargoyles?"

"Why don't we ask them?" I suggested.

"Who?"

"The gargoyles. Why don't we ask them to bring the prayers closer to the Sky?"

I was proud of myself for this idea and wondered why no one had suggested it. Other than at the cusp of dawn, we rarely thought of the gargoyles. They were so solitary.

"That is not what gargoyles were made for!" Michel said. "They must spend their precious wakening hours protecting the cathedral from l'enfer. Archangels were made for speaking to the Sky."

Michel extended his wings to their full length before letting them drop against his back with a grinding clatter.

"Why must my wings be so useless?"

Michel's beautiful falcon wings? Useless? Those wings made him Archangel Michel. Those wings inspired the people to believe in angels. I would have given him anything to make him feel better. I would have done anything to bring Michel closer to the Sky.

"I would like to talk to the gargoyles," I pressed. "Perhaps they've seen things we have not and have the answers we're looking for."

"It is no use; they won't talk to us. They won't talk to anyone. I've tried before. The Child has, too."

"Really? Marie never said so."

"Oh, yes. It would be wonderful to know what gargoyles have seen from the cathedral's other façades, but they refuse to speak with us."

"I could try."

"No, Geneviève. You should spend The Wakenings here with me. That is what I want."

Michel drew near, close enough for me to see fractures in his green eyes. He took my hands and brought them to his mouth, placing chalky kisses on each palm. I closed my eyes and knew my hands would always hold the memory of that touch.

I wanted to live on this balcony forever, with Michel, and forget Isabelle and the people and their prayers and funeral pyres. Especially their prayers. Their prayers upon prayers upon miserable prayers that I never remembered, no matter how hard I tried.

CHAPTER VIII

Feast of Saint Michel, September 1348

Just as I began to climb, Bathsheba grabbed my arm and pulled me into our niche.

"You always spend the entire wakening on the balcony now," she said. "Won't you come back sooner and tell us what you've seen up there? Those dreary gargoyles have to warn us of first light before you bother to climb down."

I tugged my hand free, frustrated that Bathsheba would try to snatch up the precious nighttime I'd saved for Michel.

"Time is short," I said, narrowing my eyes.

Bathsheba let go, showing me the palms of her hands. I turned around to continue my climb and tried to ignore Bathsheba's sunken, dejected face. I reached towards the patriarchs who stood on the wall above me.

"Geneviève," she said softly behind me.

"What is it?"

"I wish you would tell me why everything is different now."

"The illness," I said.

"No, it's not just the illness."

The patriarchs took my hands and pulled me up. I looked back at Bathsheba, and she held my gaze for a breath before turning back to Jean.

"Something's troubling you," Michel said.

Joaquim and Anne had returned to their niches, leaving Michel and me alone in the Virgin's Balcony. He sat on the railing, and I stood beside him, so close the tips of his wings brushed my shoulder.

"Bathsheba's upset with me. I understand. I've been neglecting her. I haven't been sharing my thoughts with her as I used to." I crossed my arms, careful not to flake my paint. "Bathsheba has always been my pillar. She makes me feel rooted in the earth and has always made my world feel whole."

"She's simply jealous," Michel said with a flick of his hand. "That's to be expected. You can speak to the Sky. You're special now, Geneviève. You offered yourself as grimpeuse, and she did not, because she knows she couldn't do it. She wants to bring you back to your door jamb, close to the ground, the people, l'enfer."

Michel was right; Bathsheba was jealous. But not jealous of me, jealous of Michel's beautiful singing voice. I remembered how she shrugged when I told her about Michel's prayer for the beguines.

"Of course he's an excellent singer," Bathsheba had said. "He spends all night alone in the Balcony of the Virgin. If I spent every wakening by myself in a balcony where only the Sky could hear me, I would sing and sing and sing until my voice grew strong and I sounded better than a Benedictine choir."

"You're not impressed at all?" I asked her.

Bathsheba sighed.

"If I could sing as well as Michel, would that be enough to keep you in the Portal of the Virgin each wakening?" she'd asked. "I'm beginning to miss you."

"Don't give her another thought," Michel insisted.

Breath tunneled my body as I exhaled.

"I ate a prayer, Michel."

Michel's eyebrows flickered. "I don't know what you mean."

"A prayer. An offering. A citrus. The kind the people sell for cooking.

The kind that doesn't even grow in Paris. It must have been so expensive. A young woman placed it in my hands, and prayed for her family."

I placed my hands over my mouth. I couldn't look at Michel.

"Geneviève, what are you saying?"

"I should have just held it until it rotted away in my hands, but instead, I peeled it and I *ate it.*"

Michel's smile faded.

"Then it soured inside of me—even Bathsheba and Sylvestre could smell it. On the next wakening, I coughed it up into my hands. You were there, Michel. It was The Wakening you came to tell us about the illness. I was afraid you had seen me."

He took my hand and looked at me, his green eyes wet and wondering. I thought they looked so lovely, so innocent, the way they caught the muted starlight. Smoke coiled from his lips.

"I see. When you spat out the prayer, what did it look like?"

"Putrid, black, and soft. It looked just like the sores ill people grow beneath their skin."

Michel's nostrils flared. I shook my hands and turned my back to the bewildered archangel, but Michel put his palm on my shoulder and coaxed me to turn around.

"I should have been able to control myself," I said. "Now I'm afraid I've torn the fabric of the enchantment, like L'Ecclésia and Saint Etienne. I'm afraid I've cursed Isabelle's family."

I closed my eyes and felt Michel's hand on my shoulder again. The chalky pads of his fingertips. He touched the corners of my lips. His touch! So unexpected and reassuring.

"But you've wakened, and you stand before me," Michel said. "You have not torn the fabric of the enchantment."

"The girl who gave me the offering, Isabelle, I have not seen her since the Feast of Sainte Geneviève. But her brother visited the cathedral, and I overheard him tell his friend that the illness took his family."

Michel placed his hands in mine, and my fingers were so long, they covered his.

"This youth—Isabelle's brother—was the one who was so angry he threw stones at the cathedral and shattered The Child. Of course, he did—he felt that the Church, its saints, and his faith had betrayed him. But I was the one who betrayed him. His sister prayed for their family's health, and I ate that prayer. It never reached the Sky. And all this time I've been grimpeuse, I've still been too ashamed to tell you."

As I spoke, something curious happened. For months, my thoughts had had no place to go but to turn circles in my mind. Now, they were free. It began to feel strange—presumptuous, arrogant even—to believe I had so much power that I could curse an entire family. I was one being. What if I were not responsible for every person who visited the cathedral?

For the first time, I wondered if I had been wrong about the curse.

Michel parted my lips and ran the tip of his index finger across the top row of my teeth. My mouth did not resist. I let his finger pry my mouth as much as he pleased, revealing to him each little, sculpted tooth. Smoke blew from his mouth to mine.

He touched teeth in the back of my mouth, teeth I didn't even know I had. I closed my eyes and enjoyed this friction. Heat of stone against stone.

"I am only amazed that you can eat," he said, yanking his hand away. His expression went dark.

I pulled my arms across my body.

"I suspected something was eating the people's prayers," he said, moving further away from me. "And yes, I saw that rotten, chewed-up bile in the Portal of the Virgin, but I thought it was a demon. A demon those useless gargoyles weren't catching. I didn't know it was you!"

He turned and jumped from the railing into the shadows.

"No, wait. Don't go!" I called in horror. "I haven't been eating prayers! It was only this one offering."

"Just this one offering?" Michel scoffed. "Oh, Geneviève, you have indeed committed a great sin; you have eaten, and we are not meant to eat. You courted the Great Death and now look what happened. Look what happened to The Child! How could you have been so impulsive?"

I turned away and buried my face in my hands. I felt pressure behind my eyes as if my disappointment could spill out as tears, though I had never cried before and had never seen another statue cry.

"I have no choice but to tell every guardian in the West Façade," Michel continued. "Not everyone will be gentle with you. Some might call for your destruction. They may want to drive you from the cathedral grounds or forbid you from returning to your doorway so that you meet the light of day without the cathedral's protection."

I told myself to be brave, to listen to Michel speak. I had brought this upon myself. I deserved this.

Didn't I?

"Some will want to throw rocks at you, like that mortal who shattered The Child. You would simply be damaged then, and if the right stone struck your mouth, you would never speak—much less eat—again. But you would get to live," he said. "How lucky.

"I think the stone is your best fate, Geneviève. You have been a very loyal grimpeur, so I will advocate for that punishment on your behalf if you choose, though I cannot make any promises," Michel said.

I summoned all my courage and spoke.

"I accept whichever fate my companions choose for me. But I will do whatever I can to make things right again. To atone."

"Geneviève, we are not mortals. We cannot *atone*."

"Why not? When you visited the Portal of the Virgin, you told us we must atone—that's what you said."

"I don't remember using that word," Michel said.

"Why can't we atone?" I asked.

"Because I don't know how you could have kept this from me," Michel said, hiding his face in his hands. "I trusted you."

"I'm sorry."

I had nothing more to say. Michel would tell my companions, and I would pay for my transgression. A stone to my mouth would be a suitable punishment—I would never eat again.

"Gargoyles," Michel said, breaking the quiet between us.

"What?"

"Have you ever wondered why the gargoyles can fly but the angels cannot?"

"Isn't that the way it's always been?" I reached to touch Michel's shoulder, but he shrugged off my hand.

"How is it that they have this power, but I do not? I am the Archangel Michel! If they can fly, the angels should be able to as well."

I stared up at the Rose Window, taking in the immensity of it. The cathedral was so very big, and we were all little fragments.

"Geneviève, what if the gargoyles were eating prayers, like you? What if they were the ones who were responsible for the illness?" Michel's eyes dazzled with starlight.

"What? How can you say that?"

"What if the gargoyles are snatching up the prayers and eating them before they can reach the Sky?" Michel said. "Don't you know that this cathedral was built atop the ruins of a pagan temple? What if pagan souls became gargoyles?"

"I've never heard anything like that. Marie has always said that gargoyles are the guardians of the guardians—"

"Marie," Michel snarled. "Marie thinks she understands everything there is to know about the enchantment. Marie wants power more than anything else—that is her weakness."

I inhaled, drawing back.

"I need a pair of flying wings so I can deliver the prayers to the Sky myself," he said, his expression turning thoughtful. "If I can fly, I will know for sure whether gargoyles are protecting the cathedral or swallowing prayers."

"But how will you get a pair of wings?"

He smiled at me, that smile I would do anything to produce.

"If you bring me the wings of a gargoyle, I will keep your transgressions a secret. I won't tell anyone about the citrus."

"But how? They wouldn't give me their wings!"

"You would harvest them."

"Harvest? How?" I recoiled. "You can't mean it."

He smiled again.

"I suspect you can convince one of our companion guardian gargoyles to give you their wings on their own accord."

I nodded slowly.

"You and I are a lot alike," he said, opening his hands. "You aren't satisfied to stand still in your alcove, and neither am I. You want more. That's why you ate the offering. I can see that now."

"Yes!" I said, relieved Michel understood me.

"Well, that's why I'm willing to keep your secret. You can atone for courting the illness after all, if you help me." He cupped the palms of his hands against his chest. "Do it for the cathedral. Do it for Paris."

He opened his wings and beckoned to me. I moved beside Michel again and rested my arms against the balcony railing. Michel slid his wings against my back as if to envelop me.

"Do it for me," he said, softly this time.

My mind spun faster than a ball in a game of la Soule. Not once had I watched the silhouette of flying gargoyles and thought they were swallowing prayers. And I didn't know if the cathedral was built atop pagan ruins. But now I wondered why the angels couldn't fly, and I saw how unfair that was.

"I would like to give you something in exchange for gargoyles wings," he said. "I'd like to give you my wings—angel's wings."

He placed his hands against my back, where a woman would have shoulder blades. Stone grated stone in a way that made warmth from his fingers spread beneath my mantle. I closed my eyes and imagined red and purple heat tendrilling the length of my body.

"If I gave you my wings, you could become an angel. An angel with archangel's wings. You wouldn't be able to fly, but you would be powerful. Marie would never be able to order you around again. Bathsheba would answer to you."

I frowned. Marie and Bathsheba answering to me? That didn't feel right.

"But wouldn't the others protest?"

"They will adore you. Isn't that what you want? Their adoration?"

I stepped away from Michel, not sure of what I wanted, not sure of what to say. "The people will notice."

"You must stop worrying about the people," Michel sighed. "I've told you many times, they don't pay attention to us, even the ones who know the cathedral most intimately."

Isabelle noticed me, I thought.

He perched close enough for his arms to brush mine.

"Do you still trust me?" His voice was gentle.

I nodded, and he took my hands and kissed them both.

With Michel's wings, everything would be different. I would transform. I would become an angel with archangel's wings.

I hoped I would finally forget the taste of rotten citrus.

"Until the next dark moon," Michel said. He climbed over the railing and began his descent towards the Portal of the Last Judgement. I heard the Kings of Judah greet him with reverence before they stepped aside to make room for his climb.

Now I was alone on the balcony. I wanted to stay and look out over the tangle of rooftops that sprawled on either side of the Seine. I wanted to stare at the dark spire of the Sainte-Chapelle dominating the horizon. I wanted to watch light flicker in windows as people woke. Before the illness, this had always been the hour for pushing carts through the city's winding streets towards the market in the parvis. What had happened to all those farmers, those clothiers, those leather workers and blacksmiths, those braying donkeys and chuffing horses? In the distance, from beneath the Petit-Pont, at the riverbank, I heard a single howling dog. A lonely, warning sound that made me hug my arms across my chest.

One foot beneath the other and the cathedral yielded to me. When I reached the Gallery of the Kings, I found Asa and Jehoshaphat eagerly awaiting my return.

"What did Michel say?" said Asa.

"We simply prayed," I said.

"We heard whispers," Asa said, reaching out and taking my arm.

"I have nothing of importance to share."

"I don't believe you," Asa said. "Tell me or we will not let you climb down!"

Jehoshaphat jabbed Asa in the ribs. "What are you talking about?" he said.

I looked over the gallery, staring down the long length of stone between the Portal of the Virgin and myself. Mirach had slipped closer to the horizon, winking as it faded from the night. I turned to the kings, pleading with their eyes.

"Release her!" Jehoshaphat said.

"Not until she tells us what she and Michel discussed," Asa insisted. "I heard grave-sounding whispers."

"It was none of your concern!"

"See? You just admitted it was something!"

"There's no time for this, Asa!" Jehoshaphat said, pointing heavenward. "Look—the gargoyle!"

We tilted our faces skyward to watch the shadow twist the air. The gargoyle was swift, with great wings, and moved just like a bird. If I were mortal, I would think it was a hawk or falcon at first hunt, or perhaps an owl returning to its home at night's end. The ravens also woke at this hour—I could have easily convinced myself this guardian was a common raven.

Or, perhaps, a bird that could fly between the worlds.

"It is dawn! Let Geneviève return to her portal!" Jehoshaphat said.

"Not yet, the sky is still dark," Asa sighed. "As long as the gargoyle flies—"

I did not have time to wait for Asa to step clear of my path. I nudged him out of my way, urging myself to outclimb the rising sun. In my haste, I stepped on Asa's stupid foot and slipped.

The kings called out to me, stretched their futile hands as I tumbled out of the balcony, grabbing air instead of wall. I heard a shrill, whistling sound as I fell and realized it was my own voice. It wasn't a scream exactly, but the sound of air passing through limestone.

Instead of horror, I felt freedom.

Free from the cathedral, free from the citrus, free from Michel's anger, free from the horrible task he had given me.

It would be over.

But it wasn't. Hands on my ankles. The faces in the archivolts. The cherubim and the patriarchs, grabbing me, supporting me, pulling me back to safekeeping in my door jamb. Bathsheba and Sylvestre held me upright, my limbs still soft and weak. I leaned against Bathsheba's shoulder for support.

My companions' voices swirled in a choir until I could not distinguish one from the next.

"I told you she's not fit to be *grimpeuse*."

"Next wakening, we will find another."

"There should be no more grimpeurs or grimpeuses," said Marie. "This has become a game of hubris."

I rested against Bathsheba's shoulder and felt hoary lichens on her mantle tickle my cheek. Her arms tightened around me, chalky and soft. I welcomed her embrace.

CHAPTER IX

La Toussaint Eve, October 1348

Be clever enough to figure it out—the only instructions Michel gave me. Of course. Michel didn't know how to harvest gargoyle wings either. But if I could find a way to bring him what he wanted—no, what he needed—to fly, I could prove my devotion to the cathedral and the enchantment. My devotion to Isabelle's family; I could bring her what she wanted! A bird to fly between the worlds. Michel would become that bird, and I could make myself good again.

I could climb out of the feeling that made me want to climb out of myself.

Now more people than I could count came to the cathedral to beg clergy for a dying family member's last sacrament. Each prayer was more desperate than the last, and I struggled to absorb them while I held the weight of Michel's impossible task.

The clergy fussed over the great treatise King Philip had commissioned, the Paris Concilium. According to parvis rumors, the king had taken to pulling out his hair, snapping out his long blond strands, plucking his eyelashes in fits of rage and worry. He threw temper tantrums that created bald patches on his scalp and devastated his eyebrows, according to those closest to him.

Well, those closest to him, the noble ladies and lords, the wealthy but subservient demoiselles and captains, had long left Paris for their countryside mansions, but the clergy and common people were skilled gossips. The people demanded an explanation for the illness.

The people demanded to be fed. With few left—or willing—to harvest the land, the price of bread and fruit was inconceivable. And so, the king ordered forty-nine of the finest medical masters from the university to puzzle out what had awakened the Great Death.

Of course, these sharp minds could not agree. Ultimately, they concluded that humankind would never know what had caused the illness. Still, they had their theories. Some believed it was caused by evil fumes that had escaped l'enfer after a terrible earthquake. Many others simply said it was God's wrath; they blamed King Philip himself for provoking the long war with England, they blamed the ineffective priests, they blamed the money-hungry merchants, and they blamed the people for spiritual deprivation.

Other medical scholars in this consortium believed the illness was caused by the position of the planets and stars spiraling in the Sky. That planets with names like Jupiter and Saturn could be powerful enough to influence mortal bodies and mortal decisions.

I didn't know what to believe. I didn't know where the illness came from. And as I listened to these ideas, but only halfway, as if with only one good ear, I thought about Michel. I knew these arguments strengthened his conviction that the Sky was in disarray, that only a flying archangel could sway the indifferent Sky.

I would bring him his flying gargoyle wings, or else he would tell my companions in the Portal of the Virgin that I had eaten a citrus fruit, that I had courted the illness, that I deserved to have my face smashed in and my lips pounded to dust.

Where would I meet a gargoyle, and if I managed to encounter one, how would I convince them to give me their wings?

When night fell on the eve of La Toussaint, my companions would not let me climb, not after what had happened last wakening.

"I have not changed my mind," Marie said. "You will not climb again, Geneviève."

No matter. I knew I wouldn't find gargoyles on the Balcony of the Virgin; I knew their territory spanned the cathedral's other walls as well as its roof.

But how would I reach the roof? The two bell towers that rose like great horns looked impossible to climb, even for the most lithe, skilled grimpeurs, like Michel or The Child. When I craned my neck to look at them, I saw long windows that opened into a dark maw. No easy footing. And besides, they simply reached too high.

No, tonight I would descend.

I would walk the length of the cathedral, without leaving its grounds, and try to find a stairwell that led to the rooftop. But that was where my plan began and ended. I didn't know what I would say when I met the gargoyles. I didn't even know what a gargoyle looked like; I had only ever seen their shadows. But I had heard stories about them and knew they were supposed to look like hell-haunted human nightmares. Like the monsters that roamed the forests beyond the city walls, swallowing piles of bones while sitting on piles of bones. Plucking out eyes and tongues with their long, gnarled teeth and nails. And ugly. Ugly enough to frighten real demons.

But could a gargoyle frighten another guardian statue?

Could a gargoyle eat another statue?

Could a gargoyle really eat a human prayer?

I shivered, almost regretting my agreement with Michel.

I stepped forward, confident that the stones beneath my niche would catch me. They did. The little round-faced imp carved into the wall grabbed the hood of my mantle.

"Let me go," I whispered.

He pulled hard, but I was stronger and broke free of his grasp. My other companions had expected me to try to climb up the façade, not down, so I descended the cathedral steps with ease. When I reached the ground, I slid my fingertips over the earth, admiring the rough sensation of dirt against my hands, and breathed in the smell.

Denis saw me and cried out. At once, the murmuring stopped. I crouched low to the ground, turning my head to avoid Bathsheba's puzzled stare. Marie released a weary exhale, and we locked eyes. I thought she would demand I return to the door jamb.

"Go ahead," she said. "If you're still too foolish to know that staying in your niche is what's best for you, I won't try to stop you."

I bowed my head to hide a scowl and nodded.

I couldn't make myself glance back at the Portal of the Virgin and meet Bathsheba's eyes. So, I took the air in deep breaths, let it fill my body's hollows, and I lifted my feet, ready at last to walk on earth.

How freeing it was to move in the cool, damp air! I thought I knew what movement felt like. After all, I had climbed part of the cathedral. But now I was alone, separated from the West Façade—separated from the architecture! No one to watch or touch me.

My body belonged to *me* now.

For these few exhilarating moments, I saw that I was more than the people's stories about a woman named Sainte Geneviève, ideal because the best thing a woman could do was transcend her nature and become a saint. And now I was more than an ideal statue, content to stand still and admire the same view for the entirety of my existence.

Now I understand why L'Ecclésia and Saint Etienne wanted to walk far beyond the parvis and the cathedral's boundaries. If I were not careful, I would be tempted, just like them.

But Michel needed his wings, I needed Michel's forgiveness, and Isabelle needed her bird, so I vowed to myself that I would be far more careful and controlled than L'Ecclésia and Saint Etienne.

I thought of all the people who had walked this path before me, and I pulled their faces from my memories. Nascent memories from my first days on the cathedral wall. I remembered all the masons who had come to Paris from the North, Germany and the Low Countries; the South, Tuscany and Rome and Tunis; the East, Egypt and Ethiopia; the West, Aragon and Castille. They had heard stories about a cathedral that had taken a hundred years to build, and they came to Paris seeking opportunity. Entire families came. Men cut stone, women made plaster, and children gathered supplies. Their straw-roofed huts filled the parvis, and their cookfires smoked the air.

I touched the stones they'd built and remembered so many faces. The Notre-Dame de Paris was all these people, all these languages. All of them had made me. They had taught me how to listen and speak.

I knew there had to be a way to enter those towers—those two great horns. A stairwell, perhaps. A safe passage to the roof.

Soft laughter interrupted my thoughts before I reached the North Façade. I pressed my body tight against the wall and told myself not to breathe. But soon, my curiosity overcame my fear, and I turned my head.

A Cluniac scholar with a woman wrapped in his stern black robes. They were standing some distance from me, but I could still see them clearly, hear their voices, and smell them. I recognized her, a femme de Samedi, one of the women who sold their bodies after Vespers. Sometimes, I caught glimpses of their elaborate clothing in the parvis, squirrel fur mantles and silk cotehardies that exposed the tops of their shoulders.

"There's no one here," she whispered. "Let's stay."

"My apartment is a short walk from here. No one else will wake. I promise."

"There may be illness in your home," she said.

"Then take me to where you live."

"There may be illness in my home."

"Then let's stay right here," he said.

She pressed him against the wall. I had crept close enough to touch them, but they didn't notice me. He lifted her silk green skirt, exposing one pale thigh, and I watched how she guided his hands.

In peaceful times, this scholar would have faced expulsion from the University if he were caught, but the illness had changed everything, driving away the people who would punish him. And the Saturday women? Forbidden, too, yet it was easy to look the other way when their services were valuable, perhaps now more than ever. They did not fear the body and its fallibilities. They were the merchants of forgetting all bad things. Merchants of forgetting illness and loss.

They didn't feel my presence.

They couldn't see me!

Michel would have been so impressed if he could see how I stood still, against the wall, veiled to mortal eyes, just as he did when he visited the Portal of the Virgin on the Chandeleur.

The Chandeleur. That felt so long ago now, though it had only been months. Back then, I thought Michel was the only guardian powerful enough to stand this close to people without being perceived. Now, I realized I had that power, too.

Had I always possessed such power? Or was I becoming more like Michel?

The scholar's fingers made indentations in the moon-white thigh. He pushed aside his robes, and I stole a glimpse at his ball sack. She turned, bending, her hands pressed against the cathedral wall now— my same wall, where I drew all my strength. His hood fell, exposing his bald-tonsured head.

I told myself to return to the West Façade. Leave. And yet, I heard the rhythm of their breathing and the soft rasp of skin on skin.

I wanted to watch. His face was buried into her back, and her face was nearly pressed against the cathedral wall. To my frustration, their clothing concealed most of their bodies, but I could see the bottom of her ass and the way she spread open her cheeks.

That silver face rose into my consciousness. His fingers on my teeth. His hands in my mouth. I closed my eyes, leaned against the wall, and felt my mouth open, recalling the sensation of the citrus fruit and how my body had taken what it wanted. I could smell them: the scholar, the Saturday woman, and Michel, too. Frankincense blown through red painted lips. Red-colored heat coiling through my chest.

I ran my hands down my belly. How unfair that my makers had carved my body fully clothed. The outline of breasts and legs was just a suggestion beneath limestone I could never access. What would it feel like to touch somebody? What would it feel like to be touched?

How cruel that I could only seek pleasure in a citrus fruit prayer!

An animal ran past, and I jerked in surprise. But when the creature slowed to a trot, I realized it was only a dog. She barely acknowledged the scholar and the woman, but she paced before me, sniffing the wall, mesmerized. Her soft fur brushed my legs, and I wanted to reach down and stroke the place between her pointed ears. She sniffed at the air, ignoring the scholar. When I looked into her eyes, the fur on her back stood up. She released a hellish snarl and bared her teeth.

"Quiet, Grâce!" The monk hissed.

The dog responded with a low growl.

"She doesn't like me," said the woman.

"She does this sometimes. Barks at walls."

I panted, watching my breath materialize in the cold air, curling from my lips outward. The Saturday woman pulled her skirt down over her legs and covered herself in her dark wool mantle.

"Merde, Grâce! Go away."

The dog whined but didn't leave.

"I'm sorry," said the monk. "We'll get caught here with her howling like this."

He retrieved the coins to pay her, and I caught a glimpse of his face. He looked nervous, relieved almost, that it was over. I suddenly doubted he had paid for company like this before. She counted the coins and looked content. I watched as she kissed his cheek and straightened out his robes for him.

They walked past me without looking up, and I exhaled, relieved that they could not perceive me, though the dog slinked by with flattened ears. I felt the corners of my mouth flicker into a smile. The dog had acknowledged me. A living thing had acknowledged me! For several moments, I stood with my head resting against the wall and my hand over my chest. I closed my eyes and breathed.

Eventually, I let go and took tentative steps towards the North Façade. Not far ahead, I spotted what I'd been searching for: an indentation in the wall. A doorframe. The Cluniac and the femme de Samedi had been blocking this entrance to the cathedral, but now I could pry open the door. Would I find a stairwell?

I noted the position of the stars and cursed when I saw Cygnus approach the horizon. Soon, it would be Lauds. I suddenly felt exposed standing like this with my feet planted in the earth, and I craved the safety of the Portal of the Virgin. I could avoid one distracted scholar, but I was afraid of a whole procession of monks. I was simply not as daring as Michel—not yet at least.

I would have to return to the West Façade without gargoyle wings. Next wakening, I would try again.

I tried to convince myself that it would feel wonderful to have an archangel's wings. Wings would satisfy all my needs. But something else was still there: Michel's red mouth in the place of the scholar's and how his lips had felt on the backs of my hands.

CHAPTER X

Feast of Saint Saturnin de Toulouse, November 1348

Pouring rain curtained the doorjamb, enclosing Bathsheba and I, sheltering our conversation from curious ears. I was grateful. When I told her what I saw near the North Façade, she cupped her hand to mouth. I could see her broad grin peeking through her fingers. She began to giggle and sing:

entor le moustier sanz parler

.iii. tors dire .iii. patre nostres

Another silly troubadour's song. I had no recollection of this one, but I knew it had to end the same way as the rest: with a clever woman in bed with a sneaky priest.

"Bathsheba, how do you remember them all?"

"The same way the grimpeurs remember all the prayers," she said eyeing me. "Although, I find songs far more entertaining than prayers."

So did I.

"Geneviève, please say you're done being grimpeuse now. I know I've teased you for being fidgety, but The Wakenings are boring without you here for company. No one else appreciates what I have to say or the things I notice in the daytime. No one else thinks I sing beautifully."

"But imagine, if I hadn't climbed down, I wouldn't be able to amuse you with this great story."

I didn't want to leave my niche either, not tonight. I didn't want to walk in the rain and look for gargoyles. The thought of seeing Michel made me nervous, too. I didn't know what to do with the thoughts that had come to me last wakening and had stayed with me ever since. Me instead of the monk. Michel instead of the femme de Samedi.

"I'll stay with you tonight," I said.

"Good, because I want to know everything you saw," said Bathsheba. She huddled close to the wall as rainwater pooled between our feet. I stretched my arms and cupped water in my hands. It was so cold, it burned, but I didn't mind. Bathsheba shook her head.

"You can't stand still, can you? It's going to wash away all your paint."

"I don't mind."

"Well, I want to remain beautiful," she said.

"The cathedral is immense, overwhelming in its greatness," I began. "From the ground, the walls stretch on and on into the night sky with no end. It's strange to realize we are just one part of something so big. Bathsheba, can you imagine what the cathedral looks like from the inside?"

She pursed her lips into a tight line.

"We'll never get to see that. That's why I don't like to imagine it," she said. "Tell me more about this monk and this woman."

"Everything was covered beneath his robes and her gaudy green cote. Well, mostly."

"Mostly?"

"I saw some of their asses."

I didn't tell Bathsheba how I looked away, closing my eyes as Michel intruded my thoughts. How I could hear and smell them and only see Michel's silver face and golden hair.

Bathsheba shrugged and rubbed her hands together. "I should not envy them—their sweetness is brief, and they will not live forever."

In the time between The Wakenings, I had wondered how this scholar and the femme de Samedi remained rosy-cheeked and well if courting sin was to court the Great Death. How were they in full health when so many others had died? And even if the illness did not take them, how much time did these young people have left in life?

Even under the best conditions, their years would pass them quickly. How did they wake each day with the knowledge that their time with their bodies was so limited? How could they enjoy their footsteps, the softness of their mouths, the taste of wine and each other? How could one mortal life ever be enough? Bathsheba was right. I mourned them preemptively, envious of my stone body on their behalf.

Bathsheba's eyes narrowed. "You know those people could have seen you."

"But they didn't! That's why this is so fascinating. I felt as powerful as Michel! The people couldn't see me. Only the dog—"

"The dog! There was a dog?"

"Come with me next wakening. I'll tell Michel you are going to help me—I'll tell him and Marie we need a second grimpeuse from the Portal of the Virgin."

I hadn't meant to tell Bathsheba about the dog. If she knew that another being had seen me—recognized me as a being that could breathe—Bathsheba would worry for me even more than she already did.

I wanted her to approve of me and what I was doing. Maybe if she knew what it felt like to walk free from the wall, she would understand.

"I know you want to be mortal, Geneviève. But you know, all mortals ever do is *want*. Want, want, want, and then your life is over. We get to see everything. Isn't this enough?"

The feelings Michel gave me felt like eternity, too, but I didn't know how to share that with Bathsheba.

"You know, maybe Michel isn't so special after all," Bathsheba said. "You can do the same things he can. You can walk the cathedral grounds unnoticed. You can climb all the way to the Balcony of the Virgin. And I can sing—just as well as he can, I'm sure."

Jean and Sylvestere began to make protesting sounds, loud enough to hear over the rain. Michel had sent down a message: he wanted to see me in the Virgin's Balcony.

"In this rain?" I asked.

"In the rain," my companions echoed. Sylvestre shook his head with concern, keeping one hand on his pope's crown so it would not slide off. Even the little imp face carved over my shoulder looked surprised.

I waited for Marie's reaction, but she held her face still, wearing an expression of disinterest. "Well, do you want to climb again?" she said at length.

I nodded yes.

"Go, if you think it's wise," Marie said. "If you are not concerned about the rain."

"You told me you were going to stay here and talk to me tonight!" Bathsheba crossed her arms tight over her chest.

"I know, but Michel demands it. I don't know how to tell him no."

Marie's eyes lingered on my face and for a moment, she raised a single, dark eyebrow.

"I don't know if climbing to the roof in the rain and risking your own existence is worth so many prayers," Bathsheba said. "I'm surprised Michel would expect that from you."

"Michel knows I'm capable of climbing tonight," I said. "He trusts me."

"I'm not saying that you're not capable of climbing." Bathsheba placed her hand on my wrist, but I shook her off.

"I trust Michel," I said.

"I just don't think he should have asked you to climb tonight. Especially not after what happened the last time you went up there."

As I turned towards the faces in the archivolts, my fingers trembled. Bathsheba was right, tonight was a dangerous night to climb. I knew it, and I knew Michel knew it, too. This was another one of his tests to see if I was worthy of archangel wings.

I could be a saint with an archangel's wings.

I felt Bathsheba's reluctance. Still, she offered her hand to help me steady my footing in the slick architecture. More hands reached for me. Marie's voice was just audible over the rain, "Geneviève, be careful."

I passed the archivolts, then the flat swath of wall between the archivolts and the Gallery of the Kings. The wind began to pull here, threatening to pry my fingers from the bricks. I wondered how Michel, much lighter than me, had managed his climb tonight. But Michel, I remembered, was an experienced grimpeur.

When I could just see the king's balcony, I reached for safety. Too soon. I grabbed at nothing but cold air and raindrops, my hand swinging wildly behind me by the power of its weight.

Asa caught me. When I recovered from the flurry of hands gripping my arms, pulling on my hood, I saw the thirty kings. They were gathered around me, their hands on each other's shoulders, straining to see over each other's crowns, breathing through gaping mouths. They looked so foolish.

"I'm fine," I said, unable to meet their eyes.

"You should have never climbed tonight," said Jehoshaphat.

"Michel requested me."

"Michel told us not to give her trouble," Asa conceded.

"Be careful," said Jehoshaphat.

I was growing weary of all these warnings, but I said nothing. None of them would doubt me or Michel when I became a saint with archangel's wings.

"Pleasant wakening." Michel's voice was as gentle as ever.

He sat on the railing of the Virgin's Balcony, and I stood beside him, arms pressed against the guardrail, both of us looking towards the tangle of spires and rooftops beyond the parvis. The rain had turned to mist and drizzle, and the clouds bloomed with muted light, illuminating the cracks in Michel's eyes. I returned his smile cautiously, disappointed with myself for arriving without wings.

Michel offered his embrace, and I pressed my cheek to his. Though he held no coal beneath his tongue tonight, he smelled of cathedral smoke.

"I should have never asked you to do something so dangerous," he said. "It was foolish of me to think you could harvest gargoyle wings."

"I will try harder next wakening," I said, proud of the resolve I heard in my voice.

"It is too late. You couldn't get the wings last wakening, and tonight, you wouldn't even try. That's why I called you here. To tell you to forget it. You couldn't get them even if you wanted to."

"Oh no, you've misunderstood me! I want to help you."

"You want to atone."

"I want to help *you*!" I said. My hands flew to his shoulders, to his chin. I wanted him to face me. I wanted him to see the sincerity in my eyes. Instead, he fixed his gaze on the dark steeples beyond the parvis.

"I am not even the Archangel Michel!" He cupped his hands over his eyes. "I am useless, and I am not strong enough to withstand the city's pain." He leaned in close enough to breathe on my face. "I don't even think I want to exist anymore."

I drew back. "Please don't talk like that."

"Why not?" His voice was flat and distant. He leaned out and thrust his head and chest over the railing. I grabbed his forearm, as if that would be enough to keep him from tumbling. He jerked away and stood up, balancing on his delicate toes with his wings and arms outstretched.

"Michel!"

"Why do we come to life each dark moon? Our existence is useless." He let himself sway forward. "We're useless! To be alive and aware is horror." Michel began to laugh. "Do you realize your precious Isabelle has likely perished? It's true you haven't seen her since the night you greedily *ate* her offering."

Bits of stone and crushed paint flew from Michel's mouth, spraying me. One debris struck my eye, but it was too small to hurt.

"It's your fault she's dead," he said, and lifted one foot off the railing. "Why don't you feel more guilty?"

"Please, Michel. Please come down. The West Façade needs you, even if the people do not."

"I know you do. You need me to tell you what is right and wrong. You need me to tell you not to eat. But that doesn't make my existence on this wall any less miserable. I'm trapped here and so are you." His flight feathers shook over the drop.

I wanted him to quit speaking. To quit spitting rock and mineral.

"Whatever you want, I will do it," I said. "I will bring you gargoyle's wings. I will bring you the wings of every gargoyle on this cathedral. Whatever you want."

He moved in the way of cats. Without taking his eyes off mine, he stood with his feet flat on the railing and his back perfectly straight, as if he would let himself fall back to the ground.

But he didn't.

He crouched to the railing, pulling himself to the safety of the balcony. I realized I had been kneeling, as if in prayer.

"Geneviève, I am so sorry. I should never speak to you like that. I am so, so sorry. Geneviève, protector of Paris."

We both sat on our hands and knees, facing each other. I looked past him, thinking about Isabelle. How I hoped it was not true that she had died. I didn't want her to die. She was so young.

"Do you forgive me?" Michel asked.

He was still and quiet as I brought my tentative arms around him, an embrace meant to comfort, a gesture I had learned from all these years of watching people. My hands fell across his wings, grazing his flight feathers.

"The truth is, I want to give you my wings so that you can know all the secrets I do, the secrets of angels," he said. He reached out and cupped my face in his hands. "I cannot wait to give you my wings; you deserve them. You've brought me to life. But first you must atone."

"I will atone." The words fell out of my mouth. I heard them the way I heard other people speak, as if they were not mine. How I hoped Isabelle was not dead, how I hoped she had simply left the city. I didn't want her to die. How deeply, deeply unfair that she was mortal.

Michel's expression softened. He touched the front of my neck, tapping his fingertips on the base of my throat. "I'm sorry for being so harsh with you. Do you forgive me?"

"I forgive you," I said.

"Do you really forgive me?"

Maybe it was fear and desperation. Maybe I needed to be comforted. Maybe it was because Michel looked so celestial with his golden hair and silver painted skin. He looked to me like my salvation. I pressed my mouth to his, just as I had seen people do. Like the femme de Samedi.

His lips softened; his mouth turned wet with rainwater and condensation. He sighed and returned my kiss, grabbing me towards him. I breathed in the smell of incense, felt his stony tongue meet mine. I sighed and pulled him close. My lips grazed his neck, and his breathing quickened.

"You don't know how long I've been wanting to—"

Michel suddenly pushed me away and looked at me like I was the seven-headed dragon.

"What is the matter with you?" He pinched the base of my throat. "Are you trying to break the enchantment?"

I heard the crack and felt a jab of pain. When I reached for my neck, I found a new seam.

"Oh!" I cried.

"Oh, Geneviève, you are just a simple saint, you poor thing. I am so sorry." He pressed his fingers to my aching throat. "I'm so sorry, I'm so sorry, I'm so sorry I hurt you."

I didn't know what to say, other than to repeat his apologies back to him. I had bitten into his mouth, just as I had bitten into the citrus. Of course, he grabbed me in response. I deserved it.

I was wrong.

Impulsive.

I rested my head against his shoulder, catching my breath, trying my best to understand what had happened between us tonight in the Virgin's Balcony, the great rose-shaped window as witness. He leaned against me and told me to stroke his wings—to remember the gift he would give me once I had atoned.

We breathed together as the sky turned predawn blue. I pressed my forehead into his shoulder, feeling the rise and fall of his breath until one of his feathers came loose in my hands. I inhaled with surprise, but Michel didn't notice.

"We've stayed here too long," he said, suddenly alert.

The feather. What would I do with it?

The air shifted overhead; a specter-like ripple. The arrival of another presence. Body riding the air's currents, moving the air itself. Gargoyle in flight to warn us of the approaching sun. I tucked the feather deep in the folds of my robe.

"We have to go," he said.

"Your wings—I can catch them," I said.

"It's too late, Geneviève. If you try now, you will die."

"What?"

"The sun."

He grabbed my hand and together we descended. My body was familiar with the cathedral's nuances now, and though the pain where Michel grabbed me persisted, I could climb with more ease than before.

"*You will die.*"

I heard the Prime bells and knew Paris was waking—the faithful to attend mass, the courageous bread sellers who still had something to offer the living, the collectors of the dead. Could they see me? Michel's words rang in my ears. *You will die.* The possibility of my own death implying that I was a living thing with a life to lose.

In the Portal of the Virgin, I touched the tender spot Michel had given me with his too-strong grip. There was a cold feather still tucked deep within the folds of my chemise and cote.

Would he punish me for this, too?

My throat *ached*. A seam. A crack. A fracture.

My evil throat. My evil citrus-eating throat. My hungry throat.

Had Michel pinched me to pinch out the evil? To pinch away the evil, seven-headed dragon?

I stared across the parvis and imagined Michel's green eyes and smoke unfurling from his mouth.

CHAPTER XI

Approximately Noël, December 1348

Gusts of laughter broke the stillness that blanketed the parvis. It was Terce. The bells, eager footsteps, and voices calling for companions named Marie, Agnès, Claire, and Hélène troubled the quiet, icy morning. Feminine giggles. A snort or a "Haw!" I absorbed the medley. I couldn't see this merry procession, but they sounded like a group of demoiselles and servants.

They lingered near the Portal of Sainte-Anne and the cloisters until it was halfway to Sext. Fragments of speech swirled the air, but I couldn't parse their conversation. What were they doing outside when the rest of Paris was so afraid of devils, bad stars, evil vapors, and that sick house, the Hôtel-Dieu, that few dared to approach the cathedral, not even for the week of the Nativity? I soaked up their voices. High-pitched giggles bounced off my hands and the cathedral walls; stone consumed only so much sound.

I was grateful for these visitors. I had missed the chaos of people that spiraled through the parvis most days, especially on the Feast of the Nativity. The endless rattle of dice, and the lament or yelp as players won and lost money, the smack of the Soule ball, huffs of patient donkeys with ribbon-braided manes, troubadours singing of corrupted priests, merchants bartering over glass and pomegranates, hand drums and flutes and tinny bells and cymbals. I missed the smell of hot, spiced wine, the smell of breastmilk, the smell of newly-tanned leather, stale piss in the alleys, newly-cut lumber, gooseberry tarts and eel pies, and fresh hay.

The days were so quiet, except for the bells and workers' calls to collect the dead.

Stone consumed sound; stone *ate* sound. What was the difference between my body and the rocks strewn across the parvis? Michel believed that I had eaten one prayer and that gargoyles were eating all the prayers. But didn't every guardian—no, every stone in this cathedral's foundation—eat prayers? Didn't limestone pull and suck?

We not only ate prayers; we ate everything we heard, saw, and smelled. We ate names, we ate history, we ate stories, we ate entire family lineages, we ate music, we ate laughter, we ate tears, and we ate light. We absorbed lives from our makers. Without people, we would be inert. Michel was right. We needed the people.

But how could I believe gargoyles swallowed prayers, when I believed The Wakening, our existence as stone, was so much bigger than that?

What did I mean by *that*?

A pair of women crossed the Portal of the Virgin, arm-in-arm. Finally, I could see the happy visitors. They were beguines. Michel's beloved beguines! Of course, who else was brave enough to linger at the threshold of the Hôtel-Dieu?

Red cheeks and apple-full baskets struck a contrast against undyed wool smocks and white head coverings. I understood. These women were decorating the trees and bushes lining the Seine and parvis in honor of Adam and Eve. I wondered where they had found so many apples. I hadn't seen any fruit sellers or couriers since the Feast of Saint Michel.

Red streaked past me. A basket filled with three bruised apples. I looked at the person who held them: a young woman who stood before the Portal of the Virgin gazing at all the statues. Brown eyes pressing into mine. Lips pulled into a tight, stern line. Black eyebrows furrowed. Her plump cheeks had thinned, and she had covered her hair completely in one of those voluminous hoods the ladies called wimples, but I knew her.

I knew her scent. I knew that pleading look in her dark eyes.

It was Isabelle. How could I mistake her for anyone else?

Isabelle!

She had traded her tight cote and budge-fur mantle for beguine's habits: loose garments as plain as mine. But here she was, alive, alive, alive.

Michel was wrong.

Michel was wrong, he was wrong, he was wrong!

I had eaten Isabelle's offering, but I had not destroyed her!

I watched Isabelle decorate the parvis and wondered what had happened to her in all the months since I'd last seen her. What had happened to the fiancé Celestine mentioned? Did he die? Did his whole family perish?

Or had she run away?

What shape did her days take now? Did she care for the ill and dying at the Hôtel-Dieu, like the heroines of Michel's songs? What did Celestine think? This kind of work was not befitting for a woman from a moneyed family.

The bells rang for Sext and Isabelle and her companions drifted from my sight, towards the Rive Gauche.

The parvis stilled again.

Near dusk, the beguines returned, baskets filled with candles instead of apples. I looked for Isabelle in the throng arranging candle stumps across the cathedral steps, but I could not see her. Had it really been her, or had I only imagined her face in someone else's? After all, how did a merchant's daughter come to renounce her fine, green gowns and fur mantles to live among the beguines?

Had I wanted that much for Michel to be wrong, wrong, wrong?

Dusk brought breath, fluttering eyelids, and finally, parted lips. I'd planned to ask Bathsheba if she had also recognized Isabelle de Grantrue. But Bathsheba did not wish me pleasant wakening. She reached out and touched my throat instead.

"What is it?" I asked.

I reached for my girdle where I had tucked Michel's flight feather against my waist. It was still hidden.

"What happened to you?" Bathsheba breathed.

Her fingers pressed. I slid my hands beneath hers and felt the place where Michel had pinched me. The fracture line across my throat.

"Geneviève, you can't climb and walk like this anymore," Bathsheba said. "You are crumbling!"

I closed my eyes. My thoughts returned to Michel in the Balcony of the Virgin. I remembered his astonished pout, the way his mouth formed an angry ring as if I had been the one to pinch him. Surely, this was an accident, he hadn't meant this crack. Just like I had accidentally taken his feather. These deteriorations were unintentional, weren't they? Just small erosions. Mutual decay. Michel was an archangel.

Michel was my friend.

I was Michel's friend.

We hadn't meant to hurt each other, I told myself as I remembered the way his mouth and eyes bunched into the center of his face like a furious star.

"Tell me how this happened," Bathsheba said.

I looked past her shoulder towards Marie, who had lifted her chin and looked at me with interest.

Oh Marie, I thought. *I know you would love for me to give you something to gossip about.*

But it *had* been an accident, hadn't it? And that was after the kiss. After the kiss and before the feather. The pinch was an accident. I had to believe the pinch was an accident. The feather, too.

But the kiss? The kiss had been intentional. Defiance of our limestone nature, defiance of our saint-carved bodies, our purpose.

"Oh, this is only a chip," I said, flicking my hand. "After the next painting, we'll never know it was there."

I stared at the candles burning on the stairway and remembered Michel's silver face—how radiant he'd looked, cupping fire on the Chandeleur as if the fire was something that belonged to him. I wondered what it felt like to control fire like that. How different would my existence be if I knew how to control something as ancient, as persistent as fire?

Maybe I already did.

Suddenly, I knew how I would capture Michel's wings and help him become the bird that could travel between worlds.

My hands flew to my throat.

But why? Why did I still want to help him after he'd pinched me?

I had spent so many hours with him above the West Façade. We had spent so many hours in prayer together. I couldn't help it; I cared for him.

I slipped down my niche, careful not to disrupt the candlesticks. With each wakening I grew more malleable, softer, more porous. Confident on cathedral steps. Another living thing that roamed the grounds. Bathsheba reached for my arm to stop my descent.

"You have to stop this!" She pulled hard. Harder than I expected. Where had this strength come from? "You will deteriorate until there's nothing left."

I ignored her, my eyes fixed on the tallest, brightest candle I could find. I snatched it up, inhaling as the flame warmed my fingertips. The light made long, strange shadows on my hands. I loved the tiny crescent moons beneath my nailbeds. I could never see features like this in the daylight when I stood with my hands upturned and my eyes set still. Only at night could I appreciate my hands.

I walked down the remainder of the steps as quickly as I could before Marie could call my name.

No luck.

"Geneviève, it's too early to climb down," she said. "Matins hasn't passed."

"I will remain on the cathedral's north side, away from the cloisters."

"But whose prayers are you releasing to the Sky?" Marie asked.

"The beguines," I said hastily. I covered my throat with my free hand, hoping Michel's hidden feather would not slip out from my belt. "The beguines who hung up these apples for Adam and Eve and lit these candles."

"I'm worried someone will see her," Denis said. "Michel is skilled at walking the cathedral unseen, but he's an archangel. Geneviève is just a saint. A woman."

"Denis, I am every bit as skilled as Michel." I placed a hand on my hip.

"But Michel is an archangel!" said Jean, shaking his hands and his voluminous blue sleeves that I coveted.

I decided to ignore them all. I had a promise to keep. A promise to Michel. I turned my back to the Portal of the Virgin. I felt their eyes on me as I worked my fingers over the candle, protecting the flame.

Gargoyles couldn't hold and possess fire, could they? I'd never seen them fly close enough to the cathedral steps to snatch candles on feast days. Fire would surely scare them. I would tell the gargoyles they must give me a pair of wings, or I would burn the roof to ash.

I held the candle against my chest and pressed my free hand to the northern wall for support. The errant student and his femme de

Samedi emboldened me. They had walked past without seeing me, as if I were simply part of the wall. It was true: I was learning from Michel. I was becoming just as skilled at navigating the boundaries of the enchantment. And I knew there was a door near the North Façade, and behind that door, I hoped, a stairwell that led to the upper reaches of the cathedral, high above the Balcony of the Virgin.

My breath frothed to ice. Michel's voice was in my ears again, repeating the strange thing he'd said last wakening, *"If the sun strikes you, you will die,"* as if I had already crossed the boundary between the enchantment and mortal life.

Michel.

I remembered my mouth on his, my mouth a cavern, the softening of his lips. Good Sky. I had deserved that pinch for tempting us both beyond the limits of the enchantment.

One foot before the other, I followed the path I lit before me until I stumbled on the door. It was shut tight. I coiled my fingers on the cold metal handle, but I was too afraid to tug. Too afraid I'd tug off a finger as I yanked the handle. If I came back to the West Façade without a finger, Bathsheba would never let me leave my niche again. The thought made me want to laugh. The thought that I could pull this handle hard enough to crack a finger off my hand. That would be real deterioration, wouldn't it?

How strange to grip this mortal-made thing, this metal handle. I pressed my face against the cold, damp door and inhaled wood. I wondered if it was alive the way I was. Materials the people had dug or cut from the earth to build their worlds.

"Please open," I asked the door.

It did not yield. Perhaps it followed the rules of a different enchantment; perhaps wood and metal spoke different languages. I could spend all night here, breathing in these materials, marveling at each sensation.

A gust sprinkled snowflakes on my candle, and it sputtered in response. I had to find a gargoyle before the flame extinguished. But how?

Where?

I could almost feel their eyes bear down at me from their tower perches. I shone my light high up on the walls but saw only shadows and nighttime. More snowflakes wet my face.

I knew I'd reached the East Façade when my fingers tapped on a glass window that rose into a point. Red, gold, and blue-colored panes glistened in my candlelight. Painted men and women in clerical robes, saints and angels and kings. Biblical stories painted on glass. I brought my mouth close to the window, smiling as my breath made fog. I drew lines with my fingers, nearly forgetting the approaching Matins prayer. I drew the shape of a heart and the shape of a sparrow.

Movement on the other side of the glass startled me, and I nearly dropped my candle. I stepped away from the window and pressed my back against the wall, breathing as the bells rang. The cathedral swelled with the hollow echo of footsteps and prayer chants. Sounds spilled through the windows, and I dug my back into the walls, terrified someone would see my silhouette through the glass panes. It was one thing to hide from two people fucking against the cathedral wall. It was another to escape the eyes of an entire cloister.

I waited and waited for the monks to end their prayer, which seemed to go on without end while my candle burned to a sad stump, extinguishing my plan. Why couldn't those tired monks chant faster? I had no choice but to stand still, look up at the wall beyond me, and wait.

Breathe and wait.

The West Façade was flat, but the East Façade rounded out to form the cathedral's nave. A great tower rose from the center of the façade, supported by a matrix of sweeping arches. I remembered the people called these arches buttresses, and they helped the masons grow the cathedral tall. I thought they looked like bridges connecting various parts of a great city, the way I'd imagined the bridges connected Paris' right and left banks to the Île de la Cité. But they could also be fingers, or the bars of a cage, depending on how one looked at them. An enormous oak tree grew at the threshold of the cathedral grounds. A living thing. A living thing standing all on its own, just within my reach.

While I stood open-mouthed and gawking, Matins prayer ended, and silence reclaimed the cathedral. Yet, I could not tempt my eyes from the labyrinthine wall, understanding now, for the first time, how big the cathedral was; it was bigger than I'd ever imagined, and my niche was simply one small part of it. I was one creation among many. I felt like the walls could see me and sense how out of place I stood.

The star Altair winked from the sky's dark dome, and I knew hours remained before daybreak. If I didn't linger, I could stand beneath the tree. That would feel nice, wouldn't it? That would feel nice to touch living lumber. I stepped away from the wall until my hands held only air and my guttering candle. I took stilted, unsure steps. One foot before the other until I could touch the tree with stiff, outstretched fingers.

Touch was not enough. I wanted to fit fistfuls of bark and leaves into my mouth.

I let my body sink to the base of the tree trunk, and I pulled my legs under me. My cote softened and spread as if it were made of wool. I admired the shape of my legs beneath folds of sculpted skirt. A zephyr rustled the leaves.

My idea felt foolish in the shadows of the East Façade. One pathetic candle to threaten the gargoyles of the entire Notre-Dame. I retrieved the feather from my mantle and ran my fingers across its ridges. I wanted to believe in Michel, but I remembered the way his face twisted up. Ugly. Silver paint wrinkling and peeling off his brow. The crack in my throat. I knew Bathsheba was right; this fracture line would only spread.

The flame grew short and dim and short and dim and finally extinguished. I cradled my face in my hands, sighing, calling out to the indifferent sky, calling out to no one in particular. *By the cathedral's walls,* I thought, *I've gotten myself entangled in vines with Michel.*

The branches rustled in response.

"Who's there?" I said.

I started to tilt my head to look, but then I remembered the fracture. I couldn't let it spread. I told myself this sound was just an owl, or maybe a cat. Certainly, not one of the men from the cloister hiding in the tree instead of praying at Matins. A human body would shake the branches more. I stood and pressed my hands against the trunk to support my great weight and turned on my toes to search the shadowy limbs. I remembered old pagan stories I used to hear in the parvis about malevolent deities that took the shape of wind to pursue nymphs and maidens.

Silence again, long enough to believe I had imagined the sound. Then, the crack of limbs and branches, and I knew, with no uncertainty, that I was not alone. I touched the cratered place at the base of my neck. The Archangel. He had followed me here.

"Michel," I breathed.

Finally, a low, languid voice dripped from the branches. Masculine and unfamiliar. Not Michel.

"Pleasant wakening, statue. But this is my territory."

Someone who knew the language of The Wakening. Another cathedral guardian.

"Who are you?" I asked. "Show yourself."

"I will do no such thing. You have entered my territory without my permission. You may tell me your name, or you may leave."

"How can a guardian made of stone, made to protect the cathedral, claim this living oak for their territory?"

"I simply can."

"My name is Geneviève. I was carved in the likeness of Sainte Geneviève of Paris."

"Pleasant wakening, Geneviève. My name is Corvus, carved as no other likeness than the one in my maker's imagination."

"Corvus." I held the name in my mouth.

Corvus. I sifted the layers of stories I'd heard across all my years on the cathedral wall. The Christian stories and the older stories beneath the Christian stories, stories about trickster spirits that turned to wind. I couldn't recall a Corvus.

"Which niche do you guard?" I asked.

"I perch above the North Façade."

The North Façade! One hundred years of Bathsheba, Marie, Jean, Sylvestre, Uriel, Gabriel, so on and so forth. Meeting Michel from the Portal of the Last Judgement had been the most exciting thing that had ever happened to me. But now? A guardian from another façade! My body felt light and hollow with excitement.

"I'm from the West—"

"Oh, I know where you stand, Sainte Geneviève."

"How do you know?"

No answer.

"What do you look like?" I asked.

"I look like a fantasy."

"But are you porous? Are you made of limestone or marble?"

"I believe I'm oursin boned, like you, mon calcaire. I'm porous enough to climb this tree; I will tell you that."

"But do you know which quarry you came from? Do you remember your maker?"

"You ask many questions. I think I know just as much about my origins as you know about yours."

"Are you male or female?"

The statue laughed so hard leaves rained.

"You use mortal language! Geneviève, you've absorbed the way the people talk. What? Do you talk of sin and atonement, too? Do you believe in their idea of God? Do you believe the alignment of the stars caused the illness? I suppose you can't help it—absorbing this language. I understand you, because I can't help it either. After all, we are human creations. I call myself 'he'. But when we accept their language, you and I should remember we are made of things that are so much older than all of that."

I walked around the tree, following his voice, but he slid to the opposite side before I could reach him. We circled each other many times, to my bemusement and frustration.

"You ask me so many questions, yet you do not let me ask questions myself."

"You can see me from the branches," I replied. "But I cannot see you."

"I will let you see me if you answer my questions. Why are you so far away from the West Façade? And why did you carry fire? Surely not to see in the dark. Or have you spent so much time absorbing the people's lives, you believe your eyes work like theirs now?"

I wanted to laugh. What could I say? That I came here to harvest wings from a gargoyle to please Archangel Michel? That I thought a candle stump would help me? That Michel believed gargoyles were swallowing prayers, and so he sent me to take their wings?

"I came here to pray for the people," I said. "I thought that if I walked the cathedral grounds, the Sky would hear me better."

Corvus laughed his big stone-snorting laugh. "Praying? I've been watching you since you stood huddled at the East Façade's windows, and you breathed not one prayer. No, I don't believe you."

"I was a grimpeuse from the Portal of the Virgin, but it seems the Sky can't hear our prayers. The people pray, the grimpeurs climb, and the illness continues. But you're from the North Façade—you don't know about the grimpeurs, do you?"

"Of course I do. I know more about the West Façade than you know."

"How?"

"I hear things, like you. And I see."

"But how? Do you spend each wakening in this tree? How did you get up there? Are you a grimpeur, too?"

"Absolutely not! Grimpeurs, grimpeuses. That's more ways of absorbing human language and customs. As I said, I believe we stone beings are much older—more practiced than that. I recline in this tree instead of the cathedral because it makes me happy. For my own pleasure."

Pleasure? Didn't Corvus know pleasure was dangerous?

"Who are you really, Corvus? Where is your place in the cathedral? If you let me see you, I'll give you this feather."

An impulsive, stupid idea I knew I would regret. But in that moment, beneath Corvus' tree, I did not care. Michel and the West Façade felt so far away. Suddenly, the thought of giving away Michel's stolen feather felt delicious. Thrilling.

After all, he'd hurt me.

"This belonged to Archangel Michel," I said.

"I have plenty of feathers of my own, I have no use for that," Corvus said.

"Oh," I exhaled, disappointed.

I felt damp breath on my cheek. If I turned my head, I knew I would see him; already, his breath warmed the air.

"What are you?" I asked, even though I knew.

Hot breath on my face. Then a long reptilian maw opening before me. A forked tongue and rows of jagged teeth, just visible in the gloom. He smelled like rainwater. I opened my mouth despite myself, overwhelmed by the desire to drink.

"You're a gargoyle."

"Yes. And you are an effigy of a saint."

"Michel told me gargoyles swallow people's prayers."

Corvus released his luxurious laugh, full-throated and wild. "Archangel Michel?" he said. "The owner of that sad, little feather? Ha! He should see my wings."

Gargoyles looked like nightmares. The makers fashioned them after every mortal fear. Illness and death and disgust and shame and Hell and animal and wilderness and eating a pile of bones and sitting atop a pile of bones personified in one monstrous sculpture. A face so ugly, it could scare mortal and spirit. But I was not afraid.

"Come closer, Geneviève. Why do you look so timid? Are you afraid to look at me now? Why don't you look inside me to see if there are any prayers caught in my throat? I'll show you."

He opened his mouth wider. My curiosity was greater than any fear. I looked and saw all the way down into the open groove where rainwater ran through his back. A body that was all drain, incapable of holding prayers. He smelled so strongly of water, I wanted to bring my lips to his throat and drink.

Before I could say another word, Corvus slipped back up into the branches where he could laugh at me from above. I hadn't even seen his eyes.

"Why are you in this tree and not on the cathedral wall?" I asked.

"I've already told you; I like this tree. And you shouldn't linger here," he said. "You know gargoyles are dangerous."

"You do not scare me."

"Not even with my teeth?"

"Let me see all of you," I said. "And I will tell you if I'm afraid."

I rested my cheek against the tree trunk and felt his eyes resting on places where my paint had peeled to bare stone. When he spoke again, his voice was soft.

"I've come to this tree every wakening for the past one hundred years," he said. "If you return here on the next new moon and bring one lit candle, I will let you see me in my entirety. Perhaps I'll let you stay, too, and spend The Wakening here."

"But why? Why do you want fire?"

"Geneviève, our time together this wakening must end. Look, Andromeda is low in the sky. Return to your home in the West Façade."

"But tell me why you want fire!"

I heard his wings strike the air as he retreated into the dark architecture, just a shadow, too swift for me to see him well, leaving me in the company of the tree, the delicious smell of water withdrawing with him.

I hadn't even tried to take his wings.

CHAPTER XII

After the Feast of Sainte Agnès, January 1349

Good Sky. What did Corvus look like?

I spent the restless days imagining the wings he boasted about—wings so powerful, Michel coveted them. I thought about the hidden flight feather, nestled between my cote and mantle, and wondered if Corvus' wings looked rounded and dove-like. Or if they were mightier, like a hawk's? Were they painted silver or vermillion and green, like the dragons in the spice merchant's stories?

I'd promised Michel I would harvest gargoyle wings. I still cared for him, but now I wanted to see a gargoyle in his entirety and spend another wakening beneath his oak. I hated how I always wanted something and how quickly the thing I wanted at a given moment always seemed to change. Why wasn't I content like Bathsheba? She and I were split from the same stone, carved by the same maker. Why couldn't we have shared desires?

I reminded myself of a girl on the eve of Sainte Agnès' feast day now. A maiden performing rituals—cold baths at nightfall, cinnamon and nut cakes, climbing stairs backwards—heart full of hopes that while she slept, the lovely Sainte Agnès would gift visions of a future husband. If the maiden performed the ritual correctly, of course.

I knew what it meant to want something this badly.

Mourning doves had begun to nestle with the cherubim in the archivolts, escaping the wind sheers. I hoped the painters would return soon; I hoped someone would come and scrape the shit off our cheeks. I didn't want Corvus to see me with stained, peeling paint.

Days before The Wakening, shouts flooded the parvis. Human shouts and animal sounds—bleating lambs or goats. Someone, a woman, insisted on bringing two lambs to the beguinage for the Feast of Sainte Agnès. Lambs adorned in fine ribbons.

Too nice for those girls, answered a man. He had the gruff accent of someone who had come from one of the northern towns beyond the city. Ribbons, presumably so soft and thick, they would have been better suited on the grave of the dead princess.

An inappropriate use of our savings, Marguerite.

A married pair, I realized. Wealthy enough to offer animals but not wealthy enough to do so comfortably.

The beguines are the reason your sister is still alive, Robert.
She came out of that hell-hole hospital by the grace of God, Marguerite.
She would have died if it weren't for those women, Robert.
They deserve our offering.
Your offering, not ours.

I sifted through my memories of voices. They were the fashionable owners of an apothecary nestled between the book and parchment shops beyond Rue Neuve and Rue Char-Rori. In my mind's eye, I saw round-faced Marguerite with red curls peeking from the hood she always wore with its proud, metal buttons. I liked to see people with red hair. There weren't as many of them, which made them more interesting to look at. Marguerite helped me understand what I might look like if I were soft bodied and human.

Robert was young, younger than Marguerite, who was already twice widowed. He had broad shoulders and strong arms, which he loved to show off in his short, fitted tunics. The outline of his ass was always visible beneath woolen stockings. For the maidens, a sick relative meant an opportunity to run giggling to the apothecary. That was, of course, before the illness.

I heard shutters snapping as some of the houses lining the parvis opened their windows. Busybodies sticking out their necks to join the commotion. Busybodies and gossips I had missed and taken for granted. But these faces in the windows were unfriendly.

The beguines are witches, someone said. *How else could they work at the Hôtel-Dieu?*

Give them no lambs—the women would eat them with mint. They'll curse the city—you know it's bad luck to eat a white animal.

Yelling and the sounds of physical struggle.

She's a witch too, that's why she's helping the beguines!

People wrestling for the lambs. Bleating when the animals broke free to run panting towards the bridge. Marguerite screaming at her handsome, idiot husband. Ecstatic hoots and yelps as people leapt from their houses to chase the creatures.

I slid my hands over my throat, thumbing the edges of the fracture. It didn't feel like it had grown between The Wakenings. My head and neck were solidly intact.

"Pleasant wakening," Bathsheba told me.

But what would happen if this crack spread? My breath grew shallow. Could I really lose my head?

"Pleasant wakening," Bathsheba repeated.

What had Michel done to me?

"I said, pleasant wakening!"

Bathsheba leaned over me, as if I were not there, breaking my thoughts. She, Jean, and Sylvestre laughed about the lambs.

"Pleasant wakening, Bathsheba," I said.

She laughed louder, stepping on my foot to stand closer to the other statues.

"Well, I've heard that the apothecary woman sells herbs that can end a pregnancy," Jean whispered, his voice filled with wonder, as if he were the gossipy old candlemaker who lived in the parvis years ago. "Even the nuns visit her."

"Everyone knows nuns are troublemakers," Sylvestre said.

"I'm sorry I didn't hear you, Bathsheba," I said. "My mind was somewhere else. Pleasant wakening."

"I once thought that if I were a person, I would want to be a lady or demoiselle because they get to eat whatever they want," Bathsheba continued. "Now, I think I'd rather be a nun."

"Why?" asked the little imp with a misshapen face.

"Nuns can read and write and study," said Bathsheba. "Their responsibilities are far greater than a lady's. A lady's role is to have children for carrying on the family name. I don't find that nearly as interesting. Besides," Bathsheba sighed, "nuns spend more time singing. One wakening a month is hardly any time at all to sing."

"Sometimes, I look at the ladies' pregnant bellies and wonder what that must feel like." Sylvestre lowered his voice to a whisper. "Sometimes, I wish I could be pregnant."

Bathsheba stuck out her tongue. "Not me. That would never be for me."

"What about the creatures that lay eggs?" I asked, nudging myself into the conversation. "Like the finches that built a nest in Bathsheba's arms?"

Jean made a contemplative huffing sound.

"Maybe those people are right about Marguerite, maybe she is witch," said the imp. "I hope she is a witch. I think I would like a witch if I ever met one."

"She's simply very good at her business," said Bathsheba. "She can charge whatever she wants for her herbs. And look at her clothing—always new. I've even seen her wear a velvet-trimmed surcote ouverte over her dress. What commoner can afford such luxuries?"

"Bathsheba, I'm sorry," I said. I shifted closer to her.

"I've heard velvet is worth six month's labor for most people,"

Sylvestre said. "I'm sure this surcote was a gift. A gift from someone important."

"Like a noblewoman who wanted to end a pregnancy?" Jean suggested. "She must be careful, or she'll get hung up in the Place de Grève."

Bathsheba shook her head no. "People end pregnancies all the time. It's very common—haven't you paid attention to the ladies' gossip? It would be impossible to punish every person who took herbs to bring the menses. Or punish every person who grew such herbs."

"You're not going to speak with me, Bathsheba?" I asked.

Bathsheba looked past me, chattering away with Sylvestre, Jean, and the little imps.

"You never seem to want to talk with me anymore," she said at length, her round face raised towards the archivolts. "You have more important things to do now. You'd rather spend The Wakenings with Michel, even though he asks you to do things that crack you."

She wasn't wrong, but her accusation stung.

"I would have been happy for you to join me," I said. "I wanted to show you the Virgin's Balcony and the North Façade."

"That's not true," said Bathsheba. Her eyes made grinding sounds as they rolled. "You are always in such a hurry to leave each Wakening— you want to be the grimpeuse all by yourself. Besides, you know I don't want to climb the façade."

I matched the heat in her voice.

"Well, that's the problem, isn't it? You never want to leave the West Façade, and I do. You aren't even curious about the rest of the cathedral."

"I think leaving the façade is foolish."

"Michel doesn't! That's why I've spent so much time with him. You and I want different things. We want to do different things with our time."

"I only wish you would make more time for me. You're gone from Matins to Prime and there's no time for us to talk anymore," Bathsheba said. "Furthermore, you've become reckless, and I'm worried about you."

"Reckless? I'm trying to bring prayers to the Sky," I spat. "But you wouldn't understand. You're judgmental and boring."

I immediately regretted my words.

"So be it," Bathsheba said.

"Oh, Bathsheba, I didn't mean it. I take it back! There's more I want to tell you."

"I'm tired of feeling like I don't know who you are anymore," Bathsheba said.

"Maybe you never really knew me." I crossed my arms. "I haven't changed."

Gabriel, Uriel, Denis, Marie, and the others continued chattering in their niches, but Sylvestre, Jean, and the little imps had fallen silent.

"Geneviève, don't you think—" Sylvestre began.

Whatever he had to say, I didn't want to hear it. In my mind's eye, red coils of anger unfurled along the length of my body. Bathsheba's voice echoed in my ears. *Reckless.* She would deny me the pleasure of seeing Paris from Michel's balcony, of seeing the cathedral's façades, of meeting a gargoyle. I couldn't even tell her about Corvus for fear she'd scold me.

She hadn't even tried to understand me.

If this was how she was going to be, well then, fine.

I descended from my niche, appreciating the strength in my limbs and the breath in my throat.

My fingers bumped against the entrance of the North Façade. The door was ajar but barely. I tugged the iron handle, and the door opened with a groan. I slid Michel's flight feather from my girdle and wedged it against the frame to secure the opening.

Inside was a new kind of darkness, damp and starless. I stared up a narrow winding stairwell, my breath fluttering echoes against the walls. My legs begged me to climb, and I gave my body what it wanted. Up, up, up, letting my hands feel the inside of the cathedral, imagining the people who had laid each stone. That same drive to build and create—our makers had given us some of that ambition. Why else would we choose grimpeurs? How else would Marie and Michel know to make themselves our leaders? I soon noticed shadows flickering against the wall.

I smelled the air—resin and other fuel stuffs. Fire, I realized, hardly believing my great luck.

I moved up the stairs, ignoring my terrible, heavy footsteps, and found the whimpering flame burning from a torch mounted to the wall. I could steal this, but I would have to hurry—whoever had left it here might come back for it.

In this dim light, the walls looked warm and red like the inside of a yawning mouth. I wrapped my hands around the torch's base, pulled it from the mount, and with fanning motions, I offered the little flame air.

"Stay alive," I commanded.

How could a torch stay lit in this dank stairwell? A breeze whipped through as if responding to my thoughts, and I followed the draft, sheltering the flame with my hands. I could get Corvus' attention if this stairwell led me to the roof. I would use the torch to signal him.

Sure enough, the door at the top of the stairwell was propped open. Either the cathedral had led me here tonight, or a holy brother had neglected to close the doors. The walls themselves were enchanted, that was true, they always helped me climb. But I sensed human hands had left these doors unlocked.

And someone would see me if I wasn't careful.

There was a part of me that didn't want to be careful. Part of me wanted to let the mortal eyes see me. To see what would happen. If I turned into a simple statue like Etienne and L'Ecclésia, I would never have to worry about Michel, citrus, or a disappointed Bathsheba. It wouldn't matter who I disappointed—not to me, at least—I wouldn't feel anything.

There was pleasure in courting this kind of danger, but if I let myself turn into a simple statue now, I would never get to see Corvus in his entirety.

I found myself on a balcony overlooking the West Façade—high above the Balcony of the Virgin—with a view unlike any I had seen. Dark fog blanketed most of the city, but I could make out the outline of snow-covered rooftops and labyrinthine alleys. Poor Asa and Jehoshaphat, who thought they could see the world from their niches, who believed they were truly kings.

My eyes found the Seine. Dark ovals—some massive, others small—rested on the water, and I realized these must be the boats I'd heard so much about. I'd been created to stand on still, immovable stone—this cathedral—for eternity. Terrible to imagine resting on something as inconstant as water. And then I thought about the dead collectors who—I had heard—emptied their carts onto boats that would carry bodies down the Seine and, eventually, beyond Paris. Terrible that there were boats, right now, on this great river piled with people I used to see every day. I drew my eyes from the river, which no longer looked as beautiful or romantic as when I first saw it from the Balcony of the Kings.

Next, my eyes found the grand Pont au Change, which connected the Île de la Cité to the Rive Droite, the rooftops of those lavish homes the merchants and money changers had built atop the bridge itself. Next, I searched for Les Halles, the sprawling maze of a market I had heard put my humble parvis stalls to shame. Instead, my eyes found the Place de Grève—that landmark of execution. All of Paris knew this was where the heretics were burned, hanged, or drawn and quartered. Templars, beguines, and Jews had all been killed in this place for the safety of the crown and the pleasure of the crowds.

Grotesque thoughts filled my mind. Unwelcome but persistent. I wondered what I would do if I found myself on the gibbet. Perhaps worse than the execution itself was the wait. The night before. The morning. Being led. The hope that someone would grant mercy.

I thought about the apothecary owners and the Jewish people pushed from Paris, and how easy it would be for any mortal to find themself at the center of the execution spectacle. Bathsheba was right— we were so lucky to be what we were.

Bathsheba. Our problem wasn't that we wanted different things— although we certainly did want different things for ourselves. Now, I could see that she and I had different experiences of The Wakening, and that wasn't necessarily bad. The problem was the fact that I had kept secrets from her. I'd lied about the offering and never told her anything real about my Wakenings with Michel. Secrets created rifts, and she was right to distrust me now.

I did want to share my experiences with her, but I didn't want her to tell me I was foolish and disregard them all. I wanted us to understand and accept each other. But that wouldn't be possible if I kept secrets from her and she kept trying to convince me to feel content in the façade.

I had almost forgotten about the torch warming my hands when I sensed that I was not alone. There was no hiding, not with a flame. I turned my back to Paris and searched the balcony, afraid Michel had found me. I saw movement near the spire, dark and slender as a bone. Whoever—or whatever—it was had already seen me. I held the torch outstretched, ready to protect myself. Owlish wings sliced the air, stirring the darkness around me.

"Pleasant wakening."

A porous sculpture stood before me, blocking my path with massive, outstretched wings. No owl at all. It had a human face: round eyes that tapered prettily at the corners, an aquiline nose, and delicate lips. Uncovered hair parted in the center and carved into braids encircling the head like a crown. A long neck and bare shoulders, a feminine body beneath a sculpted sheaf. Unpainted—the pinks, browns, grays, rose, and sandy-colored swirls of limestone glimmered beneath the flickering light as if this guardian were lit up from within. The most beautiful guardian statue I had ever seen, an angel if her torso didn't bulge into the hindquarters of a predatory bird.

She was not alone: she was flanked by two similar statues. I knew what they were: harpies. Half woman, half avian. The troubadours loved to sing about these monsters from the old pagan stories, and while the Church had tried to forbid them, they were far too beloved.

Imps, sirens, and sphinxes guarded the West Façade, too, but none had the breath of rainwater. Gargoyles, all three of them. Their makers had carved long, primary flight feathers attached to their wrists that extended all the way to their elbows. Short secondary feathers had been carved in a row beneath their delicate arms. They opened and closed these wings like tremendous fans.

The air caught in my throat.

Their wings were like hawk's—not angel's. No wonder Michel wanted their tremendous, glorious wings; if he had these wings, he too could fly. They eyed me with calm, curious faces.

I immediately wanted them to like me.

"Pleasant wakening. My name is Geneviève."

The biggest of the three approached me, her tail feathers fanning open, and her talons scrapping the balcony. I stepped back until I bumped against the railing.

"Pleasant wakening," she said. "My name is Hécate." The other two greeted me and offered their names: Eurydice and Perséphone.

"You have entered our territory without permission," said Eurydice.

Hécate lifted her long, slender hand. "That doesn't matter," she said. "Our visitor brought us something useful."

"Yes, you have something we want," Perséphone agreed.

The three drew near, their eyes fixed on the torch, close enough for me to see down their throats.

"I want to play with fire and light," Hécate said, reaching. "Give me that."

"You're welcome to enjoy our view, but you must give us something in return. Like that torch," said Eurydice, her claw outstretched.

I couldn't let them have it, I needed it.

"I'll leave your balcony then. Pleasant wakening."

Perséphone snarled and leaped forward, but I jerked away from her grasp.

"Why do you want this so much?" I asked, backing away.

"We've only seen fire from a distance. Candles in windows, and the torches the monks and guards carry," said Hécate. She draped her arms over the other harpies' shoulders and waists, and for a moment, the three of them reminded me of sisters or intimate friends. I felt a pang of regret that Bathsheba was not standing beside me.

"We've seen fire in the Place de Grève," said Perséphone.

"We've seen whole buildings catch flame," Eurydice added.

"But we've never been this close to flame," concluded Hécate.

"And you're not afraid?"

"Of course not!" said Hécate. "We're no more afraid of fire than you are. And you, why did you grab this torch? Why aren't you afraid?"

And I thought I could scare gargoyles with fire. I wanted to laugh.

"I won't give you this torch," I said. "It's for Corvus."

Hécate, Perséphone, and Eurydice exchanged glances. I felt pleased. The harpy sisters hadn't expected to hear Corvus' name in my mouth, and now they didn't know what to say. I straightened my back and held the torch tighter.

"That's right, I know Corvus," I said.

Then they laughed. Indulgent, ear-splitting laughter.

"Corvus? That old chunk of beat-up, weather-blown stone?" Hécate howled, releasing her grasp on her companions.

"That worn-out rock?" Perséphone asked.

"That earless dragon?" squealed Eurydice.

"Why, in the name of the cathedral's four façades are you speaking with Corvus?" asked Hécate.

They fell into giggles all over again. Eurydice laughed so hard shards of stone shot from her thin nostrils, making Perséphone laugh even harder, to the point of tripping over Hécate. The giant harpy cried out, scolding her sister for jabbing her eye. It was an accident, Perséphone retorted. Suddenly, Eurydice snatched the torch from my hands. They squabbled for the fire. I watched it pass from Eurydice to Perséphone, Hécate, and Eurydice again.

"It's mine!"

"Give me that, stupid!" A hand struck a face, and the flame hit the balcony floor, extinguishing it.

"You two are so disappointing," Hécate snarled. "Sometimes, I think I hate you."

She leaped off the balcony and threw her body into the air. Eurydice and Perséphone followed. It had all happened so fast, and I was left alone, without the fire I so desperately wanted, watching them soar skyward. Perséphone rose to the highest spire of the cathedral. As if she were a peregrine, she pivoted her body and dove headfirst, wings straight behind her back. Long before she reached the ground, she beat the air to break her descent. Then she flew.

And they were gone.

Harpies with hawk wings. I understood Michel now. What would I become if I, too, were bound to the West Façade by beautiful, flightless wings?

What would I become?

Cassiopeia at its zenith above the West Façade; soon, the bells would ring for Prime. I gave Paris another look over my shoulder, wanting to believe I could return to this balcony, and knowing I wouldn't. It had been difficult enough to climb here once. In my mind, I drew a map of the city and the streets and neighborhoods I could see. The dark rooftops, slender houses squeezed against each other, and the funerary pits smoldered beyond the city wall. Before the illness, this had been the hour of crows and bakers. I'd once dreaded dawn because it meant the end of The Wakening. Now, I missed the sounds of people stirring, rising bundled up from mattresses to feed the hearth and stir their breakfast pottage. Now, I missed the smell of bread.

I willed my feet to move, and my thoughts turned to Corvus and the harpies. I'd imagined talons and a great, tooth-crowded maw. A fork tongued and cloven hooves. Wart-covered stone with a body to match his powerful voice. A face that could turn a nightmare to ice. A gorgeous, gorgeous monster. Someone like the harpies, not an earless dragon—admittedly, I didn't know what an earless dragon was, but it sounded insulting.

Maybe Corvus wasn't imposing after all; maybe Corvus was a joke, as imposing as a fragile clay doll, and I'd agreed to help him because I hadn't known any better. I felt embarrassed and unsettled when I thought about the beautiful harpies opening their perfect mouths to laugh and laugh.

I didn't have to bring Corvus fire now. I'd wanted to see a gargoyle, and now I'd seen three. But as I descended the stairwell, hands gripping the damp walls, I knew the harpies didn't matter. I wanted to meet Corvus again.

I wanted to see *him*.

My thoughts were so fixed on the gargoyles that I hardly perceived the light snaking from the bottom of the stairwell and the footsteps echoing against the walls. Clumsy, heavy footsteps.

Human.

Approaching.

I pressed my back against the wall as hard as I could.

"Foutre dieu," a man's voice cursed. "I hate these fucking stairs."

Drunk.

I couldn't hide from him—the top of the stairwell was too far away. My mantle scrapped the wall as I pressed harder.

"Who's up there?" His voice was timid now.

The very walls absorbed his smell. Frankincense cologne over sweat.

Could it be?

I could hardly believe it—but what was Celestine doing in Paris and not Jumiéges? No, it couldn't be Celestine. Surely hundreds of other sweet-smelling boys belonged to the cloisters.

Then he was standing beside me, on the same step.

Panic, joy, and thrill all at once as I noted the particularities of his face. Dark brown eyes flecked with gold. The skin around his eyes just beginning to thin and wrinkle. Subtly crooked canines in a mouth of otherwise clean, straight teeth. Cheeks and lips as rosy as Michel's. He stared as if he felt my presence but could only see through me.

I realized he couldn't see me.

He couldn't see me!

I had disappeared into the wall again. So, The Wakening shielded us within the cathedral as well as outside of it. Did Michel know? Had he ever tried this?

There was a part of me, a loud, hungry part of me, that wanted to reach for Celestine and trace my fingernails against his neck. To kiss the place beneath his collarbone. I resisted.

We stood so close, I could nearly hear his heartbeat. If he turned his head, our lips would touch. What would it feel like to kiss a mortal's open mouth?

Celestine continued his ascent, and, as I stepped forward, my foot landed on the edge of his too-long robe.

I reached for anything to grab, anything to catch myself before I fell and shattered. Celestine's hand was the only thing I could hold. It felt so hot in mine.

Now, he saw me.

"Who are you?" he whispered. I could smell the alcohol on his breath—mead. So that's why the door had been left unlatched; he had gone to drink.

"How did you get here?" he asked.

I thought of L'Ecclésia and Saint Etienne—afraid, afraid, afraid that I would end up cold and silent like them. If I could just stand still and quiet, maybe I could mend whatever veil I'd torn separating my world from his.

"Your hand is freezing," he said.

He shined the torchlight on my eyes, and though I flinched, I didn't blink. I didn't have to. My eyes were not sensitive like his. I saw my face reflected in his shiny skin-eyes, saw my bright hair, and my opened mouth. I had never seen myself. He stepped back, dropping my hand, as if suddenly afraid.

"My name's Celestine," he whispered.

I wanted to grab his robe and tug him towards me. I wanted to press my hands against his chest.

"I am nobody to remember," I growled instead. "I am a ghost, a simple girl taken by King Death. It's best to forget you ever saw me."

I was limestone, and the stairwell was limestone, too. We were one. I was part of the cathedral, not separate, and I did not belong in Celestine's world. His expression changed. With wildness in his eyes, he searched the space around him, raising his arm high above his head to swing his torch.

He couldn't see me anymore.

I exhaled.

Celestine walked past and up the stairs, presumably to the bell tower, his light waning as he climbed. I slumped against the wall, washed in relief. The enchantment had protected me.

Finally, at the bottom of the stairwell, I found the door had shut, and Michel's stolen feather was gone. The bells pealed for Prime, reverberating through the stairwell, and I pushed open the door, desperate to return to the Portal of the Virgin. There was no time to find Michel's feather; I could only run.

Good Sky, I had lost Michel's stolen flight feather.

Halfway to the West Façade, I realized what had happened to it.

If I were Celestine, wouldn't that golden paint winking in the torchlight catch my eye? I imagined how he must have freed the feather from the door jamb to study and feel its weight between his warm fingers. Something beautiful and unexpected.

Where had it come from? He must have wondered. Who had placed it there?

CHAPTER XIII

"'Lady, I become a werewolf: I enter the vast forest and live in the deepest
part of the wood where I feed off the prey I can capture.'"
From The Lais of Marie de France, Bisclavret (c. 1155–1170)

February 1349

I had nothing to give Corvus. Days of ice and rain had extinguished
whatever feast day candles were left to gutter on the steps of Notre-Dame. I would not return to the stairwell or the harpies' balcony to
search for torches. I was lucky I hadn't been trapped inside. I was even
luckier that Celestine couldn't hold my face in his mind—that he'd
forgotten me while I spoke. The enchantment had kept me safe, so I
could wake another night.

Bathsheba faced the other way, showing me the side of her jaw and
her long neck. I watched the rise and fall of her chest and fidgeted my
hands. A hollow feeling overcame me.

"Pleasant wakening," I said.

"Pleasant wakening," echoed Jean, Sylvestre, and the imps.

"Bathsheba?"

She held out her arm so I could see the creature slithering from her
elbow towards her wrist. A snail. I traced the spiral in its shell and the
glistening trail it left along her sleeve. Two horn-like growths sprouted
from its head.

Snails were common. The last one I'd seen had been crawling

between Uriel's feet before he flicked it away, and I doubted he had taken the time to admire its shell. Shell the color of unpainted limestone.

"You're going to leave the Portal of the Virgin again tonight," said Bathsheba, a statement rather than a question.

I opened my mouth and heard the wind sigh through my cavernous chest.

"I met gargoyles last wakening," I whispered.

Bathsheba's eyes widened and another fleck of green paint peeled away. "What did they look like?"

"Like women. Like birds. Their wings—" I cupped my hands over my mouth. I could not let Michel hear about the harpies. "But don't tell anyone."

Bathsheba frowned. "Why not?"

I looked into her eyes, mostly bare and gray now, and she held my gaze.

I could repair this split between our seams. I could tell Bathsheba about Michel, the harpies, and Corvus. This terrible task to harvest wings. The kiss I'd given Michel. And the citrus.

The citrus. The citrus. The citrus.

I could offer the truth and let Bathsheba accept me. The little snail clung to Bathsheba's fingers, and she guided it towards the wall where it would find a new home.

When I finally exhaled, I realized I'd been holding my breath.

Bathsheba's gaze turned stern. I closed my eyes to avoid hers.

She wouldn't understand, would she? Why I had eaten the citrus instead of feeling satisfied to hold it. I didn't even understand.

I shook my head. "I should descend before it grows later."

As it did each wakening, the wall extended brick-by-brick to catch my feet. Behind me, I sensed movement and heard the scrape of stone. I turned around and saw Bathsheba, her mouth open and unmoving, her eyes round.

"Do you want to come with me?" I asked without a second thought. "Come! You can climb down, too, I'll show you!"

But Bathsheba shook her head and pulled away from me. She stepped back up, into the façade, and receded into her niche.

I reached the oak tree and pressed my face against its trunk, breathing its smell, not animal but every bit alive. I opened my mouth against it, my curious tongue touching the bark. A mild and dull taste, not tart like the citrus. I looked up into the branches, knowing Corvus might be hidden there. I would feel embarrassed if he saw me like this, tongue on bark, overwhelmed with craving. But the tree was quiet, and I wondered if I'd arrived before he had.

Altair was low to the earth, and I worried Corvus wouldn't visit the tree tonight after all, that the harpies had kept him on the wall, demanding that he answer how and why he knew me. Or maybe the harpies were right about him; perhaps he was a trickster and could not be trusted to keep his word. An earless dragon.

Half aware of my hands, I began to peel bark from the tree, lost in thought and the apprehension of waiting. A spider darted across my fingers, startling me. I never understood why some people feared spiders. They built their homes in cathedral crevices and were as familiar to me as faces in the archivolts. Spiders were beautiful with their many useful legs, and their lacey webs that draped across the façade like woven coverlets. Still, I had not expected the soft gray body and the ticklish feet. I crushed it with my free hand without thought.

The streak of body and still-moving legs, a greasy smudge.

I had never killed a living thing before, and though snails and spiders and birds and mice shared the cathedral wall with its statues, I had never seen another guardian kill either. This spider had been a living thing with just as much right to its life as the people. It was not my place to end that life. Nothing, not even the enchantment, could bring it back now.

I thought of Bathsheba and how much she loved the spiders. How much Bathsheba cherished the lacey webs that covered our mantles and made us shimmer in the morning light.

Bathsheba.

What was this tightness in my chest? What were these droplets clinging from the domes of my eyes? Statues couldn't cry, not even enchanted ones.

How was this possible?

Now I heard the branches shake as if inhabited by a zephyr spirit. Talons gripped and cracked the bark. Mouth open, incisors a hair's width from my face as he crawled down the tree towards me. Forked tongue. Slender, pointed ears. Gills that fanned out behind those ears. The long, scaled neck that was also a drain. The talons of a predatory bird. He had eyes like a peregrine falcon; eyes outlined in black paint, eyes so big and dark, I could nearly see myself reflected in them. He blinked, exposing a third, avian eyelid.

As he drew near, he extended his wing to their full length. At once, I understood why he laughed when I tried to give him Michel's flight feather. Great webbed wings, bigger and more intricate than any angel's I had ever seen. As beautiful as the harpies and any statues in the Portal of the Virgin. Only the most imaginative of sculptors could have created a guardian like Corvus and painted his scales red.

He had been someone's masterpiece.

"Pleasant wakening, Geneviève."

"Pleasant wakening, Corvus. But I don't have anything for you."

"You've brought me something far more interesting than fire," he said. "You've brought me a crying statue."

He was so close to my mouth that I felt unexpected intimacy in our shared exhalations. Rain dripped from the points of his teeth, and again, I wanted to drink from his parted maw. The sharp angles of his face and the symmetry of his mouth. His maker had even given him eyelashes. I had spent days and nights imagining what this gargoyle looked like in his entirety. Now here he was, so beautiful I could hardly look at him.

He coiled himself around the tree trunk, the same way Lilith twisted her body around the Tree of Knowledge, and his scales made pleasant scratching sounds as he dug his talons into the bark for purchase.

"Why are you crying?"

"I killed a spider," I said. "I didn't know we could kill, and I didn't know we could cry, and now I've done both."

He tightened around the tree and drew back as if realizing I might hurt him, too. He was right to be wary—I had planned to snatch his wings only two short wakenings ago.

"Did you mean to kill it?"

"No."

"A mortal would tell you it's just a spider, unthinking and unfeeling," Corvus said. "But we are statues, so we notice the spiders and their intelligence. How their homes are as beautiful as cathedrals. But you did not mean to kill it. So, tell me, Geneviève, is that the only reason you cry?"

I heard the hesitancy in his voice.

"I've broken the trust of my closest companion in the West Façade," I said.

"Would you like to tell me what happened?"

I saw openness in his eyes. Patience, too.

"That would take all wakening," I said. "I'd rather hear your stories. I tried to bring you a torch last wakening, but three harpies stole it."

He laughed, and his mouth split open, starlight catching on so many teeth.

"I hope the harpies haven't made you cry," he said. "They are terrible."

"Who are they?"

"Very prideful, silly sculptures," said Corvus. "They are my friends, but they are cruel. They are harpies, after all. And you came to the balcony and allowed them to be the harpies they were carved to represent. They want to be harpies. They told me what happened, and they told me about you, and I laughed."

I crossed my arms and stepped back from the tree. I could see my breath when I exhaled. "You laughed? I wanted to see you, so I tried to bring you fire. It was difficult to get, and I was disappointed when your friends took it from me. I don't think it's funny. They didn't have friendly things to say about you either. They called you an earless dragon."

Corvus laughed even louder, booming and wild, sending wind spiraling through his water-drain back. It was a horrifying, curious, and nearly musical thing to hear a gargoyle laugh. "Who said that?" he asked. "Eurydice? That's an amusing thing to say, but I don't know what that means. Do you know what that means?"

"I don't know!"

I had taken Corvus seriously, and now I only felt embarrassed.

"Why did you ask me to bring you a candle if it wasn't that important to you?" I asked.

"I wanted to see you again. I wanted you to have a reason to come back here and see me."

"Why didn't you just ask me to come back?"

"Because I am a gargoyle," he said. "I feared I would scare you so badly you would never want to. Your Archangel Michel thinks I eat prayers; you might be the only one from the West Façade who believes I am all pleasant words and loveliness. And it's true, I have so many teeth." He smiled to show them off.

I didn't mind the teeth, crowded, pointed, and animalish. Unlike the harpies, with their pretty ladies' faces and small ladies' teeth. I looked through Corvus' eyes and tried to see his maker. The inspiration and story beneath the stone. I heard the merchant boys tell big stories about four-legged monsters with muscular tails and toothy snouts. Monsters that would eat a merchant boy while sunning on the riverbank. Mon joli petit crocodile. I was not afraid.

I dug my heals into the dirt and shook my head. "I think you knew I would come back," I said. "You played a game with me."

Corvus folded his wings against his back and lowered his eyes.

Moments passed.

"I didn't think you would come back," he said. Not a trace of laughter in his voice. "But I understand, Geneviève, and I apologize."

He raised his furrowed brow, and his face seemed to open, to soften.

"The harpies, they want to be harpies," he continued. "I want to be a gargoyle. I want to terrify. But this quest I sent you on for fire—I admit, I didn't think it out well."

I uncrossed my arms.

"Does being a gargoyle mean you only want to be terrifying?" I asked.

"No. It means protecting the cathedral roof from floods," he replied, lifting his head. "I am grateful to my maker for creating me just as I am. I like what my body, this drain, can do," he said. "And you, Geneviève, are you satisfied with the body your maker gave you?"

What could this body do?

I didn't have a purpose like Corvus and the harpies. I couldn't protect the cathedral roof from floodwater. I couldn't fly. Between The Wakenings, I could only stand still and be comforting.

It wasn't enough. This existence might have been enough for Jean, Sylvestre, and Bathsheba, but it wasn't for me.

Oh, Bathsheba. Bathsheba who found wonder in the sweet lichen that bloomed across our hands and the little imps' snouts. Bathsheba who could absorb so many words and sounds and songs. Bathsheba who become a sanctuary for the birds and snails.

Bathsheba could see all that was, and that was her very special talent. I see what *could be*; I could imagine possibilities and future shapes. It was me who wondered whether Bathsheba and I were sister stone. But it was Bathsheba who first noticed identical lines of sediment beneath our paint.

Bathsheba was happy to belong on the West Façade and I was not. That's why I ate the citrus. That's why I had become the grimpeuse. That's why I kissed Michel and agreed to steal a gargoyle's wings and become a saint with archangel's wings.

I understood Michel's rage. The torch-fire-hot, blacksmith-forged rage felt more like desire. We were saints, we were angels. And still, we could not fly. Didn't we deserve flight just as much as harpies and dragons?

"No," I said, touching my throat. "I'm ravenous. I think I would eat the whole world if I could."

"Is that what happened to your neck?" asked Corvus. "Did you crack your neck trying to eat the whole world?" He pulled his face close, body coiled serpentine around the tree. "Stand still. Let me see."

My maker had given me a chemise, cote, and mantle. I was layers of clothing and paint. But now, Corvus, crocodilian Corvus, spitting gargoyle Corvus, looked at me, and I felt the paint and stone peel, peel away to bone buried beneath limestone.

"There's a fracture in your neck," he said, his voice more serious than I'd ever heard it. "If it grows, you may lose your head."

I wanted to tell him the truth about Michel. Beautiful, beloved archangel Michel. Silver-faced, golden-haired Michel. Michel had cracked me because I'd kissed him. And I'd kissed him because I'd eaten a citrus fruit.

But most shameful of all was what Michel had asked me to do: to steal gargoyle wings. And I'd agreed to do it.

I said nothing.

"I can help you if you would like," he said.

He bit his shoulder, retrieving a red scale. "Take this," he said as he placed it in my outstretched hand.

I knew it was made of stone, just like the rest of him, but it looked and felt like flesh. It reminded me of a fish's scale, curved and shimmering in the parvis market. And I knew what to do with this trick of the enchantment. I pressed it to my neck, covering the fracture, and felt it grow until it became part of me. A raised blemish, a flaw in the limestone, a simple imperfection, that was all.

Wasn't it time to start telling the truth?

But how to tell someone you'd been sent to hurt them?

How to tell someone you had come to take their wings?

How could I look into Corvus' peregrine eyes, especially after he had apologized for his pretext with fire, and tell him that Michel was dangerous? And because I'd been so eager to please Michel, I'd been, too?

I would tell him because I had to.

I was done keeping secrets.

"Corvus, I don't need you to trust me, but I do need you to believe me," I began. "Before I met you, I was willing to destroy you. But I realized how wrong I'd been. How Archangel Michel is so wrong."

I heard my eyelids rasp against the domes of my eyes as I closed them. I inhaled a fistful of air.

"What do you mean you were willing to destroy me?" Corvus asked. Though he tried to keep his voice even, I heard it lilt with alarm.

What could I say?

How could I describe what Archangel Michel meant to the guardians of the West Façade?

"Michel told us he was the Alpha and Omega," I finally began. With closed eyes, I described how Michel looked when he appeared before the Portal of the Virgin on the Chandeleur. All silver face and golden hair and eyes as green as precious stones. He knew the illness was coming, and he knew how serious it would become. But Michel offered a remedy: we needed more grimpeurs to help the prayers reach the Sky. Michel always had an answer, and the answers, I supposed, reassured us that all could be well—that all *would* be well.

"Michel was beautiful," I said. "We were all taken with him."

As I spoke, I thought about Marie and Bathsheba and remembered their skepticism. I gazed at the ground, wishing I'd listened.

"But perhaps I was taken with Michel most of all," I continued.

Corvus didn't look away when I told him about the citrus. The way Isabelle placed it in my hands. The weight of it. How I had never held anything as soft and fragrant. How I succumbed to my craving and ate.

And I told Corvus how Michel offered atonement in exchange for gargoyle's wings.

"And you thought you would threaten us with fire," Corvus huffed.

I described how alive I'd felt with my mouth on Michel's, losing all sense of the enchantment and mortality and forgetting all about citrus fruits, grimpeurs, and duties. And the moment Michel slid his fingertips across my throat, gently at first, before he pressed down hard and left a crack.

"Michel simply cannot accept that you can fly and he cannot," I said. "Because he's carved in the likeness of an archangel, he believes he is most worthy of flight. And if you can fly, and he cannot, then your powers must have come from stolen prayers. Not the enchantment."

"How did Michel's mind twist up?" Corvus asked. "Did he absorb deception and jealousy from the people?"

"I'm convinced Michel believes this is the only way to stop the illness," I said. "He believes he's an archangel. And I understand why: the people have called him archangel since he was placed on the façade. People believe he's an archangel. That's what he's absorbed."

"But you don't think you're Sainte Geneviève."

"No," I said. "I don't. People have always paid less attention to the Portal of the Virgin. Isabelle was the first person who gave me a prayer."

"You and I are lucky to be less beloved," Corvus said. "We choose who we are."

I brought my hand to my mouth, considering his words.

"But you don't really believe you've caused this illness, do you?" Corvus continued. "One statue in a city—in a world—filled with human makers? Anything could have caused it."

"When I spat the citrus, it was rotten."

"All things decay," Corvus replied, coiling around the tree. "You didn't make it rot. That is how our world works. You know that."

"I know," I admitted. "These were bad ideas I absorbed from Michel and every other statue of the West Façade. Every statue except for Marie, I suppose. We all want order and certainty, don't we?"

"In some ways, we are like our human makers," Corvus said.

"Michel must admit how wrong he was," I continued. When I clenched my fists, my nails made scraping sounds against the insides of my palms. "I think I can convince him—"

Corvus titled his face towards the sky as the bells rang for Prime.

"It's nearly sunrise," I said.

"Foutre dieu, it was my turn to fly at first light," he said.

Foutre dieu. Coming from his mouth, the swear was comical.

"You curse like the merchant!"

"The harpies taught me," Corvus said.

Tonight would be the only wakening, in all The Wakenings, without a gargoyle to warn of dawn.

"How did I let this happen?" Corvus asked, his voice soft and wandering. "How did I forget about something as obvious as the rising sun? I've never done this before!"

He turned towards me.

"Geneviève, you must run."

"I will come back next wakening!" I said. "And if the sunlight doesn't strike me, I'll return every wakening after that."

"By all means, don't let sunlight strike you."

Corvus leapt from the oak tree with extended wings. He beat them against the air once or twice as he climbed skyward, angling his body towards the cathedral, serpentine tail unfurling behind him. I took a breath, and he was gone, swallowed up by shadows.

Jean and Sylvestre awaited me with arms outstretched, anxious to help me climb into my niche. Across the parvis, I heard footsteps as the clergy approached for Prime prayer. Bathsheba's mouth was locked open, her eyebrows arched in fury and horror. I felt my own anger rise to answer hers. She was going to scold me again and I gritted my teeth. Defensiveness coursed through me.

Yet, hers were the only hands I reached for. She took them, and with strength I'd never seen her wield, she pulled me into the façade.

I fell into my niche, rejoining the wall, and held Bathsheba's hands tight. "I outran the sun," I said. Relieved. Breathless. Incredulous that I'd made it back. Bathsheba's jaw softened and she closed her eyes. We held each other's hands for moments that passed like years.

"Geneviève, I'm sorry for how I've been treating you," she finally said. "When you became the grimpeuse, I should have been happy for you. It is a beautiful way to contribute to the cathedral."

"Do you mean that?" I asked. My face softened in kind.

She nodded and met my gaze.

"I am the one who needs to apologize." I heard my voice break. "All these months, I've felt bitter because you didn't accept my nature—how my maker carved me with a sense of restlessness that even bewildered me. But I've realized I'm the one who hasn't accepted you for who *you* are. You are happy. You are happy on the cathedral wall, which is a beautiful way to be. You do not need to be more like me."

"And you do not need to be more like me," Bathsheba said. Her lips were trembling. "I admit I've also wanted you to change."

Holding her hand and speaking with her again felt good and right.

"Don't be so quick to apologize to me," I admitted. "I have more to tell you, and I don't want to keep any more secrets."

Bathsheba's eyes flared open.

"Why must you wait until The Wakening has ended to tell me," she said. "You make me wait another month to hear what you want to say!"

I couldn't apologize for The Wakening being over. As the sky paled, we let each other go, and the enchantment pulled my hands back towards the parvis to stand as I had been carved.

CHAPTER XIV

Feast Day of Saint Benoît, March 1349

I had barely taken my first breath of The Wakening when Michel summoned me to the Virgin's Balcony. The message reached me through the imps and cherubim perched overhead; they told me they'd heard the summons from the Foolish Virgins in the Portal of the Last Judgement. The imps tugged my mantle and cried, "Go to him now, don't wait until Matins has passed!" Even the Ark of the Covenant and Heavenly Jerusalem reached down from the Tympanum and grabbed my closest arm, pulling me upward.

"What are you doing?" Bathsheba yelped as she tugged my other arm.

Michel had found out about my new friendship with the gargoyles—that was the only explanation—and he was furious I'd failed to harvest their wings. If I didn't go to him tonight, would he take the wings from the gargoyles himself? I couldn't let that happen. I couldn't let Michel hurt them.

"I have to go to him," I told Bathsheba.

"You promised me you would stay here this wakening. You have something important to tell me! Why do you choose him above me? Why do you make me wait?"

"I'm afraid he will make a dangerous decision if I don't go."

"What is going on?"

"I'll return well before Lauds," I promised. "And then I'll tell you everything I've seen from the Virgin's Balcony and from the North and South Façades."

"No!" She said, shaking her fists. "Tell me first!"

But the Tympanum statues were more powerful than Bathsheba, and they pulled me higher into the Portal of the Virgin.

My climb was familiar now. I knew where to put my hands and feet and where to press the cathedral, encouraging the wall to help my climb. Lulled by routine, my thoughts drifted from Bathsheba to the de Grantrue family.

I was beginning to see more of Celestine in the daylight. He visited the parvis often now, always dressed in his black scholar's robe, his head even less tonsured than before. I had even begun to recognize his scent when he approached. Cologne and the anise he chewed to freshen his breath. Vain, haughty Celestine. I realized he had made a habit of visiting Isabelle at the Hôtel-Dieu, that she was his reason for returning from Jumièges. Vain, haughty Celestine, but a protective brother.

He had also begun to pay far more attention to the statues of the West Façade.

One morning, he stood in the Portal of the Virgin between Denis and Gabriel, as if trying to decide whether he wanted to enter the cathedral. He ran his tongue over his red lips. In this light, his eyes were the color of wheat. He stared up at The Child, closed his eyes and reached out, as if to take the broken statue's hand. I thought I heard him mutter under his breath, "I'm losing my mind."

On another day, he stood in front of the cathedral, just beyond my line of sight, but I knew him by his smell and the sound of his voice. He spoke with a young woman who I heard say, as clear as the cathedral bells, "If I'm not mistaken, I think you're falling in love with the statues. It's not as if you have any shortage of admirers; no need to seduce stone, too."

Celestine sighed and said, "What is it now? What does Isabelle want?"

"She told me to tell you she's leaving with a small entourage to petition the Montfort-l'Amaury estates for money. Thinks she can pull on the ladies' heartstrings when she tells them the beguines are hungry. She wants to see you before she leaves."

"That's a half day's journey from Paris. Please tell me this 'entourage' will be heavily armed."

"You'll have to ask her about that."

"Bon sang, she's a fool. The city walls are surrounded by flagellants. Can't you talk some sense into her, Agnès?"

Their conversation receded as Celestine continued his walk beyond the cathedral, the woman trailing behind him.

I was impressed with Isabelle. Though I still didn't know why she had left her fiancé and entered the beguinage, I could gather that her decision had deeply displeased her brother.

That meant she was making decisions on her own terms. She had courage.

It had been days since I'd seen Celestine now. No sign of Isabelle either. I tried to reassure myself. They were smart; they had both made it this far, after all. They had safety in the beguinage and the monastery, and they knew how to look out for each other. They would know how to stay safe from the flagellants.

The flagellants. I gripped the wall tighter as I climbed. The stories I heard about them were becoming more intense as the weeks passed. Cross their path on a day they felt extraordinarily convinced of their righteousness and be prepared to fight or be killed. That was according to a parchment seller, who had cautiously opened his shop again in the street behind the parvis. The flagellants were so convinced of their goodness, their moral superiority, that they would slit a beguine's throat.

I pulled myself onto the Balcony of the Virgin, where Michel stared at the sky, with his hands outstretched and wings expanded. A funny pose. It embarrassed me to catch him in such an unguarded moment. He was counting to himself. I stood still, my hands folded over each other in a gesture of serenity, unsure whether to interrupt him. Finally, he looked up.

"Pleasant wakening," I said.

If he heard the hesitancy in my voice, he didn't seem bothered. In fact, a smile stretched across his mouth, and he reached out, delighted to see me. I inhaled and met his eyes.

"I think this is it; I've found my flight path! Where to jump, how to keep myself aloft!" He snatched up my palms and squeezed them tight. My fingers engulfed his.

"What do you mean, Michel?"

"I'm studying the gulls and have figured out how they fly!" He swung out his hand, pointing at the sky. "Someday, the people will learn to fly, too. It is not so hard. One just needs the right materials."

He released my hands, and I stepped backwards.

"I am talking about flight, Geneviève!"

He closed the distance between us, all smiles, hands outstretched to cup my cheeks.

"Geneviève, you've done it! I knew you could!" He saw my empty hands. Dropped his smile. "But where are my wings?"

"I don't have wings for you, Michel." My voice came out soft and tentative.

"You don't?" he stammered. "But the gargoyle didn't fly over the last wakening. I was certain you'd taken its wings."

"No."

"How can this be? What have you been doing all these wakenings?"

"The gargoyles aren't stealing prayers. They can't. Their backs are drains."

"Everyone knows their backs are drains, you stupid thing!" Michel shook his hands in my face. "That doesn't mean they don't eat prayers."

"But they can't. There's nowhere for the prayers to go. They'd escape through their backs."

"Then what makes them fly?" Michel gnashed his teeth so hard I thought they would chip. "I need wings, Geneviève! I'm not just any angel. I'm Michel. I was made to protect this cathedral from demons. It's unfair that they can fly, and I can't!"

He stamped his feet and keened—a terrible shrieking sound.

"Gargoyles are not swallowing prayers. We can't steal from them, Michel."

He lunged forward, his eyes, mouth and nose squeezed tight, silver paint creasing into that now-familiar shape of an angry star.

"What's this thing?" he asked, sliding a finger across my neck, eyes locked on Corvus' scale. My hands flew to my throat to cover it.

His nostrils flared. He pried my hands away, gripping my wrists so tight I thought they would break.

"That's not yours; someone gave you that."

I stepped on his foot, hoping to break every toe.

He screamed, releasing me, then reached out and snatched at Corvus' scale. Though he pinched and scratched until I cried out in pain, the scale remained sealed in place.

"Fine then," he said. He leaned close and breathed into my ear, "I hope you crack all the way. I hope your ugly head breaks from your neck and falls off."

He struggled to stand on the balcony railing but managed to pull himself over.

"I don't need you. I'll get the wings myself, Geneviève. But I'll tell everyone how you stole my feather and how you hurt me," he said. "Oh, you didn't think I would notice my missing feather? Well I did. Now everyone will know how violent and flawed you are."

I stood alone on the balcony until Lauds ended, then returned to the Portal of the Virgin. I knew what I had to do.

Bathsheba looked at me with expectant eyes as I climbed into my niche. "You came back!" she said, sounding happy and relieved. I hated to disappoint her.

"I did, and I need to tell you and everyone else the truth about what I've been doing since I became grimpeuse."

Bathsheba's smile faded, and a frown creased between her brows.

My voice shook as I called out to Marie and asked for silence in the Portal of the Virgin. "I have something I need to tell everyone—about me and Archangel Michel."

Marie studied me with raised eyebrows for a long while as I fidgeted my hands. I exhaled, trembling beneath her gaze. This was it. No matter what happened next, I knew my existence would change irrevocably after this night.

"Companions, our grimpeuse requests silence," Marie bellowed. "She has something to share."

I told them about the citrus. The taste of it, the satisfying feel of its weight in my hand. The ridges in its outer flesh. That I had bitten into it. That I had spit it up. And that was why I had fought so hard to be elected grimpeuse: I'd wanted to make it up to Isabelle for eating her prayer. I'd hoped to carry her prayer to the Sky myself.

Michel took advantage of my guilt. He told me Isabelle was probably dead, and it was my fault, but I could atone, I could live up to the name of Sainte Geneviève herself, light of Paris, if I stole— *harvested*—wings from a gargoyle for him.

My companions, who had all listened with talons and hands tucked beneath sullen chins, began to ask questions.

"Michel wants to fly," I said. My voice still trembled, though I heard it strengthen.

"Why does he want to fly?" asked Uriel. He and Gabriel looked down at their wings and stretched their feathers as if noticing, perhaps for the first time in over one hundred years, that their wings were simple adornments.

"To carry the prayers to the Sky—" I began.

"Why?" asked the little imps.

"He believes gargoyles are swallowing prayers."

"What?" Marie's nostrils flared. "But how?"

"He says pagan souls become gargoyles."

"But what evidence does he have that gargoyles swallow prayers?" Marie swung out her hands while The Child hung on to her side.

"None, other than the fact that the enchantment, bewilderingly, gave them the power of flight, while it gave the angels—*the angels!* In all their staggering beauty!—no such gift at all!"

Denis, with a sour look on his face, wanted to know if I trusted Michel's motives: did Michel simply want to fly, or did Michel genuinely believe he could protect the people with flighted wings?

"I've spent many months with Michel, listening to all the prayers he shares with the Sky, and I know that he is truly terrified," I said. "Michel is terrified of the illness; he fears the flagellants. He also fears that Christians are wrongly accusing lepers and Jews of poisoning wells. He's afraid the cathedral will get destroyed; he's afraid people will get angry and set it on fire. All these fears are justified, and I know we share them, too.

"However," I continued, "he wants to fly. He's that angry the gargoyles can fly and he cannot. He feels entitled to flight because he's the Archangel Michel, and the people love Archangel Michel."

"Michel was the one who grabbed your neck and cracked it!" Bathsheba said, eyes wide with understanding.

"Forget about all of that—I'm fascinated you *ate*," Gabriel said.

"You ate and didn't break the enchantment!" Uriel said, bringing his fingertips to his mouth.

"Eating is vile!" said the Ark of the Covenant.

"Eating is beneath us," said Heavenly Jerusalem. "Base! For fleshy mortal bodies."

"We are dignified cathedral guardians! Not animals," Sylvestre spat.

The whispers began as they always did, hissed between neighbors, from the Portal of the Last Judgement to the Portal of the Virgin. The nimble angels, martyrs, and patriarchs crawling over one another to spread Michel's words. Sylvestre repeated them out loud for everyone in the Portal of the Virgin to hear.

"Michel is missing a flight feather," he said. "Michel lost a flight feather because another guardian stole it. He lost a feather, and he says Sainte Geneviève stole it."

Everyone pointed their chins towards me. Bathsheba nudged my ribs. "Tell them how he cracked your neck," she hissed.

Sylvestre's eyes met mine. It was, perhaps, the first time we had ever looked at each other directly, and I realized that he spent most wakenings facing outward, as if the parvis offered much more exciting things to watch than his companions. I saw that the paint had peeled entirely from one side of his face, revealing bare stone. His nose had chipped, and deep rivets ran between his eyes when he frowned. He turned my hands over, touching the corners of my sleeves as if he could find the feather tucked inside.

"Where is it?" Jean said, nudging me. He grabbed my shoulders and ran his hands over the hood of my cloak.

Sylvestre spoke again. More condemnation from the Portal of the Last Judgement. Sainte Geneviève, filthy Geneviève, had tried to kiss the Archangel Michel. How revolting. How disgusting!

The cherubim in the archivolts began to screech. The prophets in the trumeau shouted over each other and accused me of lying about Michel to protect myself. I felt Bathsheba pull me from Jean and Sylvestre, drawing me beneath her arms, shielding me from the congress of screaming statues.

"Throw her from her door jamb!"

"Throw her from the roof!"

"Break her head off her neck and make her hold it like Denis!"

"Make her walk straight into daylight!"

Marie's voice boomed above the din, a rolling wave of sound that crushed all conversation in the Portal of the Virgin. I was shaking so hard beneath Bathsheba's arms, my teeth chattered. I listened, without really hearing as Marie told us to say nothing more about destroying Sainte Geneviève or any of the other guardians—that included Michel and the gargoyles. Someone was not being entirely truthful, but Marie didn't know if that someone was me or Michel.

"Now tell me," Marie said. "What happened to Michel's feather? Did you take it? Answer me and answer me well."

"Yes! I took his feather, and I tried to crack his foot! But he would have hurt me, otherwise, and he wants to destroy the gargoyles."

The walls exploded into shrieks. Denis joined Marie's pleads for silence that went ignored. The cherubim—those sweet little faces, innocence embodied—sprung out of the archivolts with all the violence and exuberance of a sentient being that had been forced to hang in the same place for over one hundred years. They crawled over and under each other, little hands and feet crushing other statues as they moved down the façade.

"I think we should listen to Geneviève," Denis said, so quiet, so tentative, barely anyone heard him. The cherubs snickered at his meekness.

"I said, I believe Sainte Geneviève!" he repeated, this time with force. "It is grotesque to harvest the wings from another guardian statue! No one in the West Façade is entitled to extract from the cathedral!"

"Yes!" Bathsheba shouted, pulling me close. "We must stop Michel!"

"But Michel is an archangel!" Constantin cried.

"We must listen to Michel's perspective!" Sylvestre shouted. "Let there be a trial!"

"Yes, a trial!" echoed the statues in the Tympanum.

"No one in the West Façade is entitled to steal from another cathedral guardian!" Denis screamed. "Not even an archangel!"

"Precisely!" Sylvestre said, shaking his finger in the air. "That is why we must try Geneviève for stealing Michel's flight feather. Not even a saint is entitled to steal feathers from angels!"

The laughing cherubim swarmed the door jamb where Saint Denis stood between Uriel and Gabriel. They pinned the archangels' arms and wings to the wall and pried Denis' head from his fingers. They laughed and tossed the head back and forth between them while the rest of the guardians watched with their hands over their mouths.

"It's time to play!" the cherubim sang, either oblivious or apathetic to the conversation at stake.

"What am I going to do?" I whispered to Bathsheba. "I stole his feather."

The cherubim fumbled Denis' head—it struck the ground, shattering to fragments.

Bathsheba dropped my hand. "You must leave the West Façade," she said. "They will destroy you next!"

"I don't want to!"

She nudged me out of our niche. "But you must. Go now."

Corvus was not in his tree. I walked circles around its trunk, called into the branches, but only the wind responded. I ran my hand across my neck and thought about Michel, how he knew the shape of Corvus' scales now.

I couldn't decide whether to look for Corvus or wait beneath his tree. So, I watched Cetus arch across the sky, knowing the Lauds bells would ring soon, knowing I couldn't return to the West Façade. I lowered myself to the muddy earth, the folds of my clothing softening and making room for me to recline against the tree. I brought my arms around my legs and rested my chin against my knees.

I mourned all the time I had lost with Bathsheba while I was enthralled in the Virgin's Balcony and all the time I had left to spend with her, talking about the world we saw in the parvis. I mourned her voice, how she used to sing *Dit des quatre oiseaux*. How long had it been since I'd heard that song? I missed talking with her about the people. When promised eternity, the one hundred years we had spent together, as sister stone, was not enough.

"Geneviève?"

I opened my eyes to Corvus crouching beside me. I had only seen his body wound around the oak tree, protectively, reptilian—serpentine. Seated, he resembled a wolf. A wolf with scales and wings.

"I knew something was wrong when you didn't return, so I tried to find you," Corvus said. "I hid in the Gallery of the Kings and overheard everything your companions said about you. I watched you climb down the wall and wanted to fly after you, but I stayed behind because I had to know what they were planning. You're in horrible trouble."

"So are you," I said, pressing my fingertips against my closed eyes.

"All the portals in the West Façade have decided there will be no more grimpeurs until they determine who has been telling the truth—you or Michel. They've decided to hold a trial. Whoever is lying will be thrown from the Balcony of the Virgin."

"Good Sky," I said reclining my head against the tree trunk. "Whose idea was that? Denis'?"

"No. Denis spoke up for you, and now his head is shattered. Remember?"

"Oh, Denis." I cupped my face in my hands. "Poor Denis."

Corvus flickered his wings.

"Bathsheba spoke up for me, too," I said. "What happened to her?"

"I don't know. After you left, they grew so loud, they spoke over each other, and I could barely hear any individual—except for Marie. Marie unequivocally supports you. She believes Michel is manipulating the entire West Façade."

"Should I go back? It's almost dawn."

"You are the only one who can make that decision. You are telling the truth. Michel is the liar."

I wanted to watch Archangel Michel fall from the Virgin's Balcony. I wanted to push him myself.

"I don't think they will believe me."

"The West Façade is just as much yours as it is Michel's," Corvus said, drawing closer. "You are Sainte Geneviève, bearer of fire, friend of gargoyles. If you decide to go back to your niche, we will not let them harm you. Marie won't let harm come to you, either." He opened his wings as if to shield us both. When I looked up, our eyes met, and I saw that he was just as vulnerable as me.

"Some of them will side with Michel no matter who supports me," I said, shaking my head. "They love Michel so much that he can do no wrong."

The archer had nearly risen over the horizon. Corvus' mouth parted, revealing the edge of his forked tongue. He smelled like water, like the mineral smell of earth after rain, like the mud we kneeled in, a smell like flowering and rot. Like a warm-skinned sweating being, like Celestine.

"There might be another way," he said. "You can transform."

"What do you mean transform?"

"With water." His voice softened and he held my gaze. "The way the rains revive the earth after winter, and the rains bring the cathedral grounds to life."

I shook my head and frowned. "What do you mean?"

"I've spilled enough water to know it is a force I respect more than any other. I've seen water turn what seemed dead back to life. I've seen it create new life. Haven't you?"

"I have," I admitted, dizzy with understanding. "But is water more powerful than The Wakening? Can it transform me?"

"I believe so," Corvus said. "But it's almost dawn, and you've nearly run out of time."

If I were to change, then I, like Michel, wanted flight. I wanted to become the bird that flew between the worlds—a being that could help Isabelle and those like her. A being that could fly to Corvus each wakening.

Whispers of morning light reached the cathedral, and I saw that Corvus' scales were painted in alternating shades of pale and dark reds. And what was that—the suggestion of a belly button in the center of his scaled belly? Ridges above his eyes that gave his face a hawkish look. How terrible that the darkness had kept these lovely details hidden from me. When I looked at him, I felt alive. Nothing else mattered. I was awake. I was alive.

"I choose to change," I said. "And if you can wield water to change me into anything I choose, then change me into a gargoyle. A harpy, like Hécate."

I wanted him the way I had wanted Michel. I wanted him the way I had wanted Celestine the night I saw him in the tower. I felt body heat— was it mine or his? And I joined the ranks of the hungry living things.

He lunged towards me, eyes wide, lips curled back over fangs— and pushed me to the ground. His talons pinned my hands above my head and his weight pressed down on me. Heat tendrilled up the length of my body, and I imagined red vines unfurling and flushing my cheeks, neck, belly, and between my legs. I bucked my hips against his, expecting the friction of stone, but found that my garments had slipped aside, and I had bare legs beneath my chemise. His skin had also softened, and I dug my nails into him, pulling him closer. My legs opened. An invitation.

Was this perverse?

Was it perverse to want?

What was the difference between stone and flesh when stone came to life? When stone was made from ancient flesh?

As long as the enchantment forced me to life each month, I would want and crave. I was a living thing with body heat. Even limestone could want.

Water tumbled from his throat, filling my mouth. I should have drowned but I didn't.

"Drink," he insisted.

I drank.

Better than biting the citrus. My lips tore against his incisors.

All the water that had ever run down his throat—the memories of water—passed my lips. I could see Michel's angry star face and Marie's inquisitive face and Bathsheba's soft concern, but they slipped away as I found the dark innards of Corvus' mouth. Corvus on my ribcage and I could support all of him. I could taste all the water in the world fill my throat, threatening to drown me.

I closed my eyes, submersed in water. I tasted salt on my tongue and lips, and it stung my eyes. Waves sluiced cliff and sand. I was in the ocean's depths, and I watched creatures live and wither, calcify on the seafloor, and turn to stone. I felt the lives that lived within me: terror birds, foraminifera, and mollusks. The ache was more ancient than pain; it was the ache of separation. All that I had ever been, annihilated. Rebuilt as someone else's saint.

Who the hell was Sainte Geneviève? Who was she before she became the myth? What did she want? There were many things I knew, but Sainte Geneviève would never be one of them.

Corvus drew back. I watched his expression change: his eyes widen, and his mouth fall open in horror.

"How can this be?" he whispered. "What have I done?"

I tried to reach for him but lacked strength. I closed my eyes.

"Oh, Sky! I don't know what I'm doing at all," Corvus said. "I don't know anything!"

"What's wrong?" I tried to ask, but my voice was too thin.

I could see my makers with their lips pressed together in concentration, determining the shape of my eyes.

Rust-colored powder flaked from my teeth and clung to my fingertips. Dried paint. I ignored it and reached for Corvus, touching nothing but air. I pulled my skirts down over my ankles, half-noticing the coarse fabric between my fingertips. I pressed my hands into the earth and slowly rose onto my forearms.

"Corvus." I heard my voice, rough and thin, barely able to leave my throat, unrecognizable as mine. "Corvus, where are you?"

But no one swayed in the branches above. None of the familiar rustling as the tree bent beneath Corvus' weight. I grabbed the tree trunk to pull myself to my feet, felt bark dig into my hands. A new feeling. I knew the bells would ring for Prime, but I couldn't return to the Portal of the Virgin if I didn't know where Corvus was. Where had he gone? Had Michel taken him?

Had he left me?

No—I remembered. He had promised to change me. Where were my wings? Where were my scales and claws? Where was my peregrine-painted brow? Why hadn't he taken me to the ledge where he watched over the city? What was this ugly fabric skirt? This dirty tattered mantle?

Footsteps crunched against the gravel as a scholar swaggered towards the cathedral through the predawn gloom. I pressed my back against the tree, hoping he wouldn't see me. A youth like Celestine who had let his shaven crown grow over with dark, wild hair. Another one of the many students who was so pleased and proud of the way he looked. I could smell the alcohol on his breath. Perhaps he wouldn't have noticed me if I hadn't lost my balance, a twig snapping beneath my feet. He drew back, eyes wide.

I wanted to say, "Don't be afraid of me. I am the statue of Sainte Geneviève. I watch this city. I protect this cathedral." Instead, I pressed my back tight against the tree, remembering the way I had slipped from Celestine in the stairwell; how I had convinced him that I was a ghost.

He jerked a satchel of sweet-smelling herbs to his nose.

"Get away," he hissed.

His lips curled, and his nostrils flared, a look that stole the air from me.

"I said go away."

I mean no harm, I wanted to say, but I knew I looked like a specter. When I finally opened my mouth, I said none of these things. "Water," I said, barely recognizing the word I breathed through my lips. As if for all these years, I had known how to articulate thirst. I touched my mouth to my throat.

"Is this what you want? Take it, putain."

He retrieved a pouch from his underclothes and hurled it towards me. I cried when it hit my abdomen, and doubled over, clutching my belly. He sprinted towards the cathedral's entrance, his robes swishing behind him.

The pouch lay prone at the base of the tree, and I reached for it, curiosity overwhelming me. I remembered the citrus. That same desire. I closed my eyes. Willed myself to return to the West Façade. Realized I stood on the precipice of daylight. But I couldn't deny the dryness in my mouth, how my body wanted me to drink. I snatched the pouch up from the ground. I opened it and a musty smell overwhelmed me—the sour-drink smell on the scholar's pallid skin. Alcohol. I thought of Bathsheba and how she once longed to drink wine, long ago, before the great doorjamb statues broke the enchantment.

The liquid was tangy, sweet almost, but it stung my lips and burned the inside of my mouth. I spat and watched a trail of mucous drip to the ground and shimmer in the morning gloom.

What time was it? Had the bells already rung for Prime?

I had to outrun the sun; I had to return to my pedestal before daylight touched it! But where was Corvus? Why wasn't he beside me? He had promised to transform me, so where were my gargoyle's wings? Where was the new body he'd promised? I took a running leap and extended my arms, flapping them at my sides.

I landed with a painful thud.

I should have been able to fly—why couldn't I?

I panted until the air burned my insides. Fabric dragged the ground behind me and bunched at my feet, nearly tripping me. I ran and ran until I reached the Portal of the Virgin.

Bathsheba absorbed all the space I had once occupied.

"Help me," I said, reaching up towards her. The pedestal was too high, and the limestone did not reach out to help me climb. "Help me, Bathsheba." Louder this time. But my companions only smiled into the sky.

My eyes flickered from Bathsheba to elegant Uriel and Gabriel. Placid Marie between the two doors with the broken Child in her arms. All content smiles. I leapt up and touched the top of Bathsheba's cold foot.

My companions were solid, lifeless effigies. What was this harshness in their eyes? Why had I never noticed how big they were? The cherubim in the archivolts glared. "Just look at yourself!" their stern little faces seemed to say.

I turned my attention to my fingers, which were still long and slender and cold to touch, but soft blue veins pressed against the tops of my hands. I felt the shape of my face, felt bone beneath skin. I ran my hands over my belly and legs. Noticed I was clothed in course, frumpy robes. I ran my fingers through my hair finally understanding why my scalp itched.

I put my hand to my neck. A mound of flesh rose in the place where Corvus gave me his scale.

These once familiar faces were secure within the architecture while I was abandoned to the air and wind and sickness. This wasn't what I wanted. I had wanted to live, I had wanted to transform, but not like this.

Denis' poor head scattered on the ground. I picked up a shard and thumbed the edge until I bled. I pulled at my clothes and heard a high shrill sound I didn't recognize as my own keening. One or two solitary figures meandered through the parvis; they seemed to take care to avoid me.

I rose, dazed, and stumbled towards the Portal of the Last Judgment.

I looked at all the faces in the door jambs: male saints crowned with a stone nimbus around each of their heads. Not a single woman saint from the old stories stood here. I knew one of these men was Saint Jude, and another was Saint Matthieu, but I couldn't place names on any of their sullen faces. I glanced from the Beau Dieu, who stood between the double doors to the archivolts, where court doctors, martyrs, Wise Virgins, and Foolish Virgins thrust their bodies towards the earth. The innermost rows of the archivolts were crowded with somber-eyed cherubim, and the king of the Sky reigned from his throne in the Tympanum, the most prominent figure in the Portal of the Last Judgment. These figures passed on Michel's words with the rest of the façade whenever he had something to say, and it felt strange to finally see them with my own eyes.

The West Façade looked wholly oppressive with its rows of serious faces bearing down on the parvis—as if the architecture not only served to tell stories through sculpture but also to intimidate. Pray at this cathedral and obey its laws, *or else*.

Lucifer caught my eye before Michel did.

Lucifer's arched, mischievous eyebrows and teeth were visible over a twisted smile, a muscular body carved in fur. His maker had given him eyes that were almost comically large. Michel stood beside him; his hand raised gently to calm the souls waiting for their turn on the scales. His flightless wings soared up in an elegant arch above his halo.

He was a diminutive shadow carved into the frieze. Perhaps it was his will, his sheer energy, that made him seem so much bigger during The Wakenings. I could nearly hear his voice. *What have you done to your gift of The Wakening, you fool?*

My lips were stinging again. I had cut myself on Corvus' teeth. I pressed my fingers against the softness of my mouth. Recognized the blood as my own. I had taken water from Corvus' throat, which had turned to blood. My blood. My mortal, human blood. The shock of its color in the pale sunlight against the somber façade. But this blood wasn't an offering. It was who I was now.

I threw the broken piece that had once been Denis' eye at Michel's laughing face. My attempt was pitiful, and I missed.

The double doors began to creak open. I had to choose. Step inside the cathedral and hope someone there would help me. I touched the inside of my bloody mouth. Corvus had kept his promise to transform me, and now I didn't belong here. I ran towards the Seine, tripping over my bare feet before the doors swung open.

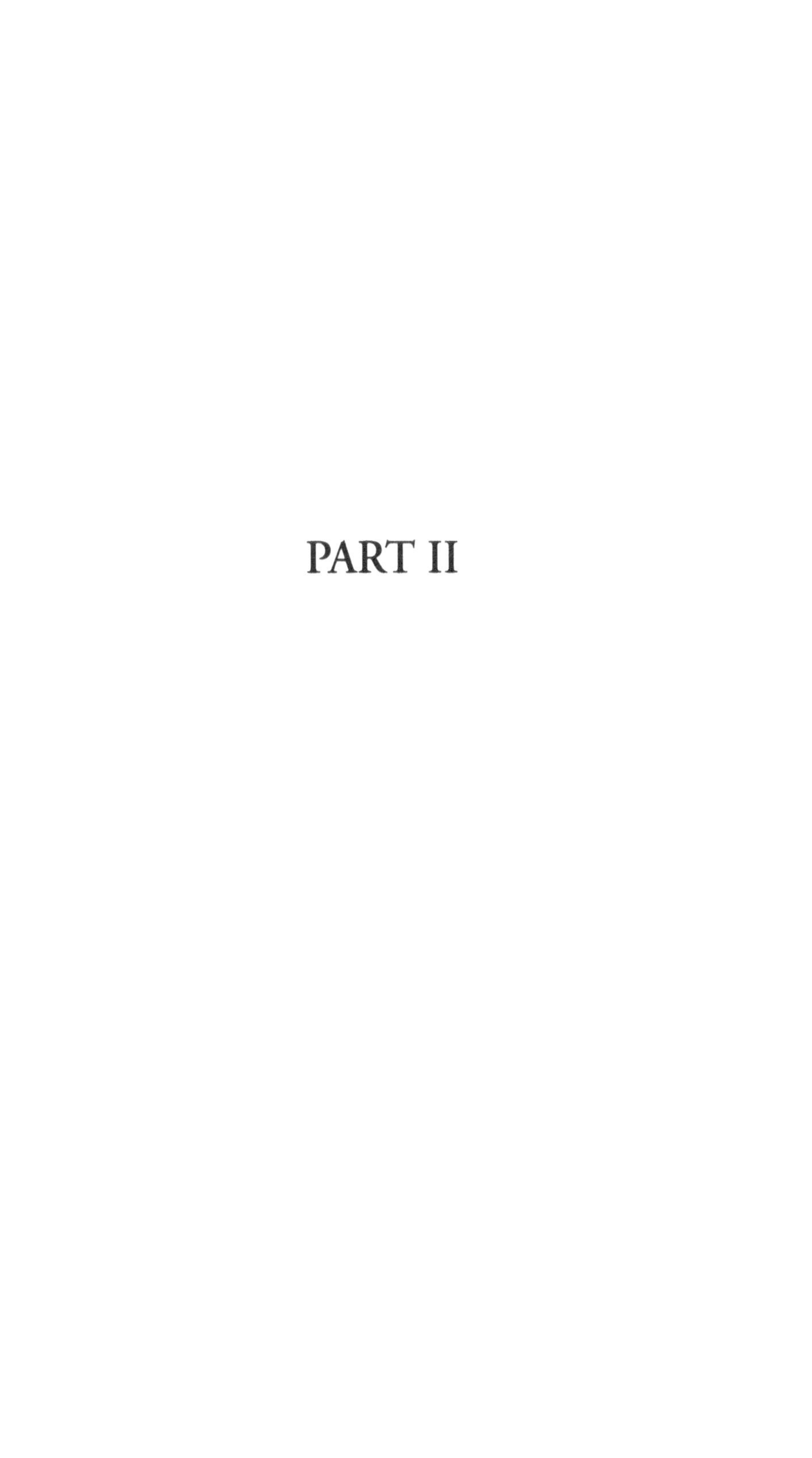

PART II

CHAPTER XV

What to do with this body I didn't want? I didn't want this hair. I didn't want this mouth. I didn't want these terrible, tender eyes that stung when the breeze flung dirt in them. I didn't want these bruised, purpling feet. I'd wanted talons. I'd wanted wings and a tail. I'd wanted a brow like a hawk's. I'd wanted to become something closer to the bird that could fly between the worlds.

I took refuge beneath the awnings of the Meson de l'Evesque, which was situated between the South Façade and the riverbank. The structure sheltered me from the harshest light, but I was afraid of the sun. For as long as I'd existed, the sun had been an enemy, a force that could take the gift of The Wakening. Obey the sun. I shirked from its warmth, pressing myself against the bishop's house and its cool walls.

I considered hiding from the sun inside the cathedral or knocking on the bishop's door and begging for charity as I had seen so many people do. The bishop wasn't there; he had joined the pope in Avignon, but the monks watching over his living quarters might open the door to me. But what would I say? How could I possibly speak to someone? I wasn't really a person.

Even if I could manage words and ask for help, I knew where the hapless clergy would send me: the Hôtel-Dieu.

No, I wouldn't enter those walls. Most who did never left. For most, a comfortable death was all the Hôtel-Dieu could offer, and though I didn't want to live with this body, I didn't want to die. Not even the possibility of meeting Isabelle was enough to lure me to that place. I sat down, huddled between the Seine and the cathedral, turning my hands over a broken piece of poor Denis' face.

Oh, Denis. One of the only to stand up for me. One of the only brave enough to contradict Michel. I thought of all the times I'd participated in his humiliation. And still, he had defended me. I wished I could have returned this kindness. I wished I could have protected him from the treacherous cherubim.

The sun rose higher, and my throat ached. Water. I stood and walked to the river's edge as if called by the Seine itself.

I thought I knew the Seine's sounds: steady breath of rippling waves, the hull of merchant vessels, and little boats rocking into the docks. Merchants and comics shouting from the Petit Pont. The riverbank was just a few footsteps from the parvis, but now I heard nuances I hadn't imagined. The startling splash of fish breaking the surface and flinging their bodies back into the depths. From somewhere far away, the sound of someone scrubbing clothing clean against a stone. Laughter—a sound I had not heard in months—sliced the air. I closed my eyes and felt droplets spray my face. Serpentine Corvus came to me in fragmented thoughts. Did Corvus know what would happen to me when I drank water?

The river curled around me with a cold, inviting tug as I leaned forward and scooped water into my cupped hands to drink. The fragment of Denis slipped from my fingers, and I watched, dumbfounded, as the river swallowed it up. What would it feel like to let the water spiral around this new skin and pull me towards the bottom of the Seine? Would I still be able to breathe—water having made me what I was? Would it turn me back to limestone?

The water smelled like rotten meat, but I was thirsty. I cupped my hands, trying to ignore the acrid stench. I drank and drank, forcing myself to withstand the smell, the taste. The water was past my knees, soaking my heavy wool mantle. If I slipped under, all the way under, I might not be able to come back.

My foot slid across a slick stone, and I nearly lost my balance. A shriek escaped my lips. My heart pounded. *Pounded.* Not just an imaginary stone heart. A real heart warmed with blood. I splashed towards the bank, panting, and fell to my knees. The sticky earth cushioned the weight of my body but soiled my clothes. This body wanted to survive.

I lay on my back, feet touching the water's edge, smelling my own soft body, and thought about Bathsheba and Marie and The Child and Uriel and Gabriel and all the faces in the archivolts and wondered what each thought of me now. Did they regret breaking Denis?

I wondered whether I could return at nightfall and squeeze back into the façade. But if I could undo what Corvus did and return to my niche, they would hold their trial. My word against Michel's. The missing flight feather. The kiss I'd given Michel.

What about Corvus? What would Michel do to him?

I looked over my shoulder and gazed up at the double towers. Sunlight bounced on those two thick horns, dazzling me, and forcing me to blink. I sneezed, a whole-body sensation that was almost pleasurable. Corvus knew exactly what he was doing when he offered me water.

Hadn't he?

I had known, too, hadn't I? This was a choice we made together. I knew he couldn't really turn me into a gargoyle—no enchantment was that powerful—but I'd wanted so badly to believe he could. This was how Isabelle must have felt. She wanted so badly to believe I could protect her family; she wanted to believe I could help her speak to the dead. Both Isabelle and I knew how it felt to want improbable things.

All at once, I remembered how Corvus pulled away from me and how his face twisted in horror. What was that look? Had he recoiled from my transformation or had the rising sun taken him?

No, if daylight had taken him, I would have found a lifeless, shriveled up statue. Instead, I woke alone.

I would have to find a way to return to the cathedral to understand what had happened. For Corvus. For my own sake.

I wanted to know what I looked like, but I was too afraid to meet my reflection on the water's surface. I felt my face. Round cheeks and high-arched eyebrows. What felt like a young, innocent-looking face. I knew a naïve-looking face was the face of someone people trusted easily and confided in, and I could use this trait to my advantage. It would take a lot to deceive me now. I tugged my hood to feel and see my hair underneath, and a long, orange braid fell out.

I unbound the braid from its string and ran my fingers through the loose waves. Bathsheba always told me my hair was painted this color, but I'd imagined it was darker, rustier—like the woman with red hair who owned the apothecary. I hadn't imagined it was *truly orange*, nor how it would feel to hold it in fistfuls. It was beautiful.

But I was no fool; I knew this color was dangerous. Some people believed fire-colored hair was evil—the mark of Hell. Most people had stopped believing such stories, but the illness had stoked old fears again. I clutched my strands protectively before binding them beneath my hood. I didn't want to inspire fear or draw attention to myself. I wondered why my maker had given me this hair. Was I Hell-marked? Was that why I couldn't resist the citrus, Michel's mouth, or Corvus' mouth? Why I couldn't resist harpy-watched rooftops? Why the most beloved cathedral in Paris hadn't been enough for me?

I turned my attention to my clothing. So old-fashioned— generations out of style. An untailored woolen cote loose in the breasts and shoulders—a nunnish, unflattering fit compared to the tighter garments people wore now. My mantle was caked with river water and layers of dust from all the years I'd spent outside on the West Façade. I shrugged it off my shoulders, wincing. Undyed wool. Simple fabric. I didn't like it. It was too humble.

I hugged my arms around my knees and inhaled. God's bones, I had never imagined something as simple as sitting beside the river and breathing. For me, this sensation wasn't so simple at all. I put my hand to my chest. How did this work? How did I breathe? Did I have a pair of lungs?

What did I know about lungs?

I closed my eyes and tried to remember conversations I'd overheard. Medical students dissecting cadavers from the Hôtel-Dieu had described lungs as soft and phlegmy, and out of the four elements, water ruled them. Lungs looked like long, pink fruit slices, and they cooled the heart.

Phlegm. Blood. Black bile. Yellow bile.

Water. Air. Earth. Fire.

My porous calcite body softened into four humors, four elements. Was this what I was now?

I was curious about this strange new animal of mine, the animal I was. I kept my hand on my chest, admiring the rise and fall. Feeling the softness of breasts. I squeezed them over my clothes, running my hands over my stomach. Pushing my fingers down over my thighs as the waves licked my ankles, feeling the discomfort when I squeezed and pinched too hard. I slipped a hand under my skirt and felt for the soft mound of hair between my legs. I tugged and pulled up dark strands, which I marveled over. Pulled the skirt up over my calves, staring down moon-silver skin with blue veins. Short red hairs. Bones I could feel beneath my skin.

Voices drifted towards me. Two women in the distance ambling along the riverbank. I ran back towards the bishop's house, abandoning my mantle in the mud, and watched the women from underneath the awnings, afraid to make eye contact. I didn't want to see myself through their eyes; I didn't want to know what they thought of me. I didn't want them to look at me the same way the drunk scholar had. And, to my horror, I realized that my hair was exposed without the mantle.

"This looks like something your great-grandmother used to wear."

"Excuse me!" The older one held it up with one hand, shielding her eyes with the other.

Cautiously, I stepped away from the wall, out into the open sunlight. I felt self-conscious as they eyed me up and down. A mother and her adolescent daughter. They both had the same beige skin, round cheeks, and pointed nose. I felt them search my body with their eyes for bulbous lumps beneath my skin.

"Good morning," the mother said, with warmth in her voice. She reached out with the mantle until I took it from her. "If we are going to say, 'to hell with the illness' and go outside, today is a lovely day to do so."

"I couldn't stand being cooped up any longer," said the daughter. She was still a maiden with uncovered hair.

I opened and closed my mouth. I didn't know what to say.

"Well, enjoy the morning," the mother said.

I felt disappointed when they walked on without saying another word. I thought I might follow them and ask them if they'd be willing to help me. What was that they held? Almond cakes? My curiosity grew. The pair walked along the Seine's soft bank, occasionally stopping to stretch. I tried to follow from a distance to avoid suspicion, but I caught their cautious backwards glances. The mother threw her arm over her daughter's shoulders.

Had my maker gazed upon my completed face with the same all-consuming fondness that this mother gave her offspring? What about the ones who sheared me from the dark, wet underground?

I saw that they meant to cross the Petit Pont into the Quartier Latin and felt excitement. On feast days, I could often overhear the cries of jugglers and fire eaters on the Petit Pont. Now, I could see the bridge for myself as it rose above the Seine. But as I neared the Rue de la Cité, I stepped onto cobblestones that had grown hot beneath the midday sun. I jerked back in surprise, retreating into the soft earth and tendrils that grew along the riverbank.

My maker had given me everything but simple shoes. Now I saw that I had stubbed my toe on a broken piece of stone, and jewels of blood seeped through skin and nail. I dabbed the wound and brought my fingertips to my mouth in wonder of my body.

Dare I follow the ladies across the scalding Petit Pont with nothing to protect my feet? The Rue Neuve and Rue de la Cité had once been lined with shoemakers' shops, but they were all shuttered now. Memories of the parvis markets swirled around me. I saw the leather merchants and clothier stalls in my mind's eye. I heard them barter over scraps of velvet and scarlet wool. Pressured arguments broken by good-natured laughter. I had taken these sounds for granted. My throat tightened, and I swallowed.

The two women hesitated at the bridge. "Come, Claire, let's be quick," said the mother.

"I think that dirty woman is following us," the daughter whispered, loud enough for me to hear. She clutched her bag of treats.

"That's unkind, Claire. Be grateful you aren't poor. By the grace of God, walk I." The mother crossed herself and nudged her daughter towards the bridge. I bit my lower lip and flared my nostrils in annoyance, but I didn't follow them.

Then, I began to laugh. The sun had slipped past the center of the sky, and I was walking beneath it.

Walking!

At the edge of the Seine! In the full-throated light of day!

The sun warmed my skin.

I had skin!

I closed my eyes and opened my mouth as if to swallow up the light. This was why the people gathered outside on summer days; it felt good. I hadn't understood before, even though I had spent one hundred years on the cathedral wall. I didn't just know; I *felt* it.

I felt cheated out of all the sensations I hadn't experienced or let myself experience until this moment. Oh, Good Sky! I wanted to feel *more*.

How many times had these two women visited the riverbank? To them, did walking here feel as natural as breathing? Did they take the river for granted? Did they take their bodies and mobility for granted? Did they believe these days of warm sun would stretch on without end?

Maybe they didn't. Perhaps the illness had taught them not to.

I wanted to ask them, but they had already disappeared beyond the Petit Pont, and I still didn't have any shoes.

CHAPTER XVI

The Hôtel-Dieu loomed over the parvis and the Seine, solemn and inevitable as a coffin. I kept my eyes on the ground as I walked the narrow street between the hospital and Meson de l'Evesque. I was afraid to look at the hospital, this house of the ill and the dead. I was scared that looking at the hospital would attract illness. I asked my skin, "How will I keep you safe?"

I turned onto Rue Neuve Notre-Dame and walked past rows of parchment and booksellers' shops, now abandoned. Doors and windows shut tight. The people had painted crosses—long, thin, and white as bones—across many of the doors. Others were marked with Stars of David. I recognized these warnings, homes touched by illness and stepped from their walls.

I squeezed through a narrow alley. There, hidden from the thoroughfare, messy drawings of erect cocks and hair-covered balls sprawled across the buildings. An elaborate painting of a nun straddling a priest confronted me. I spun around and faced a priest bent over, a nun's fist between his ass cheeks. Above this pair, a tableau of monks tongued each other between the legs. Was that pain or pleasure on the figures' faces? I couldn't tell. I stood between graffitied walls, afraid and curious and amused. The paintings were funny in their irreverence, but they were violent, painted to intimidate.

I thought of Corvus, and the breath caught in my throat. His mouth on mine, teeth shearing lips. In the predawn darkness, hidden from the cloister windows beneath the great oak tree, Corvus and I had been just as raw and obscene. Hadn't we? But now I was separate from Corvus and separate from the cathedral.

I didn't know what I was going to do.

I was *alone.*

Forget the sun! Forget the river and the ground sinking warm and soft beneath my feet. This new body felt grotesque with its skin and fats and hair and smells. This frame of bones felt obscene. Not because the priests said all women's bodies descended from a weak-minded, treacherous woman. This body felt obscene, because it was not my body. My body was made of limestone. This body was made of blood, phlegm, and bile, and it belonged to someone else.

This body would die, and I didn't want to die.

What was death? I had always accepted it the way the people did. Life was part of the journey to the Sky, according to the people. Life was transition, said the people. But these were things I had never had to think about; these were problems for people and animals. Not me. I was eternal. If the people loved us guardian statues, generation after generation, we would be cared for. I would never have to know death.

This was why Bathsheba always scolded me. This was what she'd meant when she peeled the sheafs of dead moss from her arms and mine. This was what she'd meant when she pointed to the dead sparrows. The dead people in those carts.

Dead meant dead.

"What did you do to me? I wanted you, Corvus. Not this weak body!" I tried to shout, but my voice was a thin hiss.

Why did Corvus transform me? Why did he give me water in his kiss? Now, I was good as dead.

I would keep myself alive until the next new moon, and then I would climb into the Portal of the Virgin and rejoin my companions.

I cupped my face in my hands.

I didn't know how to keep myself alive until the next new moon. I hated this body that needed things from me, and I was afraid.

Hoofbeats echoed through Rue Neuve, and I looked up. I hadn't seen many horses since the curfews were instated. The animal sounds reassured me. I was not alone in the realm of the living. I stood still, waiting for the rider to breach the corner.

Both horse and rider reared back, startled by my presence. Hoofs kicking up air. I gasped and took wide, backward steps. I'd thought I liked horses, at least from the safety of the cathedral wall. Now, I wasn't so sure. It was beautiful, that was true, with its chestnut fur, dark mane, and musky smell. But it was far stronger than I'd ever be, and I had enough sense to step out from underfoot.

The man released a cry as he calmed the animal, patting its elegant neck. He wore fine spring clothing: a plum-colored tunic over blue stockings. When he pressed his calf against the horse's belly, it pulled back its lips, showing off teeth in a big, wet mouth. Mucous dripped from its round, snuffling muzzle. The man pulled the reins and circled me in an unspoken negotiation.

I stood still, taking in his feathered hat and long, pointed shoes, and tried to see myself through his eyes. I saw a woman of nearly thirty years—not a youth but not old. The same age as the martyred Sainte Geneviève. A woman with damp strands of ember-colored hair poking from beneath her hood. I passed my hand across my face self-consciously and wiped a smudge of dirt from the riverbank. He eyed me and didn't seem to like what he saw. With these garments, I knew I looked both overly modest and deeply unfashionable.

I had seen him before in the parvis. He had been part of royal processions parading to the Notre-Dame—I had seen him on the Chandeleur. But all the other wealthy lords had fled the city—why was he still here? He narrowed his eyes. I squinted back. I crossed my arms and tried to remember his name.

"You are not going to bow to your lord?" he asked.

A blue silk purse tied to his waist caught my gaze. It bulged from the weight of coins, and I fell silent, imagining what I could buy with them. My belly protested; I needed to eat soon. I stared at the purse and licked my lips.

"Well, are you?" he pressed.

I blinked, suddenly recalling how I knew him and why he hadn't fled to some chalet in the country. He wasn't a lord at all. He was an abandoned servant from the Rive Gauche. His lords had left him to tend to the house and horses, and now that they were gone, he was wearing their clothing and spending their money. I didn't fault him for it; how could I resist trying on someone else's skin? How could I resist a full purse?

I would probably do the same.

"Who are you?" he repeated. "I know your face." His eyes softened with curiosity. His voice did, too.

Who was I? I didn't know how to respond. I didn't know what to name this human body. I didn't know if I was still Geneviève or if I needed a new name. I ran my hands beneath my hood to hide my hair, and I caught his lips flicker with the slightest smile. He had noticed my self-conscious gesture to make myself more presentable.

"Well, are you going to answer me?"

I stayed silent. I couldn't decide whether to share my name or run.

"You won't answer me? It's because you think you're beautiful, isn't it?"

Maybe he would decide to help me—a poor woman. I stared at the shape of his thin nose, the bow of his lips, his trim blond beard, and the frail softness of his throat. Broad shoulders beneath his tunic. He had a delicate, aristocratic face. A face I did not trust.

"You're not that beautiful," he huffed. "You're kind of old. You have a long neck, too."

The longer I stared, the more nervous he grew. I saw his feelings in his trembling hands.

"Your name. Answer me," he said. "I've seen you before."

I walked towards him. I knew the effect I had; he was afraid. He recognized my face on the face of a statue.

I closed my eyes and tried to recall the names and faces of his lords. There. I found them in my memories among the other nobility, and my eyes snapped open. A family from Lyon—no, was it Carcassonne? Their town didn't matter. What I remembered was that they had blamed the famine of 1321 on the lepers—that the lepers were poisoning all the wells in the land. Then, they joined the other rich families in blaming the famine on the Jews. They, like so many other noble families, used these pretexts to confiscate land and vineyards from the leper houses and Jewish families.

The man paled and his voice turned thin and tinny. "What *are* you?" he asked.

I stepped closer, taken by the horse. I wanted to reach up and pet its velvety fur. What would happen if I touched its mane?

The man's thin nostrils flared. "Get away from me!" he shrieked. "Witch! Hell hag!"

The horse reared on its hind legs and kicked the air with its two front hooves, stirring up that sweetly damp, musky smell. I watched its eyes roll in its tremendous head as its breath frothed the air. As the man clung to the reins, goading the horse forward, his purse swung on his girdle and fell. I gasped. That horse could easily crush me if caught underfoot, and I needed to retreat.

But not without that purse.

Who needed that money more? Me or this man?

Me or this man?

I grabbed the purse the moment it came within my reach. I didn't know if the man felt it slide off his belt while he struggled to control the animal. The horse carried him down the road before he could protest. Dust rose behind them, hoofbeats deafening until the horse and rider turned a corner and disappeared beyond my line of sight.

I tied the purse around my waist, marveling at my finger's strength—as if binding a purse to a girdle was the most natural thing—and secured my mantle over my shoulders. I pulled the wool tight, concealing the purse.

A terrible thought crossed my mind: what if the purse was filled with buttons or shells instead of coins? What if he had made himself a counterfeit purse to look and feel even more lordly? I held my breath as I pulled the drawstring and peered inside.

Good Sky! It was filled with silver deniers. I could afford food, shoes, and an inn for the night. I wouldn't have to knock on the Hôtel-Dieu's doors and beg for shelter. I wouldn't have to face that place. The money meant I might survive the night into the following day. I yelped with joy.

I felt a small stab of guilt for stealing the servant's purse, but I told myself to ignore it. I told myself that I wasn't stealing from a servant; I was stealing from a family that practiced stealing other people's property and lands. The money was never the servant's—he had stolen it himself.

But he'd also needed it to survive.

The sound of wheels grinding on the earth broke my thoughts. A woman's high, melodic voice cut the air. "Who did the Death King visit last night? Who did Hades take? Bring us your dead. Bring us your dead!" What a sweet voice to sing such a fearsome song. What a lovely little bell she rang as she walked. I recognized her voice, her music, her bell. I remembered the stench from her cart.

I darted into the small alleyway between two houses and pressed my body tight against the wall in imitation of spiders. It was bad luck to let these carts pass you in the street. I buried my eyes and mouth in fabric and tried not to breathe the sweet and familiar fecal smell wafting from the cart.

From the cathedral wall, I had always watched those carts with a perverse curiosity. The limp hand belonging to a once-living man never scared me. Decay interested me; I could simply watch it, because I knew I'd never decay. Now, I couldn't bring myself to look inside that cart. I couldn't look at the woman who pushed it, no matter how beautiful her voice. I didn't want to look at the children walking beside her. I was afraid I would see a body like mine among the pile. I wasn't ready to see what my body would become.

No, my body would never meet this fate. Beneath this skin and orange hair, I was still the statue of Sainte Geneviève. Calcaire. I would return to the cathedral.

Curiosity overcame me, and I decided to look at the woman and her children as they passed the alley. She and her husband pushed the cart together, and she occasionally stopped to ring her merry bell. The pair were plump and rosy with health. The children ran ahead and fought each other with sticks. They even looked jovial.

Across the street, a front door creaked open, and the pair walked inside. I strained to see the threshold, but it was dark inside the home. Shortly, the man emerged carrying a small bundle. A child wrapped in sheets with his ashen face exposed. I squinted and searched my memories. I had seen this child before, hadn't I? Trotting through the parvis on stubby legs, bare-bottomed and laughing, clutching his tin knight. That's when I looked away—I couldn't withstand more. The woman collected coins from the family and moved on.

I cupped my hands to my mouth and kneeled against the building. My belly heaved, but there was nothing inside to vomit. I coughed and gagged up the air, feeling sick and weak and frustrated.

The grim procession finally passed, and voices floated from the open windows above, filling the quiet streets. The murmur of conversation. A sob-wrecked breath. Laughter even. I thought I heard someone singing.

I left the alley and saw a shiny denier a few steps away. It winked in the sunlight, and I snatched it up. Oh, what luck! The cart pushers had dropped a coin.

But as I placed it in my purse, I reconsidered. The cart pushers were not like the false lord. They earned their money fairly—they risked their lives for it. They did the work no one else wanted to do.

I chased after them, screeching and panting and waving the coin that did not belong to me.

The man kept pushing the cart, but the woman stopped and regarded me over her shoulder. Her face looked red, and her weathered lips were pressed into a distrustful line.

"Yours," I tried to say, willing my mouth to make the right sounds. I held out the coin in my trembling fingers. "You dropped this." A harsh whisper.

She snatched the coin and turned back to her husband. The pair moved on, continuing their work, leaving me alone in the street.

Nervous the false lord would see his purse was missing, I squeezed through the narrow alleys behind Rue Neuve, where he wouldn't follow on horseback. I hoped no one had heard him cry out, *Hell hag*! My feet sank into damp earth, and I had to step around puddles. I squeezed the coins through the silk, happy to offer some to a baker or shoemaker, but all the shops were shuttered tight.

Eventually, the path led back to the parvis, and I faced the cathedral again.

Now that I saw the façade from this vantage, it really was *beautiful*. Looking at the guardian statues, each adorned with jewel-toned paint, felt like watching a procession on the Chandeleur. Wild sapphires, fuchsias, and reds all lit up and hazy by the afternoon sun. A glorious stone metropolis. The breath caught in my throat.

This cathedral was my home.

Michel, I will destroy you, I said to myself over and over until this phrase became my prayer. *I will smash your hands and mouth. I will break your foolish wings off your silly body.*

The gulls circled high above the Seine and beyond that, the rooftops of the Quartier Latin. One bird hovered without dropping longer than the others, and I watched it with mild curiosity. A hawk or peregrine, I decided, judging by the size and the way it flew. Its pearly, near-translucent feathers caught the sunlight, and I squinted; this beast was far more ethereal than any bird I had ever seen.

Was it an angel? Were the mortal stories true? Was this the true Michel?

Then I laughed; this was not a bird or an angel—just a simple kite, shaped like a falcon. Someone out there, beyond the river, was flying a kite.

A kite!

I remembered the Song of the Four Birds and heard Bathsheba's voice in my ears again. The song was beginning to make sense to me, or perhaps I was giving it a new meaning for my benefit. It wasn't about women at all. It was about hope, no? Maybe all the birds would fly away, but one falcon, by its own free will, would return to its falconer and land on her fist. Maybe there was no other feeling like that in the world—to feel this connected with *life*.

Someone out there, beyond the Seine, was flying a kite. Someone was still alive despite so much horror. It was all so beautiful and horrible, and now here I was, part of it all. And I would try my best to live.

Or maybe—I thought of Isabelle—maybe this was the bird that could fly between the worlds. This kite. Maybe this bird-shaped painted thing meant something. Maybe it would lead me to Isabelle. Maybe Isabelle flew it herself? Maybe I could still help her.

And maybe she could help me. I thought of the mother and daughter walking beside the Seine. I thought of Bathsheba. I had nobody.

I walked towards the Petit Pont. I needed something or someone to hold onto. I needed someone to wrap protective arms around my shoulders. I was ready to cross the river away from the cathedral, the somber parvis with its shuttered-up, abandoned homes, and the dreaded Hôtel-Dieu.

CHAPTER XVII

The soles of my feet itched. And right between my toes. My left breast itched, too. A million tiny sensations I had never noticed assaulted me as I crossed the Petit Pont. My crotch itched and so did my ass cheek. Little bitty gnats buzzed around my sweaty face. After every few steps, I stopped to scratch my scalp and pick my skin beneath my clothes.

More than anything, I was hungry.

Hungry, hungry, hungry.

I longed for cloth to tie around my nose and mouth, to keep the flies away and protect me from bad smells. People said King Death traveled with foul air, so they covered their faces. This bridge smelled foul; it smelled like piss and rot. I only had my hooded mantle, but I needed it to hide my hair. I would need to buy a cloth mask, a wimple, shoes, and food.

I wished I could have seen the Petit Pont last summer. The thick crowds snaking through the market stalls, browsing sweet oils and spices, young girls clapping for the dancing bears and chanteuses masquerading as princesses dressed in velvet-trimmed surcottes. Scholars sharing philosophical musings for the gathering crowds. I closed my eyes and tried to imagine. This bridge used to be alive. Not as impressive, perhaps, as the Pont au Change with its wealthy goldsmiths, jewelers, and merchants like Monsieur de Berry, who owned shops and homes on the bridge itself. Nevertheless, I'd heard that the Petit Pont had been a place to dress in fine clothes—to bare one's shoulders in a snug cotehardie. To flirt, banter, drink wine, and be seen. Now, all that remained of last summer's festivals was an old man ambling towards me, pushing a cart filled with dented onions.

He thrust one of his prized treasures in my face, and I stepped back, irritated by the sharp odor and his sudden closeness.

"A pretty, plump onion," he sang. "As pretty and plump as you!"

Was it true? Was I pretty and plump?

Was this human body pretty? The false lord had called me ugly.

I remembered my long limestone limbs. They had been perfect, hadn't they? How could a human body compare?

Was I ugly now? Or was I pretty? Did it matter?

I put my hand to my chest, flattered all the same. Flattered and relieved that I could walk among the people. My skin wasn't flaking from my body in sheets of old paint. I didn't have a mouth carved into an O, like a statue drinking water from a gargoyle.

"Come here and take a fruit of the earth!"

He thrust one of his prizes in my face, and I sniffed it. A pleasant smell, rich with humus. The people said that onions and other foods that grew inside the earth were lowly and uncivilized. The opposite of the lofty regal citrus. But I didn't care what the people said. My mouth watered; I was so hungry.

"Yes." My voice was still a thin, frustrating whisper. "I want it."

His eyes widened with obvious delight as he spied the purse tied around my waist. I happily gave him the coins he requested, far more than any onion should cost, but I didn't care. I was eager to eat.

"Now, then!" said the old man. "How about something for your teeth? Something to clean them!"

He was already trying to sell me something else.

"My teeth?"

"Yes! You can clean them with charcoal sticks. I have pumice stones, too."

I realized he had clean teeth and perfect, clean nails. I brought my free hand to my mouth, suddenly unsure about my teeth. I ran my tongue across them and longed for a mirror to see what I really looked like. The man's teeth were small and flat—the bottom row much shorter. His upper row was slightly rounded, with a gap between the front two teeth. Yet, they were clean.

"Come." A woman who looked no older than Isabelle had appeared at my side. "My cart is near the tollhouse." She took my arm and led me from the man who sold onions and clean teeth.

"You are so lovely," she said, guiding me by the elbow. She spoke with a lilt common to the merchants from Salerno. I felt like a giant beside her; she was quite petite, and I was beginning to realize I was unusually tall. Feeling self-conscious, I tried to keep my bare feet hidden beneath my heavy clothes.

"You must have beautiful hair beneath your hood. May I see it?"

My belly tightened. Had she already seen my sunset-colored hair? This was a trick. I shook my head no.

"Too modest to share your hair in public?"

"Yes," I hissed, knowing I shouldn't spend time talking with her.

"Really? Married?" Her smile looked forced. She grabbed the corner of my mantle and studied the fabric. "Why are you alone? Did you lose your husband to the illness? You're dressed like an old woman, but you have such a lovely young face. What are you?"

"A servant," I said, chastising myself for answering her questions. I needed to cross the bridge before she snatched off my hood.

"A servant. Well! If you can spare some coins, I can offer you something to make you feel beautiful."

But you already told me I am beautiful, I thought. I didn't trust this woman. I wanted to cross the bridge to eat my onion in peace.

"Look! Solutions to enhance the color of your lovely hair." She gestured to the assortment of glass jars lined up on her stand. "Perhaps your hair is plain and brown. This will turn it the color of golden wheat." She grabbed a handful of the jars. "Now, this will turn your hair as black as a raven's wing."

"Raven black," I said. My voice was still a raspy whisper. "How do you use it?"

"That will cost you a handful of whatever you have in your purse."

My belly growled in protest. I wanted to leave this bridge and find somewhere quiet to sit with my thoughts and eat. The sun slowly dipped behind the parvis and the towers of Saint-Chappelle. In this light, the Seine looked like it was on fire.

I remembered the peregrine kite. It was why I'd decided to cross this bridge, and now I'd lost sight of it. I craned my neck but could not see above the pointed rooftops that lined the Rive Gauche.

"God's bones!" I cursed.

I pulled away from the woman and began to sprint, nearly stumbling into the stone building that stood between me and the bridgehead. The tollhouse, I realized, staring up at the peak of the steepled roof. A place to collect coins from anyone leaving or entering the City. All the complaints I'd heard about this particular place over the years came to me. *Pisse-froid toll collectors always taking more than their share, I can barely turn a profit on my wine!* and *What is the king even doing with this money? I hear it's for bridge repairs, but I haven't seen shit. Trust my words, this bridge will collapse with the next flood.*

The tollhouse was now empty except for a crummy wooden stool with a broken leg. Mold grew in corners too dark for me to see and released a sweet, stinking smell. I felt relieved to save coins, yet disappointed that I wouldn't get to participate in such a daily, human ritual like paying a toll collector. How many people had passed through these walls before me?

I exited the opposite side of the building and stepped into a narrow street, looking for the kite to flash again above the rooftops. I had to trust that the peregrine kite would lead to help; I had nothing else to follow or believe in. Bathsheba would want me to follow the last of the four birds.

As I walked, I tossed the onion and caught it, enjoying the weight in my hands until it reminded me of Denis' head. I swallowed the lump in my throat. *Eat, Geneviève.* I peeled the thin, papery flesh from the onion and admired its translucence. Succumbing to hunger, I bit down hard.

At first, the flavor was sweet, but then it burned my mouth, made my eyes water, and my nostrils curl. I wanted to hurl the thing into the Seine. But I was hungry, and this was all I had. I held the onion tight with both hands and sucked and bit and chewed until there were fibers and juices on my face, and my belly ached.

Now I really stank.

In the Quartier Latin, the buildings I passed were indistinguishable, most boarded up and silent. I wondered how many people lived inside these homes, hiding from the Death King. I wondered who peered at me through slatted windows in the upper stories, like the cherubim in the archivolts.

I didn't see the kite rise above the rooftops again, so I sat in the street, exhausted and aching. I imagined what this street would have looked like even a year ago. For one, I would have been trampled sitting here like this. The road had belonged to horses, cattle, and goats just as much as it had belonged to the people. There would have been cook fires and students playing dice games on every corner. Pungent and crowded. It was hard to imagine; I had only ever known the parvis. I would never know this street. I would never know the way it looked and smelled before the illness. I had missed it all. I had arrived too late.

Sometime later, bells rang for Vespers. I startled to my feet, overwhelmed by the powerful sound. I felt like I was standing in the center of a valley, the ones I'd heard merchants and soldiers describe, with bells that rose in the place of hills.

I had dozed, I realized. This poor new body was unaccustomed to walking and already fatigued. In a panic, I reached for my coin purse and found it secured at my hips. I exhaled, relieved that no harm had come to me while I'd rested. I would have to be far more careful.

Hearty, feminine laughter rippled up over the din, pulling me in its direction.

Laughter. People. Company. Food.

Food.

I followed the merry sound, hoping for bread—hoping that the bread I smelled was really bread, hoping for good water, not murky water from the Seine. I licked my dry lips and quickened my pace. How had I gone so long without good water? My mouth and throat burned at the thought, and from the aftertaste of the onion.

A tall house with crossed timber frames greeted me at the end of the road. It looked like every other house I'd seen, nothing remarkable, but its doors and street-level windows were thrown open instead of shuttered. From inside, flickering light beckoned. I heard sounds like cups clinking and dice striking a table.

An inn.

Of course it was an inn! I'd heard stories about places like this for as long as I could remember. Places where travelers could eat and rest.

I would have cried with relief, but I was too hungry and thirsty. I followed the sounds of languid, drunken banter, wondering how these people would receive me. I hoped I really looked as plump and pretty as the humble onion. I knew I smelled like one. I closed my eyes and crossed the threshold.

I stood blinking in the common room, which was nearly empty, save for the four people playing tric trac. A warm, cozy sight. They regarded me as I stepped inside. I was eager for acceptance, but I was also afraid. I wanted to belong here and appear human enough to belong. And I wanted them to invite me to play, but I also wanted them to ignore me. I felt self-conscious in my loose, old-fashioned clothing. But I was so hungry! I didn't want them to turn me away.

"Wash your hands!" said the woman, gesturing towards a large bucket filled with soapy water near the entrance. "Wash your face, too."

I obeyed and stumbled towards the bucket, relieved to scrub the scent of onion from myself. This water was clean and smelled so much better than the Seine. It had surely come from a well and not the river. I submerged my hands for far longer than necessary, but the water felt refreshing.

I could hardly believe it. Here I was inside of an *actual inn.* I'd never imagined I would ever step inside one of these places.

The people returned to their game but cast me sidelong glances as I took the seat furthest from them at the long table. My legs were aching, and my feet were blistered. I had stubbed my big toe multiple times, and now it was bleeding beneath the nail.

A woman stood from the game and slid into a kitchen in the back of the common room. She returned with a cup of ale, a bowl filled with broth and carrots, and a chunk of black rye bread. I reached into my purse and gave her the first coin I touched.

"Who are you?" she asked. "I haven't seen you around here before."

I opened my mouth but didn't know what to say. Speaking to the people felt so improbable. Wrong, even. Would I ever get used to this? How could I?

I narrowed my eyes and studied the woman. She looked to have about thirty years. Roughly my age—well, the age of this human body. She wore her hair uncovered, and it hung over one shoulder in coarse, dark blonde curls. Her eyes were deep-set, small, and blue. Thin pink lips, pink cheeks, and beige skin. She wore a faded gray cote with tiny white flowers embroidered at the neck and edges of her long, loose sleeves. Her dress fit her far more snugly than my robes fit me. She was missing a tooth—one of the pointy ones—but her smile was warm enough. Wrinkles bunched at the corners of her eyes and across the bridge of her nose. She looked like someone who had spent her whole life working.

I looked past her to the group playing tric trac; they were watching me with expectation. They all wore short linen tunics and woolen stockings in varying shades of brown. They looked older than the woman but not by much. Two were big-shouldered men with long hair and the thickest, curliest beards I'd ever seen. The slightly blonder one had round blue eyes and an inquisitive, intelligent face. His companion had dark hair and eyes and a jovial smile.

The other person had a smaller frame, a heart-shaped face, and a crown of golden hair. They wore a pale blue tunic embordered with doves along the sleeves. Green eyes that regarded me warily. Their looks weren't masculine, but they weren't feminine, either. If Archangel Michel had turned to flesh instead of me, he would have looked like this person.

"M'lady!" said the big blonde man, raising his cup. "Welcome to the Auberge de la Mer."

"Auberge de la Mer?" I said, frowning. "The sea is nowhere in sight."

Everyone laughed as if I had told a joke.

"So, you can speak after all," said the woman, voice honey sweet. "What is your name?"

I wiped my mouth against my sleeve. "I'm Geneviève," I said. My voice was still raspy, but my tongue was stronger now. Thank the Sky.

"Your surname?"

I shook my head no. A surname? I didn't have that—what was I supposed to say? But I quickly reconsidered. "Donnadieu." Given from God. The name reserved for bastards and orphans. That was me now, wasn't it?

"We're all Donnadieu in here," crooned a merry man.

"Donnadieu," the woman echoed, peering into my eyes. "Where are you from?"

"Rue du Cloitre-Saint-Merri beside the Église Saint-Merri," I said hastily, naming the first street in Rive Droite. I knew nothing about that neighborhood. I only hoped it was far enough away from this place that this little quartet would be unfamiliar with it. I didn't want to answer any more questions. I just wanted to eat my rye bread.

"You're a long way from home," said the woman, pressing her hands on the table.

"Aren't we all?" the men hooted.

"And you're married?" the woman asked, noting my covered head. "Where is your husband? Dead? Or do you just wear that old thing for modesty?"

I shrugged and kept eating. "The bread is delicious," I whispered.

And it was. It tasted just like I'd always imagined. After an eternity of smelling bread and looking at bread from my niche, here I was finally *eating* some. Though hard against my teeth and tongue, it was still so satisfying. I felt revived.

CHAPTER XVIII

"Having lamented thus, she noticed the shadow of a large bird through a narrow window, but did not know what it could be. The bird flew into the room: it had straps on its feet and looked like a hawk of five or six moultings. It landed before the lady, and after it had been there for a while for her to see, it turned into a fair and noble knight."

From The Lais of Marie de France, Yonec (c. 1155–1170)

"Something terrible has happened to you, hasn't it?" said the woman. She placed her hand on my shoulder. Her voice was smooth as silk, but her grip was fierce. "We've all been through so much, haven't we?" Her fingernails dug into my shoulders. "You can talk about it, you know."

I didn't know. I didn't know what to say. I only wanted more broth and more carrots, more hard bread to dip in my bowl. I didn't trust this woman's sweetness, but I didn't necessarily distrust it. For the moment, this inn was all I had. This inn by a nonexistent sea.

"I need a place to spend the night," I told the woman. *And every other night this month, until The Wakening, I added silently.* I opened the purse and pulled out three shiny livres. "Will this do?"

The woman smiled until her eyes wrinkled at the corners. "Of course," she said. "Stay as long as you'd like." She snatched the coins from the table and leaned in close to the big-shouldered blond man. "Just a putain," I heard her whisper before she retreated into the kitchen. "Hiding in her granny's clothes, I guess."

I opened my mouth, but didn't know how to correct her, so I said nothing.

When the woman returned, she offered another cup of sour ale. It was tasty and satisfying, and I drank it eagerly. The woman returned to her seat, and the quartet resumed their game.

"Hey!" the burly blond shouted. "Why don't you join us?"

I didn't know how to play their game or what I even had to talk about with these people, but I wanted to join all the same, didn't I? Until today, I'd spent my whole existence surrounded by others. One hundred years of standing huddled between hundreds of companions. Companion statues all pressed together so close; we shared the same air. The separation hurt. I wanted company.

They were all smiles when I stood up. I sat between the woman and the person with the green eyes and doves embroidered on their sleeves.

"Alléluia!" said the big blond, swilling his cup.

As soon as he spoke, he realized he'd lost his round and the meager pile of coins he'd collected. He cursed and pounded the table. His gentle, bearded companion laughed and jabbed him in his ribs. The quartet introduced themselves. The blond's name was Eudes, and he and the woman were married and owned this inn. The friend with the darker beard was Josse. Before the illness, he'd built tables and chairs for lords and ladies as far away as Avignon.

"I'm Jehan," said the person with the green eyes. "Welcome to our merry hideaway. I was a student—my parents had dreams I'd become a bishop." They laughed until their face turned red. "Imagine me, a bishop! God's bones, fuck that."

The woman didn't offer her name for a very long time. She made me guess, and I drank every time I guessed wrong. I went from Anne to Marie, then to Anne-Marie, then to Isabelle to Anes, until I began to enjoy myself.

"So, looks like the five of us are among the last survivors here at the end of the world," Eudes said, lifting his cup. "The ale will sing to us! Alléluia!"

We switched from tric trac to raffle, and the woman offered her three six-sided dice. I knew they were cheaters—I had seen people play with weighted dice in the parvis. I knew they'd all caught glimpses of my stolen purse, but I didn't mind. I was having fun. It felt so good to belong to such a cozy little gathering. I slammed my cup down on the table, and the woman refilled it every time.

"What's that smell? Meli, you farted, didn't you?" Eudes said, crudely revealing her name. "I know that was one of yours."

I laughed until I snorted.

Jehan rolled first. Two, one, four.

"Damn it!"

They threw sous into the center of the table. Josse rolled next and shrugged in his sweet, self-effacing way; he, too, dropped sous onto the pile.

"You go," Meli said, smiling. She was leaning against the table, no longer seated at the bench. She smelled delicious—like lavender. I remembered the onion I'd eaten on the bridge and felt self-conscious. But if I smelled, no one seemed to notice. I gathered the dice in my hands, rolled them over my fingertips, and closed my eyes. I simply liked the way they felt.

Josse leaned over and blew hot, sour breath into my clenched hands. I jerked back. "It's for good luck," he said.

I rolled. All sixes face up. They all released cries of celebration and astonishment. Josse leaned over to kiss my cheek as he slid the pile of sous towards me. I remembered the kiss I had given Michel and touched the skin where he'd pinched me.

"I'm not going to lie," Eudes said, touching his beard, "the situation with Matthieu Phillips is veering out of hand."

"You don't say," Jehan smirked, taking the dice.

"He just finished his will, and he's not leaving a single tapestry to his wife. Not one. Have you seen those tapestries? Have you seen the inside of his parlor?"

"Have you?" asked Meli, her eyes big and wide.

"Yeah, how do you know he finished his will?" Josse questioned.

"He came here not two days ago; he told me himself."

"It's terrible how he treats his wife," Meli said, pursing her lips. "He's lucky I wasn't here when he came by—I would have sent him away."

"You'd have done no such thing, Meli," Eudes said, his eyes rolling towards the ceiling. "You know his purse as well as I do. You would have been all sweetness and 'Oui, oui, Monsieur Phillips!'"

"I don't want his filthy money!"

"Horse shit!" Eudes said. Everyone laughed except for Meli. I held my purse tight against my side.

When the laughter faded, Eudes nudged Josse in the ribs. "What are you smiling about?"

It was true. Josse held his hands to his mouth to conceal his smile, but he was doing poorly. His little round eyes twinkled merrily.

"I've seen inside that parlor," Josse said slyly. He raised his eyebrows. "Oh, it's something all right. Women and games—"

"Liar!" said Eudes.

"You know the kind of thing they're talking about, don't you?" Jehan asked me as they leaned close. "I know you must have seen *that* kind of thing before."

I shook my head no.

"Just another rich fuck who hates his wife," Jehan sighed. "Leaving her out of his will. Big scandal here in the Rive Gauche."

"He wants to ruin her reputation and leave her without a household to manage," Meli shook her head in disapproval.

"Why does he hate his wife?" I ventured.

"Probably no reason at all. Probably because he's just an asshole. His goldsmith business is failing, and who knows, he probably blames her," Jehan said yawning. "But you do know how *this kind of thing* goes. I'm sure you've seen scenarios play out like this before in your line of work—no need to be coy here. And besides, it's all very boring. With all that's going on—King Death *and* the war with England—I have no idea why we still want to discuss this. Can we just play our game and drink?"

The dice game continued. I won, then lost a round to Jehan, who took my newly acquired sous. Eudes sang 'Alléluia!' two or three more times. When Meli stood to light the candles, I realized it was well past Compline. How had I lost so much time?

I felt restless. The dark hours were the hours of The Wakening. Nighttime was for climbing. For walking. For talking with my companions *outside* in the night air. I closed my eyes and pinched the bridge of my nose. This all felt so wrong.

"Are you well?" Josse asked.

His hand grazed my thigh beneath the table. Oh! His touch was unexpected but welcomed. I slipped my hand into his and felt my body flush. If I had to choose from anyone at this table, I wished it was Jehan giving me attention, but I was drunk and willing to settle for Josse.

How was that? I wondered. It was this body. Already, this body begged me to forget names that belonged to limestone faces. Names like Corvus, names like Michel. This body begged me to absorb. Absorb touch, taste. Absorb, the way limestone could absorb light, sound, and water.

"I can't tell if you are very beautiful or very ugly," he whispered so only I could hear. "But I suppose it doesn't matter. Not here."

I laughed in his face. I wasn't drawn to his looks. I was drawn to limestone wings, carved scales, and eyes with peregrine markings. But it felt so good to be touched. To feel wanted. This grabbing under the table felt natural. I knew Josse was just as interested in my purse as he was in me—I knew he would take it if he had the chance. But God's blood, this was fun.

"You have such long fingers," he said.

"What's that?" Meli interjected. "Share your sweet nothings with the rest of us."

"I'm simply telling Geneviève that she has beautiful hands," he said. "Leave us alone."

The boldness!

"Well, I love the color you put on your lips," Meli said. It took me a breath to realize she was talking to me. "Where did you find it? I can't make a rouge stay on my mouth that long, and I've been watching you drink for hours. You know, you've got your charms. I suppose I could learn a thing or two from you."

"I didn't put color on my lips."

"And I'm the Queen of Sheba. You mean to tell me that's just your natural lip color?"

Josse leaned towards me. "Want me to find out if Geneviève's wearing paint?" He was so close, I could smell his rotten breath. But that didn't matter, not really. After all, I stank of onion.

Meli leaned in from the other side, drawing even closer to me than Josse. "I don't know what happened to your 'husband,' or what your story is, and you certainly don't have to share. But I do know that you do not need to wear that ugly hood on your head inside my business. Here, you can be free. Take that dirty thing off. Let's see your hair."

Her hand was on the fabric before I could push her away. With a single yank, the orange braid spilled out.

"Holy blood of Christ!" shrieked Eudes.

"Wow," Josse said, smiling ear-to-ear.

I lowered my head and tried to cover my hair beneath my hands.

"Well, well, well, my friends! I see we're gambling again!"

A woman stood in the common room threshold with her hands on her hips. Her cheeks were flushed, and her wimple had slipped down her forehead, revealing chestnut waves. She stepped inside and closed the double doors behind her, bolting them shut.

Jehan shook their head and muttered "Oh, good grief, not you again."

"What do you want, woman?" sighed Eudes.

"Just saving your foolish ass, Eudes," the woman said as she washed her hands. "Flagellants are nearly at your door. You couldn't hear the wailing, could you? You were too busy hollering and rolling your dice. I heard you down the street." She wedged herself between Josse and me, and Josse dropped my hand. She turned to me. She had thick eyebrows, brown hair, and a round, pretty face. "Who are you?" she asked.

"Geneviève Donnadieu."

She eyed me up and down, taking in my rough braid and loose, dirty clothing. "I know you. I've seen you before! I swear to God, I've seen you."

I realized I had seen her before, too—many times. She used to attend mass at the Notre-Dame Cathedral, but like many others, she stopped coming once the illness arrived. She was a servant in a well-respected goldsmith's house.

"My name is Geneviève, too," she said.

"It's strange how King Death has made this city so much smaller," Josse said wistfully.

"She's a—" Eudes began.

"Quiet!" Meli hissed, cutting him off. She paced the common room, extinguishing candles and shuttering the windows. "Stay away from the windows—do not let them see your shadow. And you, Mademoiselle Donnadieu, if they see your red hair, it's over for all of us."

We followed her beneath the long table, huddling on hands and knees. No one needed to explain another word to me.

Don't make a sound. Don't light one flame. This inn has been permanently closed; it was never an inn. This room has always been dark. No one has ever felt joy here, or pain, for that matter. No one has ever poured a drop of alcohol in this space. Certainly, no one has ever rolled dice. Everyone here has always lived in service of God. Flagellants have nothing to observe—there's nothing to see, nothing to worry over. There has never been a statue who turned into a woman with orange hair, a woman who loved a gargoyle.

The Other Geneviève saw the tears in my eyes and rubbed my hand. Her palms were calloused, and like Meli, she also smelled of lavender. "It's okay," she whispered. "They'll be gone soon."

The flagellants drew closer. Their voices were a chorus, like monks at Lauds, but louder and pained, almost comically pained. I heard leather strike skin and part of me wanted to laugh. I was curious, and I forgot that I was human for a moment. For a moment, the flagellants were simply a spectacle to observe. I couldn't see them or hear them, so it was hard to accept them as real.

Then I remembered I was human. I was human, and the flagellants could harm me.

They could also harm the statues on the cathedral wall. In a fit of ecstasy, they could pull down statues and shatter them. After all, they rejected all forms of artistic expression.

Whips cracked outside the inn's walls.

Rods split flesh.

The crack of knees against hard earth. Was that the sound of breaking bones? The kind of people who believed in divine self-mortification would destroy a statue. Bathsheba wasn't safe, nor was Corvus. But these chiabrenas wouldn't bother climbing the cathedral, would they? They would never notice Corvus tucked high up in the architecture. They would never see his great wings or the peregrine markings around his eyes and mistake him for a dragon or a malevolent forest spirit—a being that lived in a realm beyond mortal understanding.

I couldn't worry about myself—I just wanted to keep my companions safe.

It hurt to listen as the flagellants drew closer. I imagined my own skin splitting open. Why did they do this to their bodies? Was the pain pleasurable? It had to feel good. Otherwise, why did they keep doing it? Why break their skin with whips and rods and clubs?

They stank.

They pressed their bodies against the inn's windows and doors as they squeezed through the narrow road. God's bones, we could smell their unwashed skin and clothes. Their rancid sweat. We buried our noses into our clothing and tried not to whimper. But even if we did, even if we let out a small miserable groan, would these fevered people hear us over their laments? They were a pack of dogs, a herd of lowing cows. They were wild and loud.

The more I listened, the more I began to understand them. Self-harm as control. Grief as self-harm. Flesh breaking out of the skin, backs split open like pomegranates, pomegranate seeds of blood, pomegranate seeds. Pain was a way to feel. Pain a way in, a way to blame the grief. Blaming pain on the body because there was no way out; any one of us could get the illness.

We were all staring down the rest of our lives.

It was easy to mock them the way Eudes and Meli did. But they were also escaping into gambling and games and drinking. Everyone wanted to crawl out of their skin. Or break out of their skin, split open their skin, and crawl out.

So did I.

"It's hard not to watch them, isn't it?" asked The Other Geneviève.

The more I listened, the more I wanted to join them. I felt saved by Corvus and betrayed by Corvus. I missed him and didn't know if I would ever see him again. I was angry that we didn't have more time together. Just one more conversation beneath our tree as guardian statues. I was angry that he didn't tell me he could turn me into a human, though in my heart, I knew he didn't really know what he was doing either.

Or did he?

Did he know, or did he not know?

The Other Geneviève held my hand protectively. The flagellants passed, and we all exhaled. Only then did I realize I'd pissed myself. My chemise was damp beneath my cote and fabric clung to my legs. I was repulsed and curious and delighted all at once. I had pissed. *Pissed!*

This human body was truly human, and I felt a sudden, overwhelming sense of awe.

"Someone stinks," groaned Meli as we crawled out from under the table. "Eudes, is that you?"

"You know the way I stink, darling," he replied.

"Well, on that cheery note, I'll bid my farewell," said Jehan.

"Absolutely not! No one's going anywhere," said Eudes, pounding the table. "We have another round to play, and you still owe me coins."

"All the more reason to leave." Jehan slipped out the inn door faster than Eudes had the sense to catch them.

"Damn it!" Eudes said, swaying in his seat. "Well, nobody else leaves. We agreed on another round. Alléluia!"

"Actually, we'll take our leave, too," Josse said, grabbing my hand.

I jerked away. With his bland face beneath his beard, Josse no longer looked so charming to me. The flagellants had interrupted the moment passing between us, and I could not return to it. I didn't see soft, expressive eyes and a sensual mouth. I saw someone eager and a little desperate. He was too hungry for me. I recoiled rather than thrilled at his touch. My legs were damp with piss, besides.

He looked at me, confused and a little hurt.

"Leave with me," said The Other Geneviève. "I have room."

"No!" chorused Eudes and Josse.

"She's a thief!"

"She lives in a stolen house!"

"Don't you think for a moment I've dropped my suspicions about the well," said Eudes, pointing his fat finger at The Other Geneviève. "I'd wager the inn itself that you've dropped poison in our well."

"Don't you dare," hissed Meli.

I looked between Eudes and The Other Geneviève. This was a terrible accusation that could get the latter hung in the Place de Grève. But The Other Geneviève simply rolled her eyes. Meli and Josse behaved as if they'd heard nothing.

"Shut up with your wells, you drunk," sighed The Other Geneviève. "After everything I've done to help your little tavern this year."

"You can't trust her," Josse whispered, grabbing my hand more firmly. "Please stay here with me."

"Why can't I trust her?"

"She's a very strange woman."

Well, then, that was perfect, wasn't it? It was so perfect that I nearly spat with laughter. I, too, was a very strange woman. Maybe we could keep each other safe.

The Other Geneviève wrapped a protective arm around my shoulder and pulled me towards the door. Josse looked like a goshawk who'd lost the peregrine he'd planned to make into a meal.

"This is your fault," Eudes said to Josse. "You blew it! You made them all leave."

"Shut it, or I'll slap it shut," Josse said, pointing at Eudes' red cheeks. "The flagellants are bound to hear you with your crazed braying."

"You call that crazed braying? I'll show you braying." Eudes slapped his chest and stood. Josse returned the gesture.

"Come on, tough man. Come on, big guy. Come on, puterelle. Let's go." Eudes shoved Josse's chest.

"Back off," said Josse, pushing him back with force.

Apple red cheeks and chapped lips pulled into snarls. Eudes picked up an eating knife and jabbed Josse in the thigh. Meli shrieked. The Other Geneviève pinched my hand. Josse doubled over and groaned, but when he pulled his hands away, he realized Eudes had not drawn blood; the knife was too dull.

"Fotre dieu," Josse hissed before kneeing Eudes in the face.

"Let's go." The Other Geneviève pulled me through the doors. And I followed because she was kind and warm, and I needed someone to cling to, someone who felt safe.

CHAPTER XIX

I rushed to keep pace with The Other Geneviève, watching her hair sweep her shoulders as we hurried beneath the thin moonlight. Glass, rocks, and unknown litter cut my feet, and though I wanted to soothe them, The Other Geneviève urged me on. I longed to study the waxing moon and the position of the stars, to find Cassiopeia and Cepheus, but I could only run forward and steal curious glances at the sky. Breathing felt more natural, and my mind felt sharper. Nighttime had revived me; finally, I felt awake and alive and right inside this body.

We arrived before a high wooden door, which my host opened with an iron key. She entered the garden first, then cast a backward glance as the bells from Saint-Séverin rang for Lauds. If I followed her, I knew she would lock the doors behind me, sealing me inside. *No, not yet*, I thought. *I want to stay outside and walk under the stars.* Walking at night felt like the most natural thing. But if I did not follow, she would lock me out and leave me to the flagellants, thieves, and whoever else roamed the city at this hour. I needed this refuge, too. I needed to rest, drink water, and wash my bloody feet.

A warm, cavernous room swallowed me like a mouth and veiled my eyes. Onions and smoke filled my lungs. After one hundred years of wakenings, I expected to see well in the dark. I could not. I felt as vulnerable as a prey animal; The Other Geneviève could hurt me if she wanted to, and I wouldn't be able to fight back. Worst of all, my abdomen felt heavy once again with everything I'd had to drink at the tavern.

My host brought the hearth fire to life, lifting the darkness. As my eyes adjusted, I made out the shape of a brick chimney and a staircase. The innkeepers were right: The Other Geneviève lived in a massive house worthy of a renowned goldsmith. I stumbled into a chair placed at a round table and folded my knees beneath me, pressing the heel of my foot against my crotch to relieve the pressure.

"How long have you been alone?" she asked.

I opened my mouth but didn't know what to say. Could she see the way my lips trembled? Could she hear the hesitation in my voice? I didn't know how to make up stories, that was too much work.

"Some time now. I don't know how to talk about it."

As I spoke, I looked her in the eyes, wondering if she'd eventually recognize me for who I was, half hoping she would. I wanted to tell someone. I didn't like pretending I'd been born into flesh. This skin wasn't really who I was. I had been a beautiful statue; this skin felt cheap and fragile in comparison. For a moment, I imagined her seeing me as the limestone Sainte Geneviève—I imagined how she would *worship* me. We shared the same namesake, after all. She could help me return to the cathedral. She could help me feel less alone.

I sighed. But I didn't want to be worshiped. I just wanted to survive until the next wakening.

"I've lost everyone I care about," I said. "I'm just trying to keep myself alive."

She nodded and laid her hands on the table across from me. Her face softened, and her chest rose and fell with even, relaxed breaths. She trusted me. But why? It was dangerous to trust strangers, wasn't it? But here we were. Maybe some small part of her recognized Sainte Geneviève.

"This is my employers' house, and they're all in Lyons. Or they were—God only knows if they're still alive. I haven't received a letter from the steward since well before the Nativity. I'm like you, trying to live each day."

"How long have you been alone?" I asked.

"Bloody bad fevers, it's been months. There were others. A steward, laundresses, chambermaids, a cook. You know, the usual house varlets. When the family left, they took the steward and the head chambermaid with them. The rest of us got left behind. Last year, there were eight of us."

"The illness took them all?" I asked, even though I knew the answer.

"The last chambermaid died in January. She was my friend, and I had to drag her into the street all by myself. Now it's just me, so I invite other people—people lost like you—to share this space with me. Until my employers return—if my employers return—this is my house." The Other Geneviève slammed her fist against the table. "I don't think it's right to have this many rooms and even a garden and not share the house with people who need it. These doors would be locked in normal times, but King Death has offered some unexpected gifts. It's only right to use them. Take what we need."

The Other Geneviève looked up with a fiery glare.

"You think I'm stealing from the family, don't you?" she said abruptly. "Well, you know what? Even if they came back and sent me to the gibbet at Place de Grève, I still wouldn't regret what I've done. They left us here, Geneviève. They left us here to die while they went to the country to pass their days hawking and drinking."

"I don't judge you," I said. "I understand."

I meant it.

I saw markings on the wooden floor where it looked like there had been chests of drawers. I wondered if the goldsmith's family took them or if my host's other guests had stolen them.

"I have to piss," I blurted, unable to hold it any longer. "I can't believe I already have to piss again!"

She laughed and told me about a basin upstairs but recommended going outside if my need was urgent.

I lifted my chemise and squatted in the walled garden. This felt *so good*. I closed my eyes with pleasure, smiling at the sound of urine splashing in the dirt. Sweet relief. Now I understand the troubadours' silly songs. I felt nearly disappointed when the flow finally stopped.

I could stand up and stare at the sky. How strange to walk beneath the moon. I tried to map out the shape of the stars and constellations, but to my frustration, my eyesight was poorer now.

"Come," The Other Geneviève said, breaking my concentration to call me back inside. "You can take the eldest daughter's room. It's yours for now."

She lit candles and placed them on the windowsills. The room had been abandoned, but if I concentrated enough, I could smell the memories of other guests my host let occupy this room and, beneath that, the girl who used to live here. Scents that reminded me of honey. How strange to grow accustomed to humans, to realize skin could smell so different, one person from the next. I yawned, searching my memories for the faces I'd seen in the parvis, searching for the goldsmith's family. I wished I could remember what they looked like.

I wondered why The Other Geneviève wanted to help me. Had she caught a glimpse at the stolen purse?

She behaved as if she trusted me, but could I trust her?

"Now, I do have one rule," she said. "You can't bring anyone here to lay with you—excuse me for being blunt. You must understand, in these times, I'm cautious."

"Oh!" I murmured, surprised she imagined I would. "Of course."

"You can take a break from that kind of work while you're here," she said. "I imagine that should be a welcome relief—your work being even more risky these days."

"You're mistaken," I began. "I don't—" But she left me alone in the room before I could finish.

It took several tries for me to figure out how to pull my soiled garments over my head, and when I did, I brought the fabric to my nose and inhaled. If my host had noticed the smell of urine, she had acted as though she hadn't. The thought embarrassed me, but exhaustion overcame me before I could dwell on it.

I felt my eyelids flicker. How strange to lie on my back instead of standing still on limestone feet. How strange to feel the rise and fall of my chest in a bed that would never be my own. How odd that this woman who shared my name wanted to take care of me. I let my gaze drift across the darkened walls. What was I now? I was a woman lying in thick wool blankets, one arm behind my head, the other tucked beneath me.

I woke to the sun streaming beneath the slatted windows. I could hear my host moving around downstairs. In my mind's eye, I could see her arranging pots and kettles by the hearth. In this half-sleep, I ran my fingers over my chest, belly, and kneecaps. I was still soft flesh; sleep hadn't turned me back to stone, and I felt relieved and disappointed. I found a ceramic pitcher covered with blue-painted swans on the floor beside me, lifted it, and drank. Stood up, slowly, slowly.

I was still surprised to find pale fleshy legs and a soft belly beneath my chemise. What were these human breasts and round dark nipples? I ran my fingers over them and pinched hard. Shook them in my hands, amused and curious. I thought of all the breasts I had seen in the parvis; mine looked like them, the same but different. Individual. My own.

A glint of light caught my eye from the corner of the room, and I stumbled towards it, happy to discover a hand mirror resting on a short table. I couldn't resist it—I had to know what I looked like.

I was indeed *mortal.*

I saw soft cheeks, round golden-brown eyes, curly orange hair in a very tangled braid, freckles dotting a long, straight nose, and pink skin that was tender to touch. The sun. This was the sun's work. My neck and ears were also bright pink. I frowned at myself; I had seen what the sun could do to the skin. It peeled flesh from the face like paint from stone. I bit my lower lip, resentful again of the sun and longing for my perfect limestone face. But the wonder of myself—what I had become—called me back to the mirror.

I had all my teeth, but they were slightly crooked, especially the bottom row. These were ordinary features—who had perfect teeth, after all? Then I saw my lips. How had I not noticed them?

Bruised lips, so dark they were the color of dried blood, nearly purple. They looked like they belonged to King Death's consort. I could have been an ordinary-looking woman, if not tall, had it not been for my lips. I would never blend into the city with a mouth like this.

Corvus. Corvus gave me this mouth when I cut my lips on his fangs, when I drank water from his throat. And what was this purple mark at the base of my own throat? I touched the raised, discolored flesh, realizing this was from Corvus, too. The remains of his scale. Stone scale turned flesh. My hands hugged my neck, and tears beaded my eyes. A piece of Corvus was still with me. I hadn't lost him completely.

I stroked the side of my neck and sighed. The false lord was right; my neck was rather long. Oddly so compared to The Other Geneviève's.

And what else? What else would I find?

I moved far from the windows, kneeled on the floor, and placed the glass between my legs.

Mortals were obsessed with all that existed between their legs. An endless source of fascination they were both proud and ashamed of. An endless source of pleasure and fear, life and death, and comedy.

My maker did not disappoint me. I ran my fingers over the folds of skin and pulled gently at my hair just to know what that would feel like. All the mortal language to describe these parts, the euphemisms and profanity, all returned to me. I smiled and played with the skin beneath my fingers and the language on my tongue. Con, Belle-chose,

Quaint. Words from other places the French had made their own. Everyone had a name for the body. I slipped my fingers inside and licked them. Cunt.

One rude knock at the door. I dropped my chemise and kicked the mirror across the room.

"Geneviève, are you awake?"

Are you awake? What did sleep and waking mean to me now? It was wrong for me to be awake like this in the daylight. I should have been standing in the west façade of the greatest, most beloved cathedral in Paris. I shouldn't have been able to reach between my legs to taste something like salt. What I thought salt might taste like—how I'd heard it described. I dropped into bedding and buried myself beneath the wool coverlet.

"I hear you in there," my host said. "Join me downstairs, there's food."

I barely heard her; my eyelids were already heavy. I drifted back into the calm darkness where I had no thoughts.

The knock again.

"Geneviève Donnadieu, are you awake yet?"

I opened my eyes. Sunlight filled the dusty room, sharp, hot, and suffocating. I closed my eyes.

When I sat up again, the sky through the shutters was cool and purple. The Other Geneviève stood over me. She wore a cotton mask over her nose and mouth. She smelled like flowers.

"I had to see if you were still alive," she said.

I pressed my fingertips to my eyelids. Still soft. Still very mortal and human. I groaned.

"Are you well?"

I wrapped the sheet tight around me. My garments were somewhere in this room. I stood to look for them, wearing the sheet over my shoulders.

"I don't have the illness," I said, "if that's what you're worried about."

"We can't be so sure about that," she said grimly. She moved to the windowsills and lit the candle stumps. "I've washed your clothing—it's outside drying, but I'd like you to stay here for the night. Out of precaution. I know you understand."

I nodded, though I didn't understand until I heard her say, "Mind the bowl of soup at your feet." Then she left the room and locked the door behind her.

Candlelight reached towards me from the room's edges. Alone, in silence, I drank from the bowl. Warm and good. Cabbage, carrot, and pea flesh drifted towards my teeth, and I swallowed without thinking. The broth was flavorful and hot. Pin pricks of spice nipped my tongue. Black pepper. Such an expensive spice—how did The Other Geneviève afford it? It must have come from her employer's pantry. I wondered if she cooked with it daily or if she rationed it. I decided that if I were in her place, I'd take nothing for granted and consume each luxury I could.

That was what I would do. Between this night and the next wakening, I would do more than survive in this body. I would enjoy it. Enjoying this new body was how I'd survive.

One bowl of hot soup was not enough. But when I tried to open the door, I remembered my host had locked me up. I rattled the handle and called out to her. Though I heard her shifting around downstairs, she gave no response. I had spent the whole day sleeping, and now she suspected King Death had touched me. Very well, I knew how to be patient. Tomorrow, I would leave this room and explore the pantry. I would see what else there was to eat.

I returned to my bed and prepared to wait the night beneath the wool coverlet. I was very good at being still. I spent most days and nights still and quiet on the cathedral, after all, and tonight would have been no exception, given the growing moon.

But how to calm my restless belly? It still wanted food. I remembered the people's market stalls: the cuts of pork and beef and barrels of salted eels. I remembered hearing about plump roasted peacocks served on wealthy tables. My mouth watered, and my belly whimpered.

Tomorrow, I simply had to wait until tomorrow.

Cuts of mutton, plates of oysters, and saffron-seasoned swan! Goose stuffed with apples and candied pears. Tender meat that peeled from the bone. Plates piled up with mushrooms as fat as my fists. Gooey mulberry tarts and honeyed cakes. How had I learned the names of all these dishes? Of course, I had never tasted such rich food—the richest, rarest food I'd touched was the citrus—but now I could imagine a feast. I could almost taste it. Oh, I couldn't wait until morning; I couldn't wait to eat again. What other riches would I find downstairs?

My belly tightened. Pressure filled my gut until, despite myself, a foul-smelling fart escaped my ass. God's blood, why? Of course, I'd learned to recognize farts after standing in the Portal of the Virgin for one hundred years, especially on feast days when people crowded in the parvis so tight, they pressed against the West Façade. But I was dismayed this one belonged to me—dismayed and perhaps surprised. It smelled of rotten fruit and cabbage. Disgusting.

But also, somewhat funny in an irritating way.

The nasty little troubadours' songs that always made people howl with laughter made so much more sense to me now. The stupid little imp carved in the wall behind me in the Portal of the Virgin always loved those songs, didn't he?

My belly cramped and begged for more release.

My maker had given me wisdom and intelligence, and I was grateful for that—especially now that I was human. I found the pot at the edge of the bed and pulled up my chemise just in time to take the first shit of my hundred-year existence. My kind, thoughtful host had left me a wad of moss, and I knew what to do with it, thanks to all the bare buttocks I'd seen in the parvis.

Now, what to do with the pot? In calm times, there were laws and fines to keep people from throwing piss and feces out their windows, but who was left to watch the streets now? And if The Other Geneviève were fined, perhaps that's what she'd deserve for locking me up in here. I pulled open the shutters and dumped the moss and contents of the stinking pot down onto the street. I dunked my hands into the water pitcher to clean them, then tossed the dirty water out as well.

I felt angry at this body for creating waste. I knew all animals ate food and shat—this was what living meant. But I never expected *my body* could produce something that embodied decay.

Why hadn't I appreciated how perfect my limestone body had been?

The citrus had been equally foul, putrid, and covered in a thin gray moldy film. There were consequences to pursuing pleasure. When was the pleasure worth the grotesqueries?

I didn't have answers to questions like this.

Sleep didn't come. The door to my room was still bolted shut. I sat on the bed with legs folded beneath me and waited to grow tired, but I only felt more alert as the hours passed. Eventually, I walked to the other side of the room and retrieved the little hand mirror from where I'd kicked it. I turned it over to study the ivory case. I ran my fingers over an engraving of a man and woman on horseback. I'd seen mirrors like this sold in the parvis and knew that they were luxuries.

Meanwhile, The Other Geneviève snored in the adjacent room, and I wondered if that's what I had sounded like last night. I wondered why people snored and why human bodies made crude sounds. I placed the mirror back on the table facedown, without looking at myself. I missed my elegant body; I missed being limestone. My longing frustrated me, because limestone hadn't been enough to satisfy me when I stood in the Portal of the Virgin. I'd spent more than one hundred years swallowing a fascination with mortal bodies. Now I had one, and I didn't want it anymore.

What was the matter with me?

Neighbors in the adjacent houses stirred, their voices crossing shared walls. I strained to hear a man and woman arguing, but layers of house muffled the specifics. Was that Eudes and Meli from all the way over at the inn? I couldn't tell. From the other direction came another kind of yelp. Rope or leather striking skin and one ecstatic whimper, "*Please, please, please, God's blood, please.*" Laughter and the wet smack of kisses. This was not the sound the flagellants made; this was another way to worship.

A shrieking baby in another home and a mother or nurse pleading for silence. The woman sounded so tired, on the verge of tears. Firewood shifting as someone readied their hearth. Children running up and down stairs. An old man sobbing. Saint-Severin's bells roused the most pious for Lauds.

People were awake at night! Nearly just as active as they were during the daytime. How had the people never seen us moving on the cathedral wall? How had we kept the enchantment a secret?

Everything I heard made me wonder if I had ever been made of stone. Had I simply imagined that I was a cathedral guardian? Perhaps I was born mortal, but the illness had enveloped me with fever and made me believe I had been a statue, forgetting everyone I'd met before this moment. Maybe it had all been a dream.

No. I was a statue. I would not forget myself even though this new body wanted me to. I knew what I was. I was exactly what I wanted to be.

The candles were small stumps with pathetic guttering flames. As I searched the room for more candles and something to light them with, I found a small, unlocked chest nestled in the shadows. Inside were men's linen underpants, a woman's chemise, and a light blue cote, all made for summer weather. Tiny, stitched roses graced the cote's neckline, and the fit looked far more modern than the clothing my maker had given me. Since The Other Geneviève had taken the liberty of washing my clothing, I would take the liberty of wearing these clean garments.

I unfolded the items, and a golden comb shaped like a falcon tumbled to the floor.

The way it caught the skinny light, the fierce beak opened just enough to let a little gold tongue loll out. It was exquisite, down to the tiny rabbit carved in the falcon's claws. All this terror carved into a comb to pin in someone's beautiful hair. The ferocity of it. Who would wear such a thing? I had seen merchants sell similarly fashioned jewelry that had come from Constantinople. I knew this was a treasure, and I found myself wanting it badly. Who had it belonged to? Who had lived here? Who had The Other Geneviève served within these walls, and what were they doing now? Would they return, healthy and well, and looking for their things?

That was all to say: if I happened to keep this comb, would anyone notice?

I ran my fingers along the prongs and touched them to my hair. I loved this comb fiercely, but I knew it wasn't mine. So, I pressed the comb to my heart before placing it in its chest to await its owners.

The candles were dead now, but soft blue light began seeping through the shutters. I felt the dampness between my legs, and when I pulled my fingers from my borrowed chemise, they retrieved blood. Brilliant and crimson-like ruby beads on a necklace, stretching between my index and middle finger. A dark stain marred the fabric, too. I stared at it, dumbfounded. For a moment, I thought something was terribly wrong with me—that this was a symptom of an injury. Or the illness.

Then I understood.

I pressed my hands to my eyes, without regard for the blood, and wept. Monthly courses meant that I was truly mortal now. I had taken water from Corvus' throat and expelled piss, shit, and blood. I couldn't imagine an enchantment or remedy strong enough to return me to stone. Breaths filled my lungs and racked my body. Would I ever speak to my companion statues again? Was the West Façade still my home?

CHAPTER XX

"The lady arose…placing the beautiful flower inside the maiden's mouth.
After a short while, she revived and breathed. Then she opened her eyes:
'God,' she said. 'I have slept so long!'"

From The Lais of Marie de France, Eliduc (c. 1155–1170)

The Other Geneviève opened my door just after Matins and found me
well. That's to say, it was clear King Death hadn't touched me, and there-
fore, I should be allowed to leave the room. My host noticed my stained
chemise and sheets and offered a linen rag stuffed with absorbent moss.
Alone again in the room, I held up this accessory and noted the cord sewn
into the cloth. I realized I could tie this around my waist, like a girdle, to
hold the linen and moss between my legs to catch the blood. My host had
encouraged me to wear the clean clothing I'd found and come downstairs
to eat more pottage. As for my weeping, she pretended not to notice.

The wooden floor felt cool and good against my feet, though my
blisters broke against the floorboards. The wad of moss and linen stuffed
between my legs itched, and because I was unaccustomed to wearing
such an item, I waddled slightly. But I didn't dare remove it and risk
staining the borrowed chemise. Though the skirt hem was too short,
these new clothes fit well enough otherwise. I gripped the railing as I
descended the stairs and told myself, *I'm here now. I am a mortal woman
now. I will survive this. I'm going to keep myself alive.*

The Other Geneviève looked up from her bowl as I limped towards
her.

"Well, you are a mess!" she said, sucking the air. "Where are your shoes?"

My maker didn't give me any, I thought.

"Someone stole them," I said. I gratefully sat on the bench and rested my elbows on the table. I felt lightheaded and red in the face, realizing how much I would have to lie to this woman, the origin stories I'd have to create. How to keep the strands together and not lose any details?

She placed the bowl before me and a chunk of good, warm, black bread. I ignored her watchful eyes, losing myself in the meal.

"You are very generous," I said.

"I just want to share the good fortune that fell into my lap like a falconer's lost peregrine. I don't like to be alone either."

My eyes settled on a citrus fruit in a bowl by the hearth.

Another citrus! The fruit that had brought me to Michel's arms and Corvus' mouth. The fruit that caused me so much pain and changed my existence. I could almost feel its weight in my hands. Making indentations in the skin. Eating something so rare and so precious. A prayer. Here was another one rotting away, casual and quotidian.

The Other Geneviève traced my gaze and understood.

"Oh, that sour old thing," she blanched. "I don't know what to do with it."

"Are you going to cook it?"

"I don't know how. Do you?"

I shook my head no. "Well, if you're not going to use it, I'd like to eat it."

She scrunched up her nose and stuck out her tongue. "That's not for eating, just cooking. You'll make yourself sick."

Little blood vessels gathered around her nostrils in spidery tendrils. Wrinkles gathered at the corners of her eyes when she smiled. I found her very pleasant, but her face wasn't smooth.

I noticed things like pores and blemishes now. While the statue of Sainte Geneviève never spent much time considering human flaws, Geneviève the mortal did. I wondered how other people's physical appearance measured against mine.

The Other Geneviève was no limestone saint, but she was still very pretty. The fact that I thought she was pretty despite the flaws surprised me.

"Don't let it go to waste. It's expensive," I said. "Please, let me eat it."

She pursed her lips. "You will not like it, but if you insist, it's yours."

I curled my fingers towards her, and she placed the fruit in my outstretched hands.

I began to bite.

"Bloody bad week, take the skin off. You must peel it first. Don't you see? You can't eat that."

I watched her manipulate her knife, the way she peeled the layers. "Like this." She looked at me and smiled. "It's bitter; I promise you will not like it."

A tart burst stung my mouth. I coughed and spat out seeds, but I felt alive.

"Satisfied?" she asked.

No, I thought, laughing to myself. One citrus wasn't nearly enough, not even with mortal teeth and a tongue. No amount of food or drink would be enough to satisfy me. I wanted to taste Paris' riches but also return to the cathedral and be with Corvus. I wanted the impossible. I wanted to eat the entire city.

"You look so disappointed," she said.

Who was this soft, fleshy person with soft lips? The light on her face was so glorious—the round tip of her nose, her round brown eyes. Her hair was so dark and thick and wavy. I shied away from my host because I knew I was insatiable, I wanted to absorb the whole room, and she couldn't offer everything I wanted.

She jabbed a piece of meat from her bowl, and her eating knife glinted like a warning. "Helping you was the right thing to do," she said.

"If I were the sort of person, I could have done you a lot of harm," I said. "I hope you don't help everyone you come across."

"I help as many people as I can. Helping those in need with our resources is the only way we will survive the horror." The Other Geneviève shrugged. "You may think I'm naïve, strange guest, but I know in my heart I'm right. My personal safety? What is that? It's worth the risk. King Death wins when we abandon each other.

"Besides," she said, looking at me from the corner of her eye. "I suspect you also know what it means to have to trust strangers. It makes you more discerning, doesn't it?"

I didn't know how to answer her question, but I did know that she reminded me of the Archangel Michel, talking like that, talking about right and wrong. Though something about her was gentler, more confident than Michel ever was. She spoke simply, stating the obvious like she didn't need to convince me.

"Talk to me," she said, narrowing her eyes and taking my hands between her rough palms. "I've seen you before. You have an unusual, striking face. Who are you?"

"My name is Geneviève, just like you. I was born on Rue du Cloître-Saint-Merri beside the Église Saint-Merri."

No, I wasn't. I was born in a quarry, and I must never forget it.

"How did your lips get bruised?"

A gargoyle bit them. A gargoyle I may never speak to or touch again.

"I had the illness. I slept a very long time, and when I recovered, my skin was pale, my lips were purple, and everyone I knew was dead. I don't know what else to tell you. I don't want to discuss it."

She squeezed my hands and spoke slowly. "I understand. I, too, survived the illness. King Death left a nasty burn on my right side!"

She lifted layers of wool to reveal her thin torso, ribs moving under pale, pimpled flesh. A mark, black as a raven's feather, stretched from beneath her armpit and breast to her belly's soft folds. My lips opened in surprise, and she tapped them with her finger.

"We share a name and scars," she said.

I had overheard stories about people surviving King Death, victims' fevers breaking as they broke from his grasp by either strength or will or excellent luck. I had never dreamed of meeting such a person and felt guilty for deceiving my host. Now, she believed we were bonded over a grim and rare experience. But I *had* survived a strange transformation and wasn't quite sure what I was now. Maybe we did belong together.

"The illness also took my spouse. King Death lets us live and ignores some of us altogether. I'm not sure why that is. My spouse had a perfect heart. He was far more sincere than our friends at the Auberge de la Mer. There is no good reason why God took my spouse and didn't lay his divine hand on Eudes. More proof that prayers and saints can't save us—we, the living, must care for each other."

I squeezed her hand. Beneath the table, in my free hand, I pressed the torn-up citrus peel. Poor Isabelle. In this body, in this kitchen, it felt foolish to believe that eating one piece of fruit, an offering, could have created a force as powerful as the illness. My understanding of the world beyond the cathedral had been so limited.

Eat the offering, or don't eat the offering. I now believed there was nothing I could have done to fight the illness. We, the guardian statues, had always served the people—the living. We were their stories. We were *their* creations. They loved us so much; they brought us to life.

And weren't the elements of life in all things? In water and stone? The world was bigger and more mysterious than praying to a statue.

"So, that's why I want to help," The Other Geneviève continued. "Have you ever met the beguines at the Hôtel-Dieu? I admire their work in caring for the ill. I thought about joining them, but that would mean leaving this house, and—truthfully—I'm much too comfortable here."

The beguines! Isabelle.

"Yes, I've heard of them. I saw them in the parvis with their apples on Adam and Eve Day!"

"I was there, too!" My host was suddenly very excited. "But why didn't I see you? You are so tall. I would have noticed you!"

"We must have just missed each other."

"Well, I've heard that some beguines also survived the illness. That's why they can touch the patients at the Hôtel-Dieu and not get sick—if you've had it once, you're protected. You could go there, Geneviève."

I didn't want to go to the Hôtel-Dieu. Not just because I'd lied and hadn't really survived the illness, but because I, too, was already comfortable in this home. It was warm, and it smelled good. Outside, Paris was damp and confusing.

"Maybe," I said, lowering my eyes.

"In some ways, it might be harder than the kind of work you did before. But in other ways, it might be better." She gave me that curious sidelong glance again. "You know, you can talk to me about your life before the illness. We all did what we had to do to survive, and I judge no one."

My eyes widened with realization. The Other Geneviève thought I had been a femme de Samedi, and so did that merry little group playing tric trac in the Auberge de le Mer. But why? They'd found me wearing such comically nunnish clothing. Was it the full coin purse? The orange hair? Because I was a woman who appeared to walk through Paris alone and unafraid?

That and more, I reasoned. I was a Donnadieu, and though none of these people had ever met me, they were confident they had seen my face before in public spaces. A figure hiding in the shadows of their peripheries. It made sense.

I smiled to myself and shook my head. The likeness of Sainte Geneviève had been mistaken for a whore, and it would be prudent of me not to correct anyone who made this very understandable mistake. I wouldn't have to invent stories about my past. I wouldn't have to invent a husband and a household that had never existed.

She stood abruptly to move a kettle over the fire. "Your feet look terrible. You must be in so much pain. I'd love to bathe them for you. May I, please?"

I consented and watched her pour the heated water into a simple wooden basin. She prepared the bath with lavender and rose and gently lifted my feet into the basin one by one. I closed my eyes and exhaled. Her soft cloth rubbed away dirt and dried blood, and her fingers massaged my heels and soles. I felt self-conscious; no one had seen my skin before. No one had touched it like this. The water turned brown, but The Other Geneviève wore a small smile as if she enjoyed it. She offered a scuffed pair of leather ankle boots—the only shoes left in the house that fit me.

Later, in my room, I played with my skin.

I had the suggestion of a belly button. Just a sliver, just an indentation, enough to look convincing at first glance. The slice of a chisel into limestone. I pressed my hands to my belly and felt the rise and fall of my stomach. The softness of my hair. A suggestion of an umbilical cord that had once connected me to something like the suggestion of a mother. Some strange source of life. The suggestion of something more than a mother; I didn't have a mother the same way that other beings did, not like The Other Geneviève. My mother came from something older and ancient, something from stone, some materials made from the bones of all mothers and fathers, the bones of ancient beings.

Limestone was still my lineage. My mothers and fathers were ancient. Ancient creatures turned into stone a mortal with a good eye had chiseled into an effigy of a woman they had made a saint.

My mouth opened in the darkness, feeling saliva drip from canine tooth to lip, gasping as I reached between my legs.

Weeks passed and there was no sleep at night. I knew bodies needed sleep, but mine resisted rest until dawn seeped between the shutters. My lullabies were roosters, braying donkeys, barking dogs, and conversations in the street below at Prime. The Other Geneviève tried to break me of this habit, knocking on my door after terce. I slept through the mornings and afternoons so soundly; she often had to enter my room to make sure King Death hadn't taken me. Meanwhile, my host could never stay awake past Compline—the hour I began to feel most awake and alive. Otherwise, I was a good guest.

While I slept, my host cut up carrots, cabbages, and parsnips and turned them into stews. She used her absent employer's money to purchase household goods from the markets and our next door neighbors. She dusted the tapestries and polished the sword collection in the room once used for entertaining. She washed the sheets by the public wells, losing herself in the repetitive work.

Because I couldn't make myself rise with The Other Geneviève, I offered to be her guard and watch the house through the night's deepest, most vulnerable hours.

The Other Geneviève could take care of herself. After all, she had lived alone long before I'd met her. I even suspected she knew how to use the swords. Still, I wanted to care for my host and protect her.

While she slept in the silks draped across her employer's canopied bed, I walked up and down the stairs and through the kitchen, nursery, and children's room. Sometimes, I'd brush dust from the figures of trees and birds engraved in the gilded cradle, and I'd push the broken baby walker across the floor because the creaking sound soothed me. The children's room contained three wooden bedsteads, each nearly big enough to fit an adult. I'd press my hands against the feather mattresses and rub the fine, woolen coverlets between my fingers. In each of these rooms, windows with real, glass panes overlooked the narrow streets.

The servant's rooms were downstairs, adjacent to the kitchen and hearth. Here, straw mattresses stuffed with feathers stretched across the stone floor. The room that had belonged to The Other Geneviève contained a simple wooden desk for writing and a set of scales. She'd used these tools to manage the household expenses. A single window with a thick, cow-horn pane let in muted light.

In the spacious room where the goldsmith had entertained his clients, I sat amongst the tapestries and weapons and ran my hands over these creations. The nubby wool and cool iron. My favorite tapestry stretched from ceiling to floor and depicted a woman seated upon a scarlet canopied bed. She was naked except for the blue garment draped across her hips. A lithe man approached her, equally naked save for his winged sandals. This tapestry had been the work of many hands, woven with as much care as my maker had sculpted me. I wondered if the figures in this scene also felt and lived.

I couldn't resist the cellar pantry at night. Sugared tarts, peeled hazelnuts, and a bite of andouille sausage or boudin. Just a bite. The Other Geneviève always let me eat whatever I wanted, willing to sell a metal spoon or a piece of the lady's jewelry to keep the pantry full, so I knew she wouldn't forbid these nightly trips to the kitchen. But eating alone in the dark was thrilling. To take more than my share. Unwatched. Alone to savor. No one awake to tell me to stop, that I'd had enough.

The Other Geneviève didn't mark feast days, so I began to lose my sense of time.

We often bathed together. My host would lead me to the large wooden tub within the walled garden. She poured heated water from a jug into the basin and covered the top with a cloth tent to capture steam. Seats were carved into the bottom of this structure, and we sat in them, across from each other, enjoying the warmth with half-closed eyes, naked. We shared a cake of soap and spun-up garments made of bubbles while we washed our hair. The Other Geneviève was not ashamed of her long, gnarled scar. I always tried not to stare at it or at the dark tufts of hair between her arms and legs. I tried not to look at her short, pretty neck and the folds around her belly. The freckles dotting her upper thighs.

"Before the illness, servants were never allowed to use this," she said the first time we shared a bath.

I caught her looking back at me and felt self-conscious. Did my skin look as warm and pliable as hers? Did my blemishes and markings look more like rough stone or the work of a slipped chisel?

"You are so familiar to me," she said for the dozenth time. "I swear we've spoken before."

"We've never spoken," I said. "We must have only seen each other in passing."

We rinsed off the soap, dried ourselves with fine linen towels, and walked inside wearing only our chemises.

One evening, The Other Geneviève and I sat at the kitchen table, shelling peas for the next day's pottage. She told me she'd heard something odd that day at Les Halles market: a statue had been stolen from the entrance of Notre-Dame. One of the big statues of a saint. No one she'd spoken to remembered which saint.

I swallowed. My cheeks flushed hot.

"Why would anyone steal it?" I asked.

"To sell, of course," The Other Geneviève said.

She quickly moved to news she'd heard in the market: the hundreds of men who'd gone missing after a recent battle with the Anglo-Gascons and a king dead in the northern city of Frankfort, of either the illness or poisoning. She was especially excited to talk about groups of servants organizing to demand their employers pay them more—now that King Death had created a shortage of workers.

This routine. How long would it last? How long could I live like this in a house? Eating vegetables, eating chicken from the bone. A life of warm fires, baths, and hot food. Sneaking blood sausage in the dark.

I tried to remember the first time I climbed down the West Façade. I tried to remember how it felt to step on a cushion of wet, mutable earth for the first time. But with each passing day, it was harder to remember Corvus and my former existence. Even the weight of Michel's fury—how he twisted his round face into an angry star—had dulled.

April and May passed. A haze of warmth, comfort, and days I forgot to count. Then came June and midsummer. Becoming a creature of blood and sinews had transformed my understanding of time. A beating heart and hungry gut made the hours go quickly. I lived from one bodily need to the next.

Sometimes The Other Geneviève talked about her spouse. He was a servant who had worked for a parchment maker's family. When the two met during mass at Saint-Severin, it was love at first sight. The two had exchanged their marriage vows at dusk beside the Seine. Love was much easier for servants, after all. Their marriages did not require priests, witnesses, or lengthy negotiations between family members. The Other Geneviève's employers had not married for love—not the way she had. Oh, she had been so lucky! Her dead husband was the most handsome, kindest man on earth.

Good Sky, I didn't want to hear another word about him.

"I wish you would tell me more about your past," she said one night before Compline, her voice gentle and shy in a way I'd never noticed before. We sat side-by-side at the hearth table, warming our hands over a single candle. "Tell me more about your family. You can even tell me about your work."

Her voice trailed off and my breath caught in my throat. I felt my heartbeat against my chest. Our hands grazed each other's as they flitted over the candle flame. I didn't want to invent stories. I didn't want to lie to her any more than I had to.

"I'm just Geneviève Donnadieu," I said, trying to convince myself. Part of me believed that if I repeated my new name enough times, I could make my story true.

CHAPTER XXI

July 1349

I couldn't stay inside when the full moon lit up every chamber in the goldsmith's house. I didn't know how The Other Geneviève slept soundly through this midnight light. I wanted to wear my borrowed cote and mantle and wander the streets. I heard laughter out there. And music: flutes and drums. I wondered if it came from the Auberge de la Mer.

My host trusted me with many things—most things, it seemed. After all, she trusted me enough to sleep with me inside the house. But she didn't trust me enough to offer the key to the gate. I could enter the garden but couldn't leave the walls, not if I wanted to return.

I knew where The Other Geneviève kept her wine. She told me that she'd begun to purchase it from Eudes and would buy more cool, pale wine to balance her humors during the summer months. But lately the weather was cool and rainy, so it was beneficial to keep drinking the darker, warmer wines. If it wasn't possible to visit the Auberge de la Mer tonight (how I wanted to play a game or two of tric trac!) I didn't see the harm in enjoying a cup of wine beneath the moonlight in the garden.

I finished my first cup before I even stepped outside. Oh, it was delicious! Neither sweet, nor bitter, but satisfying like my hosts' stews.

The big clay jug felt lighter after I poured myself a second and third cup. No matter, The Other Geneviève had an endless supply of coins. She could simply buy herself another jug.

I tugged my mantle tight around my shoulders and closed my eyes against the breeze. This moment felt *so* right. I was made for full moons and stars and walking alone in gardens. I began to laugh; I realized that I was happy for the first time since I'd become skin, blood, and bone.

Two shapes propped against the house caught my eye. I walked towards them and yelped with delight, nearly loud enough for The Other Geneviève to hear. The owl and the peregrine! I had forgotten these shapes that had led me across the Petit Pont, to the Rive Gauche, to The Other Geneviève. When I'd had no direction, these kites guided me.

I possibly owed my survival to them. Now here they were, in The Other Geneviève's home, as if they'd been waiting for me all this time. I imagined her flying the kite while she wore the sun on her cheeks and her exhilarated smile.

I picked the owl first. It was made from smooth, thin fabric painted white and light brown. Silk. A wooden bar ran between the wing tips to hold the kite's shape. Round black eyes set in a heart-shaped face gave the kite an endearing, quizzical expression. I took the peregrine in my other hand. It was made from the same soft material, and its eyes were lined with severe and elegant markings.

Such delicate, wispy fabric. Nearly translucent enough to catch sunlight or moonbeams. If there were ever spirit birds fit to fly between worlds, they would look like this. Could it be true? Could these be the birds Isabelle asked me for? Could these birds speak to Isabelle's dead on her behalf?

I knew these kites belonged to The Other Geneviève's employers. That they were another luxury, bought or traded for entertainment, just like the swords and tapestries. But when The Other Geneviève flew them, they had power: enough power to draw me from across the Seine and the Rive Droite. In my hands, they could have power, too.

I had to fly one, so I chose the nocturnal animal, the owl.

I unraveled the kite string. Ran through the garden. If I closed my eyes against the breeze, I could almost convince myself I was running across the cathedral grounds. I felt the wind's pull and the string's give, as the owl climbed towards the moon for one perfect moment. She was so beautiful, so ecstatic. I couldn't believe I was flying her.

I felt so happy!

It was either a current of wind or my happy hand forgetting and letting go. One moment, I held the string; the next, the owl sailed out of my hands and over the walled fence.

God's blood, no!

No, no, no, no, no, no!

This kite was not mine to lose. The poor peregrine slumped against the wall as if grieving its companion. I wouldn't let this precious treasure get lost across the wall—I would retrieve it and bring the bird home.

I was a grimpeuse.

I closed my eyes and pressed my forehead to the wall, commanding my hands and toes to find the proper strongholds. *Show me where the gaps and ledges are—I am a child of stone, too.* But this architecture didn't speak back. There was no enchantment to guide me. No way to gain purchase. Nothing to hold onto. I climbed and fell, climbed and fell, climbed and fell until my hands, knees, and chin were scraped.

Why was this so hard? Why couldn't I speak with stone anymore?

I sunk to the ground and pressed my back to the wall, hugging my knees close. Why couldn't I make my body do what I wanted it to? My face fell forward into my hands. I hated this body, I hated this weak flesh, I hated shitting and pissing and bleeding. I missed being a beautiful statue.

"Geneviève." My host stood on the threshold with her double doors wide open. Moonlight wild on her pretty brown hair. "What are you doing out here? Why are you crying?"

She ran towards me when she saw my hands. "Bloody bad fevers, you're bleeding!" Then, she sniffed my mouth. "You're drunk! When did you get into the wine?"

"I lost your kite," I admitted.

She listened, baffled, as I explained what happened moments before she stepped outside. I slumped against the wall, hiccupping while she unlocked the gate door and entered the free, open night. I longed to follow her, but I was too embarrassed. I knew I was drunk, and I hated letting her see me like this. Moments later, she returned, holding the owl, her eyes and mouth bunched tight with worry.

Inside, she bathed my hands. Her chapped fingers felt so good against mine. I inhaled and closed my eyes, my heartbeat so hard against my chest. Corvus' mouth receded into my memories, no longer relevant. The Other Geneviève was all I saw. Now, I was grateful to be mortal; I loved this body. I felt so grateful to be *alive*. I understood! This feeling convinced me I could live forever. Nothing else mattered, just me and her washing our hands in this moon-bright house. Her hands passing over mine forever and ever.

"Again, tell me why you flew the kite."

"I saw it from the Île de la Cité. It was beautiful, so I followed it to the Rive Gauche. Maybe it's because I was so lost that I thought it was a bird that could fly between the worlds. The worlds of the living and the dead. Someone once told me some birds fly between the worlds—birds accompanying the dead. And maybe there's a way to speak to these birds—or speak through them. The kite led me to you."

"I've never heard of birds like that, but I certainly understand your wish to speak to the dead. Who are you really? Tell me."

"Geneviève Donnadieu."

"I know your name. Tell me who you really are. Share something from your past with me."

I suddenly felt so lightheaded that spots danced across my field of vision. No more lying. No more hiding.

"I'm the statue of Sainte Geneviève. For one hundred years, I stood on the West Façade of the Notre-Dame Cathedral, guarding it. That's why I look so familiar to you. You've seen me many times before."

Before she could speak, I cupped her face and kissed her dry lips. Together, we inhaled. Her mouth was soft and forgiving. She tasted like the milk and animal liver we'd eaten that evening. I knew I tasted like stale wine.

"All this time, I've been waiting for you to kiss me," she said, breaking from my arms. "Now you can tell me something real."

"I just told you."

"You drink my wine, you eat all my food—don't you dare think I don't notice—and now you nearly lost my kite. Tell me who you are really, or I'll make you leave tonight."

Her free hand clutched the dirty eating knife on the table. She pointed the edge at me, and I drew back.

"Why won't you tell me the truth?" she said, teardrops beading at the corners of her eyes. "I need to know where you came from! I'm trying so hard to feel like I know you."

"I'm telling you the truth as best I can. I don't know what else to tell you."

"I want to keep you here with me, but I don't trust you! The least you can do is tell me something about who you are. I don't care about your old profession; I just want to feel like I know you!"

"I'm telling you everything! I drank water and became human. Why don't you believe me?"

She aimed her knife at me. "Bloody bad day, I'm sick to death of being lied to and cheated. After everything I've been through, after all I've lost, after everything I've given you, I at least deserve your respect. Get your things and leave," she said, swinging the knife as if to throw it. "Don't you think for a moment I can't defend myself! I know how to use this knife. I know how to use all the swords in this house."

I ran up the stairs and retrieved the ugly, old-fashioned garments my maker had given me. My purse, which was fortunately still full. The golden falcon comb at the bottom of the chest. My feelings were as big, hot, and overwhelming as the white moon.

The Other Geneviève didn't trust me? Well, then, I would give her something to truly mistrust. That falcon comb? Mine.

Downstairs, in the common room, anger melted to tears again.

"I can't go out there at this hour; I'll get robbed. Please, please, please, don't send me out there tonight. Let me wait until morning."

"No, you won't—you know how to navigate the night. It's nearly dawn, besides," she said, pointing the knife at the door. "What happens to you next is not my problem."

I crumpled to the floor. "You don't care about me?"

"I want to, I really do," she said. "But I don't know you."

She pushed me out beyond the wall and locked the door. I stood there, uncertain, for what felt like hours and listened to The Other Geneviève cry from the opposite side of the wall. It wasn't safe for me to walk in the street before dawn. I considered returning to the Auberge de la Mer. No—Eudes and Meli would want to know what happened with my host, and I didn't know how to discuss that.

Finally, the bells rang for Prime. On typical nights, this hour marked the end of my vigil over The Other Geneviève's home. I had no bed to fall back in, so I willed myself to stay awake. But I found I wasn't alone in the street: monks rose to pray at dawn. Scholars began their classes on the fifth hour. I followed them and all the city's ringing bells towards the Île de la Cité.

I suddenly hoped I'd cross paths with the flagellants; I wanted to join them. I wanted to strike my skin with a barbed club to distract myself from my shame.

But there were no flagellants, only spiderwebs to catch the morning mist.

CHAPTER XXII

What am I doing here? I thought as I pounded the dark wooden door. *What am I doing?* While I waited for someone to appear, I answered my own questions. *I'm here because I have nowhere else to go, and I don't know what to do with myself until the next new moon.*

The Hôtel-Dieu's entrance looked like Notre-Dame's with high, rounded arches that ended in points. Formidable and earnest stone angels guarded the alcoves at either side of the threshold. I stretched my hands towards them, wondering if they had ever been enchanted. But they were out of my reach. Summer rain darkened the sky and made me shiver.

I heard footsteps and whispers behind the door. It cracked open just enough for me to see the beguine on the other side. Her skin was so pale she nearly looked translucent, and her eyes were as light and gray as Bathsheba's. Her mouth and nose were covered with a plain cloth secured beneath her plain linen wimple. Her face was almost hidden, but she was very young. She could not have had more than thirteen or fourteen years.

I spat out the line I rehearsed while walking from The Other Geneviève's house.

"By God's grace, I survived the illness," I said, pointing to my bruised throat and lips. "I'm here to give my thanks and offer labor."

The girl hesitated.

"You want to work?" she asked. Her voice sounded uncertain.

"Work in exchange for a bed."

The girl muttered to herself and opened the door. She proceeded to investigate my face, lift my arms, pull back my sleeves and feel my wrists.

"Well, you are tall," she said. "And strong! Your cheeks are still plump."

Strands of straw-colored hair poked free from her wimple, and I wanted to tuck them back in.

How did someone so young become a beguine? How did she end up at the Hôtel-Dieu? I couldn't ask her, because I knew she would demand answers to my own questions, and I didn't have a story. At least, not much of one. After The Other Geneviève, I resolved to never tell anyone about my origins again.

"I have a dowry." I held out my coin purse. "It's yours if you'll take me."

Her eyes wrinkled at the corners. I hated giving up this money. If the beguinage didn't offer me food and shelter in return, I didn't know what I would do. I kept the falcon comb from Constantinople tucked between my chemise and cote—a secret I could not part with, not only for its worth, but for its beauty.

"It's not up to me to accept that money—that's a decision for the nuns—but we're to never turn away someone who wants to work. Come inside and spend some time with us," the girl said. "Then you can decide if you'd like to take beguine's vows."

She closed the door behind me, and we entered a poorly lit chapel. The space was small and plain, with no places to sit. This room looked more like a threshold than a place to linger and worship—save for one arched window and a crucifix mounted to the wall. The glass window was the most beautiful part of the room, its multi-colored pieces fashioned into flowers. Squares and triangles of red and blue light played across the floor.

As for the crucifix, a bronze man pinned to a cross, head turned to the left in depicted anguish. Slits in the metal for a rib cage. Rather than fill me with awe and reverence, the crucifix disturbed me. It felt grotesque, like its maker had felt too much pleasure capturing this figure's pain.

The young beguine took my hand and pulled me through the chapel's back door. I was in a courtyard, blinking and shielding my eyes in the misty light. A round burbling fountain with a steepled centerpiece rose in the middle of the space. The land was divided into quadrants. The area nearest the church, where the beguine and I stood, was covered in soft green grass. Rows of herbs and vegetables grew directly across the northeast quadrant. The adjacent northwest quadrant was a row of mulberry and birch trees. Another garden of sacred plants like yew, hazel, and roses grew in the fourth section.

"I've never met you before, and I know just about everyone in Paris. Where did you come from?" she asked. "Who did you work for?"

What to say this time? What would sound respectable? I searched my memories for stories The Other Geneviève had shared about the gossip she'd heard in the markets.

"Rue du Cloitre-Saint-Merri," I blurted out. "My husband and I were the stewards in a candlemaker's home."

The beguine studied my face with narrowed eyes.

"King Death took them?" she asked at length.

"Of course," I said.

Her face softened. "You know, you do look familiar. I must have seen you in the parvis before."

"That's very likely," I said.

Seemingly satisfied, the girl continued our tour. I exhaled. At least someone believed me without needing to pry.

"This is where the sick men sleep," she said, pointing at the long rows of buildings. "There's the kitchen, and behind that, the laundry room. We need laundresses more than anyone else. Maybe that's how you can help."

"The sick women sleep over there. Those long halls are where we sleep." She spun again. "The nuns sleep here. Some male workers assist male patients, but most don't live here. They have separate apartments.

"Over there is a little woodworking shop. Some of the patients— well, the monks and nuns too—have trouble walking. Sometimes the Beghards come and make walking sticks and even some fancy supports that fit under the arms," she explained. "They even made one for me to use when my leg bothers me. It doesn't hurt today though.

"What else? Oh, the latrines. Of course, you know how to use the latrines."

I did not. I had only used a chamber pot in The Other Geneviève's home. But I would adjust. Whatever it took to keep myself sheltered. Alive.

Alive until I'd figured out how to return to the Portal of the Virgin.

I followed her through the medicinal garden and behind the female patients' hall and beguines' dormitories. "Here you are," she said, leading me to a wooden structure that jutted over the Seine. She threw open her arms and exclaimed, "The latrines!" as if she had built them herself and took personal pride in them.

The stench made my eyes water. I nodded and covered my mouth in the folds of my cloak.

"There's some blood moss in our quarters," she continued. "Take only what you need each time you use the latrines. We've found that every time we've left it in here, someone always takes more than their share."

A door swung open, and an angry face burst from the stinking hall. Another beguine half-hidden in undyed wool.

"Who is this, Héloïse?" she hissed, grabbing the girl's arm. "What have I told you about opening the gates to strangers?"

Héloïse pointed at my mouth. "She says she survived the illness and wants to help us. She was a steward in a candlemaker's house."

The beguine made a great point of eyeing me up and down while she secured a cloth over her mouth. The arch of her eyebrows looked familiar, though I couldn't place where I'd seen her. She looked older than Héloïse by several years but still very young.

Héloïse stamped her foot. "We need more workers! I can't do all this laundry by myself. Look at my hands!"

She held out her scaly, cracked hands. Her thumbnail was ridged and yellow.

"Why do you want to help the patients here?" the other beguine asked. Her voice was stern, but I knew she wanted my help, that she needed me. The eagerness in her brown eyes betrayed her.

How funny that this place I had feared so much offered my best chance for survival. I had to survive through the new moon, then I would smash up Michel and return to my pedestal—if that was still possible. I wanted to believe I could become stone again. I had to try.

Before I could answer her question, she lifted my mantle and searched the folds of my garments. I held my breath and hoped she wouldn't find the comb.

"I need to know that you're not a flagellant and didn't bring any weapons here. Héloïse, you need to search everyone who enters these doors. Do you hear me?"

"But Madam du Faut says we're to welcome anyone who longs to help!"

"Not when the laypeople and church both long to persecute us."

"By God's grace, I survived the illness, and I want to do my part to help and heal the ill," I droned.

"Pisse-froid, this place is a death trap. No one comes here because they want to help the patients," the other beguine said. "You heard stories about the payment, didn't you?"

"I don't know anything about payment."

"Liar."

"I don't think she cares about money. She offered a dowry," Héloïse said, waving my purse.

I wish I could have told them both the truth. That would have been easier than making up these stories about myself. I was tired of creating a woman.

The beguine's eyebrows lifted, and approval flickered in her eyes.

"Well, perhaps. Normally, we wouldn't be so quick to accept a stranger but, Héloïse is right—we are desperate for help," she sighed. "We especially need help with the bedding. It needs washing constantly."

"What else do you need help with?" I asked.

The beguine and Héloïse looked at each other and laughed so hard that tears came to their eyes.

"Everything," Héloïse snorted.

"Don't ask for more work. You'll find that's plenty," the older beguine said. "Everyone comes here thinking they'll make easy money and suckle the teats of the Hôtel-Dieu's benefactors. They learn, sooner or later. We might let you take on more if you can do this work."

They led me towards the long hall where the nuns and beguines slept, two a bed, six beds per room. I would share a bed with one of the beguines. Everything about this room stank of old clothes and sweat. The floors were dirty and caked in mud and so were the opaque cow horn windows.

"I'm telling you, we don't have time to clean our halls; we're too busy with the patients," the stern beguine said.

I wanted to ask for her name, but she intimidated me. I feared she would change her mind and make me leave if I asked her the wrong question. Our agreement felt so fragile.

Patients looked out their windows and watched us pass through the courtyard, and I avoided meeting their eyes. I knew I stood out with my height, long neck, and bright hair.

The beguine turned around.

"What is your name?"

"Geneviève Donnadieu."

"Donnadieu? And you said you were a former steward for some important household?"

"A candlemaker," I said, lowering my eyes.

"Donnadieus don't just become the stewards of respectable business households." Her eyes narrowed and her voice chided but not without some gentleness. She sounded tired. "Who are you really, and why did you come here?"

I crossed my arms. When I stood up straight, I was nearly a head taller than her.

"You want to know the truth? Very well then. I was a femme de Samedi. A common putain, as you would say. I'm here because everyone I cared about is dead and I have nowhere else to go."

I thought that would scandalize the smug look off this haughty woman's face. No matter what I said, the people wanted to believe I was a Saturday woman. Well, then, a Saturday woman's story I would claim.

But the beguine's expression softened.

"I figured as much," she said, sounding relieved.

Even Héloïse looked unaffected.

"Well, no need to lie about it," the beguine continued. "I'm just grateful you're not another flagellant."

My mouth opened. That was it? I hadn't expected them to welcome me so readily.

"What is your name?" I asked the beguine.

"I'm Isabelle de Grantrue."

CHAPTER XXIII

Feast Day of Sainte Marie-Madeleine, July 1349

Good Sky!

Isabelle de Grantrue! *My* Isabelle. The person who had offered me my first bite of food. Of course, it was! I had seen her with the beguines on Adam and Eve Day. In my desperation to keep myself alive, I'd nearly forgotten she was here. She hid her curly dark hair beneath a wimple now; her cheeks were thinner, her light brown skin was paler, and half-moons darkened the hollows beneath her eyes, but sure enough, this was her.

She was still with the beguines and the illness hadn't taken her!

I shook my head and smiled to myself. Isabelle did not know that the woman standing before her—the woman she thought was a femme de Samedi—was the one she'd prayed to. The one she'd believed was Sainte Geneviève.

Maybe one day, I would tell her who and what I really was, and she would believe me. But not today. Today, I only wanted to stay alive.

I lowered my head and followed Isabelle and Héloïse to the refectory, a bustling, windowless hall that reeked of sweat and onions. Isabelle and Héloïse washed their hands at the entrance, untied their face masks, and served themselves bowls of pea pottage. I followed behind and did the same. The room was filled with beguines and nuns who met my gaze with curious faces. Isabelle led me to the back of the room, away from everyone else, where we sat at the long table. I had just begun to sip from my bowl when Isabelle elbowed me.

"Wait until the prayer," she said.

An old Benedictine nun presided at the head of the table. "Oh Lord, bless this bounty," she said.

Everyone but me bowed their heads. I studied the nun's black woolen robes and veils that covered her forehead, neck, and chest. Like most nuns, she wore two veils, one made of white linen beneath the dyed black. I squinted. The white veil was clasped beneath her neck with a little gold pin. As I stared, I realized it was silk and not linen.

Isabelle nudged me again.

"Amen," we intoned.

I ate eagerly, ignoring the sounds the other beguines made as they slurped and sucked their teeth. The bog bean pottage was bland and saltless, but I ate it all anyway. I hadn't realized how hungry I was or how I'd craved the warmth of a fire after spending the night outside The Other Geneviève's house.

Laughter and the din of conversation. I overheard talk about the patients: sores that wouldn't close, moles that turned black and doubled in size, and a lot of overgrown, yellowing toenails.

"There's a fungus outbreak," Héloïse whispered to me. She covered up her bad thumb beneath her free hand. "Be careful not to walk barefoot."

Isabelle joined the conversation, eating with her back to me and leaving me alone with my humble bowl. I longed for the cuts of stolen blood sausage in The Other Geneviève's kitchen. I watched Isabelle from the corner of my eye and took in the din of voices, the shadows on faces, some grave and some laughing, all at once reminding me of the West Façade. I missed feeling part of the cathedral—part of something whole.

I counted ten beguines. Some were young, no older than twelve. Others, I suspected, had lived sixty years, if not more. Their clothing was similar, though not identical. Plain wimples covering their hair and undyed cotes fastened tight at their necks. I studied their faces. I listened to the nuances in their language and tried to pick up parts of the dialects I understood. I recognized accents from the low countries: Flemish and Dutch. I also heard Coptic and Ethiopian. Isabelle and Héloïse both spoke with the accents of the Parisian merchant class. I fiddled with my bowl, feeling out of place and self-conscious and wishing to belong.

"Isabelle, who is your tall, striking friend?" asked the eldest woman, pointing her chin towards me. She had a clear, French Flanders accent. Her tone was neither welcoming nor hostile, but mildly curious.

"Madame du Faut, this is Geneviève Donnadieu," Isabelle said, rising to stand close to her superior. "She arrived this morning and offered to help with the laundry. I was going to present her to you after we ate. I didn't know if I should consult you first—I know beguines must never turn away willing hands."

Isabelle leaned close to the older woman and whispered. I heard her say something about Saturday women.

"She offered a dowry!" said Héloïse.

I felt Isabelle nudge Héloïse beneath the table. Madame du Faut's white face turned red. "Isabelle. Héloïse. We do not belong to a monastery. Becoming a beguine requires a simple commitment, not a dowry. Did this woman offer her purse as a donation?"

Isabelle shook her head no.

"Why did you think taking this woman's money was acceptable?"

"Madame du Faut, we need the money. The patients aren't getting enough to eat, and neither are we," Isabelle said. "The royal donations have dried up; every other week we're accused of heresy. And what about the beguinage? It needs repairs, and repairs are expensive."

"Isabelle," Madame du Faut said, taking her hand. "This may be true, but taking someone else's money is wrong. That is not what we do here. If Madam Donnadieu wanted to offer a donation, that would be acceptable, but we can't demand her money as a dowry. We must keep our property and remain the lord's faithful, *voluntary* servants. That is what distinguishes us from nuns. Everything we do is voluntary."

"Perhaps she wants to repent," Isabelle suggested. "We should encourage that, shouldn't we?"

"Bloody bad day, I'll donate it!" I blurted.

My offering to Isabelle in exchange for the citrus.

The table fell silent. Two of the beguines exchanged an open-mouthed look and said, "Goodness!" Madame du Faut dropped her spoon and went all the way red. Isabelle chuckled under her breath. Soon enough, everyone was smiling.

"Bloody what?" Madame du Faut said. "Women who fear and follow God don't know anything about bloody bad days, or weeks, or anything. I don't know who taught you such crude speech, but if you intend to spend any amount of time here, you must never repeat those words again."

I bit my lower lip and closed my eyes. I wished I were still with The Other Geneviève. I wondered what she would make of Madame du Faut.

"You may donate a portion, not your entire purse!" Madame du Faut said eventually. "My daughter has a silk business you should invest in. You'll earn it all back and then some. You'll never have to do *that kind of work* ever again."

Repent. Always repenting. The statue of Sainte Geneviève had to repent. Geneviève Donnadieu had to repent.

Always repenting.

Groveling in the shadow of some past mistake.

"This silk business," Isabelle sighed. "Paris is saturated with silk. What about velvet?"

"What about crimson dye?" Héloïse asked dreamily.

"Not anymore!" scoffed another beguine. "The silk merchants keep dying, and businesses keep shuttering."

My eyes narrowed. The edge of my lip tugged upward in the beginnings of a snarl. I was so weary of everyone expecting me to repent, as if I needed to apologize for being carved into creation. I was tired of apologizing for breathing. It was not my fault that mortals and statues saw me as either Sainte Geneviève herself or as a whore, though I was neither.

"I am proud of all the work I've done, and I am not here to repent," I growled, looking Isabelle straight in the eye. "I am here to help you."

Isabelle snatched the purse from Héloïse and pushed it towards me. I opened the drawstring to retrieve an offering, but Isabelle waved my hand away.

The bells of Notre-Dame rang for Nones, ending our conversation. I exhaled, relieved that my outburst hadn't cost me my bed. The beguines talked over the clamor as we filed out of the refectory, through the chapel entrance, and into the parvis. I followed, listening to Isabelle and Madam du Faut argue over the price of bread and meat and what it would cost to repair the decrepit beguinage in the Lombard neighborhood. Their voices turned faint and tinny.

I realized we were walking towards the West Façade and the Notre-Dame.

I closed my eyes. I didn't want to see Michel's arrogant, glowering face as I entered through the Portal of the Last Judgement. Nor did I want him to recognize me; I didn't want him to know I was still alive. When I finally destroyed him, I wanted the blow to be a surprise. I pulled my hood over my forehead and lowered my eyes, feigning a pious posture. How far I'd come. I'd climbed down these walls as the likeness of Sainte Geneviève. Now, I entered these doors as a femme de Samedi.

Ahead of me, Isabelle and Madame du Faut continued their argument.

"You must learn your place. We have reasons for doing things the way we do. You are very, very young, Isabelle. You must learn patience and respect."

"We can do some things better. Hasn't the illness taught us anything?"

"Isabelle, respect!"

I followed them into the nave, where we took our place at the back of the throng amongst the Beghards, and I noticed the subtle, sidelong glances some people cast us. If Madam du Faut and the other beguines noticed, too, they acted as if they didn't. The cathedral swirled with colors, faces, and the heady scent of frankincense and myrrh. Stained glass threw flecks of color onto the floor, turning black and white marble red, blue, and green like ripe fruit. I traced the vaunted ceilings and the pointed arches with my eyes. This was humanity's idea of heaven.

Héloïse stood beside me, balancing on her tiptoes to see the choir and altar. Meanwhile, I could easily see over all those many backs of heads and realized I was likely the tallest woman at mass. A few people outwardly stared and when I returned their curious gazes, they looked the other way.

The choir and altar were positioned within the eastern side of the cathedral, opposite the West Façade's three entrances. A priest I'd never seen before, dressed in white robes, began Nones with offertory prayers. I understood the Latin, the expressions of gratitude to the Lord for so many blessings, but my thoughts drifted elsewhere. Who was that man draped in silk in the center of the nave? Could that be the spice merchant? He had grown so gaunt and gray. And that short woman standing several rows in front of me. Was that the apothecary owner, Marguerite? Her shoulders had slumped. Where was her handsome husband, Robert?

The choir sang many melodies that rose and fell together. Some voices were a low drone, and others crested the highest notes. Bathsheba had taught me how to admire these textures of sound, and I felt that familiar pang of longing, wishing she could stand beside me.

Lulled by the choir, I lost myself staring at the placid painted cherubs and statues. A world of statues inhabited the interior of the cathedral, too. A world I'd never known about before. Were they made of limestone? Cleaved from the earth's warm belly? Did they come to life on the new moon? Or were they as lifeless as L'Ecclésia and Saint Etienne?

We statues who guarded the cathedral's exterior came to life in darkness. Was the inside of Notre-Dame ever dark? Or was it always lit by so many candles?

I couldn't imagine how these statues could come to life in the face of so much human light.

If they did have wakenings, did we speak the same language?

How many times had I stood in the façade imagining what the inside of the cathedral looked like? How often had I felt frustrated and bewildered because I couldn't see beyond the parvis? I leaned against a barrel-bodied column and tried to take comfort that this was my home.

The beguines prayed, and I mouthed along. Gloria. Gloria. I wondered how this massive structure stood upright. I wondered what Corvus would look like if he could slide from the cathedral into the mortal world.

Would he look like a man?

A demon?

If I walked outside and stood in front of the North Façade, would I be able to distinguish him from the hundreds of other gargoyles? I wondered when I would get the opportunity to try.

With so much to look at, I gave up listening to the priest. My eyes settled back on the people, and I began to notice empty spots in the rows. Spots that I knew had been full just one year ago. I fought to swallow a lump in my throat. How many people had the illness taken? Everyone crossed their chests in unison, and I struggled to mimic them. The stench of unwashed clothing and bad breath mingled with incense smoke wafting through the air. This mass evoked no special feelings in me, but standing amongst the people did.

I was inside the Notre-Dame Cathedral of Paris. My home.

The realization was so overwhelming that I suddenly grew lightheaded. *Do not faint*, I scolded, willing myself to stand upright. *If you faint, they will think you have the illness.* I leaned against the column and closed my eyes. Would this priest ever cease his chanting? When would this mass end?

I opened my eyes to Héloïse's open-mouthed stare.

"What?" I hissed, louder than I should have.

"Are you alright?" she whispered, balancing on tiptoes to reach my ear. "You're so pale."

I leaned down to answer, "There are so many people."

"Are you going to faint?"

"I'm trying not to." I said through gritted teeth.

Héloïse looked between me and Madam du Faut. Then, she tugged my sleeve to pull me closer. "I have to urinate so badly I might wet myself," she said. "You can escort me to the latrines, and we can both get some air."

I nodded, grateful for the unexpected kindness from the youngest beguine. She grabbed my wrist, and we hurried out of the cathedral through the West Façade, heads bowed, eyes fixed on the ground. I didn't look up again until we were outside and standing before the Portal of the Virgin.

"Come on," Héloïse said, tugging me.

I managed to catch one backwards glimpse at Bathsheba.

Days and days passed. I fell into the rhythm of washing. I loved doing laundry. I loved the laundry hall: an enclosed courtyard with rows of slender columns and arched openings that overlooked the medicinal garden. I loved scrubbing rough linen against the flat basin stones. Removing urine, shit, vomit, and menstrual blood. Hanging sheets to dry in the sun, new again, ready to swaddle and warm the ill. I loved this repetition. The Hôtel-Dieu was not so grim after all.

I wore the humble, plain garbs my maker had given me, except for a wimple. Madam du Faut gave me one of hers, a white hood that covered my neck and forehead entirely. My eyes were my only visible feature when I wore my mask. But when I was alone in the washroom—which was often—I took the mask and wimple off and rolled my long sleeves well past my elbows. I tucked my skirts into my belt and sunned my pale, veiny legs. The sun and water on my skin felt warm and refreshing. This skin felt alive. When the water was freshly pulled from the well in the early mornings, I felt tempted to dunk my whole head in the basin. I felt drawn to swim. Instead, I tapped my feet, compelled to dance across the stone floor to a rhythm I heard only in my head.

Isabelle warned me that the laundry was the least joyful work, but the thought of the ill scared me, and I was grateful I hadn't been asked to ferry meals into the sick halls. I wanted to stay in the laundry, with sun and breeze streaming through the arches. I imagined the sick halls the way I imagined tombs. To witness death was to be reminded that this body of mine would also die.

I stopped repeating euphemisms like King Death, King of the Death, or even the illness. It didn't matter what you called this force; death was death. Dead was dead. A name did not mean the people could negotiate with it, as if it were simply the spice merchant in the parvis.

I had been closer to death when I was a statue. I had been carved from the bodies of dead things turned to stone. I was a collection of bones of many skeletons. But now I was more than bones. Blood, yellow bile, black bile, and phlegm. If I remained flesh, I would return to bone. And when I died, who would know to carve me into Sainte Geneviève again and give me back my life?

I would drive myself mad if I spent my days thinking about death, but I couldn't help it. I had spent one century believing that my days, nights, and wakenings would last without end. I had been *immortal.* Deathless. Now, I grieved my eternal life; I mourned myself.

Waking and eating watery pottage. I hid my face as I entered the cathedral for prayer. I collapsed beneath the coverlet in the bed I shared with Héloïse after Compline. Pretending to sleep between Matins, Lauds, and Prime, but staring at the wooden ceiling in the dark and thinking about death.

CHAPTER XXIV

After a week at the Hôtel-Dieu, the beguines slowly warmed to me. All except for Isabelle, who had a sullen, withdrawn demeanor. When the other women shared stories about the families, friends, and homes they'd lost or left behind, Isabelle was as quiet and guarded as me. More than once, she caught me stealing glances at her while we sat at the long table in the refectory. Sometimes, I saw her watching me, a distrustful, curious look in her golden-brown eyes.

I wondered if she was still mad that Madame du Faut discouraged my offering. When Isabelle had complained that the beguinage on the Rive Gauche was in ruins, I believed her, but I also suspected she had something else in mind for my donation. Something she kept secret.

Where Isabelle was skeptical and distant, the beguine Marguerite was open and welcoming. Every day, after Prime prayer, she visited me in the laundry to see if I needed assistance. I always declined yet she often stayed behind to share bits of gossip—usually about Madam du Faut and her daughter's failing silk business. She also told me that at least four other beguines had been femme de Samedis from the Rive Droite, and that fact made my heart sink. Did these women wonder why they had never encountered me? What kind of lies would I have to tell them if they asked me about my old life?

Marguerite looked to have thirty-five years and had brown skin and an oval face. She told me her grandfather had come to Paris from

Ethiopia to study at the university but left after a year to become a merchant. He met and married Marguerite's grandmother in Salerno before returning to Paris, where he spent the rest of his life translating medical and theological texts. Marguerite was the youngest of five children—her father, a dignitary—and the rest of her family was scattered between Ethiopia, Rome, and France.

Marguerite was the only sibling in Paris. She'd dreamed of studying at the university, but she was not allowed because she was a woman. Still, she was the most educated of the beguines—fluent and literate in five languages, including Greek. That's because she had been a nun.

When she told me, I nearly dropped the sheets I'd been washing.

"Oh yes, I was a sister at Cluny Abbey for nearly fifteen years," Marguerite explained. "For most of those years, I convinced myself I was happy. I had as many tablets and books as I could ever want. Books! Do you know the specific joy of holding a manuscript? Of tracing your fingers over those golden images and copying those sacred words?"

I shook my head no.

"Of course not, you don't know how to read," Marguerite sighed. "And I have more than my share of work cut out for me. I can't teach you. But maybe, one day you'll learn, and then you'll understand why I stayed at the abbey for as long as I did."

"What happened? Why did you leave?"

"It just wasn't enough." Marguerite shrugged. "I didn't feel the same kind of devotion that the other sisters felt. I didn't want Christ to be my bridegroom. I respected those nuns because they felt it. But I didn't. I was only in it for the knowledge.

"When the illness began to spread towards France, I knew it was time to leave. I couldn't deny my feelings—or lack of feelings, rather," she continued. "Our abbess encouraged me to join the beguines at the Hôtel-Dieu, that way I could continue to learn and live in service without pledging the rest of my life to the Church. No vows! You see, I've always felt that I was made for a bigger life than managing a household, yet joining an abbey felt wrong, too. So, well, here we are."

In Marguerite, I saw a reflection of myself. I knew what that specific longing felt like—the desire for more and the shame and confusion that came with it.

"What did your family say?" I asked. "Were they angry that you left the abbey?"

"I wrote to them as soon as I learned about the illness, but I don't know if my letters ever arrived. I don't even know if my parents are still in Ethiopia. I don't even know if they're still alive."

"How do you stand it?"

"I don't know. I'm not stronger than anyone else. I just endure, because what other choice do I have?"

Now, Marguerite had begun teaching the beguines from a series of texts about women's medicine: the Trotula. The book contained recipes for vaginal pain following childbirth: mix rue, mugwort, and camphor into a suppository; healing vaginal tears: apply comfrey, cumin, and cinnamon; relieving hemorrhoids: wormwood, southernwood, henbane, and cassia; reliving intestinal pain: cooked sesame; ending a pregnancy: asarum, yarrow, and tansy. Marguerite had successfully used some of these remedies on the Hôtel-Dieu's patients and was now scouring the texts for recipes to cure the illness.

I could not read in any language, but I understood illustrations.

"Wandering womb!" Marguerite spat, waving the leather-bound book. "What is a wandering womb? Who wrote this section? It was obviously a man. You can tell which texts the men wrote—all based on theory and superstition. Nothing practical."

The hour was between Matins and Lauds, and the half-dark moon brightened the dormitory. Marguerite sat cross-legged on the bed she shared with Agnès, an older beguine with round cheeks, merry blue eyes, and a ruddy complexion. Marguerite held the book in one hand and a candle in the other, and the three of us spoke softly to keep from waking the sleeping beguines. I knew I would become friendly with Marguerite and Agnès when I realized we were each inclined to stay awake until Prime and would have if we didn't have responsibilities during the daytime. We huddled around the book in Marguerite's lap, dressed for sleep in our chemises, our hair free of our wimples. Agnès worked braids through her thick, gray and blonde hair.

"Men think our wombs wander around in our bodies when we're not pregnant, like little mischievous animals," Marguerite continued. She pointed to an illustration of a naked woman with yellow hair, her breasts the shape of little arrows. A comically angry face scowled in the center of her belly.

"They think the womb can crawl up into our head!" Marguerite said, thumping the book. "Or our feet! And cause us to become deviant in all kinds of ways. These ideas! If my womb was able to crawl around in my body, I would feel it, wouldn't I? Have they ever asked a woman to confirm whether this theory is true? I doubt it."

"They are obsessed with women's bodies because we bring life into the world," said Agnès. She was approaching sixty years and had three grown children. She and her husband had spent their lives working for a linen maker, and she was clever with spindles. The illness took her husband, her eldest child, and the linen maker last September. "I think they are obsessed with our wombs—and life—because they are afraid of death."

"Yes! That must be it!" said Marguerite, loud enough to stir the others from their beds. "They must think they can escape death if they can figure out life."

I listened, entranced. I had come from no womb, and yet, here I was, alive. I was the child of limestone and a sculptor's vision. I was stories passed down until they became real.

"How do you think life begins?" I asked Marguerite and Agnès, my voice soft and wondering.

"I don't know," Marguerite sighed. "But I do know these men are wrong about many things. We can learn so much through observation.

We don't need to explain the world with these groundless, wild ideas." She shook her head. "These priests and university men. They believe the planets and stars caused the illness! How could the planets and stars cause an illness?"

"We are all afraid of death," I murmured.

"When people take your work, and your voice, and your stories, and your history, that is another kind of death," said Marguerite. "Women have always known how to practice medicine, and the Church wants to take that from us."

A bed on the far end of the hall creaked, then came heavy footsteps on the wooden floor.

Madame du Faut illuminated in candlelight. The shadows playing on her puffy cheeks made her features look as big and exaggerated as a statue's. For a moment, she looked like Marie emerging from the darkness.

"Be quiet!" she hissed. "God forbid one of our clerical advisors hears you—we'll be disbanded and hung in the Place de Grève!"

Marguerite scowled but extinguished her candle.

"That old goshawk hears everything," she whispered.

Agnès rolled over to her side of the bed, and I returned to my bed across the hall. I lay awake until dawn and slept through Prime.

A great commotion flooded the front gates the next afternoon.

"Chickens!" the beguines shrieked joyfully. "We finally have meat! We'll finally have eggs again!"

"These aren't for eating," said the benefactor, a Benedictine scholar from the monastery at Jumiéges. "This is a gift from the school. The court doctors have found that live chickens absorb the illness. If you place a live chicken next to the ill and the dying, they might be cured."

Silence filled the courtyard—silence except for the clucking and shuffling of animals trapped within the baskets. There must have been forty or fifty live animals.

Agnès hid her smile behind her hand. Marguerite elbowed me and whispered, "See? These men and their superstitions."

"At least we'll have full bellies," Isabelle hissed.

A soft ripple of snickers gave way to laughter. Isabelle and the scholar exchanged a look, and, for a moment, I thought they, too, might laugh. The scholar looked familiar, but I couldn't place where I had seen him before. Just another nameless face in the parvis.

"No! Please, do not eat them!" the scholar pleaded. "Each chicken absorbs sin. They absorb sin and release it in each egg! They may cure the patients!"

"God bless your soul," Madame du Faut said. She shook her head but thanked the man profusely.

"Insanity," Marguerite whispered.

I gathered one of the shaking baskets and followed my companions towards the long-empty coop. When I looked over my shoulder, Isabelle gave the monk a terse but friendly hug.

"Thank you for everything, Louis," she murmured. "Tell my brother to visit." She turned to see me staring, open-mouthed, but she walked past as if I weren't there.

Louis.

Louis!

I knew that man looked familiar. A broad-faced monk with tonsured hair as fiery as mine. This was the young man I'd seen reassuring Celestine in the parvis all that time ago, before Celestine damaged The Child. How could I have forgotten him? I knew Jumiéges sounded familiar, too.

What a curious gift.

I hurried behind Isabelle, carrying the basket with both hands.

Then, everything made sense.

Louis didn't believe live chickens could cure illness. He didn't think they expelled sin in their eggs. Isabelle had put him up to this; she must have convinced Louis and her brother to urge their abbey to share resources with the Hôtel-Dieu. Because some scholars had so many theories about animals, this might have been the only way to convince them. No wonder Isabelle and Louis had hidden their laughter.

I followed behind the beguines, smiling.

Ten of the chickens didn't survive the afternoon. I couldn't bring myself to watch the slaughter in the kitchen, but I heard it plenty. Clucking and panicking as the knife cut feather and bone, separating muscle from organ. Even Madame du Faut refused to honor the monk's orders.

"Be grateful they're foolish enough in that abbey to donate expensive food like this and expect nothing in return," she chuckled. "They think we can live on cabbage, beans, and water; they wouldn't have given us such a generous gift if they knew we were using it to feed ourselves."

My chest felt tight when I remembered The Other Geneviève's knives and pantry. I remembered how we'd lived off her employers' savings, the money she made selling his spoons. How many times she came home with a new cut of meat.

I missed both her and her kitchen. It always smelled like fire, lard, spice, and bread. I missed peeling fat from cooked lamb. I also felt a stab of guilt for all I'd eaten. I wondered if I would ever eat that well again and whether it was right to covet such luxuries when the people who needed food the most were left with broth.

But hadn't we relished spending that old man's money? We had. The Other Geneviève hadn't eaten like that when she served her employers—their absence had allowed her to live in a way she'd never imagined. For once, she had lived the way the wealthy did. Was that wrong?

We divided three hens and cooked them in a broth to share amongst the ten beguines. The other seven were split up among the patients. Marguerite and Agnès prepared great bowls for two women who had recently given birth. New life! I was so surprised that anyone could give the light in *here*, of all places. But I was beginning to see that the hospital was not only the illness' home. This hospital was full of life.

The hours and days kept blending, bleeding into one another, beading up one after the other. Some moments slipped by quickly and were gone before I'd had the chance to appreciate them. Some stretched on as if without end. But time never felt as slow, steady, and consistent as when I had been limestone.

CHAPTER XXV

After three weeks, or thereabouts, at the Hôtel-Dieu, I realized I wasn't afraid of the patients anymore. I was curious about Isabelle, and I wanted to help her. Caring for the most critically ill was her domain. The others said she had been around the illness many times but had never gotten sick. Somehow, she was protected.

Héloïse and Madam du Faut had gotten ill but survived, so they assisted her. I was afraid of death, but as each day passed, I found that keeping my hands busy was the best way to keep from becoming obsessed with it. When I was occupied, death felt far away.

I wanted to know what had happened to the young woman who had placed a citrus in my hands and whispered prayers in my ears. I wanted to know what became of her in all the days between the last time I'd seen her and now.

I followed her into the kitchen after Nones prayer on L'Assomption de Marie.

"I would like to help you carry broth to the patients," I said, tugging my wimple to show off my scale-scarred throat.

She looked me up and down as if appraising my strength. "Are you sure?" she asked. "You've had enough of the laundry already?"

"No. Well—yes," I said, trying my best to answer honestly. "It does get a bit repetitive."

The truth was that I simply wanted to help her because she had asked for my help when I was a statue. Now I could. But I couldn't tell her so; I knew she wouldn't understand.

"Very well, then," Isabelle agreed. "You'll find this work is repetitive, too, but in a different way."

I tied my mask tight around my nose and mouth and followed Isabelle to the women's sick ward, carrying all the bowls I could manage.

She twirled around to face me, balancing four bowls of chicken pottage: two in her hands, two on her forearm pressed against her chest. "Don't trip," she smirked.

I nodded obediently, holding my offerings with care.

"Do not drop those," she said, gesturing at my bowls with her chin. "No matter how disgusting these patients look to you, and no matter what they do."

"I've seen everything. I will not think they're disgusting."

That wasn't entirely true.

The hall reeked of urine and a sickly-sweet tangy feces stench. My eyes watered. I worked hard to resist vomiting the pottage I'd eaten earlier. The feeling passed. The windows were open to allow a blossom-fragranced breeze. Most patients slept, but some pulled themselves upright to greet us.

The women's hall was organized like the beguine's dormitory but accommodated many more people. There were ten beds pressed on each side of the narrow corridor, headboards positioned against the windows, feet pointed towards the inside of the room. Each bed contained at least two women, if not three. It was true; their faces were covered with open sores, but the sores didn't frighten me. I noticed rays of sunlight streaming through the room, reflecting stars on the tile floor. Most of these women would die, but some would recover.

Isabelle was so *alive* in this room. She spoke with everyone, and for the first time, I heard her laugh. Low and musical. Her eyes wrinkled at the corners, and I knew she smiled behind her mask.

I followed closely behind Isabelle, obeying her instructions and holding the bowls to the patients' lips. We had work to do; we had people to feed. Many of them spit up their pottage, so we had to clean their mouths with linen rags and encourage them to eat again. I fought my desire to gag. I knew my disgust would not help these patients heal, and I wanted, very badly, for them all to heal. Paris had seen enough death. I also knew how easily it could be me in one of those beds next.

Hours passed and I began to feel comfortable, competent even.

"It is repetitive work, and it is often very sad," Isabelle said, "but it's not lonely work."

I remembered the woman clinging to me for salvation, her breath hot on my cheek, the citrus warm in my hands. She nearly seemed like a different person now. Confident. When she gave me directions, I didn't hesitate to follow them. I understood why Madam du Faut trusted her to manage the care in this wing.

"Are your parents still alive?" I asked, eventually working up the nerve.

"Of course not, are yours?"

In my mind's eye, it was January of last year again, and she clung to me.

My voice was barely a whisper. "Did they die in Messina?"

She looked up from the bed. "How did you know they were in Messina?"

I hadn't thought of an answer to that.

"People talk," I said, finally. "They were merchants, no? Your parents, I mean."

"Were yours?" she asked bitterly.

"No. My makers—my parents—have been long dead, I suppose. I never knew them."

"Of course. Your name is Donnadieu."

"What happened to your fiancé?"

She stood upright and stared hard at my eyes.

"How do you know I had a fiancé? I know everyone loves to gossip in this damned place, especially your new friend Marguerite. But I've never told anyone about him."

I shrugged. "I just assumed."

"He's dead, too."

"Is that why you came to the Hôtel-Dieu?" I asked. "Why did you become a beguine?"

Isabelle put down her stack of empty bowls and with her free hand, wiped a strand of hair from her eyes. "Geneviève, these are painful questions. Please don't ask me more, I don't want to think about them."

I lowered my head and apologized. We didn't say another word to each other as we carried the empty bowls to the wash bins.

After my first afternoon carrying chicken pottage with Isabelle, I began to visit the women's hall late in the night. I came bearing a torch in one hand and a bucket of fresh well water in the other. When fevers broke, the water was refreshing, and fevers often broke late at night during sleep. I began to skip Matins, Lauds, and even Prime prayer as I walked between the well and sick hall. How many trips did I make each night?

Water had transformed me. I drank water nightly, too, but I never turned back into the statue of Sainte Geneviève. Water never cured the dying either, and in fact, many refused it. But for others, water provided relief, and those women were grateful for the small sips and spoonfuls. They said, "Look for the lady with the light," and greeted me when I appeared at their bedsides.

After several days, Isabelle approached me in the laundry. "I wanted to tell you, thank you for helping me," she said. "People like you here. I hope, with your continued help, more patients will be able to leave this place."

I would have hugged her if her hands had not been clasped behind her back, and she hadn't spoken so formally. Instead, I bowed my head and smiled at her praise. Something had been righted; I had finally succeeded in helping Isabelle after all this time.

Now, when I returned to the West Façade, I would be at peace.

In the following days, I caught myself praying for the patients in the Hôtel-Dieu. Not just an imitation of a prayer, like the prayers I once echoed to the Sky. But a prayer in the mortal sense. A prayer to *their idea* of a god. Now that I was mortal, I understood in my heart and humors why the people wanted to believe in a god that looked like them and spoke their language. Why it wasn't enough to accept the sky's warmth or tempests. I, too, wanted to believe that a person who looked and spoke like me could hear me and answer me.

I wanted to know that all would be well.

I wanted the certainty.

The certainty that I would live forever.

So, I prayed, but only once or twice. I couldn't make myself believe, even though I wanted to.

But no one ever spoke of birds that flew between worlds, birds that talked with the living and the dead. Not the priest at mass, the monks, Madam du Faut, the beguines, or even Isabelle.

But those kites in The Other Geneviève's house. The silky birds. A falcon for daytime and an owl for night. They looked like they might fly between worlds. If I had to have a deity and if I had to give this deity a face, perhaps I wanted it to have the face of a bird.

I knew why Isabelle gave me the citrus all those months ago. But what was the meaning of the bird? What did Isabelle know about such spirits?

After Vespers prayer on the Feast of Saint Barthélemy, I grew bold enough to ask her.

"In the parvis, I overheard someone talk about a spirit bird that could accompany the dead to the Sky—I mean, Heaven. A kind of guide," I said. We were in the refectory, and I spoke between bites of hard, dark bread. "Have you heard of anything like this before?"

Marguerite looked up from her pottage.

"That sounds like the sirens from Ovid's poem," she murmured. "Bird women who accompanied Perséphone to Hades. Not exactly Heaven."

Madam du Faut cast a stern glance at Marguerite.

"But even Ovid got the idea from someone else. Let's see, if you speak of sirens, then you speak of ancient stories and beliefs from Greece," Marguerite said. "Sirens flew between earth and the underworld the pagans believed in. Now harpies looked like sirens, but they were horrors and stole food from people's mouths. I don't know if they were the spirits you heard about, but I have seen their images on ancient artwork."

"Harpies!" I said. "Some of the gargoyles on the rooftop of Notre-Dame are harpies."

"How do you know?" Marguerite asked excitedly.

Madam du Faut crossed herself and shook her head. "Enough with this conversation," she hissed.

Finally, Isabelle put down her spoon. "You're talking about Ba birds," she said quietly. "From Egypt."

"No, those are sirens," Marguerite said, "or harpies. In any case, they're Greek."

"I don't have nearly as much education as you, Marguerite, but I know that we're talking about Ba birds. They're spirits that are half-bird and half-woman, and they're part of an old, old belief system from Egypt," Isabelle said.

One of the old nuns at the opposite end of the table turned her head towards our conversation. She arched her eyebrows, and a small smile touched her lips.

"What a scholarly conversation," she murmured.

Madam du Faut scowled and said, "I can't imagine you mean that."

"Oh, I do," the nun replied. "The boys spend all day studying Aristotle and Cicero. Let these women talk about history, too."

"They teach *logic* in the university, not heresy," Madam du Faut hissed.

Isabelle ignored her.

"You know the Greeks ruled Egypt after Alexandre and took their ideas," she continued. "So, that's why you think they're Greek sirens."

"Enough!" Madam du Faut said crossing herself. "We don't talk about things like Alexandre or Egypt within these walls."

The nun shook her head and chuckled.

Isabelle turned towards me.

"Who was talking about Ba birds?" she asked. "Did you hear anything else?"

I shook my head no.

"Of course not," she sighed.

"Are they real?" I asked her. "Do you believe in them?"

Isabelle gave me a small, sad smile. "Of course not. Just ancient pagan beliefs. I stopped believing in silly stories like that a long time ago."

Madam du Faut stood and left the table.

"Just look how she's red in the face," Marguerite said, gesturing to Madam du Faut with her lips. "Let's not talk of this anymore. We'll make her so angry, her heart might stop."

"Don't worry about her," the nun said laughing. "She's all bark and no bite."

I smelled wine drifting from the nun's mouth and wondered where she kept her supply.

That night, I asked Isabelle if she knew anything about secret caches of wine and ale while we trimmed patients' overgrown toenails.

"Tell me about the Ba birds instead," Isabelle said. "Who did you hear talking about them in the parvis?"

"I don't know. It was after mass, and it was too crowded to see."

"But you must have recognized their voice. What did they sound like? I'm hoping maybe it was a cousin of mine."

"I don't know. I'm sorry." I felt bad for my lie and for giving Isabelle false hope.

"When I was very small, my father gave my sister and me a tiny statue of a woman with a bird's body," Isabelle said. "He had bought it from a Venetian who said it had come from Rome and before that, Egypt. He called it a Ba Bird. My sister and I played with that thing until it crumbled." Isabelle sighed. "I would do anything for another one."

A statue. Isabelle's spirit bird was a statue.

A statue as intermediary between life and death.

I didn't know how to put my thoughts and feelings into words that Isabelle would understand, so I said nothing and swept up crescent moon nail trimmings.

CHAPTER XXVI

"Evil can easily rebound on him who seeks another's misfortune."
From The Lais of Marie de France, Equitan (c. 1155–1170)

Feast of the Archangels, September 1349

The feast day for the archangels marked two months I'd spent at the Hôtel-Dieu. I lived and worked in the shadow of Notre-Dame, but with each day I spent in flesh, working among the living and the dying, I felt more human. I fought to protect my memories of the West Façade from my soft-bodied self. *Mon calcaire, mon calcaire, mon calcaire.* I repeated the name Corvus had given me like a prayer, though it no longer fit.

After what felt like a particularly long Vespers mass, Agnès pulled me aside and said we were going to a tavern in the Rive Gauche.

"I heard you've been wondering where that old nun gets her drink," she said, grinning. "Well, I found out! She told me how to find the inn that serves her."

Not only would we go to the inn, but we would have a chaperone more than willing to look the other way: Isabelle's brother Celestine.

Celestine was handsome and knew it, at least according to Marguerite. All the women had a crush on him, so he was very smug.

Agnès spat. "Ha! I don't have a crush on him."

"Neither do I," said Héloïse. She gripped the walking stick she carried when the pain in her left leg flared–a condition she'd developed after surviving the illness.

"You do," Marguerite said, crossing her arms. "I've seen the way you smile at him when you think no one is watching."

"Do you have a crush on Celestine?" I asked her.

"Absolutely not!" she cried. "I don't think he's handsome at all."

"But you just said—"

"Not the kind of man I like," said Marguerite. "But he thinks he's goodlooking, and other people seem to think he's good looking. So, be careful. That's what I meant." She waited until Héloïse had passed us before she leaned in close. "He's too much like his sister. They're both so arrogant."

"They lost their entire family," I said. "I don't know if they're arrogant—I think they're sad. Isabelle, at least. I don't know Celestine."

But I did know Celestine—sort of. I remembered him in the parvis, destroying The Child's mouth and hands with stone. Celestine, and all his fury, was why I had become the grimpeuse.

And I remembered him in the stairwell. How good he smelled.

Marguerite waved her hands. "We've all lost our families—including you. And we don't act like them, like we're better than everyone else."

Agnès released a long breath. "I think Isabelle should respect Madam du Faut more, as well as the other women who have been with the beguinage since at least 1320 if not longer," she said. "Isabelle has been with us for what, a year, maybe? She's already trying to take over."

"She is good at a lot of things, though," Marguerite conceded. "Endless patience when caring for the sick. Procuring funds."

"Madam du Faut is good at procuring funds, too," Agnès said.

"Procuring funds from unusual places," Marguerite amended. "She knows how to use her name to her advantage."

"Why did she want to become a beguine?" I asked. "It is an unusual calling for a merchant's daughter—especially one so young. Even with the illness. I'm surprised she didn't try to flee the city. Does anyone know why she came to the Hôtel-Dieu?"

Agnès shook her head. "Oh no, she's never shared anything like that with us. I don't even think Héloïse knows, and their backgrounds are similar." She watched Héloïse tug the Hôtel-Dieu's heavy gates and slip inside. Agnès shook her head again. "But with Héloïse, it's different. Her father ran up his debts long before the illness, and there was nowhere else to send her. She's been here since she was ten."

After the Compline bells, we met Celestine outside the Hôtel-Dieu's gates with three other scholars from Jumiéges.

Just as Marguerite promised, Celestine and Isabelle walked outside the group with their heads close together, whispering without a smile on either of their faces. I couldn't help casting backward glances at him, wondering if he would recognize me. A shock of familiarity from the night we met in the stairwell. He didn't seem to care about anyone else around him.

"They're both so stuck up," Marguerite whispered.

But I wasn't thinking about Celestine or Isabelle; as our merry group crossed the Petit Pont, I remembered the Auberge de la Mer and The Other Geneviève. I felt so ashamed of how I had left her home, of everything I'd told her. I knew she visited the Auberge de la Mer— what if she was there tonight?

"Where are we going? Do you know the name of the tavern?" I asked Agnès.

"Oh, I don't remember the name. I just know how to get there," she said. Then, she lowered her voice. "It does have a reputation as a gambling den."

I grew quiet and slowed my pace to let them pass me.

"Come on, Geneviève!" called Marguerite.

I shook my head *no*. "I don't feel good. I'm tired. I'm going back."

"What? You're never tired at night. Are you offended by gambling?" Marguerite asked, looking genuinely surprised.

"No," I said shaking my head. "Of course not. I'm simply tired."

"But you don't even have a key!" said Agnès.

"I do," said Celestine. "I'll walk back with you."

"How do you have a key?" asked Agnès.

"She gave it to me," Celestine said, gesturing to Isabelle. Several paces ahead of the group, she walked with her arms crossed.

"Thank you, Celestine," I said. "Let's go."

"What? You can't go back!" Agnès shouted. "I planned this night for you! You wanted to go just an hour ago!"

I *did* want a cup of wine or ale, but I *did not* want to run into The Other Geneviève.

I brushed them off with a gesture of my hands, turned and slunk towards the direction of the Hôtel-Dieu, my cheeks and ears burning hot.

Celestine and I walked in silence. He was the same youth I'd met in the cathedral stairwell, but his hair was even longer and curlier now, and his tonsure almost nonexistent. I wondered how he got away with that. He no longer smelled of his frankincense cologne. Had he run out or had he simply grown bored of wearing it? I thought about Marguerite's scorn. Was he arrogant? Did he seem unhappy walking next to me? I couldn't tell. He hadn't seemed excited to visit the tavern either.

But I felt excited walking next to him. The last time I'd seen him, I was a statue. Now, I could touch him. I wanted him to remember me, too.

"You look familiar," I said. "I've seen you before."

We had reached the center of the Petit Pont. From here, we could see the spires of the Hôtel-Dieu above the riverbank. We studied each other's faces in the starlight.

"Were you ever one of the night guards at the cathedral?" I continued. "I think I saw you there before."

"I spent the last year at Jumiéges but returned to Paris once or twice to visit my sister. You were at the cathedral so late?" He suddenly frowned. "Oh, of course you were. My sister told me you were a—"

"Yes." I interrupted.

I was so tired of my lies and of pretending that I was something I wasn't. I wanted to tell Celestine the truth. I am a statue. Your sister once valued me enough to pray to me.

"I have trouble sleeping at night," I continued. "I like to pray at Lauds because I'm most awake then. I suppose you never noticed me."

I pulled off my mask and wimple to let him take in my orange hair, the dark pools of my eyes, moon-pale skin, bruised purple lips, and the terrible scar at the base of my long neck. I held his gaze, searching for a flicker of recognition. He ran a hand through his curls and chewed on his lower lip. How strange that our paths had led us to this moment, where we stood face to face in the darkness again.

"It's odd," he said. "I'll admit you look familiar, but I know that if I saw you before, I would have asked you for your name."

My cheeks flushed. Of course, the other beguines admired him. He was full lips and smooth skin and clean teeth, and he smelled good with or without the cologne. In the stairwell, I'd wanted to reach for him. Press my mouth to his lips and neck. I knew that I could not.

But now?

Were his cheeks flushed too? It was hard to see him well with these dim, mortal eyes, especially since the moon was hidden.

The moon.

The new moon!

How had I lost count of the days? How could I have been so stupid? Tonight was The Wakening.

"I'm going to the cathedral to pray now," I said, stepping away.

"Wait—I'll accompany you." He took my hand, but I no longer wanted his touch.

"Please don't. I prefer to be alone."

"Are you sure? It's not very safe."

Good Sky, Geneviève, I thought. *How will you get rid of him?*

"Wait for me at the gates of the Hôtel-Dieu."

Before he could say another word, I began to run across the bridge, my boots clapping against the stone path, bouncing echoes across the Seine. I passed the spots where I'd met the old onion seller and the woman with her beautifying wares, and I wondered what had become of them. Distracted, I nearly collided with an ambling group of monks and muttered my hasty apologies. A pair of scholars hooted when they saw me and made lewd gestures, poking index fingers through rings formed with their opposite hands. I ignored them. I had no moment to spare on fear, anger, or irritation. I entered the parvis and kneeled panting at the Portal of the Virgin, my throat raw, my chest burning.

The figures that greeted me were silent and still. They were covered in chipped paint that looked dull red in this darkness. Dirty and moss-covered. I strained to see the faces of my old companions. Poor Denis standing between Gabriel and Uriel with empty hands. Could he still wake without his head? How did The Wakenings feel now that he couldn't see, hear, or speak? Was this night of life still worth it now that he'd been pitched into darkness? Or was touch enough? His hands were free now.

I looked at my own hands. What would I do, what would I make with them if they became my only way to communicate with the world? I remembered waking up in The Other Geneviève's house and spending an entire day exploring my new body.

Denis' hands were free to touch now. But no one was moving or speaking in the Portal of the Virgin.

They weren't even breathing.

Maybe I'm delusional, I thought. *Perhaps I was never a statue; maybe I was born with this flesh.* I traced the door jamb with my eyes and chuckled softly. Staring at the cathedral in this skin body made The

Wakening feel impossible. I felt foolish and embarrassed. *Of course, I was never a statue!*

But the figures began to shift. The longer I stared at them, the more I noticed their twitching fingers and subtle smiles. Angels Uriel and Gabriel turned their elegant heads to me. They were *so* beautiful. Mighty wings dripped down their backs; their long flight feathers grazed their calves. Placid, gentle smiles on boyish cheeks. They slowly moved in the shadows as if dancing.

"Geneviève, you came back. We thought you had forgotten us."

Marie crouched low on her pedestal to hear and see me better, her stone joints grinding against her weight like tree limbs strained against the wind. The Child clung to her right side. The little figures of Lilith, Eve, and Adam climbed onto her shoulders so they could see me, too—a sound like rocks tumbling in the Seine.

And then, another voice rang out, high and melodic. Feminine. Sharp and yet hollow at the same time. A voice like wind sighing through the cathedral's walls, like a choral echo. The voice of a ghost, but human in its tenderness.

"Geneviève."

How had I never noticed the tenderness in Bathsheba's voice before?

I held her gaze and tears beaded in the corners of my eyes.

"You can finally hear me!" she cried. "I called your name three times!"

So, this was how it felt to stand on the other side of the enchantment. Mortals never heard or saw us, because we were so improbable. They didn't believe we could come to life, so in their eyes, we didn't. It didn't matter that they had carved us from the skeletons of once-living things and made us with all their love.

But now I knew how to look at the cathedral and see it as it really was: alive. The breath caught in my throat.

"How pretty you are," said Lilith, her voice a rasp. "Your cheeks are so round and red. Your hips are perfection."

"Tell us everything you've seen!" Gabriel shouted.

"Tell us what wine tastes like," Uriel said, his familiar smile curling on his mouth.

I remembered how it felt to get drunk for the first time and grinned.

"Are you happy, Geneviève?" asked Bathsheba. Her voice was gentle, curious, and concerned.

I crumpled.

"I don't know what to do," I said. "I want to return to the West Façade, but how will I ever become stone again? And what will I do about Michel?"

Bathsheba knelt on her pedestal, one slow but fluid movement, as if she too were all sinews and humors. I knew her well: she longed to embrace me, but she would not climb down the wall. She had always been afraid of breaking the enchantment.

For good reason. I'd descended the cathedral and look what had become of me.

"So much has happened since you left," she began. "The West Façade is now divided. Half the Portal of the Last Judgement believes Michel is correct about the gargoyles: that they are swallowing prayers. They believe Michel is truly an archangel who can end the illness and protect the cathedral, and they believe you have betrayed him, Geneviève.

"But the other guardians see him for what he is." Bathsheba continued, spitting each word with disdain. "Broken. Power mad. Driven by desire to rule us as if he were our human lord."

"Now, listen to this," Marie interjected, holding up her free hand. "We owe Lucifer a great deal, because Lucifer is keeping Michel from leaving his alcove. If Michel moves, even to turn his head or shake his wings, Lucifer will push him from the wall! He will destroy Michel."

"Oh!" I cupped my hand to my mouth.

"But if Lucifer dares move, Michel will push him from the wall!" Jean interrupted. "So, you see, none of them will move now. We've heard that Archangel Michel and Lucifer have stood still and silent for the past two Wakenings."

Sylvestre straightened his pope's hat and leaned forward. "This impasse will not go on forever," he tempered. "We all know Michel is too bold to stand still in the Portal of the Last Judgement for eternity. Eventually, he and his followers will grow bold enough to make moves. They will catch Lucifer unguarded."

"Mark my words," Sylvestre continued, shaking his finger. "Conflict will spill into the other portals. It will spill into the other façades."

As he spoke, old paint creased at the corners of Sylvestre's eyes and mouth, and beneath that paint, I saw fracture lines in his face and hands. When I looked closely, squinting in the dark, I saw fissures in all of my companions' bodies. And moss. So much moss.

Jean cleared his throat, a rattling sound. His once-vibrant blue mantle was faded and dull now. He looked at Sylvestre.

"We have something to tell you," Sylvestre said. "The Portal of the Virgin is on your side, Geneviève." He shifted in his niche, cracking as he squeezed and fidgeted his hands.

"We were wrong to suggest a trial," said Marie, moving The Child to her other hip. "Whether or not you took Michel's flight feather is the least consequential of crimes. Moreso, we understand why you got tangled up with the archangel: You believed he could end the illness, and you wanted to help."

Jean rocked on the balls of his feet. "You can still help us!" he said. "You can destroy Michel before next wakening."

"Climb into his alcove and smash him," Gabriel scowled.

"Hammer his body to the wall so he can never leave," hissed Uriel.

I crossed my arms as I looked between each of my companions' expectant faces. They'd wanted to put me on trial. They were the reason I'd fled to Corvus and let him transform me. If it weren't for their doubt, I'd still be Sainte Geneviève. Bathsheba and Denis had been the only ones to trust me without hesitation.

And now they all wanted my help. For once, even the cherubim in the archivolts were silent.

I closed my eyes and squeezed the bridge of my nose.

"I can't climb anymore," I said. "Destroying Michel between The Wakenings is the only thing I've longed to do, but with these fragile, human hands, I can't reach him."

This wasn't entirely true. I *had* dreamed of smashing Michel, but I'd also spent the spring and summer months enjoying my skin. I'd enjoyed eating in The Other Geneviève's kitchen. I'd enjoyed my conversations with Marguerite and Agnès, hadn't I? Walking freely in daylight. My afternoons working alongside Isabelle, though she didn't talk much, and I wasn't quite sure I could call her my friend.

There were moments when I felt deeply happy as a mortal. There were also moments when I felt miserable. And the more that time passed, the less I thought about Michel.

"There might be a way to become part of the West Façade again," said Marie, her voice tentative. She held out The Child so I could see his perfect mouth and hand.

He was intact!

"Someone has repaired you!" I said.

The Child nodded. "Yes." His red lips stretched into a smile. "Mended with blood. Human blood."

"What do you mean?" I asked.

This time, Marie spoke. "One night, not long ago, the flagellants painted The Child with blood. By the next wakening, it had dried, and he was whole again."

I recoiled at the mention of flagellants. Why in the name of the cathedral's four façades had they covered The Child in blood? And where had this blood come from?

I didn't want to know.

"Destroy Michel. I don't care how. Just find a way," Marie pleaded. She turned to face me, and I saw her left eye was still shattered. "That's how we can stop this fear of gargoyles and suspicion about prayers. We can enjoy The Wakenings again."

"Then cover yourself in blood on the next new moon," she continued. "All those church doctors with their talk about the four humors—perhaps they were right. About blood, at least, how blood sustains life. Blood *is* life. Collect blood, then you can come home."

"Home." I let the word roll on my tongue. I knew I had to destroy Michel. Not only for my companions' sake but also for the gargoyles'. For Corvus' sake too.

"There is something else we need to tell you," Bathsheba said. "We've heard whispers of a new Sainte Geneviève statue. We've heard the people discuss mounting your replacement in the Portal of the Virgin."

The Other Geneviève had repeated a similar rumor while I lived with her. And if my companions had also heard it, it was likely true. I swallowed with realization. When the people placed a new statue in my niche, I could never stand in the West Façade again. I would remain mortal for all of my days.

"Transform yourself," Marie repeated. "Destroy Michel and come back to us before you are replaced."

"Besides," Bathsheba added. "The longer you stay human, the harder it might be to return to us."

She held my gaze.

Bathsheba shifted her weight as if preparing to climb from her alcove—*our* alcove. She let her foot hang over the edge and a solitary brick extended from the wall to meet her. I held my breath as she took her first step. Then another. Fear lit up her face.

"You don't have to," I said.

Oh, Bathsheba. Sister stone. Would our limestone bodies ever fit together the way they once did? Or had our disparate decisions and experiences created irreparable differences between us?

Could we truly understand each other?

Was there part of her that judged me for desiring the things that I'd desired?

And did I judge her for not desiring nearly enough?

Love. Freedom.

But what kind of freedom was a life spent lying to everyone I met? I couldn't tell anyone the truth about myself, the source of my existence.

Was there truly freedom in forgetting where I had come from? How I'd known a gargoyle called Corvus?

She took another step, and I reached for her. I was barely tall enough to graze the tips of her fingers. They were so cold.

And then, Bathsheba was standing next to me.

I threw my arms around her, pressing my forehead against her stone shoulder. Slowly, carefully, she lifted her arms and embraced me in kind.

I no longer had seams and planes and ridges in limestone that matched with hers. Holding her felt different now. But somehow, that difference felt all right. Maybe even natural.

"I will find this blood," I promised. "I will come home to the Portal of the Virgin."

A hand on my shoulder: Celestine's.

"Geneviève, who are you talking to?"

PART III

CHAPTER XXVII

Who was I talking to?

Marie stood upright with The Child in her arms. Lilith, Eve, and Adam posed at her feet. Mossy-shouldered Bathsheba had somehow faded into the wall and watched from her niche with her serious yet inquisitive face. Their whispers receded into the shadows as if they had never spoken. Celestine stared at me with wide, bewildered eyes.

"I was praying," I said. "It's nearly Lauds."

"Not for another hour. Don't you think standing out here alone at night is unsettling? Aren't you cold?" asked Celestine.

I wasn't cold at all. Inside, I was fire. What if it was really true and I could become a statue again? I only needed blood and another new moon, and I could return *home*.

"Let's go inside the cathedral," Celestine continued, rubbing his arms. "The flagellants stalk the city at this hour."

"Why do you care what I do?" I asked.

"My sister asked me to accompany the beguines. I want to keep my word."

"No, thank you. I'd like to pray alone," I said. "We've made it across the bridge, and the Hôtel-Dieu is right over there. No one will attack me."

"You would be surprised to know how many people are robbed before the cathedral doors."

"Ha!" I snorted.

"Well, I suppose you've seen it all, given your former profession," Celestine coughed. "Still, it's not safe. No one is invincible."

Celestine didn't know that I'd watched over thieves and drunks for over a century. If someone assaulted me tonight, I would fight because I remembered that I was made of something older and more formidable than flesh; I was part of the cathedral. I'd located echoes of memories of hands cutting and separating the stone from the earth, separating the woman from the stone, and I felt powerful. No one would dare rob me.

"What is so funny?" Celestine asked. "I mean, it is dangerous."

I gave him a small smile and crossed my arms. I didn't realize I'd laughed aloud.

Celestine gazed at the Portal of the Virgin. "I understand," he said. "I used to love walking around the cathedral late at night, too. I always volunteered to patrol the grounds between Matins and Lauds—that was before it became unsafe."

"Hmm." I casted him a sideways glance.

"Does it ever sound like the statues murmur?" he asked, hiding his eyes. "By God's bones, I swear I've heard them speak. And sometimes, on nights like this, you can almost see them move if you stand very still and are very quiet." He fidgeted his hands. Even beneath muted starlight, I could see how his cheeks flushed. "Now the statue of Sainte Geneviève is missing. They say the flagellants stole it, but it's almost as if it got up and walked away."

My mouth slipped open, but Celestine didn't notice.

"Sainte Geneviève is my sister's confirmation saint. She prayed and prayed to her, but nothing changed."

Celestine's lips were so round, pink, and smooth. His angled teeth were endearing.

"Don't worry, I don't really think the statues are alive," he said. "You know how it is, nighttime plays tricks on the eyes and mind. But sometimes I like to pretend they can hear and see us. I guess that makes me feel less alone."

He shook his head and huffed. "I don't know why I'm telling you this."

I inhaled and reached for the inside of his wrist. He had been paying attention to me and my companions after all. He had been thinking about us. While so many people took the statuary for granted, Celestine and his sister made me feel recognized—cherished. I understood now why he'd thrown stones at The Child. He had felt let down, not just by God—his idea of God—but by the statues.

If he spent enough time in my company, would he eventually recognize me? Would he remember the woman in the stairwell?

Would Isabelle ever recognize me?

But why did I still care so much about this family? I had had my time walking, dreaming, scrubbing soiled linens, eating bowls of lukewarm pottage, grinding cinnamon and comfrey, trying to kiss, drinking ale, shitting, counting up the sum of stolen coins, flying stolen kites, eating cuts of stolen meat in the middle of the night, learning to read, bleeding, laughing, dancing in the laundry, gossiping, being gossiped about, wearing the same musty wimple and beguines habits, crying, breathing steam in baths, standing inside the Notre-Dame Cathedral staring up at the vaulted ceilings in awe that people had learned to build such wonders. I had done these things. Now, I knew I could return to the West Façade.

Why did I still care about Celestine and Isabelle and their Ba birds and their gods?

"Let's go inside," Celestine insisted. "I'll wait with you until your beguines join for Lauds. Then you can walk home accompanied."

I followed Celestine close as he led me through the dark nave. I couldn't help it; I was curious about him. I wanted to know what else he had seen. I wanted to know how his mind worked. I wanted to learn about his family.

We were roughly the same height, and I breathed the scent of his washed, perfumed hair. Even without the cologne, he smelled vaguely of cinnamon, cloves, and sweat. Again, I imagined kissing the back of his neck, pressing my nose and mouth into the sliver of skin above his collar. I shook my head to shake away the feeling. No. No more trying to kiss. No more making mistakes the way I had with The Other Geneviève. I knew what I needed to do: I needed blood. I didn't want to distract myself with more people and their skin.

But I was curious about him, wasn't I?

This was more than curiosity about a man's body; I had seen plenty of men's bodies from the Portal of the Virgin. This was more than desiring a man for the sake of desiring a man. I felt curious about *Celestine's* body.

Bloody bad fevers, as The Other Geneviève would say. He smelled good.

I followed him to the wall where rows of lit candles winked through the gloom. Without moonlight to illuminate the stained-glass windows, we stood in near darkness. Soon, the clergy would arrive and flood the nave with torches and candles, but I felt like I stood inside a belly for now. The tremendous arched ceiling even looked like the roof of a mouth. I didn't mind the feeling; in a way, I wanted to feel devoured. Swallowed up and safe.

Celestine lit a fresh candle, and I cupped my hands around it to enjoy the warmth. Even inside the cathedral, our breath fogged up in the autumn chill. Celestine lit his candle, passing his hands over mine, and I closed my eyes. Standing still and facing him made me feel like we were back in the tower all those months ago. Would he recognize me now? An occasional footstep echoed across the choir and transept. I knew we weren't alone; monks and nuns occupied the cathedral at all hours. I could almost feel their stares burn my skin. By now, everyone knew about the new whore who had joined the beguines at the Hôtel-Dieu.

Candles and torchlight illuminated the serious-faced statues nestled in alcoves and niches. Shadows danced across their faces, but their blue eyes and rosy lips were still. If I pushed the stern little Marie, would she react?

I turned to Celestine and said, "Your sister is kind."

His laughter broke the stillness and sent echoes trilling over columns. From across the nave, someone coughed.

"Isabelle? Are we talking about the same person? You are perhaps the first person to ever call her kind."

"She is difficult to know but very kind to the patients."

"Do not grow too fond of her; she's planning to travel. To our family home in Messina, or maybe Tunis, whenever the illness passes."

"How? Why?"

"Our mother's family came to Paris from Tunis a long time ago, after King Louis IX's disastrous crusade, but we still have cousins there. She never told you?"

"We avoid talking about anything personal."

"She hates Paris."

A stab of sorrow. Despite the long hours we worked together, Isabelle and I were not close, not the way Marguerite and Agnès and I had become. Yet, she was a presence. It reassured me to sit next to her in silence as we trimmed the patients' ragged toenails. Her presence in my mind and in my life preceded the illness. She had been as constant as the walls of the Hôtel-Dieu and the cathedral itself. I couldn't imagine Paris without her now.

"She has also talked about returning to our father's home in Messina," Celestine continued. "Our parents and sister were living there when the illness began, and sometimes, Isabelle talks about returning there to honor them. But most of the time, she just talks about getting as far away from here as she possibly can."

"I suppose she has too many memories here," I said at last.

"It will depend on whether she can collect enough funds," Celestine said. "These days, all we have is our name, and Isabelle's fiancé left her with nothing."

Now it all made sense! I understood why Isabelle wanted my coin purse—it was not to repair the beguinage after all. She wanted to leave.

"And what about you? Are you planning to leave?"

Celestine scoffed. "I'd rather not make plans beyond the next month—who knows if I'll live to see them through."

He sounded so elegant when he spoke, the way his tongue rolled over each whispered word. He had an elegant way of standing, his back and shoulders held straight as if he, too, were carved from stone. I liked the way he listened when I spoke, how he answered all my questions. I liked what he had to say. I liked the way he looked at me. He had long, beautiful hands. His mouth was so pretty. The smell of his skin.

"So…" Celestine spoke with hesitation in his voice. "I don't live in the dormitories with other scholars. I rent a room in a home that belongs to my friend Louis' family. It's on the Rive Droite. It has its own private garden entrance."

"Why don't you live in the dormitories?" I asked.

"Well, I share the room with Louis when we're both in Paris. Believe it or not, his entire family is still alive, and they think the house is especially blessed or protected somehow." Celestine raised his hands and shrugged. "You've heard how the illness spreads in the dormitories, so when Louis invited me to live with them, I said yes."

"Where is Louis now?"

"Not here. Not in Paris."

I cursed the bells for suddenly ringing Lauds. Soon, the monks, nuns, and beguines would fill the nave, and, in my mind, I cursed them too. Celestine slid his hand down my back and lowered his voice.

"Cross the Seine and pass la Gréve. You will find the house on Rue de Violeite," he whispered. "Good night."

I approached the sour-faced Marie statue nestled in the transept crossing. I really did want to nudge her, just to see if she'd respond.

Instead, I lowered my eyes. "Pleasant Wakening," I said. "Do you know how I can find blood, so I can turn back into a statue like you?"

She said nothing.

CHAPTER XXVIII

One day later, at the cusp of sunrise, the answer came to me. It was so simple, so obvious, that I laughed and woke Héloïse, who had finally fallen asleep after Lauds prayer. She groaned, rolled over, and kicked me. I whispered a false sorry and grinned at the ceiling.

Bloodletting.

Bloodletting!

Bloodletting was a specialized skill administered by doctors, and when no one else was available, monks and nuns—people more learned than beguines. Supposedly.

I'd never seen this procedure before, but it was familiar enough at the Hôtel-Dieu. At least once a week, it came up in conversation at the refectory table. I'd learned it was not to be wasted on the dying—those patients Isabelle and I cared for. Keeping those patients warm and comfortable was our duty.

No, bloodletting was for the most vital patients, those who would live, to keep all parts of the body balanced: not too much blood, phlegm, yellow bile, black bile, air, water, fire, earth. We all debated whether bloodletting was effective. Marguerite insisted it was useless at the very best and, at worst, fatal. Yet the practice was older than the Greeks. It was a prized tradition. A practice that the likes of me—a Donnadieu, a laywoman—would never learn.

But that afternoon, I convinced the Benedictine sister fond of drink and knowledge to let me observe her work.

Her patient was an old man with patches of pink, peeling skin that covered his pale forearms and thighs. He sat on a squat wooden stool by the fire and flexed his bare, scaly feet. His condition itched like a wildfire and with untrimmed fingernails, he had scratched bloody paths across his body.

It wasn't the illness; this was something else, a disease of the skin that had tormented him since middle age. Looking at the marks made my own skin feel fiery and raw. Even his eyebrows were rough, red, and peeling. I rubbed my own face.

I thought practitioners drained blood by piercing a vein in the forearm. From the illustrations Marguerite had shown me, blood squirted into a bowl. And that was my plan: collect the blood by offering to perform the unpleasant task of discarding it. Store my supply in an unused apothecary cabinet. Perhaps I would have enough to paint my entire body by the next new moon.

To my dismay, the nun used leeches.

Leeches!

Parasites that were the color of dried blood and lay flat against the skin until they drank and swelled. Some were striped and patterned; some looked like pieces of wriggling feces on the patient's arms and legs. I covered my mouth, resisting the urge to vomit, while the Benedictine sister looked at my face and laughed.

I could manage piss, shit, and blood, but I recoiled at leeches. I should have been fascinated with them, but they were so utterly unlike any other living animal I had seen. They looked evil, like rotting citrus.

Rot, decay, and decomposition were part of the cycle. Chthonic things like leeches made life possible. But the leeches were terribly ugly. I didn't understand why I hated them so much—I just knew that I did.

"Isn't it fascinating?" the Benedictine sister asked. "Come closer, look!"

With a yellowed thumbnail, she slid a swollen leech off her patient's skin and let it drop into her bowl.

"Come closer," the nun insisted.

I swallowed down bile and obeyed. The nun retrieved a tiny blade and sliced the leech from end to end. Maroon-colored blood squirted into the bottom of the bowl, filling it.

Here it was! The blood that would return me to the Portal of the Virgin. The nun wiggled the bowl before my face as if to taunt me.

"Just look at this digestive system!" she said. "Doesn't it amaze you? You have no idea how happy it makes me that some people around here actually want to learn something."

I snatched the bowl and stared inside. The leech wriggled, pumping blood and slick yellow goo. The sharp, metal odor struck me at once and made my eyes water. I began to gag.

"Oh, come on! It's not that bad!" the nun scolded.

I cupped my hand to my mouth and dropped the bowl, splattering the nun's white veil.

"God's bones!" she cursed.

"I am so sorry," I said, hands trembling.

She wiped her face with the back of her hand and removed her veil. A smudge of blood remained on the tip of her nose.

"Let me take that to the laundry," I offered.

The nun batted my hand away. "I think you've helped enough for one day," she said.

I ran from the room as the patient's laughter rang in my ears. What next? What would I do now? I'd had one good idea, and I ruined it.

I stomped down the skinny corridor to the garden, arms crossed, eyes welling with tears. Another beguine approached from the opposite direction, and she called my name as I walked past her. I didn't look up to see who she was. With my head bowed, I saw only the hem of her gray skirt. Cold air stung my face as I unlatched the door and stepped into the bright afternoon.

The Child was perfect. Intact. Able to move and speak again.

Healed by mortal blood. But how would I ever collect enough blood to become myself again?

What a terrible task.

The fountain gurgled in the center of the garden, and I balled my hands into fists as I continued past it.

Since I'd eaten that citrus, I had tried so hard to be *good* and worthy of the name Sainte Geneviève. I had climbed the entire West Façade of the Notre-Dame Cathedral of Paris as my limbs ached, the wind struck my face, and the earth threatened to shatter me if I lost my grip. I'd longed to carry the weight of so many human prayers. To give the people something to believe in, some reason to hope. Now, as a mortal, I found myself performing a similar duty. I cared for the ill and the dying. I visited them throughout the night. I was the lady with the light. And despite all of my efforts, I could not overcome my nature. I was impulsive. Hungry and desirous. I could not quit making mistakes.

I slipped through the chapel at the entrance of the Hôtel-Dieu and cast a look at the crucifix. Should I pray to become someone different? A better version of Geneviève?

No.

I shook my head. I was tired of trying to become something different. I was tired of trying to be better than I was.

I wanted a release, a distraction. An invitation.

I'd received an invitation.

I exhaled. If I could do anything I wanted, without consequence, what would I do? What would I take for myself?

I remembered that dark stairwell and how I'd seen my reflection in Celestine's eyes. The way I'd ached to trace my fingernails against his skin, open my mouth against his until we shared the same breath.

I'd spent a whole century wanting and I would resist no longer.

My heart drummed as I crossed le Grand Pont and hurried past the crowded markets in the Gréve. I had never seen the Rive Droite, though I'd claimed it as my birthplace. I wanted to explore these streets with many open storefronts, but I couldn't waste time: it was almost Sext. The sudden midday heat—or maybe it was my nerves—made pools between my breasts and tugged my chemise to my skin.

I knew better than to knock on the front door; Louis' mother would question why a beguine called for Celestine unaccompanied and unannounced. I found the alley entrance—easily, in fact—and felt both surprised and impressed with myself for remembering the hurried directions Celestine had whispered in my ear.

He opened the door wearing nothing but his linen underpants and a shocked expression.

I couldn't help myself, could I?

"Oh, it's you," he said.

He looked like someone who used to be muscular, but softness was settling around his chest and stomach. He was so pale; I could see veins snaking at his ribcage. No perfume this time, just the smell of naked skin and uncleaned teeth. He opened the door wide and pulled me towards him fast before anyone outside could see us.

The bowl of blood and leeches was all forgotten as I fell through the doorway and onto his short straw bed. In the little room with shutters pulled tight to block the sun, I bit his lips, so wet, so flushed. A mouth of my own! A mouth that wanted to be kissed and bitten back. He let me push my tongue over his. He let me fuck his mouth with my fingers. This was a mouth made for eating citrus; this was a mouth that could swallow prayers.

Celestine covered my mouth with his hands and whispered for me to keep quiet, or Louis' mother, sisters, and that gossipy old neighbor would hear us.

How would the limestone-made absorb a person with skin-covered bones? Limestone to humors, limestone to blood and bile. I would find out. This body of mine that had wandered Paris for months wanted nothing else now.

Of course, I'd heard that sex with men sometimes hurt—especially the first time. But this would not be my first time, would it? I'd had Corvus. But then again, Corvus wasn't a man. Nor had I been a woman.

"Can I bind your hands?" I asked. I didn't want him to move or touch me; I wanted to do all the touching. I remembered all the stupid troubadour songs about cocks and asses.

"What are you smiling about?"

"I can't believe I'm in your room," I said. "No one knows where I am."

"What excuse did you use to leave the Hôtel-Dieu unaccompanied?"

"None. I simply left."

He smiled with his teeth, and the skin wrinkled at the corners of his eyes. He raised his arms above his head, an invitation to bind them as I'd asked. Hot cheeks and neck. Curled hair wild and disheveled, no sign of the tonsure. This was the most relaxed I'd ever seen him.

I wanted the smell between his thighs. Hair between his legs and beneath his arms. Grabbing his hair. Grabbing his cock. Soft belly.

I threw my terrible, frumpy garbs to the floor and that ugly wimple too. Nothing else in the world, just me and him.

My two fingers pressed together, entering his mouth, running fingertips against his tongue.

"Untie me," he ordered.

I did. He turned me onto my back and pushed my legs apart.

I thought of Corvus and how similar and different it had been with him and how Celestine would never be Corvus, no matter how beautiful he was. Corvus could fly; who could compete with that? No one. No one, no matter how soft and generous.

But I felt alive.

I watched Celestine's pretty, half-closed eyes and went hot between my legs. I grabbed his hair and pushed against his mouth. His tongue and fingers found places that made me swell. I bit the filthy sheets.

I thought of the things I did the first time I found myself alone with my body, locked in that musty room in the house The Other Geneviève kept. I remembered how I'd reached between my legs and spread my new skin until I came. As I watched Celestine's dark hair, I remembered biting, sucking, drinking citrus flesh.

Our thighs squeezed against each other. My fingers found his openings. Corvus left my thoughts. I swallowed Celestine and he swallowed me, the way I'd swallowed that fucking fruit.

The bells called six times for Vespers, waking me. Celestine still slept. I knew I couldn't linger here. Surely, the beguines had noticed my absence. I rolled out from under Celestine's heavy arm and stood naked, taking in this weird threadbare room. Just the dumpy bed and a half-broken desk beneath the window. New books and wax writing tablets. Celestine had been copying a manuscript, and I ran my hand across the text. It was illegible to me, but drawings in the margins caught my eye: dogs and cats with human faces wearing pointy-toed shoes. I smiled to myself and put down the book. Then, I noticed a gold-colored object glinting from the center of the desk. Easily the most luxurious item in the whole room. I reached for it.

The breath caught in my throat.

It was Michel's stolen flight feather. Engraved and painted gold. I held it with both hands and closed my eyes, remembering the night Celestine and I met in the stairwell and how I'd lost Michel's feather. Celestine had had it this whole time.

"Geneviève?"

I returned the feather to the desk.

"I saw you throw stones at The Child at Notre-Dame," I said. "You broke him, you know."

He stared with bewildered eyes.

"What are you talking about?"

"You broke The Child. You threw stones at him and broke him."

"What are you accusing me of? I'd never hurt a child!"

"The statue!" I hissed in frustration.

Celestine rolled onto his back and blinked at the wooden beams.

"It was a little more than a year ago. You were waiting for Isabelle, but she never arrived. You got angry and damaged the Vierge Marie and the…"

"You saw that?" Celestine groaned and covered his face with his hands. "How did you see that? Where were you?"

"Don't be ashamed." I ran my fingers across his back, trailing my nails along his spine. "I understand why you did it. I understand feeling let down by the powers you've always believed in."

"God's blood. I'm so embarrassed. I was behaving like a child."

I wrapped my arms around him and buried my nose in his back. "I understand the urge to destroy the saint you've always believed in," I said.

"I was angry at my sister that day. Aside from some stuffy cousins, she's all I have left of a family, and I thought she would make a foolish mistake. But she proved me wrong."

I hesitated for a moment. Could I ask for his help? I turned him around to face me and looked into his eyes.

"I want to destroy the statue of the Archangel Michel above the Portal of the Last Judgement," I confessed. "For the same reasons you smashed The Child. But I don't know how—he's too high for me to reach."

Celestine laughed and pressed his face into my neck.

"I'm serious," I continued. "I want to destroy him—the statue. Can you help me?"

"Geneviève, you know that's not going to do any good. They're just statues."

"Just statues? You said you heard them speak."

"Don't be ridiculous." He laughed a little, but I could see concern spreading over his face.

"I know they're just statues," I said hurriedly. "But I would like to hurt the thing they represent."

Celestine kissed the tops of my hands, fingertips, and eyelids. "You don't really believe in archangels and saints, do you? You know those are just stories, don't you? The Archangel Michel didn't disappoint you because he doesn't exist."

"You're a scholar!" I said, aghast.

Celestine sighed. "I'm also a heretic. Look, Geneviève, I'm going to leave the university. I have twenty-five years, and I'm still a novice. I'm an embarrassment. I would have already excelled in my studies if I was going to, and it's too late for me to return and become a lawyer or doctor. I can write and copy manuscripts, but that's where my skills begin and end. So, perhaps I'll keep doing that for coins. But I'm not ready to renounce the world like these monks. I don't share their sense of faith."

"Well, I suppose I'm a heretic, too," I said. "I don't believe in any of their stories, either."

"I know you're frustrated and angry and have lost faith in this God we're supposed to worship—believe me, I know—but statues and cathedrals are art," Celestine said. "The people who made them cared about them, you know?"

I knew.

"For that reason alone, we shouldn't destroy them," Celestine continued. "They deserve to exist for their own sake. Forgive me, Geneviève, and don't follow my bad examples. I was wrong to damage the façade that day."

He was kissing me again. Touched by what he'd said, I let him graze my mouth and earlobes. Our lips moved across each other's bellies and between our legs. I let his desire absorb me.

Utterly useless.

Of course, Celestine didn't understand. I should have known better than to ask for his help or any other person's help. I would have to destroy Michel myself.

And if I wanted to return to my place in the West Façade, I would need blood.

CHAPTER XXIX

Approximately the Feast of Saint Jude, October 1349

"You are fucking my brother, aren't you?" Isabelle twisted her mouth and rolled her eyes. "No—don't answer that question; I already know."

When she called me into the courtyard to help her gather lilies and chestnuts for the upcoming Toussaint, I knew that she had found out about me and Celestine. I was not surprised. Celestine and I had been meeting for nearly two weeks, even taking afternoon walks by the Seine. He made excuses to deliver expensive parchment and wax tablets to the nuns, and he always asked after me. Louis' mother even caught me in the stairwell leaving Celestine's room, but because I wore nunnish robes and had—as she put it—"a rather long and unattractive neck," she convinced herself I visited Celestine for ecclesial reasons.

"Go ahead and keep seeing him," Isabelle said. "He's a terrible scholar, and I know he'll never complete his theology studies or join a monastery. You can't damage his reputation. And you're a Donnadieu, so your reputation is already damaged."

When she turned to face me, she jabbed her finger against my chest.

"But I want you to know one thing, Geneviève, if that's even your real name. You better be careful with my brother. If you cause him harm in any way, you will answer to me."

She gathered my fallen basket. "Just as I was beginning to think you had good judgement," she said, shaking her head. "Just as I was beginning to think I could trust you." She marched towards the infirmary, leaving me open-mouthed in the courtyard.

Isabelle was right about me: whatever I wanted in the moment, I took. The citrus. A falcon comb. Mouths. Kisses. Meat. Water. Now, I needed blood, and I would find a way to take that, too.

I knew that menstrual sponges and cloths would be hard to collect without alarming the other beguines, and the ones I'd managed to snatch from the latrines had dried to dust. Leeches ate the patient's blood. Though patients died each day at the Hôtel-Dieu, the idea of collecting blood from the dead revolted me, for the blood of the dead was foul. What if it made my skin blister and pop?

No, I would have to take blood from someone living. Someone living and healthy.

I spent my days in a hospital; one would think blood would be plentiful. Yet, I could not collect enough to use.

Good Sky.

Isabelle was correct about me. I was capable of hurting Celestine. I didn't want to, but I saw no other way.

I would take what I wanted, what I needed. I only hoped I would be able to forget Celestine once I'd returned to the West Façade.

But could I forget Isabelle?

When I was Sainte Geneviève again, would I be able to forget the night she came to me with an offering and asked me to protect her family?

Was this really the only way?

Celestine trusted me. I didn't want to harm him. But because he trusted me, his blood would be the easiest to take. Just a little bit, I reasoned. Not enough to *truly* hurt him or—Good Sky—take his life, but enough to allow me to return to the cathedral.

I was turning into a monster, and I knew it.

But what other choice did I have?

I entered the kitchen after Vespers mass. The two eldest beguines, Alys and Jeanne, stirred the pottage and gossiped about some so-and-so's cousin who had gotten some other so-and-so's cousin pregnant in the cabbage patch behind some no-name village outside the city walls. I smelled the ale they drank as soon as I entered the kitchen, but I didn't ask for any. The pottage bubbled and sizzled over the pot's lid. Alys gestured wildly and knocked the wooden spoon onto the floor, splattering Jeanne.

I quickly sliced up an apple, wrapped the pieces in a clean cloth, and tucked the cutting knife beneath my mantle. Alys and Jeanne never bothered to acknowledge me.

By now, I knew the Benedictine nuns kept the Hôtel-Dieu's gates open for a few moments after Matins, and again after Lauds—making it easy to slip in and out unnoticed between prayer hours. And so, for nearly two weeks, between Matins and Lauds, I had met Celestine in the darkness by the riverbank on the Rive Droite, sheltered by trees and shrubs. We were never quite alone; we always heard other couples. Laughing, drinking ale or mead, fucking. Even the cold autumn air and illness couldn't keep devoted lovers away. Smells of human sweat, dirty clothes, and drink mingling with the crush of fallen leaves and hard, damp earth.

Sometimes groups of first-year scholars came here to drink, and lit fires for warmth. No one paid attention to anyone else, though everyone knew to watch out for thieves. This dark place at the water's mouth was a wonderland, though dangerous.

Tonight, I was dangerous.

I planned to ask Celestine to pray with me before the Portal of the Virgin. I would stand before Marie, Bathsheba, Sylvestre, Jean, and all the faces in the tympanum, and I would stab Celestine. When his blood spilled onto me, I would turn into a statue. Restored, revitalized, joyful. At home again on the West Façade.

I would not kill Celestine; I would take blood but spare his life. I tried to convince myself it was no worse than bloodletting. Perhaps it would even balance his humors.

Celestine stood framed against the Seine, in near-total darkness, just starlight and distant fires. The untonsured head of curls. The straight upper back. I knew that silhouette. I knew that stance. He was alone, and he had no reason to distrust me.

Perhaps, it would be easier to take his blood here, in the darkened shelter of the riverbank. I would spill his blood and run back to the West Façade before I turned. I wouldn't have to look at him when the betrayal crossed his face. I drew my knife, felt its weight in my hands.

It would be fast.

A wave of tenderness swept over me. The way Celestine treated me was all softness. His gaze. His touch. The kind way he regarded statues and other mortal-made things. I didn't love Celestine, and I held no delusions that he loved me, either. But Celestine had shown me true affection, and I felt affection in return. That affection extended to his angry sister.

I was bound to this family.

I gripped the knife handle. Celestine trusted me. I couldn't take from him even if his blood would return me to the Portal of the Virgin and give me more than life—immortality.

Immortality!

I couldn't hurt Isabelle's last sibling. I could not spend any more intimate moments with Celestine—the temptation to take from him would always be too great.

As the bells rang for Lauds, I fled to the cathedral's North Façade and the once familiar, beloved oak tree.

The last time I'd been here, I was something else. I was someone else. The tree felt both familiar and unknowable. Like the façade of the cathedral, this old oak tree was and was not my home. I threw myself against the trunk and wrapped my arms around it.

But this feeling—this desire—was more than wanting to return to the enchantment. I also wanted to slip back through time. I wanted to live in my memories of The Wakenings I'd spent here. Why hadn't I appreciated these nights more?

This was the problem with being a statue; I had passed my days as if everything would stay the same. Infinite nights and wakenings had stretched and stretched before me.

This tree would decay, the same as I would. I rested my head against the bark and kissed it. Beautiful living bark. Bark that was as tragically and ecstatically alive as me. How terrible and unjust that we both would die. How beautifully improbable that we both had the opportunity to live.

This was why the people believed in this cathedral. This was why people desperately believed in their popes, priests, and books.

This was why those men cut me from the earth, why the sculptor cut and cut until a face and body emerged from my surfaces. Why some statues became saints and others Ba birds.

Life ended, but people turned that yearning and sorrow into something that had its own life. I was both earth and maker.

And I was not alone.

I heard the crush of talons gripping bark. But this time, I had a heart.

What would I think of him now that I was human? How would he look? What would he think of me?

Could I see him well with these eyes made of skin?

Would he think I was beautiful?

He was terrifying.

His maw opened through the veil of shadows to display those familiar rows of pointed teeth. When he breathed, he smelled of stale water, like unwashed rags in the kitchen and laundry at the Hôtel-Dieu. His body stretched serpentine down the length of the tree trunk. Talons, sharp enough to tear my skin, gripped the bark and his long tail coiled towards the boughs. Eyes painted with the markings of a peregrine. Tremendous, webbed wings. The hairs stood straight on my arms. This human body saw danger; it saw a predatory beast, a serpent with feet, and wanted to run.

I knew better.

His eyes widened as he took in my form. Scales rasping against bark as he coiled tighter around the tree trunk. I started to reach for him but stopped. I placed the back of my hand against my mouth instead, covering my lips.

Part of me wanted to kiss him. Part of me wanted to run. Another part of me wanted to fight. I was angry at him. I loved him. Most of all, I was bewildered. I had a new body while he remained entirely the same.

"You changed me. Why didn't you change, too?"

Corvus lowered his head. "I don't know," he sighed. "I've barely thought of anything else over these past many months, and I simply do not understand how or why you became mortal."

His rich, melodic voice was just as I'd remembered it. I crossed my arms and squinted to better see him through the gloom. His breathing sounded like the wind's echo through the cathedral's high walls.

We both spoke at once.

"But isn't this exactly what you wanted?" he asked.

I asked, "Do you regret it?"

I closed my eyes and remembered limestone softening to fabric, limestone softening to flesh. Wrapping my bare legs around him to pull him closer. I gasped with the sheer improbability of all of it. The fact of his existence and mine. There was no good reason why either one of us should have been alive and speaking to each other.

"I wanted *you*," I said. "I wanted to live with you. Spend every wakening with you."

"I think you wanted more than me." He rested his chin on his talons. "You wanted the whole world."

"Why can't I have both? You and the whole world?"

Corvus let out a soft laugh.

"You can live among the people, but I cannot. I am a winged wolf. I am a dragon. I am a drain. An ornate, decorated drain but a drain all the same. I gave you water to save you. Can't you see? You would have lost the gift of The Wakening and your life if I hadn't. I wanted to keep you alive, and most important of all, you wanted to live too.

"I didn't know what would happen. Water-bearing creatures like gargoyles are powerful, but we cannot control everything. I only know that I gave you everything I felt."

Everything Corvus felt. To keep me alive at all costs, regardless of the consequences. Regardless of what that meant for him.

"I tried my best," Corvus pleaded.

"I know."

Something scurried across the ground, troubling fallen leaves. Just a mouse hiding from an owl.

"Marie told me how I can become a guardian again. I need blood to return to the cathedral."

Corvus lifted his head. "Are you sure that's what you want?"

"Of course it is!" I said, nostrils flaring.

"I mean, will it be enough for you?"

I pulled out the knife I'd hidden beneath my mantle. Corvus' eyes widened. "What do you intend to do with that?" he asked.

"I am going to take the blood I need, and hopefully, I won't have to kill for it," I said. "But I will do whatever it takes to become a statue again. I want to *live*, Corvus. You are immortal and I am not. I will die if I stay in this body, and I do not want to die."

"That's your choice to make and whatever you decide, I won't fault you for it," he said, his voice so soft, I could barely hear him.

I cocked my head to the side and stared at him through the

darkness. "Are you not happy?" I said, my voice growing louder. "Don't you want me to return to the cathedral? Don't you want me to live?"

"Of course I want you to live; that is why I gave you water. But I don't know if this plan will work. I don't understand how you can become limestone again."

"Marie told me I could!"

"But you have changed so much. You are so very human now. And, what if you kill someone, take their blood, and it doesn't work?" Corvus lifted his front talons. "All for nothing."

I put my free hand on my hip and shook my head. "Well, do you know a better way?"

"I don't."

"No, of course you don't," I sighed. "You've said it yourself: you don't know anything."

"I know that it is amazing that we are here together, even if it is only for this moment," Corvus said. "I think about this often. One day the cathedral will crumble. Or perhaps there will be a fire, and the spire will snap in two. The people will rebuild Notre-Dame, of course, but one day, they will decide the damage is too great, and they will stop rebuilding. Another cathedral will replace Notre-Dame. For now, I'm just happy we were able to be here, together. Somehow aware of it all. That brings me comfort."

"No," I said, shaking my head furiously. "It's not enough. I want to be a guardian again!"

"We need to accept that you may never be a guardian again. But I will always, always, always be yours. You can visit me each wakening."

"Until I grow too old to walk and die? And then what, Corvus? And then what?"

"Don't you see?" Corvus sighed. "One day I'll turn to dust, too."

"And what is it that you want in the meantime? Tell me you are happy just the way things are. Why am I the only one on this cathedral with raging desires? Why am I the only one who seems to want everything at once? Why is everyone else so accepting and content? What are your desires? Why do you just accept whatever happens to you? Pull the stone out of the ground. Carve it up until it becomes something some holy man thinks is beautiful. Accept rituals and meaning that never belonged to us to begin with. Before you were a gargoyle, you were the same material as me!"

"I know!" he cried. "I don't know what to tell you. I don't know anything."

"Yes, you do!"

"I know just as much as you."

"I hate this," I said throwing up my hands and dropping the knife.

For a long time, neither one of us said anything. I stood with my arms crossed and my head lowered, listening to Corvus' breathing and the wind in the leaves.

"Take the knife," I said eventually. "Take it from me and fly somewhere where I can't find it. I will find a way to collect what I need so I may return to the cathedral. But I will not rob anyone of their blood. If I do that, I will be no better than Michel."

I touched my fingertips to Corvus' face and kissed his open mouth. I kissed him in a way I could never kiss Celestine or The Other Geneviève or Michel. They couldn't fly. They didn't have so many beautiful teeth.

"Geneviève! Who are you talking to?"

I turned around, shielding my eyes from the sudden light. Marguerite and Isabelle stood behind me with torches. The sight of them made me jump.

"What are you doing out here?" I gasped.

"It's nearly Prime," said Isabelle.

"I'm only talking to myself," I said, blinking. "I needed fresh air."

Isabelle rolled her eyes. "Yes, you seem mighty fond of these late-night walks by the river. Are you working again? I thought you'd left that Saturday woman work behind."

Marguerite raised her eyebrows. "It sounded like you were fighting with someone," she said.

The tree looked bare and ordinary as if Corvus had never been there. Just the bells, the singing monks, the autumn wind.

It would have been so much easier if I'd only ever been a Saturday woman.

I was so tired of lying.

CHAPTER XXX

"Lords, do not be surprised: A stranger bereft of advice can be very downcast in another land when he does not know where to seek help."

From The Lais of Marie de France, Lanval (c. 1155–1170)

November 1349

Three days passed. Isabelle sent a letter to Celestine's apartment on the Rive Droite. No one had seen him at mass nor at the Hôtel-Dieu, and she was worried. Louis' family replied that Celestine was not there. So, Isabelle sent a note to Jumiéges and waited. "It's unlike him to leave without saying goodbye," she muttered. Then, two weeks passed.

The Benedictine nun batted me away when I told her I wanted to see bloodletting again—that I could watch without fear this time. She did not believe me. Meanwhile, I kept my eyes on the cathedral, hoping someone would repaint the West Façade. If I could steal a ladder or climb into the scaffolding between the Matins and Lauds, I could finally destroy Michel. But no one had touched the façade in months, not even to repair the poor, headless Denis nor, mercifully, to install the new Sainte Geneviève.

Isabelle fretted that her letter was lost, so she wrote a new one.

When she saw me in the orchard one afternoon, she grabbed my forearm and shook me so hard, I dropped the basket of apples I'd been gathering.

"Where is he? When did you see him last?"

"By the riverbank before the Feast Day of Saint Jude," I answered truthfully. "We were going to meet there, but when I saw him, I changed my mind. I remembered our conversation, Isabelle. So, I left. I decided not to meet him; I went to the cathedral instead. That's when you saw me near the tree."

Isabelle's mouth made a tight straight line.

"It's possible he wants to punish you and that's why he's disappeared," she said, sighing. "He's like that sometimes."

What was that soft look in her round eyes?

Hope?

Regret?

"Either way, I think you were careless with him. I won't let you forget it. Nobody hurts my brother," Isabelle said. "If it were up to me, I'd make you leave the Hôtel-Dieu. Beguines are supposed to be chaste. But it's not up to me, it's up to Madam du Faut. And we regrettably, we need your help."

I bowed my head and closed my eyes. If the beguines made me leave the Hôtel-Dieu, I would have nowhere else to go. And I was running out of time. Any day, the masons could place another Sainte Geneviève in the West Façade.

Days later, the Hôtel-Dieu received a gift from the Abbaye de Fontevraud's harvest. Mainly crates of cabbage and carrots. Happily, the gift included salted meat as well—barrels of eels and a little bit of venison and rabbit—but just enough to flavor our broth, not enough four-legged beast to inspire rutting. *Too late for me*, I thought. The real luxury was the container of pears, enough for each beguine.

Pear flesh was grainy and yellow. I had to chew it carefully; my jaw ached, and I discovered a small sore spot in the back of my mouth. I swished with water and sweet herbs, like Marguerite instructed, but the pain persisted, and I thought I had an infection. Flecks of blood appeared on pear flesh.

My body was already vulnerable. Flesh for half a year and already rotting. I tapped my fingertips against my swollen cheek. Of course, this was what I deserved for wanting to *consume*. I was guilty of gluttony, wasn't I? Desirous of food and drink. I was guilty of lust, wasn't I? Desiring Celestine, The Other Geneviève, Corvus, and Michel. And greed—how could I forget the coin purse I'd snatched and the falcon comb from Constantinople? Wrath, envy, and sloth? Oh yes, I'd loved to watch the sun descend, half-dreaming in Celestine's warm bed.

"Geneviève, is there something wrong with your tooth?" Alys asked. "You've been quiet all day, and I've noticed you've touched your cheek several times. If something's wrong, there are things we can do to help."

I shook my head no but felt heat rise to my cheeks. Héloïse stifled a giggle behind her hand.

"Let me see your tooth," Marguerite said. "We can pull it if it's bad."

"Right here? In the refectory?"

"Let's see the tooth!"

The refectory fell quiet as the other beguines, nuns, and a handful of visiting monks looked up at me. I covered my mouth with my hand and swatted them all away.

"A rotten tooth?"

"Sore gums?"

"Is she going to lose a tooth?"

"It's okay, Geneviève we've all lost teeth, and you still have so many nice ones."

Even Agnès fought to hide giggles.

"Leave me alone!"

A gentle hand beneath my chin, and Marguerite leaning close to my face.

"Show me your tooth, please."

She talked to me the same way she talked to the patients. Of course, I acquiesced. I opened my mouth.

"You know, we're all jealous of your smile," Marguerite said. "No one has teeth like this at your age. How old are you anyway?"

Ageless. Older than the pope, than the cathedral, than the City, than Paris itself, than the Seine.

"Eight and twenty," I said against her fingers instead. The same age as the true Geneviève when she was martyred.

"Take a deep breath," said Marguerite.

A sudden painful tug and blood spilled over my lips. I shouted. My cheek throbbed. The monks eating stew in the back of the room howled with laughter.

"Don't worry," said Marguerite. "It was in the very back of your mouth. No one will notice that it's missing, you least of all."

She dropped the bloody molar in my hands and left me to stare at it in wonder.

It felt too precious to discard, but I did not know what to do with it. So, I placed it beneath my pillow and thought I'd keep it there. When I reached for it the following day, it was gone, and I missed Prime prayer to search for it along the floor. Eventually, I found it, covered in hair, wedged between my bed and window. I tucked the molar beneath the mattress with my falcon comb and hoped I wouldn't lose it again.

Another week passed. No Celestine.

A monk found the knife I stole, near Corvus' oak tree, and correctly identified that it belonged to the Hôtel-Dieu. Isabelle grabbed my arm and shook me again, this time in the refectory, in front of everyone. Her grip was so strong, she nearly brought me to the ground, sending my bowl of stew and eating knife along with me.

"What have you done to my brother?"

"I've done nothing, I promise I haven't seen him!"

"Explain the knife!"

I opened and closed my mouth and showed Isabelle the palms of my hands. I felt everyone's stares burn my skin.

"Marguerite, you were there!" Isabelle demanded. "You were with me when we saw her."

Marguerite frowned into her bowl. "I don't know what you're talking about."

"She was standing alone and talking to the tree in the middle of the night—don't you remember?"

"I wasn't talking to the tree. I wasn't talking to anyone; your ears were fooling you."

Isabelle went all the way red. "Hell hag, you've done something to my brother, I know it! He would never disappear without saying goodbye to me. You've hurt him!"

"I swear I did not hurt Celestine!"

"Why are we talking about Geneviève?" asked Madam du Faut with her mouth full of food. "Why do you think Geneviève has anything to do with Celestine?"

Marguerite looked at me with eyebrows raised. The refectory went silent.

"Because she was sleeping with him," Isabelle hissed. "She broke her chastity vows."

The silence was unbearable. I turned and walked out of the refectory.

Madam du Faut found me in the laundry. She touched my shoulder, begged me to look at her. Did I hurt Celestine? Of course not. Were those rumors true?

Had I laid with Isabelle's brother, our ecclesial sponsor? How was that her business? Because beguines are supposed to be chaste! Because my foolishness jeopardized Celestine, our liaison with the university. If we damaged this relationship, the consequences would be devastating.

I remembered my last night in The Other Geneviève's home, how tired and worn down I was, how I wanted to tell the truth.

Telling the truth had cost me.

But lying had cost more.

"Look at me," said Madam du Faut, gently tugging on my chin.

I lowered my eyes and bit my lower lip. This was so humiliating.

"Yes," I hissed.

"Scholars can get away with their reputations, but beguines? The rumors will destroy us." She leaned in so close, I could smell anise on her breath. "You're not pregnant, are you?"

"I am no fool," I spat. "I know how to prevent that."

Madam du Faut released a slow exhale.

"Did Marguerite show you where we grow the herbs?"

"No," I said bluntly. "He pulls out."

I crossed my arms tighter across my chest. Madam du Faut shook her head. A pained expression creased her features.

"You've done good work, Geneviève," Madam du Faut said placing her hands on both of my shoulders. "Please believe me when I say I do not want to turn you away. This hurts Isabelle, too—I know you've helped her especially."

I looked up at her. "What are you saying?"

"You can't stay here anymore," she said. "The patients need us, and we cannot risk our standing or funding. I hope you understand."

"What?" My mouth fell open. "What do you mean? Where will I go?"

She squeezed both of my hands as I stared into her pink, weather-chapped face.

"It's too risky for you to stay here," she said. "You must leave."

"But that's not fair!" I shouted. "Celestine had just as much to do with it as I did."

Madam du Faut gave me one long backwards look over her shoulder before she exited the laundry.

"I know," she sighed, shaking her head. "I know."

That afternoon, Madam du Faut returned the coins I'd donated; the only remaining kindness she could offer. In exchange, I returned the borrowed wimple.

I went to the long, thin room I shared with the beguines and retrieved the one small happiness I'd hidden beneath my mattress: the stolen falcon comb. I thought about discarding the molar but couldn't bear to part with it. After I'd become calcareous again, I would be grateful I had kept a piece of this body. I left without a word to Marguerite or Agnès.

CHAPTER XXXI

Feast of Sainte Cécile, November 1349

For three days, I sat in near-perfect stillness beneath the statue of Marie inside the Notre-Dame Cathedral—the statue that seemed to mock me with her lifelessness. I only rose for the food, water, and latrines. Crumbs from the chunks of stale, black bread that Marguerite and a few nuns slipped me between prayer hours falling from my cote to the floor. Those who saw me assumed I was repenting, but I sat here because I had nowhere else to go.

Watching life from inside the cathedral felt like watching life from the West Façade. This was practice; this was an imitation of inhabiting a calcareous body. Soon, I would be porous. Soon, I would absorb the sun's heat and the sounds of laughter and languages. Once again, I would absorb the smells of meat and eel pasties the vendors sold in the parvis after Prime. I would watch the people and not care that I didn't belong with them in their streets. I only needed blood, I told myself. I only needed blood.

There in the cathedral, I practiced sitting beneath the Virge Marie without saying a word, simply bathing in the light the color-stained glass cast to the floor. Bathing in the frankincense that wafted from the priest's censors. Bathing in Marguerite's kindness when she handed me bread.

More people were coming to mass now. The once-familiar flurry of languages began to return, Coptic, Greek, or German mingling with French and Latin. I heard talk that the worst of the illness had passed. I heard hope in the people's jaunty footsteps, the soles of leather shoes on the stone floor. The fine clothing for the ladies and men. Ermine and budge fur. Tunics and fashionable cote hardies and surcotes dyed every shade of blue. Most people still covered their noses and mouths with cloth to shield from evil vapors, but I saw people let their masks slip to share a smile.

The people all looked so different from one another, and I thought everyone was so beautiful. I would never know their individual stories, but I knew that the illness had taken something irreplaceable from each person. The thought made me feel soft. I wanted to hold each one of these people; I wanted to protect them.

But I was just a humble, silent figure in gray seated beneath Marie in the nave.

When the new moon arrived, Corvus awaited me in our oak tree, coiled around the trunk. But he was not alone: Hécate, Eurydice, and Perséphone crouched near him in the darkness.

I was startled at the sight of them, nearly tripping as I stepped backwards. The harpies looked just as I remembered them from the cathedral roof: roughly chest height, muscular limbs, and wings so long, they scraped the ground.

"We knew we'd find you here," the harpies chorused. "We know what happened to your scholar Celestine. The whole West Façade knows! Lucifer and the Foolish Virgins and the Church Doctors saw it, and they told the Kings of Judah, and the Kings of Judah told us, so we flew here to find Corvus, because we knew he would tell you!"

"Because you're mortal, you're the only one who can help him," Corvus said. "And you must help him tonight, or it might be too late."

"It might already be too late!" Hécate said. "You'll be lucky if he's still alive."

I rested my forehead against the tree, inhaling its damp, fungal scent and listened.

Outrageous.

On that night, near the Feast Day of Saint Jude, Celestine wandered back to the cathedral and prayed before the West Façade.

Prayed.

At the Portal of the Last Judgment.

"But he didn't even believe in prayer!" I hissed.

"Something must have changed his heart," Corvus said. "He prayed to the Archangel Michel. He kneeled and begged."

"Do you know what he prayed for?" asked Eurydice. She'd grabbed hold of my hair and began to braid it.

"He prayed for you," continued Perséphone, rubbing the fabric of my mantle between her fingertips. "He prayed for you to find peace and happiness."

"Oh, bloody bad fevers." I pressed my forehead against the oak tree.

The story turned wild: Archangel Michel answered Celestine.

He spoke!

"But why?" I sputtered. "For what gain?"

"When Michel answered Celestine, it shocked Lucifer to the point of distraction. Michel saw the opening and slid down the wall. Before anyone could stop him, he took Celestine's hand and convinced him to follow," Hécate continued, stamping her clawed feet. "Celestine obeyed—believing he was witnessing a miracle, believing Michel was a real angel."

I pressed my hand to my forehead.

"This is my fault," I said. "I told Celestine that the Archangel Michel let me down, and I asked him to destroy his likeness. I couldn't do it alone; I needed someone to climb into the façade and reach him. I thought he'd help because he smashed The Child all those months ago.

I didn't know he would try to *speak* with Michel! He told me he didn't even believe in saints."

"One doesn't have to believe in saints and spirits and gods to believe in statues," Eurydice said. "After all, none of the saints look like gargoyles, and yet, here we are, protecting the most beautiful cathedral in the world—or so the people say."

Corvus reached for my hand, and his claws twined my fingers. Oursin claws squeezed skin-covered bone, reminding me that beneath my skin and humors, my new skeletal structure contained some of the elements I'd kept in my former body.

"There's more," Corvus said. "Michel has set a trap for you."

Hécate took my arm in hers. It was cold to touch and stiff.

"There are catacombs and tunnels beneath the cathedral," she said. "That's where Michel took Celestine—I saw them from the roof. I can lead you to the entrance and accompany you halfway, but not all the way, because they extend far beyond the cathedral grounds—I've heard they extend past the city gates. But you can enter them and retrieve Celestine."

"I imagine Michel wants to lure you down there with Celestine," said Corvus. "So, you must either destroy him or trick him into stepping beyond the cathedral grounds."

I felt nauseous. Michel knew what the de Grantrue family meant to me. To trap me in his nets, there was no better bait than Celestine or Isabelle.

"How do you know about catacombs?" I asked.

"I've spent the past hundred years watching priests and bishops enter them from my place on the cathedral roof," said Hécate. "Then, eventually, I grew brave enough to begin exploring them."

"That is why we call her Hécate," said Eurydice. She released the clump of my hair she'd been braiding. It was so messy and tangled, I wanted to laugh.

"But you can cross the cathedral grounds," Corvus said. "So, you're the best one to search for Celestine now, mon calcaire," Corvus said.

"Though you must be careful, because Michel will surely try to trap you underground."

"The earth is unstable down there," warned Hécate.

"Geneviève?"

I turned around to face Isabelle clutching a torch and a kitchen knife.

"What are you doing out here again?" she asked, lips trembling. "Why am I always catching you here, talking to shadows?"

Corvus exhaled, his breath curling like so many smokey tendrils, releasing a low growl from the bottom of his throat, and this time, letting Isabelle see him. Then he was gone—back up into the tree and the safety of the sky.

Isabelle dropped her knife and screamed. I cupped my hand over her mouth while she thrashed and bit my palm.

"Don't touch me, you long-necked freak. What was that thing? What are you? Is this some kind of sick ritual? Are you a witch? A demon? What have you done to my brother?"

"Isabelle, I know I haven't given you many reasons to trust me, but I'm asking you to trust me now. I can find your brother."

She slapped my face. I inhaled and told myself to calm my voice, though my body shook. *Be patient with her,* I thought. *Her holy books describe demons but say nothing of living statues—statues that live because of the people who made them.*

Hécate stepped a clawed foot forward and spoke.

"I can tell you how to get your brother back," she said, extending her wings. "But you must trust me and Geneviève."

"Here is the Ba bird you asked for." I gestured with an outstretched hand.

Isabelle pointed the knife at me and stepped closer until the tip met my throat. I closed my eyes and swallowed, displaying the palms of my hand. I could smell her breath, stale with wine.

We exhaled. Our eyes locked on each other's as my heart thudded against my chest.

"This must be a dream," she said. "A terrible dream."

"I wish with all my heart it was," I sighed.

"I want to see my brother again," Isabelle said at last, lowering the knife.

"Then we must waste no time," said Hécate.

She beat her wings against the air, stirring dust and forcing Isabelle and me to shield our eyes. When we looked up again, Hécate was flying. Isabelle gasped and crossed herself, dropping the torch. Hécate was swift. She dove for the torch and caught it before it could touch the ground and extinguish.

"Follow me," she demanded, flying towards the South Façade. As her wings rose and fell, her feathers ground against each other with a sound like crumbling stone. I took off running and Isabelle struggled behind me, panting and cursing.

"Am I seeing things that are not real?" Isabelle muttered. "Am I losing my mind or am I having visions?"

"Neither," I said, grabbing her arm and tugging her along.

Hécate landed before a wooden door adjacent to the Meson de l'Evesque. When Isabelle saw the stone harpy again, she fell to her knees. "I can't," she said, covering her face.

I looked from Hécate to Isabelle, who was now huddled on the ground, clutching her knees to her chest. She was right, I could not take her with me into the tunnels. Michel had already trapped one de Grantrue sibling. I would not give him both, even if that meant I had to fight him alone.

"Go inside Notre-Dame and wait for me there," I told Isabelle. "I promise I will return before dawn with Celestine."

Isabelle looked at me open-mouthed.

"Please go," I said. "I was wrong to bring you here. Go inside the cathedral where it's safe for you."

Hécate walked past us and pushed against the door until it groaned open.

We had to bow to enter the damp-smelling cellar. Hécate swung the torch around the empty space, illuminating a cramped tunnel with a low ceiling. When I stepped inside, I saw that it stretched onward like a road.

"I believe that passage leads to Celestine," Hécate said. "And Michel."

She thrust the torch to me. "I'm afraid to go in there," I said.

Hécate laughed softly but not without some kindness. "We can't linger here; someone will catch you," she said. "I'm sure the night watch already heard us pry open that door."

It felt like climbing the tower again, trusting all the senses to lead in the right direction. Water trickled from an earthy ceiling, and my fingers traced the damp, worn surfaces; these walls were made by people. I expected the passage to open into the cathedral's interior, starlight through stained glass, but as we walked, I realized we were descending into an underworld. From high above, crevices opened just enough to allow slivers of blue, predawn light to enter the space.

"What is this?" I breathed.

"It's a tomb," said Hécate. "I've heard the monks say that priests even older than the cathedral are buried here."

Michel wanted to bury me here, too. Worse, I'd entangled Celestine and Isabelle—two innocent mortals—into the enchantment and the world of the cathedral guardians. I had been so careless with them!

The corridor twisted and forked into separate paths that all dead-ended in broken shrines and altars. Several held cracked, painted murals of the Virge Marie. One contained a stone sarcophagus. The niche that drew me in the most was a mural on stone depicting a female horseback rider with a falcon on her fist. I held the torch closer, so we could see the painting more clearly. Who was this woman? How long ago had she lived? Was her body buried here—and why? Why beneath Notre-Dame among centuries-old priests and holy men?

All of a sudden, it felt wrong to be here in this dark and private joyless place. If I stayed too long, I would never emerge. I would be absorbed and forgotten.

I heard footsteps clap behind me and echoes bounce against the tunnel walls. I straightened my back and inhaled. Hécate extended her wings protectively.

"Who is here?" she snarled.

I gripped the torch, ready to swing it, as my heart knocked against my chest.

Had Michel already found me?

"Geneviève!" a breathless voice cried out. "Geneviève where are you?"

When I heard the rustling of skirts and fabric, I turned and exhaled. It was only Isabelle.

"I told you to return to the cathedral; what are you doing here? This place is dangerous!"

"I have to find my brother," Isabelle panted. "I almost asked the monks for help but realized no one would believe my story. If I told them about flying harpies and catacombs, they would think I was either insane, a witch, or both. Another accusation like that is the last thing the beguines need."

"You didn't have to ask anyone for help," I said. "You could have waited where it was safe. I'm going to find him."

"I couldn't stand that." Isabelle gritted her teeth. "I have to know what's going on!"

"I will explain everything once I've found him," I said. "Turn back."

"No!" she cried.

Shrill echoes swirled through the expanse. *"No! No! No!"*

I shook my head. Michel would know exactly where we were now. We would not be able to surprise him.

Hécate nudged us forward. "You must keep going. This torch won't last until dawn."

I pulled Isabelle through the dark, handing her the torch to keep. Isabelle took it and crossed herself, tears shining in the light. With her free hand, she gripped the handle of her knife.

"Geneviève?" Isabelle called my name, soft and tentative.

"Yes?"

"Your name is not really Geneviève Donnadieu, is it?"

"No," I said, following close behind so she could see me in the light. Her blade made me anxious, but I tried not to think about it; Isabelle and I had to trust each other now.

"And you were never a femme de Samedi."

"No," I replied.

I followed the soft *drip-drop*, hoping the water would lead me to Celestine. A row of ancient, moss-covered statues glowered down at us from either side of the tunnel, and I knew they would never speak or wake in this blue gloaming. I could hear my heart's every thud and imagined every hair on my body upright and stiff. I looked behind me, expecting Michel, but it was always Hécate's claws dragging the ground or Isabelle, panting and bewildered. I wondered whether the gargoyles were right: if we would find Celestine and Michel here, or if Isabelle and I had senselessly entered this space.

Thin starlight entered through a crevice. Here, the corridor walls looked like the crumbling scaffolding of some ancient structure. Bits and fragments of stone deities littered the ground. I picked up a tiny limestone hand. Who had this belonged to?

"Mon dieu," said Isabelle as she spun around the corridor.

A name formed in my mind: Lutetia. An ancient Roman city. Paris was built on top of it, and the Notre-Dame Cathedral stood on top of these ruins. I was standing in the remains of the pagan temples Michel talked about. *Pagan souls become gargoyles.*

So, Michel had been right about the ruins beneath the church. How did he know? Had he come to this place before? Or had he overheard, from his niche on the West Façade, the people talk about it? Or did he learn about it through some intuitive knowledge, a map his maker had carved into his thoughts and memories? Were there memories of this place etched in his body? Had he been quarried here?

I remembered all the wakenings I spent with him in the Balcony of the Virgin and how he'd never once mentioned he could access this place, though he'd treated me like I was special and dear to him. My chest went hot with rage. I'd been a fool.

"Tell me the truth," Isabelle whispered, her voice so faint I could scarcely hear her. "Are you a demon?"

"No," I sighed. "I'm not that either. At least, I don't think I am. For now, I'm every bit as human and mortal as you."

I played with the ruined limestone hand, running my fingertips over this faceless deity's finger stubs before settling the hand back into dust.

Isabelle held the torch out, illuminating a path paved well enough to support carts and wagons.

"I will go no further," Hécate said. "I don't know for sure, but I believe this is the boundary between the cathedral grounds and the City."

"How do you know?" I asked.

"Well, to me, that road looks like it leads to an old quarry."

"But how can that be?" I pressed her. "Where's Michel? We've walked the length of this path and haven't seen any sign of Celestine or Michel. If Michel really brought Celestine here, we would have seen them by now. Hécate, if you can't cross beyond the cathedral grounds, then neither can Michel."

"This is ridiculous!" Isabelle shouted, her voice echoing. "Celestine isn't down here! You've tricked me! Both of you! You've brought me down here to trap me!"

High above ground, the bells rang for Lauds. The peeling

reverberated through the cathedral's foundation, shaking the buried corridor's walls and the ground beneath us.

"I can't stay!" Hécate said over her shoulder. "Keep looking for Celestine. He is certainly here. The gargoyles saw him descend. No one has seen him emerge."

Hécate flapped her mighty wings. As Isabelle and I stood watching the harpy navigate the low ceiling, the walls began to shudder. Old columns, foundation, and ceiling groaned around us. Isabelle ducked, dropping the torch, and I moved in to shield her body with mine, wrapping my arms around her, careful to avoid her knife. The sound of my heart was as loud in my ears as the breaking walls.

Michel, I thought. *This is Michel. He's here. He did this.*

"I went to the Hôtel-Dieu because I didn't want to live anymore." Isabelle breathed into the crook of my arm. "If I couldn't catch the illness in my fiancé's home, surely, I would catch it at the Hôtel-Dieu."

I kept my eyes on the torch, willing it to stay lit so we would not be left in darkness.

"I begged to work alongside the beguines," Isabelle continued. "Then I waited to catch the illness. The fevers. The sweats. The sores. For weeks, I waited for the first signs, but they never came. Then I realized I was good at working. I could see problems the beguines— hell, even the clergy—could not. I could raise money for the beguinage, though it was never enough."

The tunnel had stopped shaking, but we were still huddled together.

"Now, maybe I want to save all these patients because I couldn't save my family. Or maybe I like how the work absorbs me so completely, I don't have to think about anything else. I don't have to think about my family. I can forget I even had a family at all. I can pretend they're not dead."

I forced myself to stand and found I could. I picked up the fallen torch. Isabelle's voice faltered.

"But I think I might love the beguinage," she said. "Even if the other beguines don't like me, I still care about them. I want to go home. I don't want to die here!"

I closed my eyes, wishing Isabelle had stayed above ground. But I didn't tell her so; scolding her wouldn't do any good. Instead, I offered her my free hand. "You were brave to follow me," I said. "I will try my best to keep us safe."

The smell of incense snaked through the passage, subtle but certain.

"He's here," I breathed. "Michel is here."

"Who is Michel?" said Isabelle, taking the torch. "Who are you talking about?"

Michel was just a little statue. I would push him to the ground when I found him. Crush his face with fallen debris. But I could not see beyond our torch light.

And wherever Michel was, I knew he could see me.

"Michel is a statue carved into the Portal of the Last Judgement on the Notre-Dame Cathedral," I said.

Isabelle made a whimpering sound.

I grappled the air until my hands landed on a fallen slab. I wanted to push it, but I knew better. If I did, I might collapse the ceiling. My fingers gripped the surface. Chalky and porous. Rough and lined with seams.

Isabelle groaned behind me.

"It will be okay," I said. "I know what to do."

I did. These half-buried, deteriorating slabs were made from limestone. Here, beneath the cathedral, within this ancient and beloved land—beloved when it was Paris, when it was Lutetia, when it was Parisii, before that even, before it had a name committed to memory—I felt the source of the enchantment, knew the enchantment came from the land itself. All this time, I'd thought the masons gave us the gift of The Wakening. But now I knew that that wasn't true. I knew that this land had been home for oceans of people for centuries, that this love of land was as massive as oceans, that this love itself was the source of the enchantment.

I felt all of this and knew how to speak with limestone again.

I didn't have to push. The slabs yielded to my touch, shifting to create a narrow passage.

"How are we going to fit through there?" Isabelle whispered as she shone her light on the crevice.

"Just try," I said. I closed my eyes and pleaded with the stone to stay open and not crush Isabelle and I as we squeezed through.

She went first, slipping through sideways with the torch in her outstretched arm. I heard fabric catch on something and rip. "Putain," Isabelle cursed.

"Are you okay?"

"I scraped my cheek," she grumbled.

"Isabelle," I began. "After we've escaped this place, and you have returned to the Hôtel-Dieu, I think you should listen to the other beguines a bit more," I said. "Not for the sake of getting them to like you—trust me, I've found out on my own that some people will never like you, no matter what you do or what you say. What I mean is, you should listen to them for your own sake. The older ones have a lot of wisdom. You can trust them and follow their lead sometimes. Not all of the time, of course—Madam du Faut can learn from you too—but some of the time."

"Are you truly giving me advice right now?"

"Yes," I replied. "The beguines all have so much to offer—each one of you. There's so much you can learn from each other. Besides, if you feel responsible for everyone, all of the time, that's a heavy weight to carry."

"Why are you saying this?" Isabelle asked. "Especially now?"

A good question; I didn't know exactly.

I settled on, "Because I respect you."

I meant it.

Then, she was through. She shone the torchlight back through the crevice to guide me, but the light was too intense and hurt my eyes.

With my back pressed against one side of the crevice, I began to shimmy through. The slabs rocked with my movements, threatening to fall if I made a misstep. I cried out when I scraped my forehead and the bridge of my nose against the opening.

"Geneviève, hurry!" Isabelle called. Her torchlight bounced away from me as her footsteps echoed against the walls.

"Wait!" I cried. "Where are you going?"

"Come quick!" Already, her voice sounded smaller and further away.

Michel was hiding somewhere in this cavernous expanse, and I could not let him get to Isabelle. I pressed my hands on either side of the opening and grunted, forcing myself through. My mantle ripped as I tumbled to the ground.

Panting in the darkness, I stood and dusted my hands. Somehow, I had made my way through without getting crushed.

Isabelle found her brother half buried in another shallow tunnel that had collapsed into a dead end. The crumpled roof let in the sky and stars. I didn't know where we were in relation to the cathedral anymore, but I sensed we had followed a long-abandoned path for the masons who first built on this site. Isabelle kneeled beside Celestine and pressed her face close to his mouth to feel for breath. He was still alive but dehydrated and weak. He stank, soiled in his own piss and feces.

"Celestine, it's me!" cried Isabelle.

He was unresponsive, so we shook him and made his head rattle. I felt the soft flutter of eyelashes against the palm of my hand. We felt for injuries, searching for signs of broken bones along his limbs and ribcage.

"His shinbone is swollen," Isabelle said. "I wonder if it's fractured?"

"Who's this? What are you doing?" He was awake. He reached for me, felt my arms, and took my hands. "Geneviève."

"What happened to you?" hissed Isabelle.

"That statue, the Archangel Michel. He promised me paradise but pulled me through the wall instead. Something happened and I can barely move my right leg. I think he tried to bury me."

"How can this all be possible?" Isabelle breathed.

"It's a wonder you're still alive!" I said. "You've been trapped here for over three weeks!"

Celestine weakly pointed towards a cowhide knapsack at his side.

"I had provisions."

"Provisions? Provisions for what?" Isabelle yelled. "You had enough food and water to last you almost a month? What were you planning to do? Run away?"

Isabelle looked at me and I looked at Celestine.

"Were you planning to run away together?"

I furiously shook my head no. Celestine winced.

"Bloody fevers, I didn't know what I was doing," he breathed. "I just knew I didn't want to be a scholar anymore. And what about you, sister? You always talk about leaving."

"Not without saying goodbye to you or convincing you to come with me," Isabelle said. "You're an idiot, Celestine. We're going to get out of here and then we'll talk." She took her brother's hands and tried to warm them with her breath. He shivered against us.

Slow, stilted footsteps echoed against the corridor, and I looked up.

Michel in all his silver-painted splendor, luminous in the flickering light, stepped from the split in the fallen wall. Stepped towards Isabelle, Celestine, and me.

His glorious green eyes were opened wide, and the red painted lips I'd once kissed parted, as if to speak. What did that look on his face mean? What did he reach for with his outstretched arms?

Salvation? Forgiveness? Grace?

That beautiful face. Those eyes. That mouth. The paint, the glorious silver and gold paint!

Isabelle rose and turned from Celestine and me.

"That's an angel," she whispered, lowering her knife. "I know that face. I know you! You are Saint Michel."

"No, Isabelle!" I cried.

I grabbed for her mantle, but it slipped off her shoulder. Michel's lips curved into a gentle smile as he reached for Isabelle.

"Saint Michel, can you take this pain away?" pleaded Isabelle. "Can you bring my family back? I want to see my parents and sister again. Can you do that for me?"

"No, Isabelle! He's not an angel!"

I tried to scream but my voice became a whisper. For when I stared at Michel, I, too, ached to rise and follow him. Oh, wouldn't it feel so good—so heavenly—to let Michel pull us back through the crevice where tunnel walls would absorb us?

Absorb everything we'd ever felt. Absorb our pain.

Even Celestine tried to struggle to his feet, his eyes fixed on the angel's face. Michel took another step forward, his arms outstretched and welcoming.

Pain was for the living, after all. We felt pain because we lived.

Michel pointed at me and his lips mouthed the shape of my name.

The hairs on the back of my neck stood up. The enchantment gave a sudden tug on whatever force still kept me tethered to The Wakening.

"Stop, Michel," I said. "Stop!"

But he took another step and fell over, strewn on his back with outstretched arms. Mouth and eyes wide open. Simple, lifeless stone. Thresholds crossed. Enchantment ruptured.

Isabelle and Celestine shook their heads as if waking from slumber.

Bewildered and fascinated, I approached him. Even in this strange, subterranean gloom, I could see his green eyes turn dull and gray.

My fascination turned to rage. He had denied me the pleasure of destroying him myself.

What happened to you, Michel? How did you find this place? Why did you ever think it would keep you safe?

Like life and death, the enchantment was the enchantment, part of the cycle, the order of things. Not even the ruins of an ancient temple, beneath an ancient crypt, beneath a beloved cathedral could save Michel.

I began to laugh. This was what Corvus had meant. There was no such thing as immortality. Even beloved statues turned back to earth, the same as bones. An endless cycle of bones and stones.

Michel didn't answer me, and I knew he never would. He would never speak again. The same mysterious logic that had extinguished L'Ecclésia and Etienne had extinguished Archangel Michel.

Celestine struggled to stand but fell over, so Isabelle and I had to support him from either side. He remembered little of how he had entered this passage, only that the angel had pulled him down through the cathedral wall. And after the fallen wall had trapped him, he slept on and off, as if enchanted. He'd had only enough strength to eat the provisions in his bag. When that ran out, he was left with stale water runoff.

"I hate that you must see me like this," he said.

The stolen flight feather fell from Celestine's robes. I picked it up, studied it beneath the torchlight, and understood. This was where Celestine's newfound knowledge had come from. This was how he had spoken with Michel. Perhaps it had even kept him alive for all these weeks beneath the cathedral, suspended in a half-enchantment.

We followed the passage until it led up crumbling stairs, spilling out of the North Façade and into the cool, open air. I was so grateful to see the stars again, I wanted to kiss the sky.

Celestine slid against the cathedral wall, breathing hard. "Before we take another step, I must rest," he said.

I placed my hands on Isabelle's shoulders and looked into her eyes. I knew I sounded wild and desperate, but now, she was my only hope.

"Do you believe your brother Celestine?"

"He's never lied to me."

"Do you believe that you saw a living gargoyle? And an archangel?"

"I don't know."

"I'm asking you to believe your own eyes and ears. I hope you believe me. I hope you trust your own perception. I am the statue of Sainte Geneviève. I once stood on the West Façade of this cathedral, and I came to life with each new moon; I was enchanted. I broke my enchantment because a mortal taught me what it meant to want and desire and crave and feel. And not only that, but to feel needed—like I had a purpose. Even if that purpose was to provide no power higher than companionship and hope. That mortal was you."

Isabelle's eyes widened. I felt her shoulders stiffen.

"When I first became human, I thought Corvus transformed me with his gift of water. But now I know that's not true. Isabelle, it was you. You placed that citrus in my hands and taught me how to feel a grief and longing so profound, it broke limestone and turned me into flesh."

She touched her fingers to her forehead and closed her eyes. When she looked up, tears were streaming down her cheeks.

"Was it really you?" she said. "Could it be true?"

"Isabelle, I couldn't help you reach your family, because I was only a statue—not the deity you wanted to believe in. And I can't help you now because I'm only a mortal. But I will tell you that you helped me see the wonder and beauty in this world. I will always care about you, as if you were my sister. Now, I need you to help me. One final offering."

I heard wings trouble the air and knew Corvus flew above to warn of dawn. I looked up but couldn't see him with these human eyes. He could have been one of the simple crows that woke at daybreak. So ordinary, so imperceptible, Isabelle didn't even notice. But I did.

Isabelle ran her fingertips over my face and the soft place between my nose and cheeks.

"Could it really be true?" she whispered. "I want it to be true. I want to live in a world where statues come to life."

I wiped a tear from her eye.

"I don't know how to live in your world without making trouble, so now I only want to return to the wall," I said. "But I need blood. Can you spare some of yours? If enough spills over my skin, I might be able to turn back into a statue and return to my place in the cathedral. Then I can watch over you, Celestine, and everyone else who loves the cathedral and the Île de la Cité."

We stood before my empty alcove. Bathsheba, Marie, Sylvestre, Jean, and the cherubim were our witnesses. First light threatened. Already, we could hear the Prime prayers.

I looked between Bathsheba and Isabelle. The three of us together like this reminded me of moon cycles. Isabelle young and waxing with her whole life before her. Bathsheba content and full, a woman forever in her prime. Me, waning, a person who did not belong in the mortal world.

Isabelle removed the kitchen knife from her girdle and slit the inside of her arm, careful to avoid veins. The bells rang and rang, and she dripped over my forehead, face, and neck. Her blood smelled sharp—like the metal knife itself.

My heart swelled with gratitude and love for Isabelle and her family as the warm droplets trickled down my chest. I smeared her blood across my face and arms and thought about fine grain stone. I thought about terror birds, foraminifera, and mollusks withering and calcifying on the ocean floor. When I closed my eyes, I saw before me the entirety of my old existence on the West Façade. The first wakening when Bathsheba and I ran our fingertips across each other's brows, eyes, noses, and mouths to understand what we were. Claiming one another as sister stone. Absorbing languages, songs, and names. Admiring our bodies and fearing our bodies. Never daring to look beneath our clothes. The cherubim playing la Soule with Denis. L'Ecclésia and Saint Etienne twirling through the parvis. The finches with their nest in the crook of Bathsheba's arm. Marie releasing The Child to climb, stern-faced Jean, Sylvestre with his proud pope's hat. Michel shining silver beneath candlelight. Asa and Jehoshaphat lamenting the Templars. Hecáte, Eurydice, and Perséphone squabbling for my torch. Corvus playing in the oak boughs. Corvus offering his scale.

Bathsheba learning how to sing.

But my body did not transform.

I remained soft, all pulse, breath, and heartbeat.

"Do you need more?" Isabelle breathed. "Why isn't it working? I don't know if I can—"

A group of Benedictine brothers rushed towards us and Isabelle jerked her arm back. I closed my eyes and tried to shut out the chorus of questions: "What happened? Why are you bleeding? Who's hurt Celestine?"

"A thief attacked us," Isabelle said. "Celestine and Geneviève fought him off."

"Let me help you," said one of the brothers, an old man with a creased forehead.

"Help us carry Celestine back to the Hôtel-Dieu," Isabelle said.

"And what about you? You're bleeding!"

Isabelle shook her head and shooed him off. "I know how to make it stop," she said.

The old man eyed me suspiciously. I wondered what he thought of Isabelle and I, both of us smudged with blood, and Celestine, hunched against the wall with his face in his hands. The three of us were stunned, but alive.

"I said, please help Celestine," Isabelle demanded, placing her blood-streaked hands on her hips.

The sky went soft pink, and the cathedral bells burst into melody. As the Benedictines moved to lift Celestine, Isabelle and I stared at each other dumbfounded, as if this desperate moment had only been a nightmare.

"I'm sorry you can't go home," Isabelle said. "I tried my best."

She brought her arm to her mouth and sucked the wound.

"I know," I said. "We both tried."

She took my hand and led me towards the Hôtel-Dieu.

CHAPTER XXXII

The Chandeleur, 1355

Tonight, I left a candle burning between Saint Sylvestre and Bathsheba. A candle where I had stood, where masons would soon place The New Geneviève. *Now I can see you,* I thought, watching the light flicker across their faces. *I always want to remember what you are.* I never want to forget who I was and what I am. I took in their round cheeks and small lips carved into placid smiles. I inched the candle closer to their feet before I joined the congregation inside the cathedral.

I took my place next to Marguerite, who swayed with her eyes closed, obviously dozing. I nudged her with my elbow, and she opened her eyes and smiled at me. She was still hungover, and so was I. Our friends, the Benedictine monks, had gifted the beguines a shipment of ale, so we'd spent the evening drinking in the Hôtel-Dieu kitchen. Agnès sang *Dit des quatre oiseaux* and I was so drunk, I joined in. In the years since the illness, I'd come to hate that song; Bathsheba's sophisticated taste in music must have rubbed off on me, because I found the lyrics and rhythm dull now. Still, I had learned all the words and found myself compelled to sing along when I heard it in groups, like singing was the most natural thing in the world. The most human thing.

We had survived.

I had survived.

The day Isabelle brought me back to the Hôtel-Dieu, stained with blood, she begged Madam du Faut to take me in. She repeated the story that she had been attacked by thieves, and I'd helped her and Celestine fight them off. Madam du Faut did not believe her, but the Hôtel-Dieu could not turn away anyone infirm or destitute—and I certainly qualified as destitute. The nuns who managed the hospital offered me a bed. A bed I shared with two sick women in the large hall for patients.

In the daytime, I slept head to heel with my bedmates. In the evening, I rose to do the work no one else wanted. Trimming toenails. Scrubbing shit from floors. Putting more wood in the stove. Washing and combing women's hair to prevent lice from latching onto every head. After I had proven myself for a month, Madam du Faut relented and invited me to join the beguines again.

And, so, the days passed. We didn't allow ourselves many thoughts about the future. We thought about food, what we would eat and serve for dinner. Amongst ourselves, the beguines told dirty jokes and gossiped. Who had taken so-and-so for a lover. We had ideas about how to stop the illness; we tried to teach anyone we encountered about sanitation. Most people still believed sinners had woken the illness, but I knew that was wishful thinking. *Be pious, be good, and you'll never suffer.* If only following such rules could keep us safe our whole lives.

So, we lived. We lived as if we would survive, and many of us did. But not everyone.

Most days, The Wakening and West Façade became memories of a dream I grasped to hold. Most days, I felt as if I had always been Geneviève Donnadieu. But as the new moon approached, I'd wake from sleep, staring up at the ceiling in the predawn, recalling my origin to myself. I would repeat familiar names: Bathsheba. Saint Sylvestre.

Michel. Saint Denis. Uriel. Gabriel. Marie. Lucifer. Sainte Anne. Hécate. Eurydice. Perséphone. Corvus.

In 1354, Isabelle and Celestine left for Messina to honor their family. Like most people the illness had claimed, their parents and sister had been buried in an unmarked grave. Isabelle and Celestine would find this gravesite and hold a ceremony with their surviving relatives. They would also tend to and repair their parents' empty house. I gave them what was left of my stolen purse, though by the time they secured their passage on a Venetian merchant galley, that cloth pouch was almost empty.

The de Grantrue family departed on a pale April with little fanfare. I stood outside the Hôtel-Dieu's gates to see them off, playing with the falcon comb beneath my mantle. I'd had every intention of giving it to Isabelle, but when it came time to hug her farewell, I held back. I simply wanted it for myself.

Instead, I gave her my molar.

She looked at me, dumbfounded as she rolled it in her palm, and then a smile stretched across her lips. She embraced me. "This is the most peculiar gift I've ever received," she said. "But I will cherish it always. Thank you, Geneviève."

Isabelle had traded her wool beguine's garments for a tight-fitted blue cote with a high neck and billowing sleeves. Above this dress, she wore a silk green surcote with open sides that exposed the blue linen beneath. Her hair fell in loose curls along her back. Celestine wore a tunic made from matching blue linen, undyed wool stockings, and fine leather shoes with pointy toes.

For a moment, I considered running after them, begging them to let me join. I wanted to see the narrow ship with its great sails and rows of endless oarsmen. But how to say farewell to home? I would circle this cathedral for the rest of my life, though I would never be Sainte

Geneviève again. Home was the cathedral and the Hôtel-Dieu. Home was the hands that made me.

When they reached Messina, Celestine wrote to Louis and his family; Isabelle wrote to me. By then, I could read her words myself. *Thank you, Geneviève,* she wrote. *Knowing someone cared about me as much as you did helped me feel safe in this world again.* She added that she had strung my molar on a cord and wore it like a necklace.

I hoped that I would see Isabelle and Celestine again, but I knew how to let them go.

Time passed, I earned money, and I began to want a house and property in my own name—a space I could share with others, like The Other Geneviève had. If I wanted to marry someone, I could. But that would mean leaving the beguinage and the influence I had there, so I decided I didn't want to. It wasn't much, but it was more than many other people could aspire to. The beguinage had its tedium, but it gave me reasons to go into the city, often alone, and I was happiest when I walked through the streets by myself.

Sometimes I stood in the parvis and watched the masons paint the West Façade. I overheard plans for a new Archangel Michel and a new Denis, along with the New Sainte Geneviève. Now that the illness had passed, the quarries were open, and masons and sculptors had work again. Each day, I waited for The New Geneviève and wondered if she would look like me or someone new. When she looked out at the parvis, would she notice the same things I had? What would she talk about with Bathsheba? Would she ever climb down the façade?

I knew The New Geneviève would be someone else. She would not be me. Still, I worried my story would get lost, so I taught myself to sculpt. I approached the masons who set up workstations in the parvis and asked the first friendly face I saw for a piece of stone and tools to borrow. I paid a worker named Aderic three months' worth of my wages.

I wasn't an exceptionally skilled stoneworker, but I could cut the long snout, the pointed teeth. Rows of teeth like Corvus'. A female body with the feet and wings of a bird. She seemed to take on her own personality as I worked long hours into the evenings.

Sometimes, I worked alongside Aderic in his workshop in the parvis. He never asked me why I wanted to carve a gargoyle, or a Ba bird, as I called it. We had all lost too many people to the illness; it was best not to ask questions.

Sculpting became a distraction, a way to put my hands to use and forget everything that worried me. There was plenty to worry about: I could catch illness, or someone could push me in the Seine. I could be robbed. The gargoyle was a way to hang onto who I was once. The gargoyle became my everything. She was almost finished now.

I thought about her tonight as I stood with the congregation. It was stuffy in this throng, despite the frost on the ground outside. I closed my eyes, inhaled. There was a part of the enchantment still alive in me, and I longed to be out in the darkness, moving between the façades. I hadn't lost that desire, not entirely, despite the way my memories unraveled. When the congregation closed their eyes in prayer, I slipped outside. I knew which doors I'd find unlocked.

A dancing star darted overhead. Cool silver then it was gone. I almost missed it. Comets that people had seen long ago, before me, before there was limestone, before life calcified.

Corvus would see me grow old. Though I would never feel at peace with the fact that I would die long before he did, I learned to live with this sorrow. I knew that all our bodies were borrowed. Corvus wasn't immortal, not really. Eventually, he would crumble and be no more. He would become earth again.

And until then.

I would go to him each new moon, talk with him beneath the oak tree, listen to his stories, and tell him a little bit of this and that—and he would tell me stories about my companions. That was how it was.

That was how it would be. The most I could ever ask for in this world. And it was some small peace knowing we would all, eventually, fall back to dust.

Epilogue

I am Strix. I am the keeper of Sainte Geneviève's story; now, you are too.
I didn't think you would come back, day after day, to listen to me. But
here you are. I have nothing more to tell you, though your eyes plead.

What happened to Geneviève?

Well, she lived. She gave me to the sculptor Aderic, who gave me to
the Mason Guild with the rest of his statues. I waited until the pulleys
and levers sent me soaring above the city to the façade I now guard.
I awoke with all the words I'd absorbed from Geneviève, though she
continued her life without me. I met Corvus and the harpies, of course,
but I wanted to create my own self. I flew alone. Gargoyles are mostly
solitary, after all. I flew until all your lights broke the enchantment,
and then I watched the world from this wall, in silence, until you came
along.

What about Bathsheba and Marie and all the faces on the West Façade?

Mon petit chou, I'm sorry. The cathedral was vandalized during
the Revolution, and the people destroyed most of the statues on the
West Façade. I'm sorry you cannot speak with them. Nothing lasts
forever. Not Bathsheba, not Geneviève, not me, and not you.

You want to cut off all the lights in Paris so I may fly again?

Oh, ma colombe. You are kind. But you cannot do that. I'm afraid
you would have to cut the lights in the whole world, and what good
would that do? Would that truly help your kind?

No. Take this statue's story and make something with it. This is how you speak to the past: to Geneviève, to her maker, to everyone who has ever stood before this cathedral in awe of what your kind can build. If you can, make this story into something beautiful, for that is how you speak to the future.

Do you see the limestone crumble? I wondered if you noticed while you listened. Did you see the gargoyle on the other façade fall?

Remember me: I am Strix.

I am limestone and ocean and quarries. I am the creation of human hands. I am here. So are you. For now, we exist and that is enough.

Acknowledgments

The West Façade began as an incomplete story draft I brought to a workshop at the Writer's Center in Bethesda, Maryland, in 2013. There, I met the wonderfully supportive Marcia Bronstein, Lewis Cohen, and Nancy Kidder. Without your enthusiasm, *The West Façade* would not exist.

Likewise, this novel would not exist without my dream of a cohort from American University's MFA program in creative writing. Thank you, Matthew Bukowski, Yohanca Delgado, Vince Granata, Karen Keating, Karan Madhok, Emily Moses, and Bron Treanor. Long live the Blood Library! Bron, from the bottom of my heart, thank you for reading every draft of *The West Façade* over the many years and for helping me choose the title. Thank you to my thesis committee at American University: Despina Kakoudai, and Dolen Perkins-Valdez, and my professors: Stephanie Grant, David Keplinger, and Richard McCann.

Elizabeth Geoghegan and Michael Carroll, thank you for your friendship and mentorship. The summer I spent studying with you at John Cabot University in Rome changed my life.

Endless gratitude to the community at The Ruby, especially the Writing Accountability Group, and my Body of the Book cohort with Lidia Yuknavitch and Corporeal Writing. I could not have finished *The West Façade* without my WAGs and BoBs. Thank you Cari Luna and Lydia Kiesling for leading such wonderful workshops through Catapult and the Mendocino Coast Writers' Conference, respectively. A million thanks to Andrew Gifford for believing in this novel and bringing it into the world, and to my star editor, Adam Al-Sirgany for your insights, questions, and ear for language.

Thank you to my Babylon Salon co-hosts, Laurie Ann Doyle, Dominic Lim, Ryan Sloan, and Maury Zeff, and to the vibrant

San Francisco Bay Area literary community, including my writing collaborators and dear friends Sarah Broderick, Dev Bhat, Chad Koch, Yume Kim, Gaia Patience-Veenis, Kendra Schynert, and Kathleen J. Woods.

And of course, Matt Scott Carney, thank you for being my co-collaborator in art, in literature, and in life. I love you.

Thank you to Danièle Cybulskie for creating the Medieval Masterclass for Creators as well as the entire team at Medievalists.net, which I referenced countless times while writing *The West Façade*.

Gratitude to historian and medievalist, Tanya Stabler Miller, for her book, *The Beguines of Medieval Paris: Gender, Patronage, and Spiritual Authority*. While the beguines' involvement at the Hôtel-Dieu during the Bubonic Plague is purely my speculation, Miller's work inspired me to include the beguines in *The West Façade*. Madam du Faut is loosely inspired by Jeanne du Faut, a beguine who lived in the 13th and 14th centuries.

Thank you, Glyn Busby and Keith Burgess for your permission to quote your translations of the Lais of Marie de France, as well as The LiederNet Archieve for permission to quote David Wyatt's translation of "My Lady Keeps a Viper in Her Heart" by Guillaume de Machaut.

Finally, thank you to Victor Hugo; the final sentence in Sainte Geneviève's narration is an homage the last line in *The Hunchback of Notre-Dame*. Writing *The West Façade* was my way of reaching into the past while extending my hand into the future.

About the Author

Lauren C. Johnson attributes her upbringing in Florida, America's weirdest state, to her interest in the ecological and surreal. She writes speculative and place-based fiction, essays, and poetry and her writing has appeared in *The Rumpus*, *Orion Magazine* online, and more. She holds an MFA in creative writing from American University and lives in San Francisco, where she co-hosts Babylon Salon, one of the Bay Area's longest-running literary and performance series. Lauren also co-founded Club Chicxulub, a journal and reading series featuring speculative fiction authors accompanied by synthwave, dark wave, and ambient beats. She lives with her husband and her two rescue doves, Schooner and Eagle. *The West Façade* is her debut novel. Find out more at laurencjohnson.com

Also from Santa Fe Writers Project

Magic For Unlucky Girls
by A.A. Balaskovits

The fourteen fantastical stories in *Magic For Unlucky Girls* take the familiar tropes of fairy tales and twist them into new and surprising shapes. These unlucky girls, struggling against a society that all too often oppresses them, are forced to navigate strange worlds as they try to survive.

"A wonderful, truly original work."

— Emily St. John Mandel, author of *Station Eleven*

Strange Folk You'll Never Meet
by A.A. Balaskovits

With elements of psychological horror, sly humor, and the fantastic, these stories will burrow under your skin, haunt your dreams, and make you wonder what worlds lie just beyond that tiny hole in the wall.

"Written with a darkly sparkling lyricism, Balaskovits' collection is gory, gorgeous, and like nothing else you'll read"

—*Buzzfeed*

About Santa Fe Writers Project

SFWP is an independent press founded in 1998 that embraces a mission of artistic preservation, recognizing exciting new authors, and bringing out of print work back to the shelves.

  @santafewritersproject |  @SFWP | sfwp.com